One Hawaiian Morning

One Hawaiian Morning

Kelli Gard

Library of Congress Control Number:		2020901888
ISBN:	Hardcover	978-1-7960-8549-5
	Softcover	978-1-7960-8548-8
	eBook	978-1-7960-8547-1

Print information available on the last page.

Rev. date: 01/28/2020

To order additional copies of this book, contact:
Xlibris
1-888-795-4274
www.Xlibris.com
Orders@Xlibris.com
807699

Acknowledgements

A massive thanks to my great friend Alma Law who helped me develop these fabulous characters and piece the whole story together. Another heartfelt thanks to my mother who was the first to read the manuscript and was brave enough to tell me the original ending was bad. Mom is always right.

Dedication

To my beloved children Eli, Evelyn, Isaac, Elaina and Wylie.
You too can do hard things.

1

Hawaiian mornings are like no others, or so I've been told. I hardly remember mornings on the mainland. In Hawaii, the winter never brings brisk late sunrises, like those of my early childhood in North Carolina. The island sun peeks up over the water and shows its glorious face every morning by six o'clock. My daily bike rides to the beach entertain my nose with whiffs of salt water and hibiscus flowers. It didn't take me long to discover this morning delight when we moved here ten years ago. I was only eight and mesmerized by the glorious blue ocean. In the years since I've developed such a love for this mysterious water, it's like it has become part of my soul.

We moved to the island in 1930. My father was an officer in the Naval Air Corps and was assigned to assist in the setup of the new naval base. His father, my grandfather, fought in World War I as a pilot, and my father followed in his footsteps. Granddad was a high-ranking officer, as was my father. Both Dad and Grandpa are great men. They served our country gladly and with great honor. "Country first" is our family motto. "Sheplers are loyal and true, through and through," Grandpa would always say. Grandpa died a few years ago. His funeral marked our first and only return to the mainland since we moved to the island.

Daddy retired a few years ago but still works on base. He is very well respected and his presence very welcome among the officers. He shares the same love for the island as I do; I don't think he can bear the thought of leaving any more than I can. So when his time came to reenlist or retire, he chose to retire so we could stay on the island.

Our family was one of the first to be transferred to Oahu. My parents, my three sisters, and I were among the first few white faces, or haole* as the islanders call us, on the island, but now we are just one of many. When we first moved here, it was important to my father that we embraced the new culture. Our parents thrust my sisters and me into every event imaginable. We were encouraged to blend in and become as "Hawaiian" as possible. The islanders were reluctant to accept us, and the other naval families did not share my father's zeal, but that did not stop my parents from pushing. We learned hula, played daily at the beach, snorkeled, and were even allowed to learn to surf, although I was the only one who took to it. One of Daddy's local friends agreed to teach us.

Kapena and his young son, Kekoa, took us out a few times for lessons and allowed us to use their handmade longboards. My sisters claimed to be too refined for the sport even then and said it wasn't "ladylike." I always thought it was just an excuse because they were too afraid. I loved it and begged Daddy to ask Kapena for more lessons. Kekoa, who is my age, and I became good friends in all those hours we spent together on the beach. For my sixteenth birthday, Kekoa gave me the most thoughtful gift anyone had ever given me—my very own surfboard he made himself. It is still my most favorite and prized possession.

However annoying and uncomfortable it was for us girls from North Carolina to participate in those foreign activities, I am grateful for it. My best friends are Hawaiian. Hawaiians, as a whole, are lovely people, much more accepting and warm than white folks. While the other girls my age complain about the heat, the humidity making their hair frizzy, and the lack of shopping locations, I thrive in the paradise sun and soak up every opportunity to bask in the blue ocean.

The year is now 1940, it's December 12, and I am twenty years old. All the schools let out the day before for the Christmas holiday. The navy base is bustling, and the harbor is accompanied by many ships filled with eager seamen coming in and out of Pearl Harbor. Haoles populate the southern part of the island. It seems that new young seamen arrive daily, excited to be in an exotic place. I find myself almost as jaded as the locals, wishing they would go back to where they came from and leave our paradise alone. The war between Japan and China is raging, and our country's presence here and the need for the naval yard is essential, or so my father says. As long as our country's presence is needed, the navy will take up residence on the island.

I graduated from high school over a year ago now, practically an old maid by my mother's standards. I should have been married to a seaman and moved back to the mainland like my elder sister, Evelyn, by now. Not only do I have no desire to move to the mainland, but I also have no desire to marry a seaman. My sister married an enlisted man she met while he was on the island for a brief stint a few years back. Now they are stationed out of booming California, where she raises their baby son alone and spends her days pining for a time when her husband will return from whatever assignment he is on. She says she is happy in her letters, though I know she is not. She's my sister, and no matter how different we are, I know her. We spent every night of our childhood, when we were supposed to be sleeping, discussing our dreams and futures. Never in her dreams did she mention being alone. Then again, never did I in mine either.

I'd been trying to convince Evelyn to come home for the holidays, but she is hopeful her husband, Mike, will come home for a day or two this month, so she insists on staying there, just in case. The last passenger ship before Christmas left California two days ago, so it is too late anyway.

I still live at home with my parents and two younger sisters. Although with every nonsensical conversation I endure between my sisters and every unsubtle hint to "get married" that I hear from my mother, I question my reasons for still being here. But the question is, where would I go? I love my father and can't imagine moving far from him. I love the island and can't imagine leaving it either. So for now, I'm happy to attend nursing school here, not because I have great aspirations in nursing but because I don't know what else to do with my time. I can stay on the island and practice nursing, so it seems like a good plan for now.

Like all mornings, no one in my house was awake when I left. Usually, at least Daddy is awake, but with the holiday, he was still sleeping when I hopped on my bike and headed down the hill. Daddy fashioned a harness for my surfboard as a birthday present for the same birthday Kekoa gave me the board. The harness holds the board on side of my bike. Today I chose to wear my pink cover-up dress with a swimming suit underneath. The suit is like many of the other styles I see girls wearing. It has pink polka dots with white halter top straps and a tight miniskirt for the bottom. It's flattering to my curves and doesn't slide down when I get tumbled in a wave, so it fits my purposes. My long brown hair is tied up on the top of my head. Most girls are wearing their hair short with wavy curls around their face, but I like mine long; it's easier to put up while swimming.

The ride to the beach is all downhill, or Maulka. It takes me less than five minutes to get to the beach. There are only a few people on the streets at this time of day, mostly officers and seamen shuffling back and forth between shifts. I ride by cute Hawaiian huts and newly built apartment buildings. Everything in Hawaii is green. Trees and plants sprout up spontaneously and speckle the island. The plumeria trees decorate the streets with pink, white, and yellow flowers. Trees here have leaves bigger than your head and thicker than several sheets of paper. Nearly every home has some fruit-bearing trees in the yard. The Kuakahis, just down the road from our house, grow oranges, tangerines, lemons, limes, and one giant green fruit bigger than a softball that I still haven't learned the name of. We are always welcome to pick from their yard because they have plenty. The Moumaus, who live across from the Kuakahis, have mango, papaya, and starfruit. Farther down the road, there are sweet lilikoi and other exotic fruits that, after living here for so long, I'm embarrassed to ask the name of. Coconut trees are everywhere and can actually be quite a hazard. Many people and cars have been hit by a falling coconut. A few have fallen in front of me while riding my bike, but thankfully, I've never been hit.

We have papaya, orange, and banana trees in our yard. The first year we lived here, my sisters and I learned two things about banana trees. One, banana bunches can weigh two hundred pounds, which is much more than one small girl, or four, can carry. This led us to our second discovery about bananas. The sap, or juice, that comes off banana stalks stains your clothes a poop brown color that doesn't show up until the next day. My sisters and I, along with our father, learned that one the hard way. Poor Daddy ruined one of his good uniforms bear-hugging that bunch of bananas. The fruit was all so exciting the first few years, but now we take it for granted and even complain about how we can possibly eat two hundred pounds of bananas before they go bad or whine about being sick of oranges. I myself have even uttered the phrase "If I have to eat one more avocado, I will . . .," which is then followed by some verbs like "die," "scream," or "puke."

Another thing I learned the first year we lived here is that I'm allergic to the mango tree when it flowers in the spring. We used to live next to one, before we moved to our current house. I do love mangoes, but when the tree flowers, my eyes start to itch and swell up like big red cherries. Every spring, I walk around looking like I just poked myself in the eye. Lucky for me, we moved away from that first house.

When I take the time to step back and really soak in all the beauty that is Hawaii, I wonder how anyone could doubt God's existence. Clearly, this magnificent land wasn't created just by accident but through some grand design of a higher being. I try to appreciate the beautiful, bounteous scenery I see every morning, but it's hard not to take it for granted.

I parked my bike in the rack when I reached the beach, discarded my cover-up dress, and grabbed my long board and carried it under my arm. I'm a fairly short person, just 5'4", so I always look a little like I'm going to tip over when I carry my board, but I never have. I'm thin but not small framed, much stronger than most girls. I've spent so much time with my board it molds right to my side as I walk, and I hardly notice I'm carrying it. The sand is soft under my feet, not hot like it will be in a few hours.

"Howz it, Ruth?" Kekoa greeted me at the water's edge. He was just coming in, but it looked like he had been here a little while. Most mornings, we surf together.

"Are you ready for the big competition today?" he asked and kissed me on the cheek.

"Ready as I will ever be. Thought I would get a few practice rounds in this morning before heading north," I said.

"Well, these swells aren't anything like what we will see today, but best you don't bust yourself up anyway, right?" He laughed.

"Right," I said. "Let's do this!"

When my feet first touch the water, it never feels cold and startling as Evelyn describes the water off the coast of California. It is almost body temperature, and it's always refreshing. I was stepping into liquid—my favorite sensation. Everything moves, everything changes, and it feels good. I dove in face-first and fully submerged myself before surfacing to climb on my board. Kekoa was on my heels.

This is our daily routine. Before the rest of the world awakes, it's just us and the soothing ocean. Occasionally, we are accompanied by another lone surfer enjoying the morning but not today. It's Thursday, past midweek; most people are too tired to wake up this early midweek. I climbed on my board and paddled out past the breakers. A few waves crested over me. I couldn't help but smile when I came out of the wave, and it washed down my body. I maneuvered myself and my board around and waited for a big one, but I wasn't in any hurry. There was no one else to fight with for a wave or to worry about running into. I lay there on my board, drifting up and down with the swells, feeling the sun on the back of my legs and shoulders. I've been in the sun so much I really didn't have to worry about getting sunburned.

"Here comes a big one, Ruthy," Kekoa said, lining up to take the wave.

I paddled quickly to catch it. My arms were a little stiff from the night, but I loved the exercise. My arms burned with each stroke through the water.

"Now, now, now!" Kekoa yelled from behind me. I jumped on the board and embraced the freedom riding high above the waves. I rode it all the way to shore, and then we paddled out for more. We repeated this over and over, losing track of how many times we rode.

"We are going to have to get going soon," I said. "We don't want to be late to the competition."

"Eh, let's do juz one more time, Ruthy," Kekoa pleaded.

"Can't argue with that." I laughed, and out we went again.

Once I cleared the breakers, I rolled over onto my back and floated up and down and up and dull, hypnotized by rhythmic movement. My chest rose and fell rapidly, and I could feel my heart beating quickly under my chest. I was out of breath. Kekoa paddled up next to me and did the same thing. I could hear him breathing hard next to me.

The sun was off to the east, still rising, so I was able to gaze right up into the sky without it burning my eyes, and we lay there silently, listening to the waves crumbling on the shore behind me slowly, rhythmically over and over.

"I hear the winter waves are in full force up north," I said.

"Yeah, I heard dat too," Kekoa said. "You nervous?" he teased, splashing water at me.

"I always get nervous. You know that." I splashed him back. "It's not easy being the only girl."

"Ahh, but it's your secret weapon. No onz think you a threat and then you slay 'em!"

I chuckled. That was fun.

"And you enjoy it! Making a fool of all the men." He laughed. "I think this competition will have a lot of haoles. Seems like there are a lot of sailors on the island right now. Easy peazy for you."

"I hope so. Those guys are my favorite to beat!" I said.

We both laughed and fell silent again, hypnotized by the sun. I tickled my hands along the top of the water and let my leg swing off the side of the board into the ocean. I chuckled a little thinking about my daddy who called this the shark bait position. Daddy says I look just like a seal floating on top of the water. I pulled my leg back onto the board, thinking about that.

I thought about the schools of yellow and striped fish swimming below me. We've spent whole days snorkeling here. It doesn't matter how many times I've seen it; it's always so very impressive. I imagined what creatures I would see if I just had my goggles and could pop my head under the surface. Tomorrow I will bring them, I decided.

The nagging feeling of time passing eventually brought me out of my daydream.

"We need to go," I said, kicking him. As always, we lingered just a moment longer, and I enjoyed every second of peace.

"Okay, letz do it," Kekoa said, and we rode one more wave back in.

At nearly a foot taller than me, Kekoa could bound up the beach so much faster than me. He was at his truck and loading my bike before I reached to the outdoor shower on the beach. I stopped to rinse the salt and sand off, while Kekoa took my board and loaded it in his truck as well. My board looked small tucked under his muscular arms. My house is not on the way to Kekoa's, but he usually drives me home because the hill is so big. I can do it, but it is a huge task to ride home.

I didn't put my dress back on. I decided to let the sun dry me on the ride home. I don't know what kind of truck Kekoa drives, one of a kind you can say. It is blue with brown rust spots and no top, so the wind blew through my hair as we drove. We don't live on base like most military families. We live in a cute little house just off base. It has a long lani* out back where we eat most of our dinners and sit in the evening, listening to the coqui frogs and playing games. It's small for our family, but I know my parents like it that way. Kekoa lives much farther up the mountain and down a totally different street. Kekoa parked his car in the driveway and helped me unload my bike but left the board in his truck. I pushed my bike in its usual spot out back and put my board in the shed behind our house. I put my cover-up back on before Daddy could see me.

"Okay, I will comz get you at noon," he said.

"Okay," I said and kissed him on the cheek.

To any outsider, it will look like Kekoa and I are an "item." I don't mind people thinking that. It keeps sailors' attention off me. Kekoa is my little protector. We've always had an unspoken chemistry, and we enjoy flirting and teasing each other. If there ever is a man I am interested in, it would have been him. But I don't think complexities and the stigma of an interracial relationship isn't anything either of us is willing to endure. So for now, we remain very close friends.

I entered through the door on the back lani that leads into our kitchen. Daddy was sitting at our small yellow table, in the middle of the kitchen, drinking coffee and reading the paper. All I could see of him is his graying dark hair over the top of the newspaper. Without looking over his paper, he chirped out a cheery "Morning, Ruthy!"

"Morning, Daddy. How did you sleep?" I asked, getting myself a glass of water from the sink.

"Good, darlin'," he said, putting his paper down. "I didn't hear you leave this morning." I walked over to the table, leaned down, and gave him a kiss on the cheek.

"I was trying not to wake up the girls." I laughed, referring to my two sisters who sleep in the room across from mine.

I've had my own room since my elder sister, Evelyn, moved out. I miss her, but I would never want to share my room with either of the other two, Elizabeth and Marie, seventeen and fourteen, young and completely boy crazy. I can hardly stand even one of their conversations.

Daddy chuckled and said, "I think you would have to drive a truck through their room to wake them up."

I laughed too. "Is Mom awake yet?" I asked.

"Yeah, but she hasn't come out of the room. I don't know what that woman is up to in there," Daddy replied.

"She is trying to look beautiful for you, Daddy," I teased. "Would you like me to make your egg?"

"Yes, please, sweetheart," Daddy said, picking his paper back.

He is nothing if not consistent. Every morning he has two eggs, basted, with a side of rice. The locals in Hawaii eat rice for nearly every meal, so we do too. Our family of five goes through at least twenty-five pounds of rice a month. I don't even know if I like rice or not; it's just what I've always eaten.

The rice was already cooked in the pot on the stove. Every morning Daddy wakes up and makes a pot of coffee and a pot of rice, so all I have to do is prepare the eggs. I cracked eight eggs into the pan. About the time I dished them onto plates, Mom wandered into the kitchen, mumbling something about the girls.

"Morning, Mother," I said, trying to sound cheery and flashing her my "million-dollar smile" as Daddy calls it. I've never understood why.

"Hello, Ruth darling," she said, reaching around me for the coffee. "You smell like the ocean, sweetheart."

"I haven't cleaned up yet," I said under my breath. Mother isn't a fan of my surfing hobby. She tolerates it but doesn't necessarily approves. She would rather I was more "ladylike" and is really probably embarrassed that I do it.

"Hmmm," she replied.

Just then, the girls entered, arguing over who cleaned the bathroom last. They were still in their pajamas and their hair messy from a night's sleep. They share similar features as me, but we really don't look a lot alike. Elizabeth is blonde and a good inch taller than me. She is very thin and pale white. Marie has the same brown hair as I do, but she wears it short and bouncy. She and I are the same height, but she still has time to grow another inch or so. She has a beautiful baby face accentuated by the pout she was wearing.

As usual, all it took was a simple look from Daddy from behind his paper and a clearing of his throat for the girls to stop fighting. Daddy has even less patience for their bickering than I do. Mother put some plates out, I dished up the eggs, Marie scooped the rice, Elizabeth poured the juice, and Daddy said the blessing. I love our family's morning routine despite any arguments it may contain. There is something very familiar and comforting among the root pleasantries and exchanges at the table. "Please pass the salt." "What are you doing today?" "May I have some more rice?" And of course, the usual bickering between sisters: "Elizabeth stole my brush!" "Why don't we ever get to go to the dances?" and on and on.

Like many other mornings, my mother mentioned the upcoming dance at the Hickam Hall Officers' Club, celebrating the arrival of one ship or another, but I wasn't listening. I think the dances are torturous. It is a night of female-starved seamen seeking attention from the opposite sex and local girls lusting after a man in uniform. The girls are always flirting, waving, and laughing loudly at bad jokes, while the boys show off and "one-up" each other with wildly exaggerated stories from their adventures at sea. The girls eat up their stories, acting amazed and astonished in all the right places.

I've never enjoyed the events, but unfortunately, I've found myself attending them regularly lately for one reason or another. For one, it gets my mother off my back and makes it look like I am "getting out there" and that I'm not just a hermit hiding in my room. Two, I have friends who talk me into it, and three, it's a nice break from the house. Kekoa sings in the band, and I like to keep him company while he is on break, although I mostly use it as an excuse to look busy so I don't get asked to dance. He always teases me about dating him, but it's all in fun. He is safe, not a person I have to be on guard around. Sometimes I do wonder if dating and marrying an islander like him may solve all my problems. I wouldn't have to leave the island or spend my married life alone like my sister.

This morning is like all the rest but with a little extra dose of annoying. With a mouth full of rice, Marie announced, "A new group of seamen from California arrived last night. I'm sure if we are in town long enough, we will meet some of them!"

Without missing a beat, Elizabeth added, smiling, "The last group was from California too, and they were sooooo cute!" I didn't think Elizabeth had eaten a bite; she had been talking so much.

"They've been doing training exercises for MONTHS without ever making port. They are going to be so fun to talk to!" Marie said, her voice raising with every word. By the time the whole thought escaped her mouth, she was practically standing on her chair. Mother was hanging onto every word, looking just as excited as the girls. "Are they having a dance this weekend to celebrate their arrival?" she asked.

I didn't dare look up at the faces around the table, so I busied myself with squishing the last remaining piece of rice in the yoke of my egg.

Unnoticing my frozen state, Elizabeth, the elder of the two, squeaked out, "Yes, they are, Friday, at the hall! It should be the best dance yet!" Elizabeth squealed and then changed her tone dramatically, sounding pathetic. "That's what I hear anyway, not like I've ever been allowed to go." She stared at Daddy, who was casually hiding behind his paper.

Mother, in her very casual, innocent "Mom tone" that only she possessed, suggested, "Well, you are seventeen, Elizabeth. Perhaps you could be allowed to go with Ruth."

The girls erupted into a series of different celebratory squeals from Elizabeth and moans of complete unfairness from Marie. Daddy slowly lowered his paper to peer over it at Mother. He rubbed his face and looked inquisitively at Mom. I remained motionless, completely still. *Oh, why did I have to get dragged into this?*

"What do you think, Daddy? Do you think Elizabeth could go with Ruth?" Mother asked innocently.

Oh please, Daddy, no! I screamed inside my head. *No, no, no! Please NO!* Daddy looked from Mother to me thoughtfully, weighing the possibilities in his mind. I'm sure he was trying to decide who he wanted to deal with, a disappointed Mother and Elizabeth or me.

"Well, I suppose, if Ruth goes . . .," he said finally.

Ugh, I've been betrayed!! I stared at him, wounded.

Another chorus of squeals erupted around the table while Mother wore a very satisfied grin.

"Oh no, I'm not going, Daddy!" I said, trying to set my jaw and look firm.

Exasperated, Elizabeth pleaded, "Oh, come on, Ruth! Just because you don't like boys doesn't mean I HAVE to suffer! This is so not fair! Mommy, make her go—"

Daddy interrupted her tantrum with a lecture. "Elizabeth dear, these are not boys. They are men. You would be wise to remember that. If Ruth doesn't want to go, she doesn't have to go."

"Moooooooom!" Elizabeth pleaded pathetically.

Mother looked me squarely in the eye. "Ruth dear, it would be good for the both of you to go. Get out of this house, spend some time together, and have some fun."

There was no arguing with Mother at this point. I have had this conversation with my mother a hundred times. But I tried anyway.

"Mom, it's not fun. It's just a bunch of boys trying to act like men and a bunch of girls bleeding for their attention. It's disgusting and irritating. I have better things to do with my time," I said, looking resolute. Is it possible that my mother would ever understand my reasoning?

Daddy went back to hiding behind his paper, while Elizabeth looked like she was about to cry.

"What is wrong with you? Why won't you take me? Just because you've been to lots and I never have . . . You don't want me to have any fun, do you? You hate me! Just because I'm not your precious Evelyn, your 'favorite' sister, you won't take me! You won't do anything fun with me! I'm fun! I could be fun . . .," she blubbered. "What a waste too! It's so not fair you got all the looks, and you don't even use them!" She continued.

Patting Elizabeth's hand, my mother stopped her and turned to me. "Ruth," she said simply.

I sighed. It would be a worse night here with my blubbering, nagging family than at the dance, so reluctantly, I conceded with a nod.

"Fine, I'll go," I said, returning my attention to my eggs.

High-pitched screams of exhilaration erupted from Elizabeth's mouth, followed by a sigh of disgust from Marie.

"Well, then what am I going to do all night?" Marie whined.

Daddy smiled at her. "You can play chess with me!"

"Ugh, *Daaad*!" Marie wailed.

"What am I going to do all night?" I said under my breath.

2

"Well, I gotta get going," I said, excusing myself.

I hurried through the rest of breakfast so I could get washed up before the girls needed the bathroom. I cursed the situation I found myself in as I washed the scent of sand and salt off my face and neck. Another dance just meant another long night of empty conversations and frequent trips to the bathroom to avoid drunken, rowdy navy men. Elizabeth would have a great time for sure. She loves to giggle, loves to dance, and loves any attention from a man in uniform. I would have to worry about that later. I needed to focus on today. After washing my face and dressing in a fresh suit, I relinquished the bathroom to the anxiously waiting girls. They were still giddy and excited about the news of the dance. As I walked into the living room, I heard them planning which dress Elizabeth should wear and what clip she should put in her hair. I plopped down on the end of the farthest couch from the noisy hallway to wait for Kekoa.

"You nervous?" my mother asked. She rarely asked me about my competitions.

"Yeah," I said. "How can you tell?"

"You're rubbing your hands together like you always do when you're nervous."

"Oh." I laughed. "This isn't like the other competitions, you know. Bigger waves. All the best surfers."

"Ruth, you know I don't approve of you out there competing next to the boys, but, honey, you're good. You will do fine."

"Thanks, Mom." I smiled.

Just then, I heard Kekoa honking his horn and yelling.

"Come on, Ruthy! Letz go! We got some waves to ride!"

"Bye, Mom!" I said and ran out the door.

"Letz do this, Ruth!" Kekoa was leaning over his windshield, grinning at me. He hadn't changed. He was wearing the same blue swim trunks as this morning. "Come on, wikiwiki slowpoke. We got some waves to ride!" My friends Nohea and Elsie were already in the back seat. They were coming as spectators.

"Let's go kick some butt!" I said as I climbed in. "Think the Nacamoto boys will be there?" I asked as he backed us out of the driveway.

"I hope so. I love kicking their butts!" he said.

"They are tough competition though." I was nervous. "Last time they beat me, remember?"

"Eh, you got them today." Kekoa patted my shoulder.

"They barely beat you, Ruthy," Elsie said.

Elsie is a haole like me. She moved to the island a few years after my family. We've been fast friends ever since. She has bright red hair and pale skin. The poor girl is not suited for island life. She copes with it the best she can, constantly slathering sunscreen on and wearing big hats like she was now. She looked beautiful in her yellow dress sitting next to Nohea.

Nohea is a local girl with beautiful tan Hawaiian skin and long black hair. Her parents work for one of the hotels in town; they are both cooks. A few nights a week, she dances hula at the same hotel where her parents work. I can hula just as well as she, but no one travels all the way to Hawaii to watch a white girl dance. They only want girls like Nohea. We've been friends for several years and graduated together last year. She was wearing a flowing red aloha dress; no hat needed. I was also in a dress with my suit underneath. I pitched my bag in the back and climbed in the front, next to Kekoa.

"Let's go, Kekoa," Nohea said. "Take me to the beach!"

"Yeah, hang on, you beautiful wahines! This is going to be a bumpy ride!"

The drive to North Shore took over an hour. We wound past Waikiki and up the beach side, hypothesizing about the upcoming events. The road got narrower and narrower the more north we got. As we approached North Shore, cars and trucks lined the streets with bare-chest surfers wandering the roads, sitting in the back of trucks, waxing their boards, and preparing for the competition. Kekoa slowed the truck down to a crawl so we wouldn't hit anyone. The nerves in the pit of my stomach started welling up as the other competitors eyeballed us as we tried to find a spot to park. This was the biggest surf competition of the year. All the big boys would be here and lots of spectators.

"There are a lot of sailors," I said. They weren't in their uniforms, obviously, but you could tell with their buzz-cut hair and white chests. They stood out against the local surfers dramatically.

"Yeah, there are," Elsie said, giggling.

"Come on, Ruthy," Kekoa said, pulling the truck under a tree. "Some of us are here to surf." He rolled his eyes at Elsie. Both girls giggled. "Let's show them how it's done."

We unloaded our boards and crossed the street to the beach, passing a group of sailors.

"Hey, wahine, you carrying your boyfriend's board for him?" a tall blond sailor called to me. I rolled my eyes and ignored him.

"Jerks," I said under my breath.

"Don't pay attention to them, Ruth," Kekoa reassured me. "They do it because theyz like you! You're cute!" He put his arm around me affectionately, squeezing my shoulder. He is so much taller than me he squished my face into his enormous chest.

"Oh stop," I teased, pushing him away.

"You should get yourself a real man!" the sailor called from behind us. "A white man!"

Now Kekoa looked hurt. I sighed. "Don't pay attention to them. They do it because they like you. You're cute!" I teased, and I wrapped my arm around his waist, giving him a squeeze. He didn't push me away.

"Come on, bra, we're here to surf. Leave the girls alone." It was our friend Kapena walking up from behind the group of sailors.

"Hey, they don't have to leave us all alone," Nohea teased.

"Oh, Nohea, stop!" Elsie said, slapping at her arm.

"Hey, bra," Kekoa said and slapped Kapena's shoulder. Then Kapena kissed each of us girls on the cheek.

"You two ready for this?" Kapena asked.

"Oh yeah, we are. Let's do it," Kekoa said.

We registered at the booth. There were three more heats before I was up, and Kekoa was right after me. Kapena had already gone. The competition had been going on all day, but our runs weren't until afternoon. Typically, four surfers take the water at once, and they have twenty minutes to impress the judges. The surfers' best two runs are scored. High scores move to the final tomorrow. We wandered down the beach, stepping over surfboards, avoiding various legs and limbs, and chatting with other surfers. The beach was a sea of bare chests and swimsuits. The haoles' white chest stood out among the locals. Even though I am a haole, I'm not treated as such. With the exception of the few jerks like the ones we met earlier, once you're a surfer, you're in. It's an unofficial club with comradery and a love for the ocean. We all respect and love the waves. When you meet a fellow surfer, you automatically have a friend. Other surfers are a little reluctant to let me in, but for the most part, most people show mad respect for my courage. The only segregation that exists is small and is between the locals and the sailors. Sailors tend to be so cocky and so inexperienced that they are a danger to themselves and others. They think that because they sail the ocean, they know the ocean, and most of the time, they end up hurt.

There aren't any other women ever competing, so I always get thrown into the youngest group. I compete next to teenagers and kids. Kekoa found us an empty spot on the beach among all the competitors and spectators and spread a towel out, and we sat to wait our turn. We spread out our blankets and towels, claiming our spot. We settled in. Nohea spread out, while Elsie hid under the umbrella she brought.

"Great turnout, eh?" Kekoa said.

"Yeah," I mumbled. I was lying on my back, hiding my eyes in the elbow of my arm to block the sunlight.

"Come on, Ruthy, get up and watch! Diz is awesome! We're riding the giants today!"

I slowly sat up. "I'm trying not to freak myself out," I said. "These are some big waves! What if I get rolled in one and never come out!" I laughed.

"Nah, not you! Youz totally got this!" he said, patting me on the back. "Just don't think about it. Just get up and fly."

"Easy for you to say. You've done this one hundred times. This is only my second competition, and I'm doing it in THIS!" I said, motioning to the waves. They were big, bigger than anything I've ever surfed.

"None of us have surfed in thiz." He laughed. "Were making history!"

"I think you're both crazy, but I wouldn't miss watching this for the world." Nohea laughed.

"No kidding. I know you don't like them, but there were some cute boys back there." Elsie giggled.

Just then, the energy of the beach changed as onlookers started crowding down the beach. We all stood to get a better look.

"Someone's hurt," Kekoa said.

We walked down the beach to inspect more closely. The power and energy of the waves could be felt as we walked closer to the ocean. We joined the crowd just in time to see two men carrying another man out of the water.

"Oh no," I said under my breath.

"No worries, Ruth." Kekoa rubbed my back. "I watched him. He didn't know what he was doin'."

Just then, Kapena ran back over. We had gotten separated after registering.

"What happened?" I asked him.

"Oh, typical haole. He was in over his head. There are some great barrels out there, and one just pulled him in and spit him back out. Dragged him under for a bit."

I felt sick. They were big barrels. My eyes wandered to the waves. It was a beautiful chaos. I was going to have to figure out how to negotiate them or be swallowed by them.

"Don't worry, wahine!" Kapena said, squeezing my shoulder. "You got diz!"

"Easy for you big boys to say!" I laughed. They were big. Kekoa is easily a whole head taller than me and about as big around as a barrel, and Kapena isn't much smaller. Almost all locals are giants. I feel tiny next to them. "I'm going to just get tossed around out there!"

"Nah." Kekoa laughed. "It's not much different than down south. Just more awesome!"

"How did your first heat go?" Kekoa asked.

"Eh, I got rolled a few times but had one good run," Kapena answered.

After a few minutes and after the surfer was taken off the beach, we all wandered back to our spots. Over the loudspeaker, the announcer said they were canceling the kekie heat, my heat. If I wanted to continue, I would have to go against the big guys.

Kekoa sat next to me on the sand. We just looked at each other. I sighed. I didn't have to tell him what I was thinking. He knew. I studied the waves, watched them swell, roll, and crash over and over until I was almost hypnotized by the methodical movement and sound. I imagined riding each one, when I would pop up, where and when I would cut back.

"I can do it," I said finally.

"Yeah, youz can," Kekoa said, punching me in the shoulder.

"Come on, I gotta go change my heat."

We walked back over to the registration table.

"Excuse me, auntie," I said to the large woman behind the table. "I was in the kekie heat, and I need to change to another one."

She raised one eyebrow at me and signed. "You sure, honey?"

"Yes," I said.

"Okay, well, all the heats are full. We will just put you in the next one. There will be five surfers."

"Okay," I said. "That will be crowded. Will the judges be able to see us all?"

"Take it or leave it," she said.

"Well, I will take it!" I said.

"You best hurry, Ruthy. They will start it soon," Kekoa said, grabbing my arm and pulling me back to the beach. He carried my board to the water's edge for me. The other surfers were already paddling out. I tied my hair on the top of my head while Kekoa gave some last-minute tips.

"You're going to have to paddle extra hard, Ruthy. Give those last two pumps all youz got, pop up, and don't hesitate. Got it?" I nodded.

The tall blond sailor from earlier ran up beside me. "Oh no, I don't want to beat such a pretty thing. Maybe you should stay with your boyfriend," he mocked.

I rolled my eyes, ignoring him while he ran out into the water, surfboard under his arm. His back was already turning pink from the sun. I giggled to myself. I tore off my dress and handed it to Kekoa.

"Go get 'em," Kekoa said, handing me my board.

"Thank you," I mouthed as I fell in behind the sailor. I caught up with him just as he laid his board in the water and started paddling out.

I could feel the energy of the water as I began paddling. "Big long strokes," I said to myself.

My arms were tired. Maybe surfing this morning wasn't a great idea. I focused on my form, cupping my hand, making the most of each stroke, and I tried desperately not to stress about the huge waves I was paddling toward. A very large swell built in front of me. I grabbed my board and duck dove under the wave. The water rushed over me. It was cooler than the water south, where I usually surf. My sailor friend was no longer next to me. I peeked over my shoulder to see the wave had pushed him sideways and back to the beach. I chuckled to myself.

"Haole," I said under my breath.

I know I shouldn't call people that, seeing as I am a haole myself, but he truly fit the description. I joined the other surfers in the lineup past the breakers, and we waited for blondie to try and fail again to paddle out. He was pushed back to shore three times before he finally made it. Two of my fellow surfers were the Nacamoto brothers, and the other was a sailor.

"Hey, wahine!" one of the brothers called. "How's it? You're with the big boys now!"

"Yeah, try and keep up with me!" I yelled back over the roar of the waves.

The other sailor was the farthest from me, and I couldn't see him too well. From where I sat, I could tell he was large—tall and muscular, that is. He looked nearly as large as the two Hawaiians, which is rare.

"Smooth," I said to blondie when he finally joined us. "Are you sure you can handle getting beat by a girl?" I teased. The Nacamotos laughed.

The horn blew, and the clock started. We had twenty minutes to get in our best runs. I didn't waste any time. I needed time. The Nacamotos were closest to the curl, so they took the first wave, a surfer's etiquette to give them the right-of-way. I held back and waited for the next one. Blondie hung back way behind us, but I could see the other sailor had the same idea, and we both took the next wave. I paddled hard, stroked twice like Kekoa said, popped up, but I hesitated. I wobbled, and the energy was so strong I couldn't hold it. I tucked in a ball and dove backward, covering my head. For a moment, my body tumbled in the chaos, but I surfaced, unscathed and intact. I wasn't far from where I started, and I lined back up near blondie, who still hadn't moved. The other sailor was riding in, and the Nacamotos were on their way back in.

"Uh! You got this, Ruth," I said to myself and hit it again.

Stroke, stroke, stroke. I pulled through the water. Two big paddles and I popped up. I didn't hesitate; I stuck with it, and I was flying. Riding on the shoulder, the power under my board was more than I felt before. I cut once, twice hard, and it felt good. There were a few moments when the energy of the water scared me, and I felt the nerves rise through my belly, but I pushed them down and finished flawless.

Running back out again, I passed a Nacamoto brother. He looked good. He was obviously not new to these size waves. I wanted to get in at least two more runs before time was up. I lined up for my second run, and I was out of breath.

"You gonna go, Erikson?" I heard the other sailor yell to blondie.

"Y-Y-Yes, sir," he said. "Just waiting for the perfect one, sir." I caught a glimpse of the sailor blondie was talking to. He reminded me a little of the Captain America character I had seen in some comics.

"Well, get on it, or I'm sending you to the brig!" he yelled back.

I didn't stick around to hear the rest of the conversation. The set wave was coming, and I wasn't going to miss it. I paddled, popped up, and I was flying again. I had no idea how the others were doing. I was only aware of my moments. I knew there was a crowd watching, but there was no place in mind that I could linger on that thought.

It was a big and beautiful wave. I was able to stay in the barrel a long time. I cut to the top of the wave and caught some air before cutting back down. I felt spectacular. I heard a rumble from the crowd, no doubt cheering for my run. No one else was coming in at the moment. I gave the crowd a little wave and ran back out. One more, I wanted one more, not because I needed the score but because I just wanted to do it.

I reached the lineup as a few of the guys rode in. Blondie was still lying on his belly, waiting for the "perfect wave." I positioned myself closest to the barrel so I had the right-of-way. I didn't wait for the set wave; I just took the next acceptable swell, popping up and flying to shore.

Out of the corner of my eye, I saw blondie drop in on my wave.

"You ass!" I yelled, knowing no one could hear me.

Surfing etiquette says to never drop in on someone's wave, and if you do, bail backward and get out of their way. He knew neither of these things and was cutting right under me. I tried to angle my board away. If I could just out surf him, we wouldn't collide. The idiot had no idea what predicament he had placed us in. He had no idea he was surfing right into my path. Unfortunately, it was a closeout wave, and all at once, the whole section of wave broke, sending me careening into him. I tried to jump away when I knew the collision was inevitable, but he kicked his board upward, shoving it into my legs. We were tossed and rolled in the wave, our bodies wiping each other. I lost consciousness; everything went dark. I came to with my head propped under Kekoa's leg and the sound of him, Kapena, and few others yelling at blondie.

"You idiot! What were you thinking?" one of them yelled.

I slowly turned my head to the commotion. The officials were in the middle of it too.

"You could have killed her!" someone yelled.

"Me?" blondie said innocently. "She ran into me! This is her fault!"

My head dropped to the sand as Kekoa jumped up and bounded over to him.

"Morons like you don't belong here! You have no business surfing in this!" he yelled. His voice was shaky but terrifying. He was several inches taller than the sailor. He shoved the sailor backward into the officials and clenched his fists. The sailor looked terrified. I tried to call to him, but I had no voice.

"Hey!" a booming voice called, bringing instant order. It was Captain America. He had clearly just ran in. He stood between Kekoa and blondie. He nearly rivaled Kekoa in size, probably the only man on the beach who could stand toe to toe with him. "Now we aren't going to lose our heads, gentleman," he said calmly, demanding authority. "We all know Erickson here is a jackass and an idiot." Blondie, or Erickson, looked hurt. "You are," he said to blondie. "You dropped in on her wave, and she had nowhere to go. Let's not lose sight of what's important here," he said to the crowd. "Erickson, you need to get off this beach now," he said, shaking his finger in his face. "Peterson and Galloway, get him out of here! Now, you boys," he said to Kekoa and crowd, "you need to take care of that young lady."

Everyone looked at me, lying on a heap in the sand. I must have looked pathetic. I felt queasy and a little confused. Kekoa rushed back over, picking me back up.

"Ruthy, how's it? You okay?" Kekoa asked. I moaned.

"Now that you mention it, my head hurts." I paused, assessing. "And so does my leg."

I looked down. My leg was bleeding. His board had cut me. "There is a first aid station up top," one of the officials said. "Follow me." Kekoa swooped me up effortlessly and hauled me off. I closed my eyes and rested my head on his muscular chest.

"That was an amazing run," I heard him say before I passed out again.

I woke up this time on the medic table. I rolled over and vomited.

"I think his board hit her head too," I heard Kekoa say behind me.

"Yeah, bra, I saw it," Kapena said. "Shoot, I think I heard it. She is pau, bra. Pack it up."

"No!" I blurted. They looked at me, bewildered.

"Well, yes, I am, but, Kekoa, you still need to go. Wikiwiki. Don't miss your heat."

As if on cue, the announcer boomed through the loudspeaker the start of Kekoa's heat.

"Go. I'm fine," I said. "I'm just going to vomit a few more times. I'm good!" I tried to smile reassuringly. "I got my girls," I said, not actually knowing where they were.

On cue, they both appeared. They had probably been there the whole time.

"We got her. Go," Elsie said, taking my hand.

Kekoa looked at me reluctantly. I nodded, and he reluctantly trotted away.

"Thanks, girls," I said.

"We got you, Ruthy." Elsie smiled at me.

"That was amazing, Ruth!" Nohea said, sitting on the other side of me. "The crowd went crazy for your last run."

"Really?" I said.

"Oh yeah!" Elsie said excitedly. "You are going to become a legend!"

"Oh stop!" I laughed. "You exaggerate. I will only become legend from that wipeout."

"Well, that's probably true too." Nohea laughed.

I laughed too, but it made my head hurt.

"You're shaking," Elsie said.

"First stage of shock," a voice said from behind her. It was Captain America again. He had a blanket and placed it over me. As he tucked the blanket under my chin, I got a glimpse of his deep almost gray eyes. "Just rest," he said. The medic had already bandaged my leg, but it seemed like there was nothing to be done for my pounding head. "It will pass, but you're going to feel lousy for a while."

"I'd say," I said sarcastically.

Nohea and Elsie stood silently, awkwardly next to me. None of them really knew what to say.

"Uh, Ruth, do you want us to go get your bag?" Nohea asked.

"Uhhhh." I hesitated. I didn't really want them to leave me, but I really would like my towel, dress, and brush. "Sure. That would be great."

"I will keep an eye on her," Captain said.

"We will be right back," Elsie said, and they ran down the beach. Captain pulled up a bucket and sat next to me.

"Your boy is doing well," he said after several moments of silence.

"Oh good," I said nervously. "Doesn't surprise me. I wouldn't be surprised if he won the whole thing."

"He's that good, huh?" he asked.

"Oh yeah. Taught me everything I know." I laughed.

"Well, then he would have to be good. I didn't see much of your runs, but it's all I've heard about since our heat ended." He laughed. "He your boyfriend?" he asked after a few moments of silence He was nodding at Kekoa.

I sighed. "No. Just a good friend," I said hesitantly.

"Well, I imagine that will make a lot of my sailors happy to hear that."

My eyes went wide, and I opened my mouth, but before I could speak, he interrupted me.

"Don't worry, I won't tell them."

"Thank you," I said gratefully.

He smiled. He had a gorgeous smile.

"You're something of celebrity around here, I take it."

"Oh no." I waved off the thought. "People are just surprised to see a girl surf," I said.

"No, I think it's more than that," he said with that gorgeous grin again. He was making me kind of nervous.

"How was your run?" I asked, deliberately changing the subject.

"Terrible!" He laughed. "I'm just glad I didn't drown! I'm not much of a surfer, but the boys wanted to come. They need supervision, and I didn't want to just sit on the beach, you know!"

"Yeah, don't miss a chance to surf in this, right?" I giggled. My head was feeling a little better. "Think I can sit up now?" I asked the large medic who was sitting away from us.

"Yah, but eazy doz it, Ruth," he said. How did he know my name?

"Let me help," Captain said, propping me up with his arm behind me, steadying me.

I felt dizzy. I wanted to push his arm away and tell him I was fine, but I couldn't. I kind of needed him.

"Give it a second," he said. "I think you hit your head pretty hard. It's going to take some time to get your bearings."

"I'd say." I was swaying back and forth.

"I'm sorry. I feel like this is partly my fault. I shouldn't have let him enter. He said he was good though . . .," he trailed off.

"Oh, all you sailors think you're invincible," I said sarcastically but with a hint of disdain that I couldn't hide in my voice.

"Oh, now come on!" he said, overly offended. "I just said I was terrible!"

I laughed. I focused on the water just long enough to watch Kekoa come in on his last run.

"He killed it!" I said, not hiding the admiration in my voice.

"He did," agreed the sailor.

"We got your stuff, Ruth," Nohea said, running up to me. They both paused, noticing the sailor's hand propping me up.

"He-He's just helping me sit up," I explained.

"I see . . ." Elsie giggled. I rolled my eyes.

"I'm going to let go," he said. "Think you can handle it?"

"Actually, do you think you can help me up? I would like to walk over to the shower and rinse off," I asked.

"You sure, Ruth?" Nohea asked.

"Yeah, I really want to get off this table and be walking before Kekoa comes in. He should be able to celebrate and not worry about me."

"Okay, we will all help you," Elsie said, coming to my side. I swung my legs around the side. Elsie took one arm and the sailor the other. I placed my legs on the sand.

"I feel good!" I said and took a step. Immediately, my knee buckled, and I would have fallen if they didn't catch me.

"Just give it a minute," the sailor said. "Stand still, get your bearings, and then walk."

"Yeah, okay, okay. I think I'm good now." I took a few steps, still wobbly but feeling good. I was gripping his arm pretty tightly and didn't notice it. I relaxed my grip and tried to lean on him less. He was solid though. I felt secure next to him.

"Think we can make it to the shower?" I asked.

"Sure, we can," Nohea said. She was walking behind me, carrying my stuff. We walked toward the showers located just off the beach against a rock wall. They had two concrete walls, so it was semiprivate, better than the beach down south.

"Ahhh!" I squealed as Kekoa swooped me up from behind, breaking my hold on the sailor.

"Did youz see me? Did you see that?" he asked excitedly, spinning me around.

"Oh stop!" I pleaded. "I'm going to throw up!"

"Oh sorry, Ruthy," he said and put me back down.

"I only saw some, but what I did see was amazing. Great job!" I said.

"Yeah, that was amazing, man," the sailor said. Kekoa turned to him. He hadn't noticed him until just then. "I'm going to leave you guys to it. I need to get back to my men. You going to be okay?" he asked.

"Yeah, we got her," Elsie reassured him. He gave me a nod and a half grin and left.

"Who was that!!" Nohea asked as soon as he left.

"Yeah, who wuz that?" Kekoa echoed.

"You know," I said slowly, "I never asked his name. He competed in my heat and was the one who broke up the fight—"

"We know THAT!" Elsie said. "But who is he?"

"He is drop-dead gorgeous is what he is!" Nohea said. "I mean, for a haole," she amended.

"Really?" I said. "I hadn't noticed."

"Well, of course, *you* didn't," Elsie said, exasperated. "You never do, so I will tell you. That man is to die for! He seemed pretty keen on you too."

I rolled my eyes. Truth is, I had sort of noticed.

"What? Him? Gorgeous?" Kekoa laughed. "He's nothing compared to me," he said, puffing up his chest proudly. "The guy can't surf either. So where we going, ladies? You're up walking. That's good!" he said cheerfully.

"We're taking her to the shower to get cleaned up," Nohea explained. "Why don't you go check your scores and meet us back on the beach?"

"No," he said hesitantly. "I think iz best to walk you to the shower."

I swayed a little, and Kekoa caught my arm.

"Oh okay. I guess that's a good idea," I relented.

Kekoa picked me in his arms again, this time a little more gently, and carried me to the shower, placing me under the nozzle, and turned it on.

"Yow!" I squealed again. It was cold.

"All right, keep herz upright, and I will be back," he said and trotted off, presumably to get his score.

I was able to get showered and cleaned up with minimal help. The girls held up a towel so I could actually take my suit off and change. I was covered in sand, in every crack and crevice and all through my scalp. It felt so good to get cleaned off.

"Ouch!" I yelped.

"What's wrong?" Elsie asked.

"Oh, that cut on my leg stings, is all," I said.

"Well, hurry up," Nohea said, getting impatient. "Kekoa is on his way, and I don't know if he will wait for you to be dressed before he swoops you back up!" She giggled.

I slipped my dress over my head just moments before he rounded the concrete corner.

"Perfect score! I'm in the finalz!" he shouted.

"I knew you would be! Great job!" We all cheered for him.

"Howz about some food? I'm starving. Aunt May has some laulau and poke she said she would share," he said.

"Sounds great. I'm hungry," I said.

Auntie isn't actually any of our aunt. "Auntie" is a term Hawaiians use for all respected women. She is a friend of Kekoa's family who lives nearby. She is large and jolly, always wears an apron, and is always cooking up a feast. No one can cook like Auntie, and she loves to feed people. We stuffed our bellies, thanked her for the delicious food, and went back to the beach.

We spent that night on the beach with all the other surfers and friends. There were a few fires started, a few sailors brought out their guitars, and there were a few squealing girls and couples making out. Not very many spectators stayed, but it was just too far for us to drive back. My parents already knew it was likely we would stay over. I think they wished I would stay out more and be home less, so they weren't worried.

"Youz made it too, Ruthy!" Kekoa said, hopping around and through the people sprawled out on the beach over to our fire.

"I did?" I sat up, surprised.

"Yeah, your scores were high enough youz made it to finalz!"

A wave of grief washed over me. "But I can't surf tomorrow," I said, touching my head. "Well, maybe . . ."

"No, Ruth, you can't surf," Elsie said, firmly rubbing my leg.

"Well, I thought you would want to know," Kekoa said, sitting.

"Daz pretty awesome, Ruth!" Kapena added. "First wahine ever!"

"Yeah, too bad I can't actually do it." I was disappointed.

"Hey, wahine!" I random surfer yelled across the beach, recognizing me. I half-waved back at him. That had happened all evening—surfers spotting me, slapping me on the back, and telling me what a great ride I had. It made me feel good, but I also hated the attention.

"You're somewhat of a celebrity!" Nohea pointed out.

"Seems so," I said, rolling my eyes.

Across the beach around another fire, I spotted the surfer who broke up the fight between Kekoa and blondie and who had helped me. He saw me too. We made eye contact.

My stomach lurched into my throat, and I felt nervous and awkward, and I quickly looked away.

"You are like the most popular girl on this beach, Ruth," Elsie said, giggling. "You could have any guy on this beach!"

"Oh stop!" I protested.

"Nah, I'm de only guy for Ruthy!" Kekoa said, squeezing my shoulder.

"Ha," I said, sarcastically swatting at him.

"No, Ruth just doesn't like guys," Nohea teased. "Which works out good for us!" She and Elsie giggled.

"Oh stop!" I said, slapping at Nohea. "It's not that I don't like boys. I just don't like any of *these* boys," I said, motioning to the beach.

On cue, two rowdy sailors ran by. One tackled the other and shoved his face in the sand.

"Maybe I will feel better tomorrow . . .," I said, changing the subject.

"Ruth, even if your head feels better, you can barely walk across the beach," Kapena pointed out. "Howz can you get up on a board?"

"It's better this way," Kekoa said. "I hate to beat you in front of all of thez people." Kekoa laughed.

"That's true," I admitted. "I still wish I could do it," I said. I was really bummed out.

Kekoa pulled me in with his big bear arms, and I rested my head on his chest. He was still bare-chested. The guy never wore a shirt. My eyes met the gaze of the sailor across the beach again. This time he looked away. For a moment, I felt guilty that Kekoa had his arms around me. What a weird feeling he gave me. I ignored it, pushed it away.

"I'm tired," I said.

"Lie down, wahine," Kekoa said.

I laid my head down on the blanket and closed my eyes. I didn't sleep soundly. I drifted in and out of sleep while the noises of the beach woke me up over and over.

I woke up in what must have been the wee hours of the morning, and I had to go to the bathroom. I tried to ignore it, to sleep through it, but I couldn't. I pulled my feet under myself and gingerly stood. My leg hurt, my head ached, but I was able to shuffle through the sand. The beach was quiet, eerily quiet. I've never liked the dark, but the sound of the rhythmic, lapping waves was soothing to me. I could hear a few coqui frogs singing in the distance.

The bathrooms were located on the far end of the beach because they were really just a hole in the ground and pretty gross. Most people probably just peed in the ocean, but I thought that was kind of gross too.

It was difficult to navigate through all the sleeping people, but I was doing it. The longer I stood on my leg, the better it felt. I imagined by tomorrow it would be feeling a lot better. I tiptoed and balanced and hopped over the arms and legs of many surfers, around the embers of fading fires, and over towels and blankets without too much trouble.

About midway across the beach, I took an extra big step over a cooler and landed on an unsuspecting sleeping man's toes.

"Yuch!!" he yelped, startled from sleep, and pulled his foot quickly out from under mine.

This, of course, tipped me off balance, and I fell directly on the poor guy. I began to scream, but before the noise could escape my lips, he covered my mouth with his enormous hand.

"Shhhhhh." He chuckled deep in his throat. "You're going to wake the whole beach!" he whispered sleepily.

I was literally lying chest to chest with the man with just a small blanket between us. It was, of course, Captain America, the same dang sailor I'd been bumping into all the previous day and who broke up the fight with Kekoa. I was probably going to have to figure out his name eventually. No time for that now though; I was WAY too embarrassed.

The hand that wasn't covering my mouth was behind my head, holding me still.

"I'm going to let go now," he said. I nodded.

He slowly released both hands and smiled at me. We both laughed. I felt so ridiculous, but it really was funny.

I awkwardly put my hands on each side of him but couldn't push myself up without literally straddling him. I didn't want to do that. I fumbled around for a few moments before he rolled me to the side of him, stood, and then offered a hand to me, pulling me to my feet.

"I'm so sorry. I didn't mean to . . .," I tried to apologize.

"No worries," he whispered. "That's the best wake up I've ever had. May I escort you to your destination?" he said, offering me his arm.

"I couldn't. I mean," I protested. "I didn't mean to wake you," I whispered.

He chuckled again. It was a deep, sleepy chuckle. "Well, I'm awake now. Where are we going?" he asked, taking my arm.

"To the restroom," I whispered.

"Okay, let's go."

He pulled me through the sleeping beach, zigzagging around the sleepers. We passed one rather large Samoan man sprawled out, snoring loudly. In an effort to avoid him, I tripped over a thermos and nearly falling again before he caught me. I nearly erupted into a fit of giggles.

"Shhhh!" he said, laughing too.

"Did you see that guy?" I said between laughs.

"Yeah, but be quiet. I don't think you want to fall on him."

"If I did, I would bounce right back up!" We both laughed, and we scurried across the rest of the beach, laughing not so quietly.

I was still giggling when I felt my way into the dark restroom, hoping I didn't touch anything nasty. He was waiting for me when I came out.

"Did you survive?" he asked.

"Barely." I was still giggly.

"I'm Will, by the way," he said, offering me his hand.

I shook it gently. "I'm Ruth," I said.

"I know who you are. The whole beach does. Where did you learn to surf like that?"

"My friend Kekoa. I told you that. You met him earlier, remember? He's the one that tried to clean that sailor's clock."

"Oh yes, I remember. He wasn't too bad himself. He made it to finals, didn't he?"

"He did. Last year, he came in third. I think he has a pretty good chance this year."

"Well, that's good to hear." He smiled sweetly. "Back to bed?" he asked.

I was pretty awake. I couldn't imagine going back to sleep. I should go back to sleep. I shouldn't stay up any longer but couldn't imagine settling my brain down now. I looked out at the water. It was beautiful. The moon was full and reflecting a huge stream of light across the surface. The waves were calmer than they were during the day.

"What are you thinking?" he asked, studying my face.

"I'm thinking"—I smiled—"that I should go back to sleep but that the water looks really inviting."

He raised his eyebrows. "Midnight dip?"

"Yes." I hesitated. "I think so."

"Let's do it," he said, taking my arm and leading me to the water.

No one was sleeping near the water's edge, so we weren't in much danger of waking anyone. Of course, there were a few people awake. You could see people sit up now and then readjusting, a few people walking around, but most everyone was out. I slipped off my cover-up dress. No reason to ever be out of a swimming suit here. He pulled his shirt off and offered his hand to me. What on earth was I doing?

"How is your leg?" he asked, looking down at my bandaged calf.

"It's okay." I winced as the water touched it. "The salt stings a bit, but it is feeling better."

"And your head?" he asked skeptically.

"Well, considering I'm going for a midnight swim with a strange man, I'm going to say my head isn't quite right."

We both laughed.

"Well, I will enjoy it while you aren't thinking straight." He smiled.

The only word for his smile would be beautiful. Combined with his eyes, he was nearly hypnotizing. I tried to shake myself out of the trance by diving in face-first. If Nohea and Elsie knew I was doing this, they would flip. I let the water envelop me in its serenity and slowly swam to the surface. Will was close behind me. Even though the waves were smaller than during the day, they were still too big to swim past the breakers without the help of a board. We stayed in close, the water never going higher than our shoulders. I floated on my back, looking into the night sky. Will watched me for a while. I felt nervous with his eyes on me, but I tried not to make it overly self-conscious.

"So how long have you been on the island?" I asked.

"A long time," he said. "Well, off and on for a long time. How about you?"

"A long time." I giggled. "How long have you been surfing?"

"Not long at all. I don't know if you can call it surfing. I do a lot better on a ship than on a board."

"Well, why are you here then?" I asked.

"My men wanted to come, and they need a babysitter—clearly. You saw that."

"I did. They could use some more babysitters." We both laughed.

His smile was captivating. I'd never really looked at sailors before. I had always avoided them. They usually forced their presence and cocky attitudes into my space, but Will was different. He was unimposing. I found myself actually enjoying being with him. We spent a few moments in silence before we decided to go back to the beach. I held onto his arm, and we dried off in silence. He walked me to my campfire, surrounded by all my sleeping friends. He waved a silent goodbye so we wouldn't wake anyone up, and he walked back to his campfire.

It was silent and dark. I lay quietly on my towel and looked at the stars. I didn't remember falling asleep, but my next coherent thought was, why was my mom shaking me? It wasn't my mother, of course; it was Kekoa.

"Ey, wake up, Ruthy! We're going over to Auntie's for some breakfast. She's got a big spread for us!"

"Uh, okay," I said sleepily, rubbing my eyes and sitting up.

Most of the beach was awake too, just a few remaining sleepers. A couple of people were swimming. Most people were presumably getting breakfast somewhere. My leg felt a little achy but better than even a few hours ago. Kekoa helped me to my feet, and we started shuffling down the beach with the rest of the gang.

"So whoz did you sneak off with last night, Ruth?" Kapena asked.

"Who? What? I-I didn't sneak off . . .," I stuttered. I was sweating. Why was I sweating?

"Howz it I heard you laugh and saw you two swimming last night then?" Kapena asked.

"Ruth! No way our Ruthy snuck off with a guy! Sure it wasn't someone else?" Kekoa asked.

"No! I saw it wid my own eyez!" Kapena said.

I pressed my lips together. I was so sure no one saw us. How did he see us?

"No way Ruth snuck off!" Elsie laughed.

"Well, Ruth, explain! Tell us! Tell us!' Nohea was bouncing.

Everyone was looking at me. I felt sick. I had no idea what to say.

"I just got up to go the bathroom, and someone else was up too. They helped me to the bathroom."

"Well, I would have helped youz. Youz should have woke me up," Kekoa said. He sounded a little hurt.

"I didn't want to wake you. I thought I could do it," I explained.

"So he helped you to the bathroom, and then you went swimming?" Nohea raised her eyebrow at me.

"Well, I went swimming. Just . . . just a dip. He just happened to be swimming too. Nothing happened!"

"We believe you, Ruth," Elsie said, giggling. Everyone laughed.

"Is it so impossible that something would have happened?" They all laughed again.

"So who was it?" Nohea pressed.

"It was nobody," I said.

Nohea elbowed me. "How could it be nobody?" she asked.

"Well, it was somebody. It was that sailor. You know, Captain America, the one that broke up the fight."

"Oh, he's cute!" Elsie squealed.

"Oh stop!" I insisted. "It was nothing."

"You said that," Kapena said.

"Leave her alone, guys," Kekoa said. He didn't sound very amused.

No one said anything else about it. We went to Auntie's for breakfast. By the time we got back to the beach, the first round was getting ready to start. Kekoa was in the second round. The Nacamotos were already heading out to the breakers. Kekoa was getting into his "surf mode," so Kapena was helping me cross the beach, although I hardly needed any help. He plopped me down in the sand with Nohea and Elsie, where we were going to watch the event.

"Eh, wahine!" A group of locals walked by. "You waz something yesterday!" one of them said.

"Yeah! You can surf with me any day!" Another one laughed.

I waved at them casually and went back to listening to Elsie's story about her brother's friend who came to their house the other night.

"The Nacamotos aren't doing so great," I said, interrupting her.

"Huh?" Both Nohea and Elsie looked up. They hadn't been watching.

"One of them has fallen twice, the other once," I said.

"It looks pretty choppy out there," Nohea observed.

"It does," I agreed. "Worse than yesterday."

They finished rather unimpressively, and Kekoa and two other surfers took to the water. The horn blasted, sounding the beginning of their heat. I watched Kekoa like a hawk. The choppy water didn't seem to bother him. He got on top of his wave and rode it in effortlessly. The only sailor who made the finals was hot on his tail but looked wobbly. His next two runs were just as seamless.

"He might have this," I interrupted Nohea and Elsie again. I had lost track of what subject they were on.

After four runs, the buzzer sounded, signaling the end, and Kekoa stood in the surf, watching the judges' table. I couldn't see the scores when they held them up, but Kekoa's fist pump was all I needed.

He won. He won the whole dang thing. We didn't know for sure until after the last round's scores were in. When it was announced, the beach erupted into a roar of applause as he jumped. He beat his chest a few times and hollered loudly. Nohea, Elsie, and I stood next to one another, cheering. After a few moments, he ran over to me and lifted me. The crowd cheered even louder. I held onto his neck as he twirled me around a few times. The energy of the beach was amazing. My cheeks hurt from smiling. This was his moment, and what a great moment it was. I saw Will as Kekoa set me down. He was clapping and smiling kindly. I felt a twinge of guilt for being with Kekoa but didn't understand why. Kekoa ran around the crowd, high-fiving people and receiving pats on the back.

We celebrated and cheered for a while longer, and people started to clear the beach. Kekoa was still pumped as we gathered our stuff and loaded the car. People honked and cheered as they drove off, but everyone was anxious to get back home. It had been a long two days.

3

The next morning, I was tired. No, tired wasn't the word for it. Exhausted, drained, spent, done, or maybe just dead was the right word. Surfing was out of the question. I lay in bed well past nine o'clock. I could hear the family at breakfast but couldn't pull myself out of bed. I wiggled my toes and legs, testing how they felt. After a quick analysis, I determined I felt pretty good. Today was our shopping day. I loved going to town and didn't want to miss it because of a silly hurt leg.

By the time I ping-ponged my sleepy body down the hall to join the family, Daddy was gone. I flopped myself down at the kitchen table. Mother just smiled and handed me a plate of rice. I poked at the white kernels for a minute while Mom clanked around in the sink.

"Geeze, Ruth, nice of you to join us," Elizabeth said, walking into the kitchen.

I shrugged and started eating.

"Kekoa's mom dropped off some items you left in his car this morning. She said Kekoa won the whole thing!" Mom said.

I nodded.

"You didn't think to tell us that?" Elizabeth snapped.

I shrugged again. I didn't say anything last night. I went straight to bed after Kekoa dropped me off.

"She also said you got hurt." Mom stared at me, eyebrows raised.

"Oh yeah, but I'm okay now. Did she happen to tell you how I did as well?" I was curious if Mom even cared.

"She did." Mom nodded. "She said you did well, would have made it to the second round if you hadn't been hurt."

"Wow, nice job, Ruth." Elizabeth actually sounded impressed.

I couldn't help but smile. I was proud of myself.

"So were there any cute sailors?" Marie asked, bouncing into the kitchen.

"There were sailors," I answered.

"Like Ruth would notice," Elizabeth said, rolling her eyes.

"Well, it was a sailor's fault that I got hurt, and I certainly didn't think he was very cute when he crashed into me," I said.

"He crashed into you! How exciting!" Marie giggled. "For someone else, that could be the beginning of a love story!"

"Nothing romantic about being knocked out," I said, remembering how much my head hurt.

"Do you want to stay home from town?" Mother asked. "I could take the girls."

"No," I insisted. "I want to go. I'm just moving a little slow this morning. Give me a little bit of time."

And I took my time getting ready. I was recalling the last two days in my head as I got ready. It was a lot of fun. Thinking about Kekoa winning and about my nighttime dip with Will made me smile.

After I was finally ready, I sat on the couch to go over the shopping list. Our living room furniture was made out of white wicker with burgundy cushions and white flowers. Two couches and a single chair circled around the big radio my dad got us a few years back.

Thinking about shopping was always fun. This was an excited day for me and my sisters. Twice a month, we walk to the market to pick up bags of rice, flour, sugar, and different fruits from the vendors. Today we get to go without my mom, which made it extra exciting. Mother was allowing us to go on our own more and more often, and we all enjoyed the freedom. My sisters looked forward to it because it is unadulterated time to walk among the seamen without dragging Mother behind, which allowed for more opportunities to giggle and flirt with the men who wanted to stop and chat.

I look forward to the walk too. I love shopping in the market. We often walked longer and farther than we needed to without Mother with us, who is always tired and wanting to go home. We liked to walk by the harbor and watch the men working on the boats. As much as I don't want their attention, I enjoy watching the sailors work. They are so organized, thousands of men coordinated together to run one giant vessel, for one cause and for one common good, heeding whatever orders they are given. They accomplish so much. It's an amazing thing to watch. Even as a daughter of a higher officer, I am not privileged to hear the comings and goings of the navy. They keep all the good stuff classified.

Daddy worked on the naval air base, which is the home for all the aircraft. That in itself is a sight to see, rows and rows of bombers and fighter planes all lined up, ready for battle at a moment's notice. Men run from one to another in a coordinated fashion, fueling and adjusting each plane. My favorite thing is to watch them all take off together. Daddy always comes home smelling like fuel and exhaust. I know even less about the sailors since they were not in my father's field. Even though I live next to the ocean, I've spent very little time on the water, unless you count surfing.

Mother walked into the room, joining me on the sofa, but before sitting, she yelled to the girls in the back, "Hurry up! It's time to get going!" Mother sat on the couch opposite mine. She had changed out of her pink nightdress and was wearing a green light cotton summer dress.

"Ruth, do you have eggs on your list? Last week, we didn't get enough from the Nacamotos' farm, so be sure to pick some up."

"Sure, Mother." I added eggs to my list.

"I'm glad you are taking Elizabeth to the dance tomorrow. It will be so good for the both of you," she added casually.

I had completely forgotten about that.

"Yeah, sure it will." I still didn't want to go. I forgot I had to go. "So do we need any sugar or honey from the market? Last month, I saw someone selling fresh honey."

Mother didn't even look like she heard me.

"Maybe you will meet someone really nice at the dance. I would so like for you to meet a nice man. Have some fun, and fall in love!" she said, looking off in the distance dreamily.

I let out a sigh and looked up at her.

"Ohhhh, Moooooom! Come on. Why do you do this every time I go to a dance?" I asked.

Her eyebrows rose, and she sat forward in her chair. I could tell she was upset.

"Why do I do this?" she asked innocently. "Why do *you* do this? Just what is your plan for life, young lady?"

Mom scooted all the way to the edge of her seat, looking at me seriously.

"Are you going to stay here with us, surfing every morning, for the rest of your life? Well, if you think that's how it's going to be, then you've got another think coming. You can't live here forever! You have to grow up someday! Maybe if you just gave it a chance, went on a date, you might actually find you like it!"

I was trying mightily not to turn this into a big fight. I worked up a calm voice.

"Mother, it's not that I don't want to fall in love and move on. Just think about it for a minute, will you? These are just a bunch of young boys, fresh to the navy, excited to be away from home and on a beautiful island. They aren't looking for marriage or to settle down, Mother. They are looking for a girl to have some fun with while they can before they get back on the ship. I don't want to be just some 'good-time girl.' Please, Mother, try to understand," I begged.

"Well"—she sighed, falling back in the couch, defeated—"just promise me you will try. Don't be one of those stuck-up, too-good-for-you girls, or you will end up all alone," she said, looking at me sincerely.

"I promise I will try," I said, surprisingly calm.

Just in the nick of time, Elizabeth and Marie emerged from the back room. Elizabeth was wearing a modern baby blue, knee-high dress that Grandma Beth gave her last Christmas, and Marie was in a yellow identical one. Both were wearing their short hair curled and under flowered hats. They were wearing white gloves and carrying a pocketbook. Elizabeth's dazzling blond hair actually made her look quite sophisticated and beautiful. The red lipstick she chose to wear today looked great against her pale skin. Marie could easily pull off being fifteen or sixteen in her getup (though I would never tell her that). She was dressed much like Elizabeth, her brown hair done similarly. She looked beautiful, but she still looked like a girl in woman's clothes.

They were both smiling wildly, clearly proud of their outfits. They looked more like they were ready to go out to a fancy dinner than a walk to the market. I was sure I would look strange next to them, in my sleeveless flowered dress, wearing my straight hair down the middle of my back. I am also tanner than both of them. They try to avoid the sun and keep their skin white, while clearly, I am no stranger to the sun.

I pulled myself off the couch.

"Okay then, let's get going. Marie, I think it's your turn to pull the wagon," I said, walking toward the door.

Marie shrugged disappointedly. "Oh come on, Ruthy! I'll get my white gloves all dirty, and the wagon is so heavy!" she complained and stomped her foot.

"Okay, fine, I'll pull it." I sighed. I really didn't mind anyway.

We left through the back kitchen door off the lani to get our old wagon out of the shed that Daddy had modified to be our "grocery getter" cart. After waving to Mother, we walked down the driveway, me towing the wagon, followed by the two chattery girls. We rounded the corner, where we were out of sight of the house, and started down the hill toward town. The girls were practically bouncing with excitement. I could feel their energy, and it made me excited too. It wasn't long before we were all laughing and teasing one another. We stopped a few houses down the hill, at Nohea's house. She normally joined us on outings to market.

Nohea bounced out her front door, her hair flowing behind her and wearing a beautiful smile and a soft red dress that wrapped around her neck. Elsie followed after her. They were both wearing flowers over their ears, white plumerias. Nohea's flower stood out against her jet-black hair and looked simply dazzling. Elsie's flower blended against her short blond hair. Nohea ran up to us and slipped a flower over each of our ears and kissed us each on the cheek.

"On the right side, of course, to show all those sailors that we're looking," Nohea said, emphasizing the word "looking."

When a girl wears the flower on the left, it means she is taken, much like wearing a wedding band or engagement ring.

"A new shipload of seamen arrived yesterday, ladies!" Elsie squealed and hugged each of us once she caught up. The girls all squealed too, even though we were all well aware of this fact.

Elizabeth and Marie responded enthusiastically, "We know!"

"My dad says they are off of the USS *St. Louis*," Elsie explained.

"Does that mean they are from St. Louis?" Marie asked.

"No, that is just the name of the ship. The men are from all over," Nohea answered.

"Well, I don't care where they are from as long as they are cute!" Elizabeth said as she adjusted the bust of her dress.

A chorus of squeals in agreement broke out again, and we started skipping down the street. The five of us were a giddy group of laughing girls. We would turn any sailor's head. There wasn't one among us who wasn't easy on the eyes. What seaman could walk by us without taking a second look? Whenever Daddy sees all of us together, he just shakes his head and mumbles something like "Lord help me." I never quite understood the meaning of that, but I think it means we are a sight to see.

My sisters were in heaven, along with Nohea and Elsie. They came along for the same reasons as my sisters. I enjoyed the good company and sights. With the sun in the sky, the smell of salt water and flowers, it would be hard not to enjoy myself. Elsie and Nohea updated the girls with the events of the last two days.

"And Ruth snuck off in the middle of the night with a sailor!" Nohea said.

"What?" the girls asked in unison.

"I did not!" I insisted. "He helped me to the bathroom."

"And then for a dip!" Elsie giggled.

"No way!" Elizabeth said. "No way!"

"Ruth could have had any guy she wanted." Nohea laughed. "They were eating out of her hand."

"What a waste," Elizabeth said, disgusted.

"Excuse me?" I asked. I was really kind of hurt by that.

"Well, you know," she stammered. "Any of us would kill for that attention, and you don't even want it."

"I don't want it. And neither do you really," I insisted. "They are just dumb sailors. They don't know what they are doing."

"Well, anyway," Nohea continued with her recount of the last two days, "it was like being with a celebrity. Which was good for the two of us." Elsie and Nohea giggled.

We reached the bottom of the hill and turned left toward the market and harbor. We were nearly a half-mile away, but we could already see sailors strolling in and out of the marketplace. Some were wearing dress blue uniforms, but most of them were in their navy white work uniforms or a plain white T-shirt. They all wore crisp white seaman caps on their heads and black silk neckerchiefs tied around their necks. I didn't know much about the uniforms, badges, or what signaled a rank. All I knew was that a white stripe around the shoulder identified them as a deckhand, and a red stripe meant they were an engineer, though I don't remember where I picked up that bit of knowledge.

Blue and white speckled the street before us. The sight ignited another round of giggles and excitement. When the seamen weren't on duty and not at the beach, they frequented town, looking at all the exotic fruits at the market and buying trinkets to take home to their loved ones. The market was located just outside the harbor. If it weren't for the seamen, I don't think there would be a market. I could see the ocean from my house and part of Ford Island, but the trees block the view of the ships. Now that we were a mile down the mountain, I could see all of them moored up on Ford Island. I've heard people call it Battleship Row. We all agreed; the fleet was very impressive today. Elsie tried to count how many ships were moored up, estimate how many sailors came with each of the vessels, and guess how many were on the island today for us to meet. Elizabeth grabbed Marie's hand excitedly.

"We should go to the beach later today and lie out. I just got a new swimsuit," she said with glee.

Marie nodded in agreement. "That would be so fun! Let's do it!"

Everyone else agreed as well. I can never pass up a trip to the beach, even if I don't have a new suit. So I agreed to go along, after we got our shopping done.

By the time we reached the edge of town, we passed our first group of sailors. They both smiled and tipped their hats at us.

"Morning, ladies!" they said with silly grins.

Everyone pretended to be shy and surprised by their greeting, before Nohea bravely spoke up.

"Good morning, boys. Aloha," she said sweetly.

One of the sailors completely turned around and was walking backward, watching us walk away. I peered over my shoulder to see he was wearing the biggest boyish grin I had ever seen.

"Oh, we will! It's been great so far!" he called back to us. "See you at the dance?"

"If you're lucky," Nohea said smugly, turning back around. She always knew just what to say to the sailors. None of them could resist her charm.

"Oh, I'll see you, honey. And I'll see you, and you, and you," he said, pointing to each of us.

The girls burst into a fit of giggles as we scurried away from them, myself included. Nohea linked arms with my free one and with Elsie on the other side.

"How do you talk to them like that? I always get so shy and nervous," Marie asked.

Everyone looked at Nohea, interested in her response.

"I just open up my mouth and talk. That's all. There's nothing scary about it. They won't bite." She laughed.

We had several more encounters, much the same as the first, as we made our way through town. There were lots of giggles and promises to see someone at the dance. No one was actually brave enough to break off from our little group and talk to a sailor all on their own. There was safety in our tight group.

I've learned from our past trips to town to keep my eyes fixed forward. If I look at the sailors and accidentally make eye contact, inevitably, one will wink at me, wave, or, worse yet, try and pull me aside from this safe little group to talk to me. At first, I tried just looking at the ground to avoid eye contact, but that was sometimes misread as being shy. I've met several seamen who enjoy the shy type and still seek after my attention. I'm not shy; I'm just not interested.

So today I walked with a purpose, looking straight forward like I was in a hurry to get where I was going. If ever I can't avoid eye contact, I usually can lean over to Elsie or Elizabeth and point out the sailor looking at me and tell her the sailor is making eyes at her. Then she generally turns red and starts batting her eyes, which usually diverts the attention off me.

The store where we needed to buy the flour, milk, eggs, and rice was up on the left and the market with fresh produce to the right. Standing in front of the market was a large group of sailors. They made an informal semicircle with their backs to us, gathered around one man, listening to orders, or so I presumed that was what they were doing, but I really couldn't see who or what they were standing around. All we could see of them as we walked was the back of their heads. I knew the group would look very promising to my company, and I wasn't interested in hanging around for any of it.

Elizabeth noticed them first. "Oh, I think we should go to the market first, Ruth," she said with a silly smile.

"I agree!" Elsie said, eyeing the crowd of men with the same look as Elizabeth.

Our little group of girls started moving in their direction, but I didn't want to have any part in this charade.

"Elizabeth, you guys go buy the produce, and I will go into the store," I said, slowly breaking away from them. I wasn't sure if the girls even heard me; they were so fixed on the sailors.

I was only a few feet from the girls when the group of sailors said, "Yes, sir!" in unison, and then their circle broke off into different directions.

A few sailors turned around in our direction. Upon seeing my friends, a tall dark-haired sailor, who looked like he just graduated high school and fresh off the football team, smiled and was first to approach them.

"I bet these ladies know where the best beach is," he said casually to a few of his buddies.

I kept walking in the direction of the store and ignored the spectacle behind me. I could hear the girls tell him where to catch the best waves, like they really knew anyway.

Then to my dismay, I heard Elsie's innocent voice chime up bravely with "Oh, you should ask Ruth. She is a real surfer!"

Oh no! My heart sank, and I stopped mid-stride.

"You're a surfer, sweet thing?" he said, turning around, calling after me.

I could feel everyone's attention on the back of me, including most of the other sailors from the group. I stood motionless for a moment in the street. I had to respond. I couldn't just walk away. I would have to answer the waiting, obviously surprised that I could surf group of men.

I turned around slowly to reply to him and was slightly surprised at the number of men looking at me. The officer who was obviously the one who had just been addressing the whole group of sailors just a moment ago was also looking at me. He was standing in the center of the mass of men. The sight of him, looking curiously at me, took my breath away for a moment. I paused briefly to study this tall, lean, strikingly handsome sailor looking at me with a pleasingly puzzled look.

He had dark hair, slightly bleached by the sun, poking out from under his cap. He had deep blue eyes noticeable even from the twenty-foot distance I stood from him. He was probably a few years older than the rest of the sailors. He was wearing a blue officer's uniform, his chest ablaze with ribbons and patches, but I had no idea what any of them signified. They didn't look like my father's fighter patches. He was probably a higher rank than the rest of the group, an officer of some kind, I thought. He had a big kind grin that I couldn't help but be captured by for just a moment, and then I realized who it was. It was, of course, Captain America, or Will. I mentally corrected myself. I hardly recognized him in uniform and not in swim trunks. I shook the moment off quickly and diverted my eyes from him to the sailor who was still talking to me.

"Well, you must have a board then, sweetheart, if you surf. We are looking for someone to teach us to. Our buddy Frank acquired a surfboard, but we could use another person with a board. What do you think? Would you like to teach us to surf, honey? Some of us are from Alabama and had never seen the ocean before we joined the navy."

I could hear the Southern drawl in his accent. The girls were all smiling at me encouragingly, with hopes that I would say something fantastic and worried that I was going to ruin everything for them.

"Of course, she knows," another sailor standing from behind him said. "She's the girl from the competition I told you about." I didn't recognize the sailor. At least he wasn't the one who crashed into me.

"Really!" the first sailor said, noticeably impressed. "Well, that is something. How about you teach us, honey!"

"I'm sure you can find someone much more qualified than myself to teach you," I said politely. "If you go up this road"—I pointed at the street we just walked down—"and stay to the left when the trees part in about a mile, there is a great keiki beach."

"Do you go to that beach often, darling?" he asked condescendingly.

"Oh no, I haven't been there since I was twelve. But I'm sure you will enjoy it," I replied.

"What does keiki mean?" one sailor asked.

"It means child," another sailor said. "She is sending you to the children's beach."

All the sailors laughed, and a few of them slapped the football player sailor on the back. My eyes involuntarily wandered back to Will, but he was gone. Strangely, I felt a twinge of disappointment, but I brushed the thought off.

The girls quickly engrossed themselves in conversations of giggling and showmanship with the men, so I gratefully left them without another word and crossed the street to the general store with my wagon in tow. I could hear the guys' deep laughter and the shrill sound of Marie's giggle even as Mr. Comesario, the store owner, held the door open for me and my wagon.

"Aloha! Howz it, Ms. Ruth?" Mr. Comesario asked, kissing me on the cheek.

Greeting with a kiss was strange to our family in the first few months we lived here, but now it is so natural, and I think nothing of it.

"I'm doing well. How are you today?" I asked, wearing a genuine smile.

"Oh, good, good. Doin' your shoppin' today, Ms. Ruthy?"

"Yes, sir," I replied.

"Well, don't forget da rice. Your father would be very disappointed," he said and walked behind the counter.

"Oh yes, he would, sir. Thanks for reminding me."

"Well, let me know if you need any help." He smiled kindly.

"Thank you," I said politely and proceeded to pull my wagon up and down the small aisles, which were just wide enough for me.

I started with the rice since it was the biggest and heaviest. I heaved two twenty-five-pound bags into the bottom of the wagon, leaving a little room on the side for the milk. Then I walked down the next aisle. The wheels were already squeaking under the weight of the rice. I put a small bag of sugar on top of the rice and oats for the rare occasion we ate oatmeal for breakfast. Squeaking again, down the aisle, I walked toward the milk. I had to put the milk in before I topped off the cart and balanced it with all the last few bags. I squished two glass bottles of milk between the rice and the side of the wagon and walked over to the aisle with the flour, squeaking the whole way.

The flour was on the third shelf up. I was taught it would be easier to put the wagon right under the flour so when I pulled the heavy bag off the shelf, it would fall directly onto the wagon. I situated the wagon between me and the shelves of food, leaning over the wagon to pull the flour toward me, hoping it would land nicely in place on top of the rice, oats, and sugar.

I stretched over the wagon and grabbed onto the edges of the bag, and just as I began pulling the bag toward me, I felt, more than heard, someone walk up behind the right side of me. I was leaning precariously over the wagon, and out the corner of my eye, I could see a pair of white pants and black shoes standing next to my own sandal-clad feet. I jerked around to see who it was. Unfortunately, I had already pulled the flour far enough off the shelf that it was in the grips of gravity. In the process of twisting to see who was beside me, I pulled the flour off the shelf and across the wagon, so it fell on the ground to the side of the wagon, taking me down with it. I fell over the top of the wagon, careening head-first toward the concrete floor.

When I opened my eyes, all I could see was my legs in the air for a brief moment before they landed on the bags of food in my wagon. I braced for the impact of my head on the hard cement floor, but strangely, the moment never came. I didn't have time to ponder why. My only concern was my dress. I grabbed at my waist in case it had slipped down in the horrific tumble. Sure enough, with my legs up high on the wagon and my body on the ground, just as I feared, gravity was at work, and my dress was nearly to my navel, revealing all my legs and a portion of my white cotton undergarments.

I gasped.

"UH!" I yelped and quickly pushed my dress up over my legs.

I heard a low, warm chuckle coming from the stranger next to me, who, I had just become aware, was the object the left side of my body was resting on and whose hand was holding my head off the concrete. It all happened so quickly, and my eyes were closed nearly the entire time I didn't notice he had caught me. I could hardly imagine just exactly how I ended up in this position. Did he just see my panties?

Slowly, reluctantly, and unwillingly, I turned my head to look up at him. It was Will, of course.

"Nice," he said, looking down at my legs that were bare just a moment ago. "No tan line," he said through his smile, referring obviously to the little peep show I had just given him. "We have got to stop meeting like this," he said. "I don't think your head could handle another injury."

"I don't think so either. Captain America to the rescue again," I said flatly.

He tilted his head, confused.

"Just . . . just a nickname . . . a nickname I have for you."

He half-smiled so handsomely I almost melted into a big gooey humiliated puddle.

I was so mortified. I wanted to curl up into a ball and die. I hid my eyes under my hands and tucked myself against his chest, catching my breath and hoping to disappear. My heart was beating fast.

"Now come on," he said kindly, trying to pull me off his chest. "It wasn't that bad," he said. Gently touching my face, he pulled me out of my hiding spot to look at me.

He was wearing a huge smile, which softened his stubborn chin, and his beautiful kind eyes burned into mine. He looked thoroughly amused at this precarious situation. I was very aware that our faces were so very close I could feel his breath on my cheek. He was kneeling beside me, holding me against his chest in a pretty intimate position. I was dazed, but I couldn't tell if it was because of the fall or because of my proximity to him.

I had never been so close to a man before, other than my father and Kekoa's bear hugs. He smelled different, although I thought I recognized his aftershave. He didn't smell like salt water like he had before. He was clean-shaven and had a strong chin, not like my father's, which was soft and round. His cheeks looked smooth, and he had a bright white smile.

I had to just laugh it off, but I was so embarrassed I wasn't sure how to get out of the moment gracefully. So I hit him in the chest playfully.

"You planned that on purpose, didn't you? You were just trying to get a show!" I said, pointing an accusing finger at him. But my giggles were giving away my insincerity.

He chuckled again.

"Who? Me?" he asked innocently. "I'm not that clever, but it was a great move." His smile softened. "Hey," he said, lowering his head and looking serious, "are you okay? That was quite the tumble."

"I'm fine," I said, rubbing my head. "Thanks to you, the only thing hurt is my pride."

"Ahhh, don't be embarrassed. This is the most fun I've had in months!" He laughed.

"Ohhh," I moaned. "I'm so mortified."

He laughed more loudly now, so I covered my face again to hide from the embarrassment.

"I'm just going to close my eyes," I said through my hands, "and you walk away. Then when I open them, it will be like this never happened."

I waited a few moments before peeking through my fingers. He was still kneeling beside me, crooked grin, raised eyebrows, and all.

"Why didn't you leave?" I whined.

"I can't leave without my hand," he said, referring to the hand still holding up my head. "Plus, I'm too much of a gentleman to leave a pretty damsel in distress."

Pretty? He just called me pretty?

In one fluid, effortless motion, he lifted me, swinging my legs off the wagon and placing me on my feet square in front of him. I forgot how tall he was. He must have been nearly six inches taller than me. My eyes looked straight into his chest, and he was certainly much broader than me. I straightened my dress and checked to make sure nothing else was showing. I could hardly raise my head again to meet his eyes. I was still so embarrassed. But when I did, he was still smiling, so I hit him again.

"Hey, hey"—he laughed, blocking my hits to his hard chest—"I'm the hero here, remember?" he said, laughing and dodging my pitiful jabs. "I just saved you from a possible head trauma . . . You should be thanking me."

He grabbed both my clenched fists and held them still in front of him. His hands were so much bigger than mine I could hardly see my own under his. I was acutely aware that he was holding my hands. My stomach flipped inside me, and I swallowed hard as we looked at each other for a small quiet moment.

I pulled my hands out of his grasp and looked down. I couldn't stand to hold his gaze anymore. I was still too embarrassed. I forced myself to look up. His smile was less goofy and more kind and concerned. His finger briefly touched the bottom of my chin, making my stomach flip again.

"You all right?" he asked quietly.

"Yes, thank you," I said honestly, smiling back and feeling awkward. "But you know, that really was your fault. You startled me!"

"I know, and I'm sorry. I didn't mean to. Let me make it up to you," he said. He bent and picked the discarded bag of flour and placed it on top of my wagon effortlessly. Grabbing hold of the handle of the wagon, he said, "Now let me help you finish up your shopping."

"Oh no, no, no. No need. I'm quite fine. Thank you," I insisted.

I wanted to grab the wagon handle from him and walk away, but I was too afraid of brushing my hand up against his, which was firmly placed on the handle. I was very aware of the proximity the aisle forced our bodies to stand in, and I didn't want to take another step toward him. I wasn't this nervous with him at the beach. Why was I now? Was it the uniform?

While my mind mulled over how I could get out of this awkward situation, he bent over to pick something off the floor. It was my shopping list and the flower that had fallen out of my hair. He studied the items in his hand and the contents of my cart.

"I'm assuming that this flower goes over your right ear?" he said, twirling it between his fingers.

I nodded.

"I already told you I don't have a boyfriend," I said.

"Yeah, I know, but it's kind of hard to believe, especially with your big Hawaiian friend always around."

He tucked the flower behind my ear. I couldn't look at him while he did it.

"Hmmm, it looks like you still need eggs, yeast, beans, and baking powder," he said, looking at my grocery list. "Let's do it." And off he went, squeaking down the aisle with my wagon of groceries following him.

William loaded the baking powder and yeast. He worked much faster than I could, and it didn't seem to take any effort for him to pull and load my heavy wagon. Normally, by the time I finish shopping, I'm out of breath, and my sisters have to help me drag the wagon back up the hill.

"All we need is the eggs, but I have no idea where to put them. This thing is full," he said, looking puzzled at the full cart.

"Oh, I usually just carry the eggs in my arms so they don't fall off," I replied.

He looked amused. He stopped the wagon, turned to me, and rested both hands on the handle. "You do this often?" he asked.

"Yes, at least once a month," I said.

"So tell me, really, how long have you lived here?" he asked.

"For eleven years," I said and crossed my arms. "How long have you lived here?" I asked, challenging him.

He just chuckled. "On and off for a few years. You do this by yourself every month?"

"No, my sisters help me," I replied.

"I don't see any sisters around here," he said, motioning to the rest of the store. "I just see you," he said, pointing at me.

"Well, they are outside, talking to the sailors," I said, pointing toward the door.

"Oh yes." He nodded. "I saw you all walking down the road. Why aren't you out there with your friends?" he asked.

At that moment, as if timed intentionally, someone walked into the store, allowing us to my sisters' high-pitched squeals from across the street carry into the store. I shook my head and laughed.

"Why aren't you out there?" I asked.

"Fair enough," he said, laughing. His smile and eyes seemed to say we had a mutual understanding as to why we both weren't out there with the crowd.

"Brothers?" he asked, curious.

"Nope, just us girls," I said.

"Hmm, your poor father," he said, smiling. "Okay, well, let's buy these groceries, huh?" William pulled the wagon to the register, and I followed awkwardly after him.

"Looks like you found more dan just rice today, Ms. Ruth," Mr. Comesario said, nodding to William and winking at me."Yes . . . it does," I said quietly.

I had no idea what else to say. I searched my brain for something funny to break up the awkwardness of the situation, but I came up with nothing, so I just paid him for the items in silence. William bought a notebook of paper, a pen, and a pack of gum.

"Big spender," I said as he passed the money to Mr. Comesario.

William smiled sweetly at me, and we gathered our items and walked toward the door.

"Aloha, Ms. Ruth," Mr. Comesario said, waving to me with a smug smile.

"Aloha!" I said back, and William and I left.

I tried again unsuccessfully to get the wagon back from William. Instead, I ended up holding the door for him as he towed it outside. I carried the eggs and his notebook.

I swallowed hard. We were outside on the street where everyone could see us. I reassured myself, thinking that the girls were too involved in their conversation to notice what company I was keeping across the street from them.

"Well, thank you very much for your help, and it was good to meet you," I said. "Enjoy your stay here on the island."

I bravely grabbed the handle of the wagon, touching his warm hand. Half of my hand was on top of his hand, but I was determined not to back down this time.

William didn't move his hand away from mine like I had hoped. *Why doesn't he just move his hand?*

"Aren't you going to go join your friends now?" he asked, motioning toward the spectacle of my sisters and the sailors.

My mind was racing. I couldn't pull the wagon up the hill all by myself, especially with my small limp, but I didn't want to get my sisters.

"I'm just going to pull this down the road and wait for them at one of the shops," I stuttered. It sounded like a good plan, but I knew I could be waiting a while, and I was worried the milk was going to go bad in the heat.

"I'll wait with you and keep you company then," he said, smiling.

"You know, actually, my milk is going to go bad in the hot sun, so I'll just go ahead and start for home." I smiled back.

"If you think I'm letting you pull this thing home by yourself, you've got another thing coming, miss. My mother would box my ears if she ever found out I did something so ungentlemanly. Now let's go, and please quit complaining," he said. I thought for a moment. It wouldn't be so bad if he helped me get the wagon home. It would be nice not to have to pull it all the way up the hill, and conversation with William really hadn't been so bad so far. I was really enjoying his playful energy. I had never before talked to a man who was so easy to be around.

"Well, in that case, you can help me, for your mom's sake," I said, giving in.

I was actually kind of excited. That is, until I remembered my sisters, Nohea, and Elsie. Was I going to have to tell them I was walking home with a sailor and then have to face a brigade of questions afterward?

As if reading my thoughts, William asked, "Do you need to tell your sisters to not wait for you?"

"I don't want to," I said, scurrying around to hide behind him, hoping my sisters wouldn't spot me.

William smiled, looking amused. "Fair enough. They are looking right at you anyway, so I'm sure you don't have to tell them I'm taking you home," he said, waving to them across the street.

"They are?" I asked, peeking around him. Then I saw them, all four girls' hands to their sides, mouths, and eyes wide open, gaping at me. "Oh geez!" I said under my breath.

But then I noticed that the soldiers standing next to them had a similar look on their faces. When my eyes met the sailors' gazes, they each tipped their hat and nodded to me politely.

Acting oblivious, William continued to casually wave at them and yelled, "I'll take her home, ladies! She'll meet you there!" His next comment he directed to the seamen. "You boys treat those ladies right, you hear?"

I heard a few quiet "Yes, sirs," and the girls waved awkwardly as we walked away.

After a few moments of silence, I asked, "Are they still looking at us?"

"Don't know and don't much care to turn around to find out," he replied. His big smile made me blush.

"Why did those guys look so shocked to see you walking with me?" I asked.

"Why did your sisters look like their eyes were going to pop out when they saw you walking with me?" he asked in the same tone.

"Fair enough," I said. I laughed. I wasn't going to make him answer a question I myself didn't want to answer.

His pace was so quick I was out of breath when we reached the turn up the mountain. William wasn't even breaking a sweat, and he was the one pulling the wagon.

"Up THAT hill?" he asked, pointing to the road.

"Yeah, do you need me to take a turn?" I tried to look serious, but I couldn't keep the grin off my face.

"Noooo," he said emphatically. "I'm just impressed you do this!"

"My sisters do help, and it really doesn't get steep until the very top."

"I saw your sisters. They don't look like they would be a whole lot of help," he said.

"They can be, when they have these guns behind them," I said, flexing my muscles, trying to look tough.

"Wow, that is impressive." He laughed. "I'm glad to know I have your help."

While we made our way up the first part of the hill, he tried to make a little small talk.

"So you've been here eleven years?" he asked, and I nodded. "Your family must have been one of the first ones here when they established the naval yard."

"Yes, my father was an integral part of the initial organization," I answered.

"How is it that he hasn't been transferred elsewhere by now?" William asked.

"He loves it here, so he retired and took a civilian job on base when it was time to reenlist. I doubt he will ever move back to the mainland," I said.

"Do you like it here?" he asked.

"I love it here! I love the beach. I love the sun. I can't get enough of it. I hope I never have to leave either," I said. I smiled thinking about how much I really did love it here.

"That would explain your amazing tan and no tan line," he added with a mischievous smile, reminding me of the embarrassment in the store.

I smacked his arm, feeling mortified, and he laughed playfully.

"And it would also explain why a beautiful girl like you isn't married off to a handsome sailor yet," he said more seriously.

I bit my lip.

"Oh, I've hit a sore spot," he noted solemnly, acknowledging my frown.

I shrugged. I couldn't think of a funny thing to say in response. "And you? I mean, apparently, it always has to come to this subject. Why haven't you got yourself a nice young bride in all your travels?"

"Who? Me?" he said sheepishly. The mood between us suddenly became less playful, and I didn't like it. "I guess I'm just waiting for the right girl," he said with a shy grin.

I laughed. "You just want to get a peek at all the girls' undergarments when you trip them in the store," I accused.

"I'm not going to lie. I didn't hate that. That was a pretty ingenious move on my part," he said, smiling again.

"Yeah, you should go tell all your buddies," I said and bumped my shoulder against his.

Am I flirting with him?

"No way. That's my move. I don't want any of them to steal it." He laughed.

I laughed too, trying hard not to sound like my sisters when they giggled.

When we finally reached the steepest part of the hill, William started showing signs of fatigue.

"You doing all right?" I asked.

"Oh yeah, sure," he said, wiping his forehead. "Whew, this is quite the hill. Lesser girls would struggle just walking it, you know? I'm impressed you pull this wagon up it," he said. He tried to smile through his labored breathing.

"Yeah, well, I'm not most girls." I flexed my muscles again. "Lucky for you, you're with me today," I said, and with all the courage I could muster, I grabbed the handle, our hands touching, and began marching up the hill, pulling the wagon right along with him.

The warmth of his skin against mine sent tingles up my arm and down my spine. I was determined not to let it faze me. I would not be some weak, silly girl who swooned at the touch of a handsome man.

Right?

William was chuckling, his eyes fixed curiously on me. I couldn't help but let a full-scale smile spread across my face as our eyes met. We pulled the wagon up the steepest portion of the hill in silence except for a few grunts and heavy breathing from both of us. We stopped to catch our breath just a few feet from my driveway.

"Well, thank you again very much," I said, catching my breath. "I really would have had a difficult time without you."

"Somehow I think you would have managed," he said between breaths.

"I actually had a great time," I added, not really sure what else to say. Part of me was hoping he would actually ask to see me again. What would I say if he did?

Instead of appreciating my honesty and actual hopefulness to see him again, he looked irritated.

"Are you really NOT going to invite me in for a glass of water after hauling your groceries up this hill in the hot sun?"

He actually wanted me to let him into my house? Why didn't I see that coming? I couldn't invite him in! I tried to hide my anxiousness.

"I . . . uh . . . I'm really sorry. I just don't think I can ask you to come in." My mind was racing for a believable reason why. "Our house is just a disaster, not suitable for company. But I truly am grateful for your help . . ."

I tried hard to pull the wagon out of his hands and walk to the door, but there was no budging it from his grasp. I started feeling frantic.

William folded his arms across his chest, still holding firmly to the handle. He looked just like Captain America. He tilted his head sideways and asked, "Just what is your problem, Ms. Ruth? Don't think I'm so dense that I haven't noticed you putting me off since the moment I caught you in the store. Just what do you have against me?"

"It's not you," I said too quickly. "It's just . . . It's just . . .," I trailed off. I'm sure I looked like a big idiot mumbling and stumbling over my words. I felt like a little kid trying to come up with a good fib to tell her dad, until the thought crossed my mind.

Why not tell him the truth?

"Look," I said, "it would take me much too long to explain WHAT exactly my problem is, but basically, right now, if I take you into my house . . ." I hesitated, already embarrassed by the words I was about to say.

"What?" he pressed.

"Well, you just don't understand. If I walk into my house with you, my mother will go ballistic and have our whole . . ." I started to speak in a whisper, hesitating, embarrassed to say the words. I looked down at my feet. "She . . . she will already be planning our wedding by the time you leave!"

William smiled; he looked relieved. I couldn't help but smile too, but I was still irritated.

"You think that's funny, huh?" I said with a chuckle. "You don't have to live with her!"

"Oh, come on, it can't be that bad!" he said, laughing.

"Not that bad? I'm glad you think it's not that bad." I felt my face turning red with embarrassment.

"Now come on, get over it," he said. He paused. He stopped smiling and studied my face. "You're really embarrassed, aren't you?"

My face grew even warmer, and I looked back down at my feet. How could he see through me so well?

William smiled and wrapped his arm around my shoulder. "Come on, it won't be that bad," he said, putting his arm around me and leading me toward my driveway.

I had never walked with a man's arm around my shoulder like this before, and I was acutely aware of every inch of his arm that was touching my shoulder and back and where our hips touched. My stomach jumped into my throat again. I was sure he noticed how stiff I had gotten under his touch; he squeezed my shoulders, trying to reassure me.

Once we reached the corner before my driveway, I slipped out from under his arm so my mother wouldn't see us from the window. He let me go without any protest. I looked up my driveway and saw Dad's '38 roadster.

"Ugh!" I accidentally said out loud.

"What now?" William stopped, pretending to be irritated.

"That's my dad's car. He must be home for lunch. Great!" I said sarcastically.

"All right, now I get to meet your dad!" William looked thoroughly amused.

I rolled my eyes as William pulled in front of my increasingly slow walking speed. I drudgingly pulled one foot in front of the other up the driveway. William cheerfully pulled the wagon all the way around to the back of the house and amazingly up the two stairs onto the lani.

"This is a cute little house," he observed as he waited for me to catch up with him.

"Thanks."

All I could think about was the moments that would follow upon opening the door. I felt sick to my stomach, dreading what was behind that door.

4

I took a deep breath and reached for the door. William flashed me an encouraging smile, making it hard for me to remember why I was upset. I stepped into the kitchen with William in tow. Daddy was sitting at the table eating lunch, and Mother was standing at the sink with her back to us.

"Hey, Ruthy!" Daddy said cheerfully, not looking up.

At the sound of my dad's pet name for me, William's grin got even bigger. Daddy looked up, choking a little on the water he just sipped, obviously surprised by our visitor. He grabbed a napkin quickly and dabbed the water off his mouth. After composing himself, an unfamiliar smile grew across Daddy's face as he looked from me to William. He looked surprised, shocked, and like he had won some kind of bet.

"Well, Minnie," he said, addressing my mother, "look what we have here!"

Mother was engrossed in whatever task she was involved in at the sink and just responded with a "Hmm?"

Daddy stood, closed his dropped jaw, stepped around from behind the table, and reached out his hand to William. "Welcome, Commander . . . ?"

William took his hand with a firm handshake. William's whole demeanor changed, and he suddenly looked like the officer his uniform presented him as.

"Lt. Cdr. William Wellington. Good to meet you, General Shepler."

Lieutenant commander!?

My jaw dropped. I was flabbergasted. Daddy must have recognized his rank by the patches he wore on his jacket. I couldn't believe I just let an executive officer haul all my groceries up the hill to my house. My heart sank with embarrassment.

"Oh, please call me Wendell," Daddy said. "I'm retired now."

At the sound of William's voice, without hiding one bit of shock, Mother whipped around to see who the strange man was. She stood there, leaning against the kitchen counter, bracing it for support, speechless, gawking at William.

I couldn't help it. I hid my face behind one hand. William let out a small chuckle, obviously amused by my embarrassment.

"Good afternoon, Mrs. Shepler," William said with a warm smile, but he still looked officerly. He took a step toward her and shook her hand.

"Lieutenant Commander," Mother said softly. She looked like she was staring at a ghost. Her whole disposition changed as quickly as it fell, and I could see her mentally pulling herself together, smiling politely. "To what do we owe the pleasure of your company?" Mother asked, looking from William to me, trying to solve the riddle of William's presence.

"Ruth looked like she needed a little help with the groceries, and I just couldn't resist, so I offered my assistance. Now where would you like me to put them?" William asked, acting like he didn't notice the awkwardness in the room. He turned around to pull some items off the wagon, which was still outside when Mother uncharacteristically dashed across the room to stop him.

"No, no, no! You've done quite enough, sir!" Mother pulled out a chair and motioned for us to sit. "Now please sit and let me get you lunch. You've done quite enough already."

Daddy had already sat back but was still smiling triumphantly.

"Well, I am certainly glad I came home for lunch today," Daddy said with a goofy grin.

"Ruth tells me you've been here for ten years," William said, trying to make casual conversation as he joined Daddy at the table.

"Yes, we have. How long have you been stationed here?" My daddy has always been good at acting causal in uncomfortable situations. My mother, however, is not and was hovering over every word as she threw some chicken and rice on plates for me and William.

"I've been on this island on and off for the last few years," William answered.

"Are you assigned to a battleship?" Daddy asked.

"No, sir, I'm lieutenant commander on the USS *St. Louis*, over the gunnery division. But lately, I've mostly been running training exercises here and in California."

All I could hear were the words "lieutenant commander" echoing over and over in my head. I'm sure now I was the one who looked like I'd seen a ghost. I slowly got up from my chair to get some lemonade.

Lt. Cdr. William Wellington. I foolishly had made him carry my groceries a mile, uphill, to my house. My mind went back to the surf competition. I fell on him! I felt like such an idiot.

I sat back and placed two glasses in front of us and filled them. My hand was visibly shaking. William reached for the glass and smiled sweetly.

"Thanks, Ruthy," he said, still amused.

"You look very young to be a lieutenant commander," my dad observed. "Do you mind me asking how old you are?" I felt my mother's eyes boring down at us, hanging on every word.

"Not at all," William said casually. "I'm thirty, and I am young."

"So, William," my mother prodded, "where is your family from?" I could practically hear the wheels turning in her head as she considered all the possibilities of future in-laws.

"My parents live in Wyoming, on our family ranch," William answered.

"Really?" my mother said. "That sounds lovely. Ruth loves horses. She has always said she wants to visit the Parker Ranch on the Big Island, but I bet your family's ranch would be even better."

"Mother!" The words escaped from my mouth before I could stop them. I shot her a piercing look. She didn't notice.

William looked like he was enjoying every moment of my shame. Daddy looked amused as well. *How can he be enjoying this too?* I let my head fall on the table, resting it on my hand.

Mother walked behind me and rubbed my back. In a lower voice, she said to William, "Don't mind Ruth. She's a little funny about boys."

"Ugh," I whimpered into my arm. Maybe if I closed my eyes long enough, I would wake up, and this would all be just a bad dream. No such luck.

"Yes, I've noticed that already," William said.

I could hear my mother walk back to the sink. She was still talking. "So how long have you two been dating? It must be a while for Ruth to bring you home to meet us. This is just like her to be hiding it from us," Mother said over her shoulder.

I refused to move, though I could feel William looking at me and my puddle of shame. *He can deal with her,* I thought. *He's the one who wanted to come inside in the first place.*

"Oh no, ma'am—" William tried to correct her, but my mother interrupted.

"Please call me Minnie," she said.

"Yes, Minnie." He cleared his throat. It sounded like he was the one getting a little antsy in his seat now. "We really did just meet in the market today," he said. "Well, no, we met the other day at the surf competition," he corrected.

I peeked up over my arm to whisper to him "See? I told you this would happen!"

William was still smiling but looked a little more wary. "Yes, you did," he whispered back.

Daddy noticed our little exchange and smiled too.

"Well, Ruth is going to the dance this Friday. Maybe you will see her there," Mother went on.

"Mother, please!" I insisted, sitting bolt up in my seat.

"Oh, calm down, Ruth. I'm just helping," she replied.

I rolled my eyes, exasperated.

"Actually," William interrupted, "I was going to ask Ruth to go with me. I'm in an uncomfortable situation, being the only executive officer without a date. The other officers are all married."

Oh no! Why did he say that? This was worse than I could have ever imagined. My mother squealed with delight, like she was the one who had just been asked to the dance. William's eyes never left mine but bore straight through me and like he was staring into my soul. I felt exposed, vulnerable, and like I was going to throw up.

"So what do you say, Ruth?" he asked seriously. "Will you accompany me to the dance?"

I swallowed hard. I felt like I was about to cry. This was so much more than I bargained for. William looked at me sweetly and very sincerely. How could I possibly refuse Captain America in this situation? But I felt tricked. He had put me on the spot. I couldn't say no.

"Of course, she will!" Mother said, giggling like Elizabeth.

"It's settled then," Daddy said very calmly. "What time would you like to pick her up?"

"How does seven o'clock sound?" William asked. He was still looking at me. He was waiting for me to answer. I appreciated that he was trying to talk to me despite my parents' interruptions.

"That will be fine," I said weakly.

I was so dazed and confused I couldn't focus on the conversation around me after that. I think they talked about his parents more and some of the ships he had served on. Daddy talked about a few air force adventures, and he and Mother prodded more into his family life.

After a while, I got up and placed our two empty dishes into the sink, and William walked up behind me with his glass. I heard giggling coming up the back steps.

"Oh no, it gets worse!" I said under my breath.

"What could possibly be worse?" William whispered in my ear as we rinsed our dishes. I felt his breath on my neck, sending goose bumps down my spine.

"My sisters," I said as they walked through the door.

Elizabeth, Marie, Nohea, and Elsie walked into the kitchen, immediately noticing William. Their faces formed into the same shape we left them in the market, their mouths opened and eyes bugged out like fish again.

My mother, so proud of me, introduced them all to William. He politely shook each of their hands as Mother told them he was a lieutenant commander and that he would be taking me to the dance on Friday. With the word "dance," they seemed to break out of their trance.

"Oh, we remember *you*." Nohea giggled as she shook his hand. "You're Captain America!"

Daddy's eyebrows raised, but no one else seemed to notice.

Elizabeth piped up, "Oh, Mother! I was asked to the dance too by a sailor! Can I go with him? Please, please!"

Mother looked to Daddy, who was gathering his things to go back to work. "The agreement was you could go with Ruth," Daddy answered evenly.

Mother looked almost as disappointed as Elizabeth.

"Well, maybe we can double," Elizabeth said hopefully.

Both William and I stiffened at the idea. I think he might have hated the thought as much as I did.

"No, it would not be proper for an executive officer to socialize in that way with an enlisted man," Daddy said without missing a beat.

"But, Daddy!" Elizabeth moaned. "What if I went with Nohea and Elsie too? Ruth will still be there. Everything will be fine."

"You may go with Nohea and Elsie," Daddy said, and Elizabeth looked relieved. "But you may not go with that sailor. You can dance with him while you are there, but that is it."

Knowing that was the best she would get, Elizabeth agreed.

Taking advantage of the opening, William announced that he needed to get back. I offered to walk him to the road, grateful for the chance to get out of the house. William politely thanked Mother for the lunch and shook Daddy's hand again. He said goodbye to the girls, and we left through the back door.

The minute the door closed behind me, I blurted, "Executive officer! Lieutenant commander! Just why didn't you introduce yourself to me as that?" I scolded.

William looked at the ground sheepishly. "Well, when most girls hear the words 'lieutenant commander,' followed by the fact that I am single, they tend not to focus on anything else other than my rank. So I like to keep it quiet."

I admitted I could understand that reasoning. I wanted to get off the lani to keep my family from hearing any of our conversation, so I led him down the steps and around the house.

"I guess I can understand that. But you made me feel like an idiot! I'm going to a dance with an executive officer! I brought an officer to my home and made him lug my groceries up the hill! I'm going to have to go to the dance and socialize with commanding officers! I can't do that! I feel like you tricked me!"

We were walking slowly to the road. I could feel my family's eyes on me through the front window, so I was trying not to make a scene.

William stopped to face me and placed his hand on my cheek. I heard a chorus of "ahhhs" from the window where they were spying. Funny, that's exactly what I felt when he touched me. If he heard them, he didn't show it.

"I'm sorry," he said sincerely. "I didn't mean to trick you back there. Although," he said with a smile, "it did turn out nicely for me." He tucked a stray hair behind my ear and then continued on walking toward the road. "I never thought I would see you again after the surf competition, so I didn't bother to mention it, and it was just too surreal when I saw you again. I didn't want to ruin anything. It's not like I hid it," he said, tapping his patches.

I rolled my eyes. It wouldn't take genius to look at his brilliant coat and figure something was up.

When we reached the corner, I stepped behind the big tree on the edge of our lot to hide from the window. William knew exactly what I was doing and laughed.

"Are you sure you don't need someone to swab the decks? I'd gladly do any kind of work to get out of walking back into that house," I asked.

"Oh no, you're much too pretty to be scrubbing the decks," he replied softly.

Daddy's roadster fired up behind us and backed down the driveway. We stopped talking to wait for Daddy to pass us. Instead, Daddy stopped at the corner, opened his door, and poked his head out.

"Can I give you a ride back, Commander?" he asked.

"It will be out of your way, sir," William pointed out.

"I don't mind. I have the time," Daddy replied.

"Well, I would love one then," William said.

Daddy shut the door and waited for William to get in. "Should I be worried about getting into the car with him?" he asked.

"No, no," I assured him, "Daddy's just fine. Its Mother you have to worry about."

"Okay then, I'll pick you up tomorrow at seven o'clock."

I gulped. "Yeah, okay, seven," I said weakly.

"You'll be here, right? You're not going to skip town on me?" he asked.

"I'm not going to lie. That thought has crossed my mind," I said, only half joking.

William laughed, not picking up on the partial truth in my statement, and got into car with Daddy. With William waving one hand out the window, I watched them drive down the hill, dreading walking back into my house and trying desperately not to worry about what he and Daddy were talking about. My mind kept wandering back to their conversation as I walked back to the house. My feet felt like they weighed one hundred pounds as I tried to lift one in front of the other. The laughter inside the house got louder and louder the closer I got to the door.

I rested my hand on the front screen door for just a moment before opening it, and then I walked into the living room, where everyone had moved so they could watch me and William walk down the road. After closing the door, the room erupted with their high-pitched cheers.

"Ruth, he is so cute! I can't believe you found him here!" Elsie said.

"Where, how did you meet him?" Elizabeth asked.

"How did you do that?" Marie asked, baffled.

"Did you see how he smiled at you? I think he really likes you!" Elsie said, looking way too shocked for it to be a compliment.

"You are going to have so much fun! I'm so jealous!" Nohea gushed, a touch more calmly than the other girls, and gave me a hug.

I couldn't keep my face from turning red under the attention. I flopped onto the couch and threw my arm over my face.

This is more than I can take.

I couldn't drown out the feeling that I was also kind of enjoying it too. Admitting that to myself made my face grow even warmer.

"Well," Mother said calmly after the chatter died down, "I think we definitely need to go shopping."

More squeals erupted, and I groaned. It just kept getting worse and worse. It was true that getting a store-bought dress was a treat, even for me. I've only owned three dresses that I didn't make on my own, but under normal circumstances, picking a dress that both Mother and I agreed on is downright painful. With the upcoming dance, this was sure to be a disaster. I just wanted to get out of the house and hide from everyone.

From under my arm, I protested. "Mother, I have lots of pretty dresses. I don't need to get another one, and we've already planned on going to the beach today . . .," I pleaded in vain.

"No," she said firmly. "You will be dining at the executive officers' table. You must look your best. Your loose, homemade Hawaiian dresses simply will not do."

I could see there was no arguing with her, but that was not my main concern anymore. I hadn't realized it would be dinner too and with other officers to boot.

"What?" I said, shooting straight up in my seat.

"Ruth, it's not just a dance when you go with an officer. You will be sitting at one of the officers' tables and eating dinner as well with the other officers and their wives."

The other girls grew quiet. The magnitude of my dilemma sunk in. Their faces changed to that of worry. Suddenly, my mother looked very wise, and I felt like I was going to throw up.

"Dinner?" I squeaked again. "Wives?"

Apparently, I had been reduced to one-word sentences. Gathering my thoughts, I went on, "Mom . . . what am I going to do? What on earth am I going to talk about with them? I can't go!" I proclaimed. I felt myself start to hyperventilate.

Mother walked behind me and started rubbing my back with her soft, plump fingers. "Honey, don't get upset. This is going to be a great night. Don't let yourself get worked up so much that you don't enjoy it."

Too late.

Nohea and Elsie announced it was time for them to head home.

"What? You're leaving me now?"

"Sorry, hun, gotta go!" Elsie said.

"I thought you guys were going to go lie out on the beach!"

"I think we better let you get ready for tomorrow," Nohea said.

They each gave me a kiss on the cheek and made their escape through the front door.

"Mother, may I get a new dress too?" Elizabeth asked hopefully after the door closed.

"No, you have plenty of dresses suitable for your evening."

"Everyone, get your things together. We will leave in a few minutes," Mother announced and walked down the hall to her and Daddy's room.

"But we just got back from town!" I protested. "My leg seriously hurts here." It did. I really didn't want to walk BACK to town. A nap was sounding pretty good.

"Ruth, please join me back here," she called from her bedroom. She was ignoring my petitions.

My sisters meandered back to their room, proclaiming the unfairness of their life, and I wandered into Mother's room and plopped on my belly in the middle of her bed. I skimmed through the *Post Magazine* she had lying on her nightstand while she got her hat from the closet. Deborah Kerr was on the cover, holding a golden retriever. I felt the bed sink as Mother placed her bag down on the other side. I knew she had something she felt was important to tell me; otherwise, I wouldn't be invited back to her bedroom. So I turned around to look at her and waited for the lecture.

"Mom, is this really necessary?" I said after a few moments of silence. "You know how much I hate this kind of attention and trying on dresses," I pleaded.

"Sweetheart," she said with a sigh, "you aren't just a girl anymore. You are a beautiful twenty-year-old young woman who has just been asked out by a thirty-year-old lieutenant commander in the United States Navy. It is time for you to grow up a little and act like the person you really are."

I wasn't sure exactly what Mom was getting at.

"Mother, what are you saying? I do act like myself," I said. It made me angry to realize that she thought of me that way. I was one of the few girls my age who didn't speak and act like a child. I was just being sensible.

"I know you do, honey," she said. "But I also see you running from everything in life. You're afraid to have fun and afraid to like anyone. You're a gorgeous, fun, amazing woman who deserves more in life than living with your parents and surfing. Go have fun with the commander. Get to know this man. If you don't like him, then don't see him again. But at least give yourself the chance to find out. Don't write him off before you get to know him."

I wasn't sure how to respond. Part of me was angry, while part of me thought she might be right. I also realized I kind of already liked him.

"Just promise me you will try," she urged.

I looked up into her sincere, honest eyes and sighed. "Yes, Mother," I said.

"Okay then. Part of trying includes looking your best, so let's go find you a suitable dress for the dance."

And with that, we gathered our stuff and went out the door.

I was still dragging my feet when we reached the bottom of the hill, mostly because I was exhausted, but I was trying to be enthusiastic like Mother asked. How bad could one night be? William had already proven to be good company and was gentlemanly enough. Mother and the girls were chipper and excited, and their mood rubbed off on me. It was either them or the warm sun on my face and the smell of the ocean. It has always been hard for me to stay in a sour mood when I am outside. The sights and smells always make life feel wonderful. As always, the closer we got to the market, the more sailors we saw. The crowd that had gathered across from the grocer was gone now, but there were plenty of other sailors for my sisters to bat their eyes at. I found myself searching among their faces for William. Did I actually hope to see him?

I walked next to Mother, and we were a few steps behind Elizabeth and Marie. The women's clothing store was farther down the road, past the grocers. We walked along the market side so we could stop and look at some of the produce and merchandise. That also put us among more sailors, which was by no accident on my sisters' part. The opposite side of the street had more professional businesses that the seamen didn't frequent. I concentrated on the items on the table and avoided the sailors' gazes. I bought some orchids and bird-of-paradise flowers from one of my favorite merchants. I could always pick my own, but she arranged them in such a pretty vase I couldn't resist.

"Ruth," my mother said to me quietly after we left the table, "do you not notice all the looks you get?"

"Oh, Mother, they look at any female with two legs under the age of thirty. It's not like I am any different from any other girl."

"No, sweetheart. All the sailors are looking at you. You can stand right next to both your sisters, and most of those men don't even know they are there," she said. "It's part of the reason your sisters get irritated with you so much. You get all the attention, and you don't even want it."

"Oh, you exaggerate, Mother!" I said playfully, elbowing her.

"I do not." She smiled. "This is what I'm talking about. I want you to act as the person you really are. You are a radiant, beautiful, confident young woman."

"Oh, Mom," I said, blushing. "Don't say this stuff to me. Humility is beautiful too, and you're just exploding my ego too far. Stop the flattery," I said, teasing.

We crossed the street just after the grocers and walked past a few more businesses before we opened the door to the clothing shop. The bell on the door jingled as we passed through it, alerting the shop owner, Auntie Gwen, that we were here.

"Ohhh," Gwen said, delighted to see us. "Aloha! How are you, ladies, and to what do I owe this pleasant surprise?" she asked, embracing each of us firmly against her large frame.

"Hi, Auntie Gwen! We're here to buy Ruth a dress," Elizabeth said, rolling her eyes.

"Ruth! Oh wonderful! For what occasion, dear?" She giggled.

This is just another reason why I hate shopping for a dress. I can never buy anything in private. Auntie Gwen will pry out every detail until she has enough information to gossip about to her bridge club friends.

"I need one for the dance," I answered flatly.

"She's going with a lieutenant commander!" Marie chimed in. She sounded proud of me.

I tried to shoot Marie a warning glance, but she was oblivious to my warning.

"Oh, come right over here, dear. I just got a new shipment of dresses yesterday. I'm sure we will find you the perfect one!"

Auntie Gwen led us to a rack full of frilly, lacy dresses with coordinating hats, umbrellas, and gloves. Elizabeth and Marie went straight to trying on the big brimmed hats and posing with pink umbrellas. I took one look at the first ensemble Gwen held up for me and held my stomach. It was a cupcake dress, one that was fitted and strapless on the top and puffed out at the bottom, making the wearer look like a cupcake.

"Uhhh," I began before, surprisingly, my mother came to my rescue.

"I think Ruth is more interested in a classic look," Mother said. I looked at her, bewildered. Usually, this is exactly the kind of dress my mother likes. "You will want to wear something you are comfortable in, something you can dance in and that is more 'you,'" she explained under her breath.

I was shocked at my mother's sudden awareness of my taste but also wary. She didn't usually treat me this way, and I didn't know she paid so much attention to my likes. She actually knew I didn't like those kinds of dresses? It makes no sense to me to wear layers on top of layers accompanied by more layers. It's sweltering in these humid conditions on the island. I can never understand how women can wear that stuff here. The only women who will dare wear something like that are haole women.

We worked our way through one rack and moved on to the next one. There, I spotted a few promising dresses and went to the dressing room to try them on. After trying on a navy blue shirt and a bright green empire waist, I settled on the last dress I had brought into the dressing room. I liked it the minute I tried it on. Before walking out to show my mother, I knew it was the one I wanted. It was red, calf length, and made of a satiny material. It had a halter top that tied behind my neck and had a lovely red shawl to wrap around my arms and shoulders. It also came with long white gloves, but I wasn't too sure about those. It was very simple, flowing, and elegant. It wouldn't stand out too much as "store-bought" among the other girls at the dance but looked fancy enough for the occasion.

I took one step out of the dressing room to model it for everyone, and Mother let out an excited gasp.

"Oh, that's the one, Ruth dear! You look simply beautiful!" She was smiling.

I was relieved that she agreed with me, and I sneaked a look over my shoulder to take one more peek in the mirror. I did actually look pretty good, I thought. Elizabeth and Marie still looked cross at me, but they agreed that it was the best choice too. So I went back into the dressing room to take it off. As I placed it back on the hanger, I wondered, *Will William like it?*

I shook my head, irritated with myself for being concerned with such a trivial thing.

The walk home was much the same as the walk to town except I was towing a dress over my shoulder. I couldn't stop my mind from wondering about the upcoming event and the reason for buying this dress. I also kept looking around in hope that I might catch a glimpse of William at the market, irritating myself again for being so silly.

"I am NOT a silly girl," I said to myself.

The rest of the day seemed to drag on, and my stomach never quite calmed down. It was as if there was a constant excitement in the air, making me very aware as the hours grew closer to night, which would then lead to day, which would then lead to night again, and the dance. I tried desperately to occupy my mind with other things, but my usual daily habits seemed to bore me and allowed my mind to wander again back to Lt. Cdr. William Wellington.

I read my book, took a nap, and helped Mother with dinner. I pulled the meat off some chicken to serve over rice, but the task was so monotonous it dragged on and on so that my mind went back to the events of the day, of William, of swimming with him that night and the possibilities of tomorrow.

Mother and the girls were still excited, but conversation about the event had died down some since we had discussed every possible topic relating to the dance at least twice. We talked about what Elizabeth would wear, how she would do her hair, how I would do my hair, what shade of lipstick we should wear, what Marie could possibly do while we were gone, what Elizabeth should talk about while dancing with her sailor friend, what she should not talk about, what she should say in this situation, what she should do in that situation, and on and on until every topic was exhausted.

That was until Daddy got home, and we had to talk about it all over again. Daddy sat in his chair in the living room and smiled politely, listening to the girls. I stayed in the kitchen and finished preparations for dinner. By the time they all joined us at the table, outside on the lani, the girls seemed satisfied with the amount of information they had given Daddy. After the blessing, the table grew quiet except for the sounds of chewing and sipping and the coqui frogs that sing to us every evening.

I desperately wanted to ask Daddy about his drive with William. What did they talk about? Where did he drop William off? Did Dad say anything embarrassing about me? My mind wandered, but I was determined not to succumb to begging Daddy for details. I was a grown, mature woman. I don't need to know every word spoken about, to, or from Lieutenant Wellington.

Although I really wanted to know.

As if reading my mind, Daddy smiled at me. "I had a nice conversation with William when I drove him back to base," he said.

All eyes shot up from the plates. They didn't know Daddy gave him a ride. I shrugged, faking disinterest.

"That's nice," I said, taking a bite of rice.

"You drove him to base?" Marie asked with a mouthful of chicken, a few chunks falling out as she spoke.

"Yes, I did. He is a very nice young man," Daddy said casually. "He said that he is picking you up at seven. Is that right?" he asked.

"Yes, I believe so," I answered.

"Well, I give you permission to stay out as late as you need, Ruth dear. We will not be waiting up for you."

"What?" I said. I was shocked. Why would Daddy say such a thing?

"You're a woman now, Ruth. You can determine how late you want to be out. Lieutenant Commander Wellington is a gentleman and will treat you as a gentleman should, so I have no worries or reason to place a curfew on you for the evening."

I stared blankly. What made me a woman all of a sudden? This was becoming a recurring thing today.

"Do I have a curfew, Daddy?" Elizabeth asked hopefully, batting her eyelashes and smiling.

"Of course, you do. You're lucky to be going at all. I expect you home at 9:30 p.m. and no later."

"At 9:30 p.m.?" Elizabeth gasped, appalled. "The dance will just be getting started by then!"

"No," Daddy said calmly. "The dance starts at 6:30 p.m., and if you ever want to attend another one, you will be home on time, not a minute later. Is that understood?"

"Yes, Daddy," she said sadly.

And that was the end of the conversation from all parties. Daddy had given me all the information about their car ride that he would volunteer, and I would not let myself push for more. Elizabeth was now in sour mood, again, and amused herself with pushing around the contents of her plate. Mother was chipper and happy and began talking about the last letter she had received from Evelyn in California.

I missed Evelyn. I wish she were here.

5

Finally, after clearing the table and doing the dishes, it was an acceptable time for me to retire to my room. I tried to go to sleep early, but my mind wouldn't rest. What was it going to be like dining with the officers? What would we talk about all night? Question after question plagued my mind. Once I finally fell asleep, my sleep was restless, full of short, strange dreams, mostly featuring William in one way or another. I hated it that any one person's premier into my life had such an impact as to consume my thoughts so much, let alone that person being a man. It drove me crazy wondering what I was becoming. Finally, the morning broke, and I could hit the beach and drown out my nagging irritating thoughts.

The morning brought a clarity to my mind. I felt at peace, although there were moments when a thought would pop into my mind out of nowhere. *The dance is tonight! The dance is tonight!*

I quickly squelched such thoughts and focused on the day—on riding my bike, on the refreshing morning air, and on gliding through the salty water.

I was extra early this morning. Kekoa wasn't there yet. It was a relief to be alone. I was still pretty tight and sore, but the wind, water, and sun could always clear a muddled mind. I stayed an extra long time this morning, dreading more than ever going home but not caring what Mother thought about it. I was sure she would be more tolerant today of all days. I had remembered to bring my snorkel mask, so when I got tired of surfing, I bobbed along the shore, watching the beautiful fish. I followed a school of fish as they danced along the coral and into the shallows. I floated, so still, for long enough to see a small octopus walking along the bottom. It was fascinating to watch it walk a few feet and then pause for a moment while its body changed to the color of the new surface it stood on. I've always thought that the creatures of the ocean are truly awesome.

I dove down under the surface to get a better look at the creatures on the ocean bottom, but I've never been a great diver. I got within five feet of a beautiful coral formation before the pressure from the water pounded my ears so much that I had to swim back to the surface. I gasped for a breath, drinking it in, and was greeted by Kekoa's smiling face.

"This doesn't look like surfing!" he said.

"Thought I'd try something new!"

"Sounds good to me! Let me have a go."

I gave him the snorkel mask and hung onto his board while he disappeared into the deep blue below. He could dive so much deeper than me and stay down longer. I lay back and floated, letting the hot sun bathe my bare shoulders and legs. Kekoa popped up moments later, splashing me.

"Howz long you been here?" he said after he caught his breath. We each had one elbow on his board and were bobbing along with the swells.

"A long time," I said. "Couldn't sleep."

"Dreaming about beating everyone next competition, eh?"

"Something like that." I laughed. I didn't want to tell him what I was thinking about. I was tired of thinking about it.

"Youz done?" he asked.

"Yeah, I'm pretty tired, but I still want to hang out. You ride." I shoved the board at him.

I went back and sat on the beach while Kekoa did a few runs. After a while, he joined me on the sand. I leaned my head against his broad shoulder.

"Not in a hurry to get back, eh?"

"No." I sighed.

"Well, youz got to go back some time. Nohea will be waiting for us."

"Oh shoot! I nearly forgot I told her I would help her with her routine!"

"No worriez. We still have time."

Kekoa drove me home a little bit later. I expected Mother to say something about my exaggerated beach excursion, but she just smiled at me when I walked in and continued humming the melody, humming while she cleaned the kitchen.

I took an extra long time doing everything. I soaked in the bath longer than usual, took longer to wash my face and brush my hair. I wasn't really sure why I was doing this. It was hard for me to be lazy with my morning preparations, but I was trying to avoid any idle time. I nearly forgot again that I was supposed to meet Nohea.

I quickly dressed in my blue wraparound skirt and a white shirt, tied a sash around my waist, put a flower in my hair, and hustled off to the studio.

The studio was malka* from my house set back among some beautiful trees. It really was just an enclosed stage with a wood floor and windows that never closed, so you felt like you were outside. Even though it was higher up and farther away from the ocean than my home, the view was open and spectacular. I parked my bike and hurried in to find Nohea already there. She was practicing, while Kekoa sat cross-legged on the floor, playing the rhythm on the ipu. An ipu is a large gourd the player held by the neck and beat a rhythm on the base. I love the sound of it. I am still so amazed that a dried gourd can produce such a beautiful inspiring beat.

"Ey, Ruth!" Kekoa said as I walked through the doorway. "Howz it?"

"Good," I said. He kissed my cheek.

"Little late, eh? Maybe I shouldn't have left you at your house. I should have stayed there and made sure you didn't forget again, yeah?"

"Yeah, sorry about that. I've been a little distracted, I guess."

"Could that be because you have a hot date tonight?" he said with a big grin.

"I thought youz waz my girl. What da deal? And why didn't you tell me this morning?"

I felt a little embarrassed that he knew.

"Oh, you know, a girl can only wait so long for her Hawaiian boy to sweep her off her feet before she has to settle for a haole sailor," I teased.

"Diz true." He wrapped his big dark arms around me in a bear hug, lifting me off the ground and pressing me against his bare chest.

"But still," he whispered, "it's me. Why didn't you tell me?"

"I don't know." I shrugged. "Didn't really want you to know, I guess."

"Well, I waz going to find out. I'm singing at the dance!"

"Hey, you two!" Nohea barked at us. "Hello, are you going to help me?"

"We better get to work!" I laughed.

"Yeah, diz wahine means business."

Kekoa sat back. He was dressed for practice, shirtless with a blue wrap around his waist, revealing his taut, strong chest and abs. This was the way he usually dressed even when he wasn't surfing. I'm always surprised if I see him wearing a shirt. He works a lot doing gigs for the base and at hotels, so he is usually always in costume. I think he knows he looks good too and likes to make the girls swoon when they see him. Lots of the locals wear their hair long, but Kekoa keeps his trimmed and short, which I prefer.

I took my place next to Kekoa on the floor and placed an ipu in front of me so I could join in with him. We started beating out the rhythm. Kekoa sang, and Nohea danced beautifully as she ran through her new routine a few times. The dance was a story about Pele, the goddess of the volcano. When she was satisfied with her practice, the both of us practiced an old favorite of ours together while Kekoa played the ukulele. Kekoa was a fantastic dancer, but he usually just played and sang. I love watching him dance the Polynesian dance of the warriors. He portrays a beautiful, strong, powerful dance easily.

Kekoa drove us both home. We didn't talk anymore about the dance.

I spent the rest of the afternoon wandering around the house, half-heartedly helping Mother with the chores. At five o'clock, when Elizabeth started getting ready, my stomach cramped up again. The last thing I wanted to do was sit around, all ready to go, waiting for Captain America to pick me up. So I helped Elizabeth with her hair and her dress instead of getting myself ready.

It really was pretty cute how excited and nervous she was. She picked at every part of her face, hair, and blue checkered dress, making sure everything was just perfect, adjusting the belt three or four times and reapplying her lipstick over and over.

"You look beautiful, Elizabeth! You are going to have a great time. Don't stress about it, sis," I said.

"That's easy for you to say. You're going with a handsome prince charming and staying out as long as you want. You're the one who is going to have a great time," she complained.

"I'm not so sure about that," I said under my breath.

Not wanting to miss a minute of the dance, Elizabeth, Nohea, and Elsie left the house at 6:00 p.m. Elsie and Nohea stopped by to pick Elizabeth up on their way. They each wished me good luck and kissed me on the cheek, and we promised to see one another when I got there.

After closing the door behind them, the house was eerily quiet. I turned around to see Daddy and Marie sitting on the couch reading and Mother standing at the other side of the room, looking at me.

"Do you need any help getting ready, dear?" she asked pleasantly.

"No, I don't think so. Thanks, Mom," I answered.

There was no more putting it off; it was time to get dressed for the dance. I went down the hall to the bathroom, where I made my preparations. I pinned my hair up on the top of my head with a small black hat on top and curled the front few hairs. As I transformed myself with lipstick and eye makeup, I started to get really excited. I didn't know if it was just nerves, anticipation, or true excitement for the date with William, but I was anxious for him to arrive. I slipped my dress on with just a few minutes to spare and walked down the hall to join everyone in the living room and see if they approved. Marie squealed with delight.

"Ruth, you look a-maz-ing!" she said as I rounded the corner into the living room. "Oh, when I get old enough, can I borrow that dress? Can I? Can I?" she begged. "Your lipstick matches the red perfectly!" she went on.

"You do look lovely, Ruth," Daddy added.

"Thank you, Daddy," I said, feeling a little embarrassed.

The dress fit me perfectly. It was tight on top down to my waist, where it flared out only slightly and flowed down my legs, stopping just under my knees. I left the gloves and just put the shawl on. Only a few more minutes and he would be here.

I can't believe I'm actually doing this.

"Why don't you go get a drink or something, Ruth?" Mother said, noticing my panic setting in.

"Okay," I said and shuffled quickly into the kitchen to fetch a glass of water.

My heart was racing, and I braced myself against the counter. Why was I so nervous? I wasn't there long before I heard a knock on the door and Mother answering it. I couldn't make out what William said, but whatever it was, it made Mother laugh. I stood in the middle of the kitchen, frozen, water glass in hand, for just a moment.

Marie came hopping in.

"He's here! He's here, Ruth! Come on!" she squealed and grabbed me by the arm and pulled me into the living room.

I straightened my dress and composed myself from the assault before I looked up and saw William standing in the front door. He looked dazzling. He was wearing his dress whites and cap, holding a small plumeria flower in his hand. His slacks looked neatly pressed and his shoes recently shined. His dress coat was white and adorned with all the patches and insignias befitting a lieutenant commander. Like the rest of his uniform, his hat was crisp white except for the shiny black bill. I doubted there was a speck of lint or dirt anywhere on him. His face matched his flawless uniform, clean-shaven with a sharp, firm jawbone and sharp angles. Suddenly, I understand the phrase "Can't resist a man in uniform." That was exactly how he looked, irresistible.

This is going to be a long night.

"Good evening, Ruth," he said. I hoped he didn't notice me staring at him like a goon. "You look beautiful." He cleared his throat. I thought I picked up a hint of nervousness in his voice. That gave me courage enough to break out of my trance. I put on my loveliest smile.

"Thank you, Lieutenant Commander. You look nice as well."

"Thank you, ma'am," he said, tipping his hat at me.

My family stood awkwardly beside us, listening and watching our every movement with anticipation.

William turned to Daddy, who was easily the most casual-looking person in the room. "I'll try not to keep out too late, sir," William said.

Daddy slapped William's shoulder kindly. "Don't worry about it. You two just have fun," he said with a warm smile.

William held out his elbow for me, I linked my arm through his, and he tucked the flower he was holding behind my ear. I looked up at the handsome sailor standing next to me and smiled and then looked behind us to say goodbye to my family. Mother looked proud; Marie was wearing a giddy, goofy grin; and Daddy just waved goodbye and closed the door behind us as we walked out.

William led me to the navy-issued jeep he drove. I was glad we weren't walking. He commented on what a lovely evening it was as he opened the door for me. I agreed and tucked my legs and dress in so he could shut the door. We exchanged a few pleasantries in the car as we drove down the hill. I wondered if our conversation was going to be this formal the whole evening or if we would fall back into the type of dialogue we exchanged yesterday and at the surf competition. Between the two of us, the small car was bursting with nervous energy. I noticed him fidgeting out of the corner of my eye. William gripped the steering wheel tightly before releasing his right hand and whipped it on his crisp clean slacks. He rubbed the back of his neck and let out a sigh.

I let out a small giggle and smiled.

"You're nervous!" I accused him and clapped my hands together.

"Oh, and you're not?" he said defensively.

"Yes, of course, I am, but seeing you nervous makes me feel tremendously better!" I said, laughing. "Now just what does Lt. Cdr. William Wellington have to be worried about on a night like this?"

"What do I have to be nervous about? You, of course," he said.

I laughed loudly at the thought.

"Me? Well, that's the most ridiculous thing I've ever heard."

"I'm glad my weakness amuses you," he said.

I let out a sigh, so I felt so relieved.

"Answer my question truthfully, Lieutenant. What exactly do you have to be nervous about?" I prodded.

"More than you know, ma'am," he said quietly.

"Oh come on," I said, exasperated. "You can do better than that."

"Well, to be honest, Ruth, I don't take dates to these very often. As an officer, I don't have to go to very many, just the first one after making port in a new area or sometimes when one of our boys gets married."

"Ya right, I don't believe that for one minute," I said. "You can't expect me to be that naive. You, Lt. Cdr. William Wellington, doesn't know his way around a dance floor with a date. That's ridiculous."

"Well, it's the only answer you're going to get," he said.

By the time we pulled up to Hickam Hall Officers' Club, the parking lot was nearly full of vehicles, and many sailors were walking through it to the dance. The other seamen, mostly privates, were wearing their dress whites as well, but they didn't have any patches like William, and they wore blue neckerchiefs tied around their necks. They looked nice but not near as dazzling as William in his officer's uniform.

We walked from the car the same way he escorted me from my house, with my arm linked in his. As soon as we opened the front door, we could hear the music from inside, and we both let out a nervous sigh. I looked up at him, puzzled, wondering why he really was nervous. William smiled at me and patted my hand that was resting on his arm.

"Let's just have some fun tonight, okay? Don't worry about anyone else," he said, reassuring me.

"Okay," I said hesitantly, wondering just what he meant, but it sounded like a good advice.

As we made our way into the main hall, we passed a few sailors. He nodded to each of them, stating their last names in greeting. He stood tall and professional-looking like he did when he first met Daddy. William led me across the dance floor, not to dance. We were headed to a certain destination. I noticed that the reactions of the sailors as we passed were slightly odd. Some of them smiled sheepishly and then looked down to avoid eye contact, while others nodded with big smiles when they saw me on his arm. A few more confident sailors looked at me and then slapped William on the shoulder and offered a playful greeting of some kind. One group of rowdy sailors were goofing off and laughing loudly but stopped when we walked by. They straightened up and nodded. "Sir," they all said respectfully to William as we passed. "Ma'am," a few of them said to me, tipping their hats.

William remained serious as we walked together. His jaw was set, accentuating the sharp, handsome angles of his face. He wasn't the relaxed, clumsy surfer I met on the beach. He looked like a lieutenant commander, and the men gave him the respect of a commander. I looked up at him in awe, feeling like I was walking next to a different man than I knew even just a moment ago. I chuckled under my breath as I realized this was the man everyone else knew. I was one of the few who was getting to know William as a kindhearted, pleasant man he showed to me. I wondered who he really was. *Is he the silly helpful sailor who helped me take my groceries home and waded in the ocean with me in the middle of the night, or is he the hard-respected lieutenant commander whom the sailors of the USS* St. Louis *know? Surely he is some of both, but which one is he really underneath it all?*

After pushing through the crowd, I saw where we were walking. There was a circular table at the back of the room where a small group of mature sailors wearing similar uniforms to William were sitting. They were each accompanied by a classy-looking lady, most likely their wives.

I took in a breath and stiffened slightly at the sight of our destination.

I stopped in the middle of the dance floor. "Is that our table?" I asked in a whisper as couples danced all around us.

"Yes, that is correct," William said quietly. "But not just yet." A goofy grin grew across his face, and the hard lieutenant commander washed away, and there was Will. I knew he was up to something.

William wheeled me around, so I was facing him, and began leading me back and forth and under his arm. I smiled and laughed out loud as he twirled me around the dance floor. William laughed and smiled too as we danced among the other couples. He was a great dancer. I didn't have a problem following his lead or keeping up. I felt slightly self-conscious when he placed his large hand on the small of my back and held my body close to his. My stomach fluttered with butterflies while I twirled around the dance floor, while in his arms, and when our faces drew close together. By the time the song was over, our faces were flushed, and my cheeks were sore from smiling and laughing.

The song changed, and the band played a slow beautiful love song accompanied by Kekoa's beautiful harmonic voice. William pulled me close to him. His right hand tightened behind my back, and we started dancing again. I hadn't even noticed that the music had changed until I was encircled in his arms. We were both still slightly out of breath, our hearts racing from the last song. I bravely looked into his eyes, our bodies close, chests rising and falling as we tried to catch our breaths. He gazed down at me so intensely I couldn't hold his gaze. I looked away. His smile was softening as we waltzed around in small circles, avoiding the other couples around us, but in clear view of our assigned dining table. I didn't have the courage to look over at the table, nor did I want to take my attention off the gorgeous man in front of me, but surely by now, those seated at our table had noticed me and William. I was relieved to put off meeting them for a few more moments and tried to soak up every bit of tenderness I felt gliding alongside of William. I felt safe like my legs could give out and William would still be able to twirl me around in his arms.

William looked like he was enjoying the moment as much as I was. When the song ended, we stopped dancing, and William slowly and silently led me toward the officers' table. I felt my mind come out of whatever spell I was under and my sanity return when a young sailor stepped in our path.

"Good evening, sir," he said shyly. "It looks like you've found a lovely date for tonight." He continued politely.

"Yes, I have. Galloway, this is Ms. Ruth Shepler. Ruth, this is my right-hand man, Ensign Walter Galloway," William said.

"Good to meet you, Ensign Galloway," I said to Walter.

"You too, ma'am," he said, nodding to me, and then turned back to William.

"Commander, my parents are in town this week. Do you mind if I bring them by to meet you?"

"Sure thing, Walt," William said with a friendly smile, slapping his shoulder.

"Thank you, sir," he said and left us to join a group of sailors on the other side of the hall.

"Well"—William sighed—"we've put this off as long as we can. Let's get it over with." He took my hand in his. I looked down at our intertwined fingers and then back up at him.

"Come on, let's go," he said, and with that, we made our way slowly to the officers' table.

Suddenly, I wasn't so worried about meeting the other officers; I was more worried about why on earth I was holding hands with this man. I'd never held hands with a man before, so why on earth was I doing it now? What on earth was I doing? William must have felt my uneasiness or noticed my face starting to fall. He shot me a wary look as we approached the table.

There were two open seats, presumably for us. William led us to the open chairs, but before he could say anything, a skinny black-haired woman with a big hat and long nose sitting across the table spotted us and stopped midsentence in her conversation with the woman next to her.

"Well, well," she said smugly. "Look who has a date." I could tell already this woman did not want to make friends with me.

An older gentleman to our left stood. At least he looked happy to see me.

"Lieutenant Commander Wellington, what a delight to see you here," he said. "And in such good company," he added, looking. He shook William's hand.

Out of the corner of my eye, I could see the big-nosed woman rolling her eyes.

"Why, thank you, Captain. This is my date, Ms. Ruth Shepler."

William turned to me. His face was strong and firm again. His jaw was set, commanding the respect and presence of the table.

"Ruth, this is Capt. Wallace Peterson."

I shook the captain's hand. All eyes were on me. He clasped his other hand on top of mine. He had a very friendly face that reminded me of my grandpa. His hair was a beautiful silver color, and he stood about an inch shorter than William, though he was not as slender. I could feel the eyes of the big-nosed woman bearing down on me from my side, scrutinizing every movement I made. It felt like she was looking for me to slip up in some way. I wouldn't let her have the satisfaction of intimidating me, and I vowed at that moment not to let her get the best of me. I would not let this woman have power over me, I told myself, and with all the courage and politeness I could muster, I straightened my shoulders, stood tall, and gave the captain the most charming smile I possessed.

"Wonderful to meet you, Captain," I said.

"Now let me introduce you," he said, motioning to the table. He put his hand gingerly on the shoulder of the woman to his left and said, "This is my wife and the mother to the 888 men on board the USS *St. Louis*, Mrs. Ginny Peterson."

"I am so glad to see you here tonight," she said with a big smile. She wore a lovely brimmed red hat that matched her dress and bright red lipstick. She was more mature in her years with graying brown hair like the captain's but had a youthful look in her eyes and smile.

"I'm very glad to meet you, Mrs. Peterson," I said politely.

"This here is Cdr. Jackson Gibbons and his lovely wife, Sarah." The captain continued, motioning to the couple to the left of his wife.

They both greeted me with warm, friendly smiles. The commander was a tall, slender brunet. His wife was obviously much shorter and petite than him and also brunette. They made a beautiful couple, but they must be at least five to ten years older than William.

"And around the table there, this is Lt. Cdr. Edward Smith and his wife, Theresa."

The captain was pointing to the long-nosed woman and her husband. They both nodded. She was actually quite a beautiful woman, probably in her thirties. Her husband was a short, stocky, imposing man. I wondered if she would be taller than him when they stood. I tried to smile back, but she scowled at me.

"He loves being called Eddie," William teased.

"Untrue!" the commander said, his face turning red.

The captain carried on. "And last but not least, Lt. Theodor Jackson and his wife, Elaina." Theodor stood and shook my hand enthusiastically.

"Great to meet you, Ruth. Really great," he said, slapping William on his shoulder.

It felt like he was congratulating William on bringing me to the dance. I wasn't sure if I liked that or not.

After introductions, William pulled out the chair next to Elaina, the lieutenant's wife; she was a tall, slender woman like her husband, and she wore a dazzling yellow dress. Elaina leaned over to me after I sat.

"You'll have to forgive us and our enthusiasm, but it really is great to see Will here with a date. I don't see him bring very many women to these," she whispered.

"Really?" I whispered back; I was honestly surprised. He was telling the truth then. I was curious to talk to her more. She seemed like she knew William well, but we were interrupted by Captain Wendell.

"So, Ms. Ruth, where has William been hiding you all this time, and why haven't we met you before?" The captain leaned back in his chair, studying me. He was still wearing a warm smile, and I felt very comfortable talking to him. All eyes were on me again. I tried to keep the conversation light.

"Oh, sir, I just met William. I met him at the surf competition and then again yesterday in town. He helped me with my groceries and tricked me into coming here with him."

William chuckled beside me. Will was at ease and comfortable with his friends at the table but still possessed an air of professionalism in his exchanges.

The captain looked shocked. "You could not just met him. I saw you two dancing," he said, raising his eyebrows at me and winked. "Our good lieutenant here doesn't just pick up girls in grocery stores or on the beach, Ms. Ruth. Surely you are just playing with us."

William didn't say anything. He just watched me for my response.

"Well, apparently, he liked something in my wagon because it certainly surprises me to hear that. He didn't back down at any of my refusals."

"You must have ol' Will here confused with someone else because that is like nothing he has ever done before. Usually, he will see a pretty girl and run the other way," Theodor said playfully.

Will wadded up his napkin and threw it across the table at the lieutenant.

"I'm not that bad," William protested.

"I don't think you truly know the lieutenant," I said to Theodor and the captain. "This guy here tripped me in the grocery store, swindled his way into my house to meet my parents, who forced me to accompany him to the dance!" The table erupted into even more laughter.

"Well, Ms. Ruth, you certainly have brought out a new side of William if that is all true," the captain said.

"Is it possible that the lieutenant has found a girl worth pursuing?" Elaina asked.

"Or it means she knows how to play a sailor," Theresa said, looking down her nose at me while she sipped her wine.

Luckily, the conversation was interrupted by waiters in black-and-white shirts and vests, placing full plates in front of us.

It looked delicious. I took my fork and poked around my plate at the lovely items arranged meticulously on it. There were breaded chicken cordon bleu, rice pilaf, and green salad drizzled with red raspberry dressing. The waiter walked around the table, pouring red wine into everyone's glass. When he got to mine, I smiled politely.

"No, thank you. I don't drink," I said.

"You are just a baby, aren't you?" Theresa said.

What is her problem?

"Yes, ma'am, I'm young," I said simply, not wanting to let her get to me. "But I just choose not to drink though."

"Can I get you anything else to drink, miss?" the waiter asked.

"Yes, do you have any sparkling water?" I asked.

"Yes, miss."

"I would love that," I said politely.

"So just how old are you, baby?" Theresa pressed after the waiter left.

"I'm twenty, ma'am . . . How old are you?" I smiled slightly. Everyone else seemed very occupied with the contents of their plate, but I'm pretty sure I saw a smile on William and the captain's face.

"Don't you know a woman never reveals her weight or age?" Theresa said.

"Oh, that's just something old fat women say," Theodor said. The whole table chuckled.

I smiled at Lieutenant Smith. Theresa glared at the both of us.

"My wife just finished nursing school last year," Theodor said proudly.

"Really?" I asked, excited.

"Yes," Elaina said. "I work at the military hospital."

"The big pink one on the hill?" I asked.

"Yes. I'm sure I will see you when you do your rotations," she said.

"That will be so nice to know someone up there. Perhaps we will even work together," I said.

Elaina smiled sweetly.

"Perhaps," Theodor interrupted. "But we just found out we are expecting, so I don't know how long I want her to continue working."

"Really!" the skipper's wife exclaimed.

A chorus of congratulations erupted around the table, with the exception of Theresa and Lieutenant Smith, who didn't change the frowns on their faces.

"That's wonderful," Sarah said.

"You will be wonderful parents," said Ginny.

"Well, it's about time!" the skipper teased.

The enthusiasm and happiness was contagious. It felt like everyone at the table was family. I felt a little out of place but happy to be a witness to this special moment.

Edward mumbled, "Kiss your freedom goodbye. Nothing but crying babies and diapers from here on out."

"Oh, lighten up, Eddie," the captain said. "How would you know anyway?"

Edward and Theresa remained silent and agitated as the rest of the table joined in congratulations. I wondered if they had kids. She didn't look like she could possibly be a mother.

The excitement wore down after Elaina told us her due date and that she was three months along and a few other details.

Elaina was still beaming while the conversation moved to more technical issues concerning the management of the USS *St. Louis* and the sailors aboard. The captain asked William about some of the men in the gunnery division who needed training. The commander and First Lieutenant Jackson talked about a young seventeen-year-old loader who was too small to pick up the shells and needed to be moved to powder instead. They all discussed the last war games they played target practicing on the USS *Utah*.

The women didn't pretend to be interested in the men's conversations. They broke off into their own discussions, leaning over their husbands to talk to one another. Sarah asked Elaina if she liked living on base and how she was adjusting to the humidity. Theresa was particularly annoyed with a new woman who moved in just across the street from her. Apparently, her small children were always in Theresa's yard, stomping on her hibiscus flowers.

"And yesterday I found a cockroach in my sink!" she explained. "I don't know if I can take this any longer. I need more sanitary living conditions."

"There are cockroaches all over the island. You can't avoid it," I tried to explain.

Her scowl made me instantly regret butting in. The conversation carried on as if she said nothing.

The captain's wife, Ginny, was very polite to all the ladies. None of them seemed particularly fond of Theresa except for maybe Sarah, but I couldn't quite tell if they were really friends or if Sarah was just tolerant of Theresa's complaining.

Elaina, who sat next to me, was the nicest of all. She noticeably tried to include me in the conversation, even though I had nothing to add to their discussions as their lives were very foreign to me. I was used to identifying with children of sailors, not the wives of sailors, so I was mostly content to just listen. I was in an uncharted territory. Elaina asked me a few more questions about how William and I met and told me how she and Theodor met back on the mainland when he was training in San Diego. She told me she was twenty-six, and she was obviously the closest to me in age at the table.

After fifteen to twenty minutes of conversation, most of our plates were cleaned. My stomach was deliciously satisfied, and the waiters began clearing our plates and replacing them with small glass bowls of sherbet ice cream, a real treat.

"I don't often eat ice cream," I remarked to William.

"Well, there isn't a large supply aboard the ship either," William replied.

"I assume the boys should be happy with this," Commander Gibbons added. "That is, if they take the time to stop flirting with the girls and eat some." He laughed.

"Oh, can you blame them, Commander?" Theodor said. "After three months at sea, they are only granted a Cinderella leave. They are making the most of each moment, and I would too!" All the men chuckled.

"Well, some of them went with Will to the surf competition. That was pretty damn generous if you ask me!" the captain boasted.

"Sir, that was six men. The rest are so cooped up they looked like windup toys, ready to burst," Theodor said.

"What is Cinderella leave?" I asked.

"It means all the boys have to be back on board by midnight," the captain answered. "The boys get a little restless after being at sea for a while, and I find if I don't place restrictions on them, they go plum crazy and all and end up in the brig the first night after making port." Noticing my confusion still, the captain explained, "The brig is like the ship's jail. Anyway, we have to ease them back into a little bit of freedom, or we don't get anything done."

"Ruth's father works on the naval air station, so she is more familiar with planes than boats," William explained.

"It's true," I confessed.

"Well, you should bring her along tomorrow when we give the women a tour," the skipper said.

"That's a fantastic idea!" William said.

Theresa snorted, disgusted at the thought of me accompanying them.

"Uhhh, what are we talking about?" I was confused.

"The ladies have never seen the inside of the grand *St. Louis*, so we are going to give them a tour tomorrow. You should join us," the captain explained.

"Oh, I don't know if I should," I tried to protest.

"Oh come on, Ruth," Sarah said. "Pleaseee."

"Yes, come. I guarantee you will never get an invitation like this again," Theodor said.

"So what do you say, Ruth?" William asked.

"Well, I don't know how I could possibly refuse. Thank you, Captain," I said graciously.

"Wonderful! William, you arrange to pick her up," the captain said, slapping his shoulder.

"I think I can do that, sir." William laughed.

Theresa rolled her eyes. Her husband, Lieutenant Smith, busied himself with licking his spoon and scraping ice cream out of his bowl noisily.

The music changed; it was no longer swing dance music. Kekoa and his band were in place, singing and playing Hawaiian favorites on their ukuleles and drums. I loved listening to Hawaiian music, so it was a welcome change for me. Without the loud swing music and jiving couples on the dance floor, the room took on a slightly calmer tone. Couples swayed back and forth to the romantic music. I took this chance to scan the room for my sister. I hadn't even thought about her since we walked in. As if reading my mind, William pointed her out.

"Your sister and friends are over there against the back wall to the side of the stage," he said.

I looked in the direction he was pointing, and sure enough, Elizabeth, Nohea, and Elsie were near the band, talking to a small group of seamen. I was curious if Elizabeth had danced with anyone and if she was having fun. She looked up and noticed me looking at her. She gave me an excited quick wave from across the room. William waved.

"Who is that, Ruth?" the captain asked, bringing my mind back to the table.

"That is my sister and some of my friends. I was supposed to be with them tonight, before William roped me into being here, that is." Everyone chuckled again. "I am glad I joined him though. It's been fun," I added, not wanting to really offend.

"Are you sure you wouldn't rather be over there with the squealing teenagers?" Theresa asked.

"I think Ruth would rather be anywhere else than with a group of teenagers, and that's ultimately how I convinced her to accompany me," William said.

A group of three seamen came up behind William. One of them put both hands on his shoulders.

"Good evening, Lieutenant Commander," he said.

"Good evening, Petty Officer. Didn't get enough of me all day, huh?" William asked, turning around to face the three of them.

"Oh yes, sir, we did. We just all wanted to come over and thank you for tonight's leave," the gunnery sergeant replied. "And wish the skipper a happy birthday."

"Well, don't thank me. Thank the skipper," William said.

I'd been having a hard time picturing William as a strict, feared lieutenant commander as he had been nothing but sweet since I met him, but I was beginning to see that the boys under him treated him with such respect that he must possess those qualities.

"I think we all know why you boys wandered over here. What kind of bet did you all lose?" he asked. "Or were you three brave enough all on your own?"

"What?" the sailor said, looking unconvincingly innocent. "I assure you we don't know what you are talking about."

"Well then, have a great night, boys. Enjoy the time you have. There is only a few hours left," William said and turned around.

"Lieutenant . . .," the sailor stuttered.

"Gunnery Sergeant, you can tell the rest of your squabbling hen buddies that no details or even the name of my date will be revealed to any of you tonight," William said. He didn't even turn around to address them. He suppressed a mischievous, crooked smiled and looked at me.

"Oh come on, Lieutenant," the sailor pressed.

"No," William said finally. "Now get back to your fun," he ordered. His firmness startled me. I would never argue with such a tone of voice. The men obeyed and sulked away, mumbling to themselves.

"But, Lieutenant," I said under my breath, "you already told that one man, Ensign Galloway, my name," I reminded him.

"Yes, but Ensign Galloway is different than the rest of those clowns. Sometimes they are as bad as a group of women looking for something to gossip about," he snorted.

The song ended, and there were a few moments of silence from the band. I looked at the stage to see some sailors talking to Kekoa and his band. Kekoa was smiling and laughing with them. I could hear his low chuckle from across the room. He started looking around the large room, looking for someone. I was curious what was going on. Kekoa nodded and smiled one more time at the boys and walked over to the microphone.

"Aloha, all you lovely navy ladies and gentlemen," he said. "We have a group of fine sailors here new to the island, and they are hoping to see a little traditional hula. So where are my hula wahines?" He paused a moment, searching the crowd. "I know you're out there, so come up the stage."

Nohea, Elsie, and Elizabeth, who were already close, ran up to the stage, excited for their moment to shine. A few other local girls followed behind them, taking their place next to them. This wasn't the first time Kekoa asked for hula dancers. The sailors are always curious about island culture, especially ones that involve dancing girls.

Every person at our table was watching.

"Oh, there you are. I knew you waz out there," Kekoa said when my sister and friends joined him. "But youz missing someone . . . I'm looking for one more special wahine to gitz up here," he said, searching the crowd. My face started to flush red, knowing who he was looking for. I looked down at my ice cream. "I'm looking for the beautiful Ms. Ruth Shepler. Whez are you? Ruthy, youz can't hide from me."

Everyone at my table stared at me. Theresa was scowling; everyone else looked surprised and curious. William looked a little worried, anxious to see what I was going to do. I was just hoping no one noticed how red my face was.

"Ah, there she is," Kekoa said, spotting me. "She is sitting right over there, next to Lieutenant Commander Wellington, I believe."

Now everyone in the room was staring at me.

"So much for the sailors not finding out my name," I said under my breath. William gave me a quick encouraging rub on the shoulder.

"That's all right. To see this, I would give up even more details about you." He grinned.

I stood quietly. The room was so silent everyone could hear the screeching of the chair legs rubbing on the hard floor as I stood.

"Please excuse me," I whispered. "I hope you don't mind, but I think I have to go up there," I said with an uneasy smile.

I removed my shoes quickly; scooted them under my chair; placed my shawl on my seat; unpinned the small hat on my head, letting a few loose hairs to fall on my face; and placed my hat on my chair.

I tried to look confident and was hoping no one could see through me into my terrified Jell-O insides. The whole room watched as I crossed the floor to the stage. When I got closer, a few sailors playfully punched one another on the shoulder excitedly, and there were even a few "woot" and catcalls from another group. I knew, for some reason, they were enjoying seeing the lieutenant commander's date on stage. I prayed I wouldn't fall and embarrass us both.

I put one hand on the stage, hiked up my dress, and swung myself up onto the platform, showing off some of my athleticism. More catcalls and laughter came from the audience, and I gave a little wave to the crowd. Kekoa offered me his hand and kissed me on the cheek when I stood.

"I knew I'd get youz up here," he whispered in my ear as I hugged him. "Howz da date?"

"Going well until now," I whispered.

"I can't have a hula without you. These girls need you," he said.

"All right, boys," Kekoa said, walking back to the microphone, bringing the crowd back to order, "you are in for a treat. Let's pick it up a bit. We'll start with a little traditional hula then move into the Tahitian style," he said, emphasizing the word "Tahitian," which was my favorite dance. It involves a lot of hip movements to drumbeats and is a lot faster than traditional hula.

Kekoa gave a hula skirt to each of us, not a traditional grass hula skirt. These were shorter, puffier skirts that emphasize the hips when we shook them. They were made of red and yellow fabric. They looked a little silly wrapped around our evening dresses, but they still gave the desired effect. He also handed us each Haku head lei, a ring of flowers that looked like a crown, and leaf bracelets. I suspected Kekoa had this planned from the beginning. We stood in a line at the front of the stage; Kekoa placed Nohea and I in the center. Nohea squeezed my hand, and it made me glad I was next to her.

The drummer and ipu player began their beats as Kekoa played the ukulele and sang with his deep, captivating island voice. The girls and I moved rhythmically together as we've done many times before, our arms and hands telling the story of the waves and rising sun. I didn't dare let my eyes wander to my table of scrutinizers, to any of the men in the audience, and especially to William. I transported my thoughts and mind to the movements and the story we were telling, letting my arms take control, swaying side to side with my legs following along, side to side, back and forth.

When the hula song ended, a half a second later, the Tahitian dance began. The drummer beat one time loudly and then again and again increased the speed, fast and strong, and our hips followed along. I couldn't stop a smile from creeping across my face as my heart rate and movements increased. The seamen responded to the change with whistles, catcalls, and laughter. Not only was this my favorite dance but most of the sailors too. At the end of the song, we all turned our backs to the audience and shook our hips, keeping up with the increasing tempo of the drums; paused; and hit three slower distinct beats and then faster and faster and faster for the finale. The audience was in a roar of whistles and yells, I was smiling from ear to ear, and then we ended with a look over our shoulder, which was when I finally saw William. He had moved near the stage and was leaning against a pillar with his arms folded across his chest and smiling approvingly at me. My heart leaped into my throat at the sight of him. I had nearly forgotten the company I was in. It was a great release, but now I was eager to get back to him. I waved politely to the audience, and we all took a bow.

I took my skirt off and placed it in the pile of skirts from the other girls. I tried to give Kekoa my Haku lei back, but he shook his head.

"Youz keep it, Ruth. You look lovelier than ocean sunrise with it on." He smiled, but something in his eyes made him look sad.

I kissed him on the cheek. "Thank you, Kekoa," I said.

"I guess you won't be hangin' with me during my break, aye?" he asked softly.

"I guess not." I sighed.

"Hez waiting for you," he said, nodding to William. "Better go."

I squeezed Kekoa's arm and made my way off the stage. When I reached the edge of the stage, William was waiting for me.

"That was fantastic," he said, grabbing my waist and lifting me off the stage. He lowered me down in front of him, our bodies rubbing against each other as I descended. He didn't release his hands but moved them around to the small of my back.

"Why, thank you. It was a lot of fun too," I said, trying not to show my uneasiness in his embrace. I could feel Kekoa's gaze behind me. I was uncomfortable being affectionate to William in front of him. William noticed and guided me farther away from the stage.

The audience was coupling off and dancing to the new song Kekoa started singing. I could hear my sister and friends behind me laughing. I turned to look at them. Elizabeth was joining a sailor on the dance floor as well as Nohea and Elsie.

"You ladies sure know how to draw a crowd. Those sailors will be eating out of their hands all night," William said.

"I know. It's one of their secret weapons," I said.

"Well, it worked," William admitted. "Let's dance."

"I need to go put my shoes on first," I said, pulling myself from his grasp and walking toward the table.

William grabbed me by the hand and pulled me back. "Oh no, you don't."

"Yes, I do. You'll step on my feet," I playfully accused.

"No, I won't. Just put those cute naked toes on my feet," he said, pulling me back into his arms. My heart was racing; I could feel his breath on my face again. I swallowed hard. I glanced at Kekoa. He wasn't looking at us.

I had no choice but to put my feet on William's, raising myself a few inches when I stepped on his shoes, putting our faces even closer together. We were dancing so close our bodies were touching; he really would've stepped on my feet if I weren't standing on his. We swayed back and forth, William guiding us to the back of the room, farther from the stage and Kekoa. Under normal circumstances, I would push myself away, but I found myself wanting to be even closer to him, though I didn't know how it would be possible to get any closer to him than I was at this moment. I hesitantly placed my chin on his shoulder.

I laughed in his ear, and he pulled his head back to look into my eyes.

"What?" he asked with a crooked smile.

"This is how my daddy and I would dance when I was young," I explained. "For some reason, it's not quite the same though," I admitted, blushing.

"Well, I would hope not!" he said, making me laugh. He lowered his head so his mouth was nearly touching my ear. "Kissing me won't be the same as kissing your father either," he whispered.

My head jerked back in surprise. I looked up into his eyes, my face divulging my utter shock and embarrassment at the thought of kissing him. I had not expected that. Immediately, I felt like an idiot gawking at him, my eyes wide with fear, but I couldn't force the muscles in my face to change shape. Moments later, I recovered and forced out a laugh, but my mind was still racing.

He wants to kiss me?

The thought made me scared and excited all at the same time. Different emotions were swirling around inside the pit of my stomach. I felt my anxiety rising and sweat forming on my forehead. I wondered if

I should slap him for being so forward or if I should think it was funny. I started sweating and wiped some perspiration from my forehead.

"Well, I didn't really expect that reaction. You looked like you might throw up. I didn't think the thought would be so revolting." William was still smiling, but he looked a little concerned.

I couldn't think of anything to say. I couldn't let him know how close I was to vomiting, not because I didn't want him to kiss me, I think.

Do I want him to kiss me?

My stomach churned again. I let out a sigh and gave a weak smile.

"I'm sorry," I muttered. "You just surprised me. I don't know if I've made this obvious, but I've been avoiding the gentleman callers up until this point."

"Up until this point?" he interrupted, smiling victoriously.

"Yes, up until this point," I admitted. "And," I said, slowing, not sure how much information I wanted to divulge, "I really haven't ever kissed a man other than my father." I immediately felt embarrassed for it.

"Well," he said kindly, "if you haven't noticed, I don't spend a lot of time 'calling' on women myself."

"But you have kissed a woman?" I asked, half-teasing.

"Yes," he said matter-of-factly, still leading me around the dance floor on his feet. "I am a thirty- year-old sailor," he said with a chuckle. "It comes with the territory."

I swallowed hard considering this, and oddly, I felt a tinge of jealousy thinking about him with another woman. As the subject turned a little more serious, our moods both became soft. Tired of talking, I hesitantly tucked my forehead into the nape of his neck and rested it there, breathing in his musky aftershave and, for a moment, felt at peace. William pulled our outstretched hands in close to our bodies and caressed my hand with his thumb. We swayed back and forth in more of a hug than a dance. My mind was tired, tired of stressing about the night, the conversation, what William was thinking, where our relationship might end up, what I was thinking, if it was stupid to be here with him, and on and on. I let my mind rest and enjoyed the moment.

We held our embrace for a few seconds longer after the song ended. The crowd around us began jiving to the new music while I collected myself from my daze, and we walked back to the table.

"Let's grab your things and head outside," he said, taking my hand. "Does that sound okay?"

"Sure. Is it okay to leave everyone?" I wondered. "I don't want to be rude."

"No, we're just fine. We've fulfilled our obligations, and you did fantastically, I might add," he said with a proud smile. "We can come back a little later."

The captain rose to his feet and applauded as we approached the table. The commander, his wife, and the lieutenant followed his lead. I couldn't imagine what they were applauding for until the captain reminded me.

"That was some great dancing, Ruth!" he declared enthusiastically.

"That was really beautiful!" Elaina said. "I've never seen the hula danced so beautifully."

Most of the table nodded their agreement, and my face blushed under their attention.

"Thank you very much," I said as they returned to their seats.

William grabbed my shawl and wrapped it around my shoulders, and I slipped my shoes on and grabbed my hat.

"Well, thank you all for a lovely evening," William said gallantly.

"Leaving so soon?" Theodor asked with a mischievous grin.

My face flushed again, embarrassed about where everyone at the table must be thinking we were going. I didn't even know where we were going; my face burned a little brighter, wondering exactly what we were going to be doing for the rest of the night.

"Oh, I'm just going to give Ruth a little break. We'll be back in a bit," William answered. "I can only expose her to you old fogies for so long. We have to ease her into this, you know," William said, making Theodor laugh.

"We'll see you later then," the captain said.

"You kids have fun," the captain's wife, Ginny, added.

"Thank you," I said.

6

We left through the back door, joining many other couples who were breaking off from the party. We walked along a path that skirted the back of the building and trailed off toward the water. We passed couples leaned up against the building and fence along the path. Most of the men were leaning in toward the women, the women gazing longingly into their eyes. Some couples were kissing; some were working up the nerve to do so. None of the sailors even noticed William or me walking by. They were engrossed with the girls standing in front of them. I could only imagine the immoral thoughts running through their heads.

I suddenly felt ill.

"What are we doing?" I wondered out loud.

"Right now, I'm just trying to get away from all these couples," he said.

I let out a relieved laugh. I was glad to hear the disgust and embarrassment in his voice, but I was still feeling a little cautious.

"Right up here is a real pretty spot," he said, pointing down the path. "You can see all the ships moored up on Ford Island. I didn't anticipate having so much company," he said sheepishly, nodding toward another couple making out against a tree a few feet off the path.

I laughed right out loud seeing his face turn a shade of pink, and immediately, I felt much better. I released my arm from his and let my hand drop into his hand. It wasn't intentional or thought out on my part, just something I did. We walked hand in hand, swaying our arms between us until we reached the end of the path. We leaned against the railing and looked over the harbor. Looking down, I could see the water lapping against the shore about fifty feet below. I rested my arms on the railing and played with my hat that I was still carrying. The ships were an impressive sight. We could still hear the music from the hall behind us, but it was very faint. The sound of the lapping waves was louder than the party.

"You are right. You can see almost all the ships from here," I said. It was twilight; I couldn't make out the distinct characteristics of the ships, just their outlines above the water. The moon reflected off the ocean, making it look like glass and sending a stream of light across the surface. "I love the ocean. I never grow tired of it," I said.

"Hmmm. Me too," he agreed. "You would think we might. You living here so long and me spending the last thirteen years working on the ocean."

"Yeah," I admitted, "but I think there has to be something wrong with you if you ever get bored of looking at this. Just looking around the ocean air makes people do crazy things," I said, referring to the couples we'd just passed.

He nodded in agreement and laughed.

"You've really worked on the ocean for thirteen years?" I asked after a moment of silence.

"Yeah, I'm an old guy. What can I say?" He chuckled.

"You don't seem old to me, and everyone says you're so young," I pointed out.

"I am young for a lieutenant commander. I'm just not young compared with you," he said.

"Oh well, perhaps you are too old for me," I teased.

William laughed. "Oh no, I'm not letting you get out of this that easy. You don't seem that young to me. That's why I like you," he admitted.

I laughed. It was very easy to be with him. I hardly remembered to be cautious or guarded.

"I am having a good time too," I admitted. I felt a little guilty for all the times I made him feel like I didn't want to be with him. "Thanks for inviting me."

"Not all of us seamen are alike, you know," he said, moving closer and putting one of his arms. He stood behind me with his chin almost resting on my shoulder.

"I'm not so sure," I teased. "You seem to have some of the same intentions. Maybe if I was smart, I would demand that you take me home."

"You know, the problem with the islands is there is never a good excuse to wrap your arms around a girl. She never gets chilled, never needs to be warmed up. You just have to be a man and do it," he said, laughing in my ear.

I felt a little uncomfortable being so close to him without the excuse of dancing, but I also didn't want to break his embrace.

"I'll let go if you want me to," he said seriously.

I was too embarrassed to say I didn't want him to. "I've felt uncomfortable since the moment we met, Will," I said.

His brows furrowed.

"But sometimes . . ." I paused. "Sometimes you have to go out of your comfort zone to find something you never knew you wanted," I admitted.

William didn't say anything; he just studied my face. I didn't know what else to say, so I changed the subject.

"So which one of these boats is yours?" I asked. "Is it over there on Ford Island?"

"No," he said. "First off, it's a ship, not a boat, and it's moored up off the pier next to the USS *Utah*."

I looked in the direction he was pointing but wasn't sure which of the three ships he was pointing at. They all looked alike lined up together in a neat row.

"The *St. Louis* is the smaller one," he said, watching my face as I searched the shoreline.

"Why is it smaller?" I asked. "It's a light cruiser. It's bigger than a destroyer and smaller than a battleship. We are faster and maneuver better. We work more independently than the battleships. We run reconnaissance missions, but our main role is in attacking enemy merchant vessels. We may be small, but we pack a big punch."

"So what exactly do you do on the ship for months on end?" I asked.

"Me? Lots of stuff. I'm in charge of the gunnery division, which is exactly what it sounds like, guns. Mostly, I make sure the men working the guns are trained properly, the weapons are maintained. I run war exercises with the men, set their schedules, and do whatever the skipper wants me to do."

"Hmm," I thought out loud, "it's a strange foreign life to me. I've only been on a ship a few times, just when we moved here and once when we went back to the mainland when Granddad got sick. I remember it being really cramped and pretty boring. They wouldn't even let us go up on deck."

"Well, it can get boring, but we keep busy. Mostly, you just get lonely," he said.

"Lonely? How is that possible with a thousand people on board?" I asked.

"It's easy. You miss family, you miss the people you actually care about, and like all the other sailors, I miss women. Men can get a little tiresome. I miss my mom, miss my sisters, and just plain miss seeing females," he said with a chuckle.

"Well, I'm glad you are here now," I said. I was surprised to hear myself say it. I gave his arm a little squeeze. "So do you have your own room on board, or do you share one with all the men?" I asked.

"All the officers have their own room. The captain has the largest. Our rooms are on the starboard side of deck 2. We call it officers' country. The commanders, first lieutenants, and chief petty officers all have their own rooms," he explained.

"Where do the enlisted men sleep?" I asked. I was fascinated.

"The crew sleeps in virtually every open area on and above deck 3. They are berthed as near to their assigned stations as possible, and they are each assigned a locker for their belongings. Personal space is a premium for enlisted men," he explained.

"Interesting," I replied. "And you all live there, eat there, and sleep there all year long?"

William nodded.

"I have a hard time imagining all of it," I said honestly.

"Well," William said, straightening up, "you'll get to see it tomorrow!"

"Yeah, I guess so." I had almost forgotten about that. "I'm excited to see it," I said.

"I'm glad you agreed to come. I was afraid you would say no."

"I thought about it, saying no, but Theodor is right. I will never get another opportunity like this again." I smiled and gazed across the water. I felt like I was speaking prophetically about myself. I had the overwhelming feeling that I would never have the opportunity to be with a man like William again.

"Come on," he said. "What do you say to joining me on the dance floor for a few more songs?"

"Are you sure you want to go back to that room of hooligans?"

"Oh, nonsense," he said, taking my arm. "Let's go have some fun!"

We walked arm in arm back down the pathway.

"So how did you end up in the navy anyway?" I asked as we walked.

"Oh, you know, what else is a poor nineteen-year-old farm boy from Wyoming going to do? A few months out of high school, I had no job. There was only one thing I knew how to do: work cattle. So I did what any inland mountain boy do. I joined the navy."

I laughed. "That makes no sense, William! What did your parents think when you told them?"

"I think they were glad to see me go, though I don't think they thought I would be gone this long. They didn't have enough money to send me to college or provide me with a living. Who would have thought a farm boy would fall in love with the sea? It made one less mouth for them to feed, one less pair of hands too, but I think they were glad I was venturing out. So I hitched a ride to Cheyenne, took a train to Denver then on to San Diego, where I went to boot camp and basic training. The rest is history."

"And now you are a highly decorated officer. I think you missed a few things in that story."

"Oh yes. My commanding officer in basic saw something in me. I don't know what it was. I was just a clueless rancher. Regardless of what I thought, he recommend me for Officer Training School, and I went."

We walked back through the door of the hall, where William led me to the dance floor. We swayed back and forth, dancing slowly.

"Do you ever regret it?" I asked.

"Excuse me?" he asked.

"Do you ever regret leaving Wyoming and joining the navy?" I clarified.

"No. I do miss the mountains and country though. I wish I could go home more. That is my only regret." Will looked a little melancholy and homesick as he explained it to me.

"So you were a farmer?" I said, trying to picture him working the fields and riding horses. "Like you rode horses and everything?"

"Yep, slept out under the stairs, cooked my meals on a campfire—the real deal."

"Could you still ride a horse now?"

"Oh, I'm sure I could. I'd be awfully chaffed for a while. I haven't done that kind of work in a long time. Navy can be tough and a lot of work, but nothing is harder than making your living off the land."

His past was incredibly foreign to me. Growing up in North Carolina and Hawaii, I had no idea what any of his upbringing was like.

"That's fascinating," I said. "I would love to go there someday," I said. "I have only seen a few horses in my life. That must seem crazy to you."

"No. My family has never seen the ocean. That must seem crazy to you, right?" I smiled. "We just come from different backgrounds. Maybe I will take you there someday," he said.

I laughed uneasily.

We danced a few more songs. William made me laugh. He made me feel special like I was the only girl in the room. I was actually getting comfortable with him. I'd never felt this way before. I'd never wanted a man's attention before, but I was basking in his. I believed him. I believed that his intentions were pure, that he was a good man and believed he just might be good for me.

By the time we decided to find the officers' table again, the party had started to die down. People were coupling off, and local girls like my sister were going home. It was getting late. The officers' table felt more secluded as we sat since the party had shifted toward the other side of the room.

The waiters had cleared the table, and the men were playing cards. They dealt William in, and I was content to sit and watch and to visit with the ladies. It was getting late, and I was tired. Sarah excused herself to go home and tend to their children. She kissed Commander Gibbons goodbye and said she would see us all tomorrow.

My mind wandered. I couldn't follow the conversation. The men were loud. They were laughing and joking loudly with one another. William joined enthusiastically but still attended to me. He didn't ignore me but quietly made me feel part of the group with his smiles and pats on my arm.

"Well, I reckon you better get your date home, Lieutenant, before she turns into a pumpkin," the captain said about an hour after we sat. I hadn't even realized my eyes were shut.

"I do believe you are right, sir," William said, sliding his cards across the table. "What do you say, Ruth? Are you ready to go home?"

I tried not to answer too enthusiastically; I didn't want to offend. "Yes, I think I am ready."

"Ruth surfs early every morning," William bragged. "I don't suppose you usually stay up late, do you?"

"Oh no. I'm usually pretty worn out by ten o'clock," I admitted.

"Well, thank you, gentlemen. It's been fun," William said, pulling my chair out for me.

"Yes, thank you all. I very much enjoyed meeting all of you," I said.

"Believe me, Ruth, the pleasure was all ours," the captain said, standing, shaking my hand.

"Good night, everyone," I said.

The table bid us goodbye. Elaina and Theodor left with us. Elaina looked sleepier than me.

"Pregnancy wears me out," she explained as we walked to our cars.

Once the car door shut behind me, I rested my head against the window and closed my eyes. The purr of the engine and the rhythm of the road lulled me to sleep, and I drifted out of consciousness.

7

I woke up to the sounds of a busy, bustling house. I could hear my sisters giggling in the bathroom and my mother stacking dishes in the kitchen. For everyone to be awake on a Saturday, it must be at least 8:00 a.m. I've never had a hangover, but lying there in my bed, I imagined that this must be what it felt like. My head was pounding. I felt like I could sleep a million years longer. A sunbeam sneaked between a small sliver of space between the fabric on my window and onto my bed. I rolled over, trying to avoid it.

Covering my head with my thin sheet, I reflected on the night before. It slowly dawned on me that I couldn't quite remember getting into bed. I looked down at what I was wearing. I was still in my evening dress; my shoes were on the floor, my shawl and haku on my dresser. I went over the events of the evening before trying to recollect how I got to bed. The last thing I remembered was getting into William's car.

"Ugh," I moaned and flipped the sheets off. I must have slept the whole drive home. How did I get into bed? Did he carry me to bed? Did I even say good night to him? Were my parents awake when I got home? I felt so embarrassed; I hoped I didn't snore or, even worse, drool!

I pulled myself out of bed, trying to rub the headache between my temples. I searched my top drawer for a bathing suit and slipped into the first one I found. I was so tired that surfing didn't even sound fun, but it was more appealing than explaining the events of last night to my family. I pulled a loose dress over my suit and slipped on my sandals. There was no way I could sneak out of the house unnoticed by my parents, but I might be able to get down the hall past my sisters if I tiptoed by the bathroom. Elizabeth was telling Marie about one of the sailors she danced with. They were both so engrossed in the story they didn't notice me walk by. When I entered the kitchen, my parents were waiting for me. Daddy was in his usual spot at the table and Mother standing by the sink.

"Good morning," I said casually, clearing my throat as I walked into the kitchen.

"Hello, Ruthy dear," Daddy said, smiling up at me happily.

"Good morning, Ruth. I've never known you to sleep so late. You must have had a fun evening," my mother said, fishing for more information.

"Yes, I did. Thank you. It is rather late, so I better hurry, or I'll be surfing with the afternoon crowd," I said with a hoarse voice, hurrying toward the door.

"Ruth!" Elizabeth's voice came from behind me. "Tell us all about your night!" I turned around to see Elizabeth and Marie pulling out their chairs at the table; everyone was looking at me while I backed toward the door.

"We saw you leave the dance. Where did you go?" Elizabeth asked.

"We just went outside for some fresh air," I said, probably too quickly.

"Did you have fun?" Mother asked.

"Um," I stuttered, "I had a great time. I met the captain and the other officers at the dance. They were all very nice," I said, rubbing my neck nervously.

"How was William?" Elizabeth asked, excited. "You two looked very cozy dancing together."

"Really?" my mother squealed, clapping her hands, looking eager to hear more.

"William was a gentleman. I had a good time with him," I answered truthfully. I was trying to reassure Daddy, who was looking wary.

"Did he kiss you?" Marie giggled, sitting at the edge of her seat.

"Ummm . . ." I was so embarrassed. "Ummm . . . I . . ."

"He did!" Elizabeth exclaimed, getting up from her chair and jumping. "He kissed you! What was it like? Did you kiss him back?"

"No, no, he didn't!" I insisted, stopping her. Raising my voice hurt my head.

"You lie!" Elizabeth accused. "You didn't get home until really late. "I heard you come in after eleven."

"Really?" Marie looked shocked. I looked at my parents; they didn't look surprised.

"So what did you do all night?" Elizabeth asked, sitting back.

"We just visited with the other officers, danced a bit. I don't even remember coming in. I fell asleep in the car."

"William carried you to bed, sweetheart. He was very sweet and apologized for keeping you out so late," Mother explained. "He felt bad that you were so tired."

"He did! Ugh, how embarrassing!" I slumped into the kitchen chair.

"Well, some date you are, Ruth," Elizabeth said, disappointed.

"Are you going to see him again?" Marie asked.

"Yes, he is going to give me a tour of the ship later today," I said.

"He is!" Elizabeth, Marie, and Mother all said in unison.

"That's remarkable, honey. Not many people have that privilege," Daddy said.

"Yeah, I'm kind of excited." I got up and walked to the door.

Marie started in with more questions before Daddy interrupted.

"Let her go, girls. If she is going to have time to surf and get ready to see William again, then you better let her go."

I thanked Daddy and stepped out as fast as I could.

Breathing a sigh of relief, I waved a quick goodbye and ran out the back door to my bike. I rode hard and fast to the beach, letting the wind and fresh smells ease the tension in my shoulders and throbbing in my head. I tried desperately not to think about William, but my mind wandered to his face every other moment. Question after question bombarded my thoughts, making me feel sick all over again.

Was he feeling some of the same things I was? Did he really want to kiss me? Did William think about me last night and decide he didn't like me? Did I disgust him while I slept in his car? Were my feelings for him real, or was I just being naive? And the biggest question plaguing my thoughts was, why on earth did I care so much about any of this?

When I got to the beach, Kekoa was waiting for me. He was sitting on the beach, his back to the road.

"Good morning. Have you been here long?" I asked, sitting next to him.

"Nah, I was afraid youz wasn't coming. Must of had a long night, eh?"

"Oh yeah. It was a little late when I got home. I'm not used to staying up much past ten, you know?"

We both laughed and sat in silence for a few moments. Kekoa rubbed his hands in the sand, making a small pile between his legs. I rested my head on his big shoulder and closed my eyes. It was nice to feel at peace again. No worries with Kekoa.

"So," he said, hesitating, "it looked like youz had a good time last night."

I sighed. "I did," I said, keeping my eyes closed.

"Come on, lazy bum. Letz hit it."

Kekoa stood slowly. He appeared to be tired as well. He held his hand out for me. He pulled me up effortlessly, and we walked silently to the water's edge.

"I've never seen you danz so much," he said as we stood at the shoreline.

"Yeah, I don't think I ever have before," I said, rubbing sand off my board. I felt uncomfortable talking to him about it.

I didn't say anything else. We walked out into the water up to our knees. Putting our boards in, we swam past the breakers on our bellies and rode in and out a handful of times.

I was supposed to meet William and the skipper at 10:00 a.m., so I only had about a half hour if was going to have time to get dressed. I didn't really want to tell Kekoa why I needed to leave.

I might not have felt like surfing when I woke up, but as always, the water was invigorating and refreshing. It made me grateful I came.

I waited for Kekoa to paddle back out to me past the breakers. Straddling my board, I watched him effortlessly pull himself through the water, one arm stroke at a time. He was extremely handsome. Why hadn't we ever dated? I loved Kekoa, as a friend, but it wouldn't take much for it to be more. Did he feel the same way I did? Now that William was in the picture, I had an awful feeling things with me and Kekoa would never be the same again.

"Youz done?" he asked out of breath, pulling himself up next to me.

"I . . . I'm going to have to go soon," I explained.

"Big planz, huh?"

"Yeah, I guess." I shrugged.

"Howz it, Ruth? You don't seem yourself."

He looked at me with his sweet white smile. I pictured myself leaning over and kissing him but quickly shook the image away. I couldn't think of Kekoa like that. I never had before. Why would I now? He was my friend, my really good friend.

"I don't know," I said honestly. "I feel weird, I guess." It was a lame explanation. "Maybe I'm just tired." I smiled weakly.

"Oh, Ruthy." Kekoa laughed. He grabbed the edge of my board and swung me around to face him. Our knees touched.

"It's that sailor boy. Whatz he done to your head?" He was teasing, and then a look of seriousness washed over his face. "Did he do anything to you?" he asked earnestly. "He didn't take advantage of you, did he? If he did—" His voice was getting louder, and he was visibly upset.

"No! Nothing like that!" I said, slapping him on his chest. He grabbed my wrist.

"Then what?" he asked gently.

"I don't know. I think maybe I like him." I cast my eyes down. I didn't like telling Kekoa.

Kekoa was silent for a few moments.

"I see. I thought you might," he said quietly. "Shouldn't that make you happy?"

"I am," I said, forcing a smile.

"Not convinced, Ruthy."

"I'm just confused, I guess. I've been so set on not liking anyone. I don't know what to do. I feel like I'm betraying myself." I laughed a little. It sounded like a stupid problem.

"Youz and me both. Iz never thought you would either." His eyes looked sad again.

Was he thinking the same thing I was, that he should have been the one who finally convinced me to fall for a man, not a sailor I barely knew?

"So where are you going with him today?"

"How did you—"

"What else would you be doing?" he said, interrupting me. "Youz alwayz tell me what youz doing. You tell me more things than Iz ever want to know. So why elze would youz be keeping something from me?"

He knew me better than I even thought he did. I held his hand in mine.

"He is taking me on a tour of his ship."

"I never pictured you falling for a sailor, Ruthy. I didn't knowz who it would be to finally turn your head, but thiz was the last thing I expected."

"You and me both," I said. "Let's stop this though!" I said with a wave of my hand. "I've gone on one date with him. That's all. We are getting way ahead of ourselves."

Kekoa didn't look convinced.

"We better be getting you back, Ruth."

We rode one more wave into the beach. Kekoa took my board from me and carried both our boards up the beach to his truck.

"I will give youz a ride so youz won't be late," he explained.

He effortlessly loaded the boards and my bike in the back of his pickup and reversed the process in my driveway when we got home, parking my bike in the shed for me.

"Thank you," I said as he shut the shed.

"Anything for you, Ruthy," he said, putting his arm around my shoulders. We were both still in our suits as we walked around to the front of the house. We stopped in the middle of the driveway. Kekoa took both my hands in his and turned to face me. "Have a great time today," he said with his carefree grin and kissed me on the cheek.

"I will," I said and hugged him. He wrapped me in his bear hug arms. I released him finally, and he walked back to his truck.

I had no idea how long William had been standing there, but there he was, standing in the yard, watching me.

"Hey der, bra!" Kekoa said, opening the door to his truck.

"Hello, Kekoa, right?" William asked. He crossed the yard and shook his hand.

"Yeah, bra," Kekoa said, slapping William's shoulder. "Ruthy said she had a pretty good time last night!"

"Yes." William nodded. He was ever so polite. "You were great last night!"

"Yeah, bra, thankz! Well, you two have fun today! Iz gotta go!" Kekoa gave a little wave and hopped into his truck.

I smiled at William.

"Hi," I said. I didn't know if I should hug him or how to greet him. "Come on in. I can be ready in just a few minutes."

We started walking to the front door when Kekoa yelled out his window.

"Ruthy!"

I looked back quickly. He made a motion tapping his shoulders. I shook my head, not knowing what he meant.

"Put some clothes on before you go in!" he yelled.

I looked down at my suit. "Oh shoot!"

I quickly pulled the cover-up I was holding in my hand over my head.

"My dad." I rolled my eyes in explanation to William. He chuckled.

Daddy stood to greet William as we walked in the front door. They shook hands. Mother was the first to speak. "Good morning!" she said.

"Good morning." He nodded. A moment of silence followed as we stood awkwardly in the entryway. "We are kind of in a hurry," William said politely.

"Yes, absolutely," I said. "I will go change."

"Have a seat, young man!" Daddy said to William, motioning to the couch.

I hustled down the hall and shut my door behind me. I could hear the muffled sounds of William and Daddy talking in the front room. I sighed. What a weird turn of events I'd found myself in. I started to fret uncharacteristically over what to wear. I couldn't decide which dress to put on. I tried on at least three or four. Why on earth was I having such a hard time deciding? Frustrated with my indecision, I chose to stay in the current blue dress I was wearing at the moment and fussed with my hair for a few minutes, brushing the long locks until they lay straight.

My hair was already dry but a little sticky from the leftover salt water. I thought about putting it up but decided to let it hang down to my waist.

I hurried down the hall into the living room, where William was waiting. He was a picture of perfection—crisp white pants and dark blue jacket blazing with patches. The whole uniform was frosted with his white cap and shiny black shoes. My sisters sat on the floor, gawking up at him like they couldn't believe he was actually in our house. That was kind of the way I felt.

Upon seeing me, his smile broadened sweetly, revealing his perfect white teeth, and he stood. He gave me goose bumps.

"Are you ready, ma'am?" he asked, tipping his hat to me.

"Yes, I think so," I said. "Do I look nice enough to tour your ship?" I asked.

"Yes, you look lovely, nice enough to make the other ladies jealous." He smiled his goofy smile.

"That's sweet." I blushed.

"We better go though. We only have fifteen minutes to get there," he said. He held out his elbow so I could take his arm. "Thank you, Mr. and Mrs. Shepler," he said, nodding to my family.

"Have a good time, kids," Daddy said.

"Bye." I waved.

"Bye." My sisters giggled in unison.

We walked down the stairs and back to his truck arm in arm and drove down the mountain to the harbor. I fidgeted nervously in my seat, smoothing out my dress and twirling my hair between my fingers. I was excited to take the tour, to be with William, and to see some of the women from last night. But I was worried about seeing Theresa again. She gave me an uneasy feeling, and I felt like I needed to watch my back around her.

I was lost in thought when William squeezed my knee, startling me.

"Hey, it's going to be fun," he said.

"Oh yeah, I know. I'm excited," I said, trying to sound convincing.

"Then why do you look a little ill?" He chuckled.

"Oh, no reason." I smiled.

"Did you really carry me to bed?" I asked after a few more moments of silence.

He chuckled. "Is that what you are fretting about?"

"That, among other things."

"I did. You were out! I've never seen anyone crash that quickly."

My face started to burn red.

"You were cute as can be curled up in the corner there," he said, nodding in my direction. "I hated to disturb you. The worst part is I had to wake your parents. I didn't know if I should just walk in or keep knocking until they woke up. I really didn't want to guess which room was yours though. It would have been terrible to pick the wrong one." He winked. "So I waited for them."

I laughed. "How long before one of them came to the door?" I asked.

"Not too long. Your dad answered, grunted the direction of your room, and went back to bed."

"Really? That surprises me."

"How come?"

"I don't know. He is usually so distrusting of sailors. I can't hardly imagine him willingly let one into my room alone."

"Welp, he surely did! I had a hard time getting the door open while holding you, but I managed. Got your shoes off and tucked you in and everything." He flashed a goofy grin.

"I can't believe I slept through all of that!" He was in my room, intimately tucking me in, and I was completely unaware. The thought gave me goose bumps.

"I'm willing to do it again if needed!" he teased.

"I'm planning to stay conscious all of today," I reassured.

Once we drove past the guard station, where William showed his ID, we parked the truck next to a row of other navy-issued vehicles. William ran around the front of the car to open my door and help me out.

"Okay, we just have a few minutes, so let's hustle down the dock," he said, taking my hand.

My hand instantly felt hot and sweaty in his grasp, but I didn't complain as we ran through the parking lot toward the dock.

There were rows of ships and boats moored up in the harbor, towering over us all down the shore. They each looked like large permanent buildings.

"I always have a hard time believing these are seagoing vessels," I said between breaths as we jogged together. "They look like buildings, too big to even float," I said, inspecting one of the boats as we hurried down the harbor.

"They are big buildings in a sense, but believe me, they are masters at navigating the water. It takes several men to do it though. Not just one person can steer these ships," he said. He wasn't breathing nearly as heavy as I was.

"It is amazing," I said, in awe of the sight around me.

"Yes, I think so too," he admitted.

Now that we were closer, I could see the USS *Utah* that he was talking about last night. It was ahead of us, and just past it, I could barely make out the words "USS St. Louis" on the boat moored up behind it.

We turned right, down a small strip of the dock and walked past the USS *Utah*. I grabbed onto William's arm as we walked down the narrow, creaky pathway. I felt out of place as my sandals clinked along the wood planks with every step. William looked perfectly comfortable navigating the two of us around the ropes and pulleys along the dock next to the *Utah*. He looked confident, stately and perfectly at home in the surroundings. No one seemed to be on board the USS *Utah*. It towered over us in the silence, looking luminous in the bright blue sky.

There was a crowd of people just ahead standing next to the *St. Louis*. It was undoubtedly the officers and their wives. The men stood comfortably among the pulleys, planks, and ropes, while the women looked awkward and completely out of place.

"Well, what have you two been up to?" Theodor teased once we joined them.

"Good to see you again, Ruth," Elaina said, smacking her husband's shoulder. Elaina was wearing a cute pink summer dress and dainty white gloves.

"It's about time," Theresa mumbled. She was wearing a constrictive green dress and large brimmed black hat. She looked the most out of her element of the four women.

"We're glad you made it!" the skipper boomed, shaking my hand.

"Good to see you again, Captain Peterson," I said and nodded to the other ladies standing next to their husbands.

I definitely felt like the odd one out, dressed in my loose aloha dress with my hair whipping in the wind next to the other women meticulously groomed standing next to their stately husbands. What on earth was I doing here with these people?

"Well, that's all of us, so let's go aboard. We'll go up to the deck first. I'd like to let William shine and show his expertise of all the weapons on board this ship, but we would just get in the way of our boys working, so we will go straight to the lower decks," he said.

We formed an informal line, walking up the plank to the deck of the boat. William and I hung back and let everyone go first.

"After you, Lieutenant Jackson," William said as Theodor walked by.

Theodor gave Will a smack on the arm. Theodor, the skipper, and Commander Gibbons were very attentive to their wives as they maneuvered their way up the plank. Theodor took his wife's hand, guiding her so she wouldn't fall. Lieutenant Smith stepped in front of his wife, Theresa, walking ahead of her, letting her navigate the rickety ramp in her teetery shoes all by herself.

William and I hung back, watching the precarious parade of officers and women gently maneuvering their way up the ramp.

"What do you think? You ready, pretty lady?" William asked.

"Sure. What are the men going to think of us parading around the ship?" I asked.

"Oh, they're not too excited about it. Women on ships are bad luck, you know," he said with a silly grin.

"Really? Why is that?"

"I don't know. Maybe a sailor's mind isn't quite right with a woman on board," he said. "That's just a guess though. I came up with it all on my own."

"Oh okay. That doesn't really make sense but okay."

"Well, may I assist you, miss?" he said gallantly, holding his hand out for me.

"I think I got it," I said, grabbing the railing and pulling myself onto the ramp. Our party had already made it to the deck, so I ran the whole way up the narrow walkway with William on my heels.

We were laughing and giggling by the time we caught up with our group. Elaina and Sarah smiled at us, while Theresa rolled her eyes. The skipper was explaining a few of the features of the deck. I let my eyes scan the scene before me. White and blue uniformed men speckled the deck, moving in and out from behind large iron structures and weapons. One man looked like he was loading heavy ammunitions into a container. Another man wound a section of rope around his arm. They each eyed us cautiously and nodded respectfully to the officers.

"Okay, ladies, let's not linger on deck too long. We're already distracting the men. Let's go down to the lower levels," the skipper said, gesturing toward a door on deck.

After walking through the outer door, it took my eyes a moment to adjust to the dim light inside. William led me to the left down yet another narrow passageway.

"We entered on the starboard side of the ship, and this is the upper deck. Up here is the main galley and kitchen," William said, motioning to the different areas of the boat.

"Okay, everyone, follow me," the skipper instructed.

We followed obediently, William and I taking up the rear, giggling as we straggled behind. We glanced back and forth at each other nervously as we walked. Curiously, I wished we were alone.

After a few moments of walking the passageway opened into a large room; it looked like the crews' dining quarters. The whole ship seemed cold to me. Everything was flat, concrete, metal, or wood; I'm sure it was that way to make cleanup and work on the boat easy.

"Is this where you eat?" I asked in a whisper as the captain explained the different features of the galley. The couples broke off together, wandering around the tables. The men looked proud to be showing off the ship; the women looked curiously fascinated. Theresa looked bored.

"No, I eat on the second deck with the officers," William said.

"It's kind of cold feeling in here," I said.

"You get used to it, and it gets nice and warm when there are eight hundred men in here. Now come on, it's a big ship with lots to see."

"Don't we need to stay with the group?" I asked.

"Oh, we'll stay close enough. The ship is too cramped in spaces for all of us to see everything together."

William led me through the galley.

"Where are you two going, Lieutenant Commander?" Commander Gibbons called from across the room.

"We're going to go on ahead. We won't be far," William answered. Commander Gibbons and Lieutenant Jackson laughed.

"Have a good time," Lieutenant Jackson said as William led me to the port side of the ship through another passageway.

"This is a watertight hatch," he said as we walked through a narrow doorway. I had to take a big step and hike my dress up a little to clear the bottom of the door. William had to duck his head so it wouldn't hit the top of the doorway.

"It closes tight," he said, pointing to the steering wheel–like lever on the door.

"There are several of these through the boat so we can seal compartments if they flood."

I tripped on an uneven spot on the ground near the door. I was off balance for just a moment until William caught me, and the whole weight of my body landed against his chest. I quietly laughed at my clumsiness.

"You have to watch where you step around here," I said, swallowing hard.

"Yes, you do. There are lots of things to trip and hit your head on." He chuckled as he helped me steady my feet. I didn't want to let go of him. He straightened me up, and we continued on our way.

He was right. The boat was neatly organized, and dirt seemed nonexistent on the ship.

"Okay then," he said with his charming smile, "let's take a look at the lower decks."

William led me a little farther toward the bow of the boat to a ladder leading to a lower deck.

"Ladies first," he said, motioning to the hole in the ground in front of us.

"Oh no, I'm not going down there first. I'll fall straight down. You go. Then at least someone will be at the bottom when I fall," I said.

"As you wish," he said gallantly. In one fluid motion, William grabbed ahold of the small railing above the opening in the floor and slid down the steel ladder as if there were no steps at all. "Your turn, angel," he said after he landed. My heart skipped a beat at the sound of the pet name he'd just given me.

I moved toward the hole, about to put my foot on the first rung of the ladder, when I noticed a flaw in my plan. William was staring straight up at me. I was wearing a dress and about to climb down the ladder. I hesitated and took a quick step back. William laughed from below.

"I said ladies first, remember?" he reminded me, followed by more laughing from the lower deck.

"Oh geez, I didn't even think about this stupid dress," I said, frustrated. I wasn't about to let a little more embarrassment get the best of me, so I kicked my flimsy shoes down the hole at him. They landed with a "thud thud," followed by even more laughter.

"Come on, I saw more of you this morning when you were standing in your swimsuit in your front yard," he teased.

"Yeah, that was different! You will mind your manners around a lady, Lieutenant!" I said, playfully scolding him. I tried to look down at him menacingly, but I was all smiles.

"Different?" He scoffed. "The only thing different about that was you were in the arms of another man," he tried to tease, but I could hear a little hurt in his voice.

"Now come on!" I said, feeling bad.

"You come on!" he said, changing the subject. "Get down here!"

With a deep breath of bravery, I pulled the middle of my dress together between my legs, making my skirt tight around each thigh and pulling it up a bit in the middle. I held my dress together with my right hand, the railing with the left and took two brave steps down the ladder through the small opening.

"Oh yes, this is much less revealing," he said sarcastically. "I'm really going to have to catch you if you're coming down that way." William chuckled as he watched me struggle down the ladder.

I slowly felt my way down the ladder one foot at a time until I felt a tug at my hair.

"Oh, ouch!" I squealed. My long hair had gotten caught in the top rung of the ladder. A shrill giggle came from the level above me. I looked up to see Theresa walk by. She noticed my precarious position, glared at me, and kept on walking.

I sighed, frustrated with my predicament. I could reach up and un-snag my hair, but I would have to let go of my dress, giving William a good show below. I could climb back the steps, but I would still have to let go of my dress when I got to the top.

Before I could decide on an acceptable solution, William was up the ladder, standing on the rung under mine with his body pressed against my back and his long arms reaching above me, pulling my snagged hair free.

I wrapped my arm around the ladder, holding it in the crook of my elbow, and turned to face William the best I could. William leaned to the other side, doing the same until we were virtually face-to-face, our eyes and our mouths level to each other's. I couldn't help but let my eyes drop to his perfect mouth for a moment before looking him in the eye.

"Captain America to the rescue again," I said. "You've saved me once again. I do believe you may be my hero," I said sarcastically.

"Does a hero get a reward?" he asked. We both laughed. I was getting light-headed standing, or hanging, so close to him. I could feel his warm breath on my face, and he smelled captivating. How could a person ever get comfortable being so close to him?

"I would do anything for you," he said seriously, looking irresistibly sincere.

I looked at him curiously, studying his face. "I believe you would," I responded without a thought.

We didn't move; we stayed face-to-face, our bodies close together, hanging on a ladder in the middle of a US navy ship for a few sweet moments. I had no idea what to do or say. All I knew was I liked where

I was. My heart felt like it was going to burst. His body was warm and inviting. I felt oddly comfortable pressed up against him. I wanted to be even closer. My breath got shorter and shallower as my heart raced in my chest.

William placed his free hand on the side of my face and stroked my cheek sweetly with his thumb. I could tell he was thinking about kissing me. Part of me wanted to shake him away and scurry down the ladder like a scared little girl, but a larger part of me wanted to stay right where I was and kiss him before he had a chance to kiss me. His body possessed a powerful pull, like gravity, pulling me into him. I couldn't fight it. No rational thought could combat the force his presence played on me. It was like we fit together perfectly. I'd never felt so comfortable but yet so completely uncomfortable all at the same time.

"So what is it about me that's so different than all the other men buying for your attention?" he asked. "Why haven't you ran away from me like I see your mind considering?" he asked.

"I don't know," I said, quietly biting my lip. It was the truth. I really didn't know why I was still standing. I didn't know why all good sense had left me. What was it about him?

William smiled at me, looking encouraged. I giggled, knowing he was reading every thought that crossed my face. He moved his face just a fraction of an inch closer to mine. I took a quick involuntary breath in, but he didn't move again for a moment; he stood motionless, looking into my eyes.

Is he waiting for me to kiss him? I wondered. There was no way I could. The trepidation was killing me. I couldn't will myself to kiss him if my life depended on it. So I smiled sweetly, bit my lip harder, and let my cheek rest against his hand and my eyes fell downward. I couldn't hold his commanding gaze a moment longer.

"So what about Kekoa?"

I looked up quickly. "What about him?"

"What's your relationship with him? You run from every man but him."

And you! I wanted to yell, but I didn't.

"We're friends. Always have been since I moved here. He taught me to surf, gave me my first board. We've just always been friends. Why?" I asked cautiously.

"I just wanted to know if he was an obstacle for me. If I haven't made it abundantly clear, I don't want to be just friends, Ruth."

I nodded slightly. He pulled me in closer, drawing my face to him, our lips less than an inch apart. I drew breath in quickly, my bottom lip trembling with fear and anticipation.

William let out a light understanding chuckle and pressed his warm lips against my forehead. It was sweet. His lips felt warm and soft against my forehead. I let out an involuntary sigh of relief.

He didn't stop there though. He lifted my chin slightly and kissed my cheek softly and slowly twice; moved across my face, brushing his lips briefly against mine; and kissed the other side of my face just once.

I exhaled a low breath, and I felt so dizzy I could barely open my eyes. My insides were churning with excitement and nervousness; I swallowed hard.

"Come on, angel, let's get you off this ladder before you fall and break your neck," he said, holding my arm and guiding me down the next few steps. William jumped down the last three and lifted me down the rest, placing me in front of him. With his hand around my back, he said, "Let me show you around down here."

I was a little disappointed but followed obediently.

We were standing just in front of another passageway. I felt dizzy, light-headed, and it took a moment to adjust to my new surroundings. It looked like we were moving to an area where men were working. William led me a few feet and pointed out a small room to the right. It had a few small stools in the middle and gadgets and levers all over the walls. There was a small desk with more levers and earphones.

"This is the radar room," he said. "Very important, and this is the ears of the place, Petty Officer Mason," he said, introducing me to the man sitting at a table of controls. He pulled one of the earphones off his ear.

"Well, good afternoon, ma'am," Petty Officer Mason said, looking me up and down with a goofy grin. I stood awkwardly for a few seconds while the sailor grinned dumbly at me.

"All right, back to work, squawk box," William said, flicking the earphone on his head and escorting me farther down the passageway.

"Ahead of us," he said, "to the left is the medical office and operating room." A few men walked by, nodding to us as they passed.

"Operating room?" I asked, puzzled.

"Sailors get hurt," he said plainly. "We are lucky to have operating facilities. It's very small though, much smaller than one you would see on a battleship," William said and continued on with the tour, passing sailors nodding and introducing me to them as we went.

"To the right is the barber, one of the busiest places on the ship. There are lots of heads to shave," he said, removing his hat and rubbing his head.

I peeked into the small quarters. There was a large man standing in the middle of the room. He was probably as big around as he was tall, making the quarters look even smaller. He was cutting a sailor's hair while three other sailors waited their turn. They looked up at us, surprised. I waved shyly.

"Morning, miss," the barber said. The sailors smiled goofily at me from the other side of the room. "When the skipper said he was giving the wives a tour, we didn't expect you to have any company, Lieutenant Commander," the barber said.

"What can I say? I'm full of surprises, Buzz," Will teased. "Boys, this is Ruth. Ruth, this toe head in the chair here is one of my guys, Gunnery Officer Brown. Behind him are Petty Officer Davis, Petty Officer Eli Troutman, and Gunnery Sgt. Mike Thompson, and this beast of a man is the ship's barber, Buzz."

"Oh, I'm more than just a barber, miss," Buzz corrected with a loud, booming voice. "I'm the ship's therapist. I'm the guy these clowns come to when they are having trouble with the ladies. You wouldn't believe the stories these boys share with me while sitting in my chair!"

I giggled along with Buzz, whose whole chest heaved with loud laughter.

"Why, I bet I'm the only man on this ship that already knew your name. You see . . .," he said, speaking quietly, "the lieutenant commander was in my chair yesterday."

"Okay!" William interrupted. "Time to go!"

Buzz laughed loudly. The sailors in the room chuckled quietly, obviously trying not let William see them laughing.

"Well, it was lovely to meet you, Buzz." I smiled. "Maybe we can talk more later," I said in a whisper. Buzz winked at me. "Goodbye, gentlemen," I said to the other sailors.

William took my arm and led me out of the room. Once we passed the barber, the passageway opened up to a larger room.

"Keep going to the left, and that room is the sick bay and isolation space. To the right is the laundry, and past that is some crew space."

We walked a little farther down the hall to the crew space until I saw rows and rows of hanging beds, each four deeply hanging in every nook and cranny. They were plain white mattresses hanging from the ceiling connected by chains. The area was empty. The men were all working, leaving their bunks deserted.

"The men really sleep one on top of another like that?" I asked in amazement.

"Like I said, space is at a premium. We aren't even to full capacity. During wartime, the lineup of beds reaches clear in front of sick bay, and this is just a small portion. You'll see beds all over the ship in those situations."

I walked ahead of Will in between the rows, trying to imagine that many sailors cramped together in this one space. The highest bed of each four was nearly a whole foot above my head.

"How do the sailors sleeping on the top get into bed?" I asked.

"They manage. It's better than sleeping on the bottom with your face on the floor and the other men crawling on you to get to their bed," he answered.

"Sounds like you are talking from experience." I laughed.

"Yes, ma'am. I've earned my solitary quarters, believe me." William chuckled.

I couldn't help myself; I had to try one. I walked up to a line of beds, put one foot on the bottom mattress—it was only a foot of the ground, placed my other foot on the second bed, and lifted myself and flopped on the third bunk and lay down on my back. The bed above me was probably a foot and a half above my nose. I giggled, thinking of the tough sailors tucked into such tight quarters.

"What is funny about this?" William asked, observing me from a small distance.

"This is just really cozy. I would get really tired of sleeping like this. The mattresses aren't even that comfortable," I said, adjusting my weight, trying to find a cozy position.

William walked over to me and stepped onto the bottom bed so his face was level with mine. He placed his right arm over me on the other side of the bed so he wouldn't fall off. Goose bumps shivered up my arm, and the hair stood on the back of my neck, having him hovering over me so. I swallowed hard, realizing I liked having him so close to me.

"It's hard to get used to sleeping like this, but I'll tell you one thing," he said in a whisper, moving closer to my face. "If the sailor assigned to this bunk knew you were lying in it right now, he would have some great dreams tonight." A strange mischievous smile crossed his face.

I smiled too, a little puzzled, not really understanding what William meant. Changing the subject, I looked at the far wall with lockers against it.

"That must be where they keep their belongings?"

"Yep, that is the only personal space they are allowed. They aren't allowed to bring very many belongings on board anyway, so it is usually enough."

"Oh," I said.

"Come on," he said finally, "I want to get you out of another man's bed. You don't belong here," he said casually.

I didn't dare ask where he thought I belonged. I just swung my legs over the side of the bed and let William help me the rest of the way down.

I walked over to the lockers to take a better look. They were just small cubbies, hardly big enough to hold anything.

"So what do you think of your tour so far?" he asked, putting his hands in his pockets and leaning against the lockers.

"I love it," I said, leaning my back against the lockers. "It's very fascinating. You give many of your dates tours like this?" I asked.

"No, never!" He laughed.

"So what makes me so special?" I asked, leaning my head against the lockers next to him.

"The fact that you have to ask that question makes me like you even more. I've never met any girl like you before."

I blushed.

"What about you? Have you taken many tours with sailors before?"

"No!" I giggled. "You know that. Just about everything I've done with you has been a first for me," I said.

"So do you still feel the same way about sailors?" he asked, scooting closer to me.

"Yes," I said certainly. William looked disappointed. "But you're not just an ordinary sailor, William. You know that."

He smiled, looking encouraged again.

"I'm here against all my better judgment because apparently, I just can't resist you," I said, blushing at my forwardness.

William's smile grew even bigger than I'd ever seen it before. "I like that," he said, leaning closer to me. "I think I like being irresistible." He stepped in front of me and placed his hands on the lockers on either side of my face. "Because heaven knows that I can't resist you."

William lowered his head so our noses touched together softly. I drew a quick breath in like I did on the stairs, and my heart leaped into my throat. This time William didn't move. He held his face close to mine, moving one hand to my cheek, stroking my jawline gently with his thumb and the other on my waist. Every inch of my skin that he was touching tingled with electricity. A small hum echoed through my whole body. He was so close I could feel and taste his breath. Nerves and anticipation boiled inside me until I thought I would literally explode from the inside.

My mind was racing. This was it. He was going to kiss me. Was he going to kiss me? Did I actually want to kiss HIM? Why wasn't he kissing me already?

He moved his face slightly, rubbing our noses together. He looked from my wide eyes to my lips and kissed the corner of my mouth. My stomach lurched, and my heart beat even faster. He moved his lips across mine and kissed the other corner of my mouth. I wanted to kiss him so much, but I was frozen. I closed my eyes, and his lips met mine softly. It was followed by another kiss and then again another. Each kiss was soft but a little more demanding. His lips were soft. Since I'd never kissed anyone before and really wasn't sure what to do, I followed his lead. My lips responded and moved with his. My knees felt weak like they might give out at any moment. My heart was singing. Had I known how wonderful this would feel, I would have been anticipating this moment so much more. We kissed a few more times until he rested his forehead against mine and chuckled softly.

My head was spinning. I grabbed onto his arm to steady myself so I wouldn't lose my balance. I couldn't believe I just kissed a man! I bit my bottom lip, trying to hold back a giddy smile.

"You're right. That was nothing like kissing my dad," I whispered.

"Well, I certainly am glad to hear that," he said.

We both straightened up quickly, startled by the sound of giggles coming from the passage. William stepped back, and I smoothed out my dress in case it had wrinkled.

"Well, we caught up to them!" Lieutenant Jackson said, appearing through the hatch. "I found them! They are hiding in the bunks!" he called back.

Elaina, the skipper, Ginny, Sarah, Commander Gibson, Theresa, and her grouchy husband, Lieutenant Smith, shuffled into the room.

"Well, it's about time. We've been waiting for you, guys," William said, walking casually over to the group.

"William was just showing me these luxurious sleeping quarters you all have for the men," I said, joining him.

"Yeah, I'm sure he was." Lieutenant Gibbons laughed.

"Oh, these are just lovely," Elaina said. "The US Navy spares no expense, do they?" she said dryly.

"I can't wait to see where you all sleep," Sarah said to her husband.

"Well, that will be next, ladies," the skipper said. "I hope this gives you all a little respect for what your men go through. They each had to put in their time on these bunks too."

"It is impressive, Captain," I said. "These are very tight quarters. Do the men ever get on each other's nerves?"

"Oh yes, of course, they do. It's all part of the experience," the captain said, smacking Theodor on the back. Theresa and Lieutenant Smith rolled their eyes.

"Some have more conflicts than others," Theodor said, nodding to Lieutenant Smith. Lieutenant Smith snorted. Everyone else laughed.

"We will walk back through the portside passageway," the skipper said, leading the group to other side of the boat.

I wondered how William could act so casually. He was laughing and joking with the other officers, addressing the sailors we passed, giving some of them orders. My mind was reeling at the thought of what we just did. My legs felt weak as we maneuvered across the ship. I was afraid they might give out on me. Space in the passageways was tight. When sailors walked by, we would all shuffle to one side to let them pass. At one point, William placed his hand on my stomach, guiding me to the side to let a pair of sailors by. My heart fluttered under the warmth of his hand.

Once we entered the far passageway, the skipper pointed out the soda fountain, post office, and engine office. Every room had a peculiar metal and oil smell to it.

We reached a set of stairs down to deck 3, which were much easier to navigate than the ladder to deck 2.

"Why on earth didn't we use these on the way down?" I asked in a whisper as we walked up them.

"Oh, I thought the ladder would be more fun." He smiled. I hit him in the arm.

"You made me wrestle that ladder when there was a perfectly good set of stairs!" I exclaimed.

"Hey! Hey!" he said innocently. "You have to admit that was more fun," he said.

Theodor chuckled from behind us, hearing our conversation.

William led me around and through and around each watertight door and past the bulkheads, making sure I didn't trip on or bang into anything. He explained some of the features of the ship. He told me that the walls of the ship were never called walls but bulkheads, hallways were passageways, the decks were painted red so the men would be used to the color and not shocked at the sight of blood spilled on it, and all kinds of interesting and slightly unsettling facts.

On the third deck, there were more crew space and rows of beds. The skipper showed us the brig, which was basically several jail cells for disobedient sailors to rethink their motives. They showed us the machine shop, exhaust blower, main radio room, and other workrooms, which were all filled with busy sailors. We moved farther back in the ship, where we'd been before, and walked back up to the second deck through a different set of stairs.

"This is where I spend most of my time," William whispered once we reached the top of the stairs. We turned down another passageway, where the captain began to explain the different rooms on either side.

"On the right here are the administration offices, and on the left here is my room and first lieutenants' rooms." He didn't lead us into the rooms but allowed us to look through the door. The captain's room was fairly large with a big rectangular wood table in it and access to a kitchen in the back.

"We spend a lot of time planning around that table, and it's where I eat my meals," William explained and then grabbed my hand to lead me to our next stop. "We're in officers' country now. My room is the last one on the end, the executive officers' cabin."

"Why don't you boys go down and show the ladies your quarters?" the skipper suggested, taking his own wife to his quarters.

"Oh, I can't wait to see your room, dear!" Elaina said.

"Me too!" agreed Sarah.

It felt a little awkward being the only unmarried couple.

We walked together down the passageway with the other couples. I peeked into some of the open doors as we walked past. They were modest rooms with a bed and a desk. Most of the desks held neatly stacked papers, books, and other personal items. Each bed was made meticulously with crisp tucked corners and folded blankets. I've heard it said that in the navy, cleanliness is next to godliness. Looking at these rooms, I understood why people say that now. One by one, the other three couples peeled off into the other rooms, the women commenting on the cleanliness of their husbands' rooms and how small they were. William's room was the last one in the passageway.

William's door was closed. After opening it, he led me inside. I stepped in hesitantly, feeling awkward about being in his room. His was bigger than the other officers'. It had a bed and desk like the others, but it also had a mirror, closet, and cupboards and more floor space than the other ones did.

"It's not much but better than the hanging bunks," he said, standing in the middle of the room, his hands in his pockets, rocking back on his heels. He appeared to be a little embarrassed.

"It's great, much roomier than the other officers' too," I said.

"Well," he said modestly, "it's not very homey." He banged his hand on a large pipe running across the ceiling. "But it's a place to hang my hat and get a little privacy."

It was cute to see him a little embarrassed. I walked over to the mirror and looked at a small picture taped in the upper corner of it.

"Who is this?" I asked, pointing to the family in the picture.

"That is my mom, dad, two younger brothers and their wives and kids, my sister and her husband, and of course, my dog, Jack. This was at my sister's wedding last year. Everyone was there but me. As you can tell, they are quite a crowd. I don't even know some of my nieces and nephews in that picture," he said.

"Great-looking family," I said. "I bet they are a lot of fun. When's the last time you saw them?"

"It's been a few years now," he answered.

"Do you miss them?" I asked.

"Of course, I do," he said. He was standing behind me. "But this is where I belong right now. They understand."

I had the strangest desire to meet them. I didn't know what to do next. I sat at the desk and looked around the room. William sat on the bed, which was next to the desk chair; crossed his hands behind his head; and rested against the wall.

"Well, I guess that about concludes our tour," he said with a yawn.

"I really enjoyed it," I said. "I've lived here so long, and I've never had a clue what it was like on one of these ships."

"Yeah," he agreed. "I'm really glad you came."

"I am too, William." I wondered if he wanted to kiss me again. I was pretty sure I wanted to kiss him again, but it seemed inappropriate to do in his room. "Well, we better get back, huh, before they come looking for us," I suggested.

"You in a hurry to get out of here?" he asked.

"No, not really. I rather enjoy being with you," I said shyly.

"Really?" he said, leaning forward, resting his elbows on his knees.

"If I didn't like you, I wouldn't still be hanging out with you, Lieutenant," I said, leaning forward too. Our faces were inches apart. We smiled silently at each other. I held his gaze for just a moment before letting my head drop into my hands.

"Hey, where did you go?" William asked. He grabbed one of my hands, pulling it away from my face and held it in his. He moved his face so he was looking into my eyes. His smile took my breath away. His deep blue eyes gave me goose bumps. I could feel his breath on my face.

"I am in big trouble!" I said.

"I have no idea what you are talking about," he said.

"I do not know what has gotten into me. What on earth am I doing here?" I laughed, but I was serious.

"You just said why. You like me!" he said.

"Why do I like you? I've never liked any man before. Why do I like you?"

"Well, I can't answer that for you. I have no idea why you like me," he said. "But I know why I like you. You're beautiful, you're smart, you're athletic, you're independent, you are not like any girl I've ever met." He paused. "And now that I've found you, I don't want to let you out of my sight," he said sweetly. He put both my hands together, taking them in his hands, and kissed the back of my fingers. "So as long as you allow me, I'm not letting you go."

"I think I'd like that, William." Did I really just say that? Did I really mean that?

William closed the two-inch gap between our mouths and kissed my lips softly. My lips melted into his. I could hardly believe I'd gone my whole life not experiencing this feeling.

"Hey, lover boy, you coming!" a voice called from down the hall. It was Lieutenant Smith.

Our lips broke. William let out a disappointed sigh; I giggled. "All right, we better get going," he said, rubbing my arm.

"Do we have to?" I asked.

"I like you," William said, rubbing my grinning cheek.

"I like you too," I said.

William stood, taking my hand. We walked out the door and down the hall to join the others hand in hand. Elaina and Sarah smiled when they saw us holding hands. I smiled too, a little embarrassed. They were standing in front of the skipper's quarters.

"Well, we are in for a treat this afternoon," the skipper said to our group once we joined them. "Cookie has cooked up some of his finest grub for you, ladies, if you would like to join us for lunch at the officers' table."

"Good. I'm starved." That was the most I'd heard Theresa say all day.

We all shuffled in through the skipper's door and took our seats around the large dark oak table. Sitting at the table, I understood the captain's quarters a little better. We were sitting in a large room, large for the US Navy. On one side of the room, there was an opening that led into another galley, where a man in a white coat was working over what I presumed to be our lunch. On the other side of the room was a closed door, which when I asked William about it, he said it was the skipper's sleeping quarters.

"So what did you ladies think?" the skipper asked ones we were all settled.

"Oh, I thought it was fantastic," Sarah said. "Thank you so much for allowing us to come on board."

"Yes, thank you, sir," Elaina said. "I really enjoyed it."

"And how about you, Ms. Ruth?" the captain asked.

"Oh, I thought it was extremely fun!" I said.

"Yeah, she did," Theresa said. "How was that ladder, Ruth?"

William and I both laughed. The table stared at us, confused.

"You took her down the portside ladder?" Lieutenant Gibbons asked.

"Well, sure," William said casually. "I wanted to give her the full experience," William said through a devilish grin.

"Yes, and I really appreciate that, Lieutenant Commander," I said, smacking his arm.

Lieutenant Jackson and Commander Gibbons both laughed.

"Ahh, there he is," the skipper interrupted. "What do we have today, Cookie?" the captain asked when the very slender man wearing a white coat came in from the galley.

"Today, Captain, I've made a lovely kalua pork roast, I got the recipe from some locals, and scalloped potatoes," he said and turned around, leaving again.

"Sounds great, Cookie. Dish us up," the skipper called after him. "How does that sound, ladies?" he asked.

None of them said anything for a moment. They looked like they had never had it before.

"Sounds delicious to me, Captain," I said. "I love kalua pork."

"Oh, so this really isn't a treat to you, Ruth. You must eat this often," Commander Gibbons said.

"Oh no, it is a treat. We don't eat this too often at my house," I said.

"Well, good," the captain said.

Cookie came in and served us each a plate full of delicious pork and potatoes. It was good. The only thing that would make it better would be if they served it with rice. Everyone at the table chatted as we ate. I mostly just enjoyed the contents of my plate. The ladies talked about the dance last night. They all lived on base, and Sarah was excited because she was moving next door to Elaina.

Lieutenant Smith was irritated because one of the men he was over wasn't reenlisting next month, and another was being transferred to another ship. William participated a little in the conversation, but mostly, he just ate. When his plate was clean, he leaned back in his chair and placed his hand on my thigh!

I was so surprised I straightened up, my back stiff as a board. William began laughing and covered it up by coughing in his other hand. I held my breath and tried to act casual like him so no one would know what was happening under the table. I relaxed a little but had to hold back an uneasy laugh. It felt like his hand was burning through my dress. I didn't want him to move it, but I couldn't feel comfortable with it there either. My forehead started to sweat, and my stomach flip-flopped uneasily in my belly. Slowly, I looked at William through the corner of my eye. He was smiling, and his chest was shaking as he laughed quietly. No one else at the table seemed to notice us. William stroked his hand gently up and down my leg, trying to settle me, but it just made it worse. I simply had no experience with this kind of physical contact with a man. I forfeited the rest of the contents of my plate, leaned back in my chair like William, and put both my hands on his hand. Immediately, my stomach settled, feeling like I had a little control, but not completely because now our fingers were intertwined, and his thumb was stroking my hand.

We stayed this way for the remainder of the meal. By the time lunch was over, it started to feel more natural. I liked it when he touched me, I liked it when he smiled at me, and I liked the little secret affection he was showing me. I liked feeling like I was the only person in the room he really wanted to be with. I liked it that he was respectful of me. I could tell in the last hour we spent together in the ship that he wanted to kiss me more, to hold my hand more often, but he was a gentleman and holding back, waiting for me to be ready. I never thought I'd feel this way about a person. I couldn't tell if I was surrendering all beliefs and standards about sailors because I was attracted to him or if it was simply because he was an extraordinary man.

"Well, I suppose we should get back to work, boys. What do you think?" the skipper asked after everyone appeared to be done.

"I think it's time, Captain," Theodor said.

"Why don't you all take your wives and girlfriend," he said, looking at me, "home and report back here in an hour?"

"Yes, sir," the boys said in unison.

William stood and pulled my chair out for me. I stood and gathered up my plate, along with William's, and carried them into the kitchen area and set them in the metal sink.

"Never in the six years that I've been on this ship has a guest of the skipper lifted a dish to help me," Cookie said, standing at the door. He spoke slowly with a lovely Southern drawl.

"Well, I'm sorry to have broken that streak for you, sir," I said apologetically.

"No apologies, ma'am," he said. "You are welcome in my kitchen anytime, miss," he said with a crooked smile, taking one of the plates from me.

"Hey, Ruth!" William called from the doorway. "Are you coming, or are you going to help plan dinner?"

"Ah, no, no, I'm coming," I said. "Thanks, Cookie. Lunch was great," I said, and we rejoined our group congregating outside the captain's room.

"Okay, boys, take your wives home and report back in an hour," the skipper said as we shuffled out the door.

"Lieutenant Commander Wellington," the skipper said quietly as we passed, "I understand Ruth lives off base, and it may take longer to get her home. So don't worry, you are excused from your duties for a couple of hours," he said with a wink.

"Thank you, Captain," William said politely while my mouth fell open at the unsubtlety of the captain's gesture. William laughed and took my hand in his.

"Come on, Ruthy, let's get you home," William said, smiling happily.

We wandered back out through the ship and bid farewell to the members of our party after we got onto the deck. William and I ran down the plank before everyone else so we wouldn't have to wait for them to slowly maneuver their way down. This time I let William help me a little. We held hands as we ran down the ramp to the dock and continued to hold hands until William opened the door to the car and helped me in.

William started up the car and drove us out of the parking lot and past the guard tower. Instead of turning left and driving back up the mountain toward my house, he turned right into town.

"Hey, this isn't the way to my house!" I said.

"I know, but I thought since the skipper gave me a little time, we could go get shaved ice, unless you're sick of me."

"No, I'm not sick of you." I laughed. "But I am a little full from lunch."

"I know, me too. But I'm not ready to let you go just yet. We can share one," he said, putting his hand on my knee again.

I don't think anything thrilled me as much as hearing how much he liked me. I would hate it if he didn't reciprocate my feelings. I wasn't ready to go home either. I was turning into a silly girl like my sisters.

William drove us to the Mauna Loa Café, where we sat at a booth, sipping a delicious strawberry coconut shaved ice that Auntie Nani served us. It had delicious vanilla ice cream in the middle. We sat close together, slurping through our separate straws, drinking out of the glass, and laughing about the last hour we spent together.

"Did you see the faces of the men as I paraded you around?" he asked.

"They did look a little surprised to see all those women on the ship," I said.

"Not the other women, just you," he said. "They've seen the wives before but never you. Those were the looks of jealousy." William laughed. I blushed.

"Stop it! You like making me blush, don't you?" I asked.

"I just like to see you smile," he said.

We slurped the last few drops of ice until there was nothing left, and still, we lingered. It was easy to be with him. Conversation flowed naturally. William asked me about my family, about growing up on the island. I asked him what Wyoming was like and what his sisters and brothers were like and about the girls he dated in high school. I'd never dated anyone seriously, so I didn't have anything to talk about in that department.

"So I've heard about a few girlfriends from a while back, but what about recent girls?"

"Recent girls?" he asked, clearing his throat. "No, no recent girls." He chuckled.

"So it's true then? This is an unusual behavior," I said. William nodded. "Hmm. Well, I guess I feel special then."

"I think you're special."

"Okay, I think we better go. Things are starting to get a little cheesy, buddy," I said. "Come on, you paid the check like twenty minutes ago. It's time to take me home." I stood and grabbed William's arm to pull him up. Not only was I surprised by how large his bicep was, but he also didn't budge when I pulled. William laughed. Instead of standing, he pulled me onto his lap and kissed me softly.

"Oh okay, you're right. We better leave before they kick us out," he said quietly. We stood, and William took my hand and escorted me through the restaurant.

"Thank you, Auntie!" I called to Nani as we left.

"Aloha, Ruth! Aloha, Lieutenant," she said, staring after us.

We walked back to the truck slowly, holding each other's hand. I didn't want to go home, but what else was there left for us to do? Some of the serious conversation we'd been having made me nervous too. Not only was I really falling for this man, but I think he was falling for me too. That terrified me.

William drove me home, and I was smiling the whole time. I couldn't help smiling when I was with him. We pulled into my driveway and didn't get out right away. William didn't say anything; he just held my hand. I felt like I should say something. I didn't know if he knew how much I liked him. I also couldn't decide if I wanted him to know how much I liked him, but the thought of not seeing him again made me sad. For the first time in my life, I wanted a man to keep pursuing me.

"I . . . I had a lot of fun today and last night," I said hesitantly.

"Are you upset that you had a good time?" he asked.

"A little." I giggled.

"Why?" he asked, taking my hand in both of his.

"I don't know." I shrugged and looked at the floor. It was hard to talk openly to him and look into his powerful eyes. When I looked at him, I only wanted to say things that made him happy. "It's easier if I don't like you," I said quietly. "Things are a lot less complicated when all the sailors I meet are just how I've stereotyped them. Liking you complicates my life." I paused to look at him.

Out of the corner of my eye, I saw the corner of the curtain on the front window of my house pull back and Elizabeth and Marie's eye peering out from behind it. William noticed it too.

"I think we have an audience," William said, laughing.

"Indeed we do." I laughed as well. "You have no idea how much I don't want to walk into that house right now." I sighed.

"Well, you can always stay with me!" William said.

"No, I can't." I laughed. "You know that. Eventually, I have to go in there and answer their brigade of questions," I said.

"Come on, angel, I'll walk you inside," he said, opening his door.

I waited for William to walk around the front of the car to open my door and watched Elizabeth and Marie scramble away from the window, trying not to be noticed. Will held my hand again and walked me up my front steps. I was getting more comfortable, but holding his hand in mine still gave me goose bumps.

"Are you surfing in the morning?" he asked when we got to the front door.

"Of course, I always do," I said.

"If I could get the whole day off, would you mind if I spent it with you?" he asked.

"No"—I smiled—"I wouldn't mind."

"Okay then." He flashed his brilliant grin. "I think I will go in with you and say hi to your folks," he said.

"Okay," I said and opened the front door. I led us into the front room, where my family sat, trying to look casual. The only person who looked convincing was Daddy.

"Hi, everyone," I said.

"Hello," Daddy said from his chair.

"Good afternoon." William nodded to my parents.

"How did it go?" Mother asked. She was sitting on the couch with my sisters. I couldn't tell what they were doing before we came in. From the looks of it, they were doing nothing but waiting for us.

"It was fun," I said.

"Thank you for sharing your daughter with me," William said politely.

"You are most welcome," Mother said. "Will we be seeing you again, Lieutenant Commander?"

"Yes, at least I hope so, ma'am. I hope to see you all tomorrow," William said. "I will keep coming around as long as Ruth allows me," he said. Mother smiled triumphantly hearing this.

I smiled too but couldn't help thinking about how that statement wasn't entirely true. He would stop coming around once he was deployed again.

"Well, I will have more time to chat tomorrow, but I should be getting back to the ship," William said.

"Thank you for taking care of Ruth this morning," Daddy said, standing. He walked across the room and shook William's hand. "You are welcome in our home anytime, Lieutenant Commander." Daddy slapped his shoulder.

"Thank you, sir," William said.

"Minnie," Daddy said, turning to Mother, "what do you say we invite this young man to dinner tomorrow night?"

"I think that is a wonderful idea," Mother said.

"How does that sound to you?" Daddy asked William.

"That sounds wonderful, sir," William said.

"Well, we will see you tomorrow then," Daddy said.

"Thank you, sir." William turned to me and waited for an awkward moment.

I wasn't sure what he was waiting for, so I just smiled until William made a small nodding motion toward the door.

"Oh!" I said suddenly. "I'll show you out." My sisters giggled as I awkwardly opened the door and stepped outside with William.

"Goodbye, Lieutenant Commander," the girls called as I shut the door behind us.

"I will see you tomorrow, angel," he said with a sweet smile. He took a step closer to me and wrapped his arms around my waist and kissed me just once before letting go.

He skipped the first two steps and jogged down to his car. He waved once before getting in and beeped his horn twice as he backed out of the driveway. I walked into the house, closing the door behind me. I didn't realize how big I was smiling until I noticed my family looking at me.

"Ruth has a boyfriend! Ruth has a boyfriend!" Marie chanted, making Elizabeth giggle.

"Oh stop, Marie," I said, tossing a pillow from the couch at her. I was still smiling when I sat between Mother and Elizabeth.

"Well, it looks like you had a good time," Mother said, picking a knitting project.

"Yes, it was fun," I said.

"Ruth's gonna get married!" Elizabeth giggled.

"Elizabeth, that's enough," Daddy hushed her.

I got up and went to my room. I was glad to be alone with my thoughts. I was still smiling. My cheeks hurt from smiling so much.

I heard Elizabeth and Marie shuffle down the hall an hour or so later, and my door opened in a burst of noise and excitement. Nohea and Elsie were with them. I was sitting in my window reading when they all burst into my room and flopped on my bed.

"Soooooo," Marie said with anticipation, "what was it like?"

"Tell us EVERYTHING!" Elsie begged.

"It was interesting," I said. "The ship was bigger than I thought it would be."

"Oh, who cares about the ship? What about Will!" Elizabeth exclaimed.

"We want to hear about the dance, about everything!" Nohea clarified.

"Shhhh," I said. I really didn't want my parents hearing anything about this conversation. I didn't really want to talk about it, but then again, I REALLY needed to talk about it.

"Ruth, he is so dreamy. I have never seen a man so handsome. I can hardly talk around him. I get so nervous," Elizabeth went on. "How do you stand it?"

"Well, it's not easy," I admitted, closing my book and moving onto the bed. "I get nervous too."

Elizabeth and Marie ogled at me, longing for more information. Nohea and Elsie were just as excited.

"So what did you do? Did he hold your hand? Did he kiss you?" Marie asked.

"Start with the dance," Nohea ordered. "You looked really cozy dancing, and then you went outside for a while! Did he kiss you out there?"

"No." They were all visibly disappointed. "He didn't kiss me . . . at the dance."

"But he did kiss you!" Elsie asked a little too loudly.

"Shhhh," I pleaded. "I really don't need Mom and Dad to hear this!"

"Answer the question!" Elizabeth demanded.

"Yes, he kissed me."

An eruption of squeals followed. After they quieted down, I continued.

"We just danced at the dance. He took me outside for a walk, and we just talked to know each other."

"Do you like him?" Nohea asked.

"I do," I said. Another eruption of squeals followed the admission.

"The ice queen actually likes a man!" Elizabeth sounded shocked.

"Hey now!" I protested.

"It's pretty shocking you have to admit, Ruth," Elsie pointed out.

"I know. I'm surprised myself. I can't hardly believe it actually. What am I doing?"

"You are finally living, Ruth!" Nohea said. "Tell us more. Elizabeth said you fell asleep, and he carried you to bed?"

I nodded. The girls swooned.

"That is sweet!" Elsie said with envy. "He is so handsome, Ruth. How do you stand it?"

"Tell us about the kiss!" Marie demanded.

I laughed. It felt like a dream. How could this be my life? I had never been this girl. But there I was with four sets of eyes, demanding to hear about my love life.

"Well, I toured the ship today with Will but also the skipper and the other lieutenants' wives," I explained.

"Oh." They sighed in unison, looking disappointed.

"But we did break off for a bit on our own," I said.

"Really? What happened?" Elizabeth asked.

"Well, he held my hand, but we held hands last night at the dance too," I said.

"Really? You held hands? You held hands? What was that like?" Marie prodded.

"Well, it was like holding someone's hands, only a really special someone. It made my heart beat fast and my palms sweat."

"Eww." Elizabeth made a face.

"I know, but I couldn't help it!" I explained. "I don't know how to describe it. It wasn't like just shaking someone's hands or holding Daddy's hand. It was like there was this electrical current running through us. It made my whole body tingle."

They all moaned and giggled.

"What's it like to be in love?" Marie asked.

"Who said I was in love?" I asked defensively.

"How could you not be in love?" Elizabeth asked. "Have you not seen that man?"

"I don't think I can fall in love with a man this quickly," I said.

"Well, exactly how long does it take to fall in love?" Marie asked.

"I don't think there is an exact amount of time," I said. "I guess I've never thought about it. I never *really* thought I would," I explained.

"Well, Mom said it was love at first sight for her," Marie said.

"Daddy said they only knew each other a month," Elizabeth added. "Do you believe in love at first sight, Ruth?"

"I . . ." I hesitated. "No, I don't think so." They looked disappointed. "There is something about Will though." The girls perked up. It made me laugh seeing their anticipation. "I do really like him," I admitted. "I feel something with him I've never felt before."

Marie looked at me dreamily. "What does it feel like?"

I thought about it a minute.

"Well . . ." I paused. "It's like I've known him a really long time. I feel really comfortable with him but at the same really uncomfortable. I feel really anxious and really aware of his body and whenever he gets close to me. Like I want him to touch me, but when he does, it makes my stomach flip-flop, and I feel queasy."

"The kiss!" It was Nohea demanding this time.

"What are you girls doing?" Daddy asked from the doorway. We all jumped.

"Nothing, Daddy," we said, trying to hold in our giggles.

"Let them be, dear." It was mother's voice coming from behind him.

"Hmmm," Daddy said, leaving the door open a crack.

"Don't stay up too late," Mother said from the hallway.

"Night, Mom. Night, Daddy," we said in unison and then broke into a fit of giggles again.

"Tell us more! Tell us more!" Marie begged, bouncing.

"What was kissing him like?" Elizabeth asked.

"Oh, I don't know." I blushed.

"You have to tell us more," Marie demanded.

"How and when did he kiss you?" Elsie asked.

"Well, I thought he was going to kiss me when I was climbing down the ladder. My hair got stuck, and he had to climb up the ladder and untangle it. Our bodies were pressed together." They all drew breath in, and I continued. "We were nose to nose. I think he was going to kiss me then, but he could tell I was nervous, so he just kissed my cheek."

Elizabeth shook her head disappointedly at me.

"But then," I continued, "when we were in the men's quarters, he pressed me up against the lockers."

"Oh my gosh!" Marie giggled.

"And he kissed me there."

"More details." Elsie's eyes looked like they were going to pop out of her head. She was so intent on every word.

"Well, he kissed me really softly here"—I pointed to the corner of my mouth—"then he dragged his lips across mine." I traced the path, remembering the burning sensation. "Then he kissed me here."

I pointed to the other corner of my mouth. "And then he laid one on me . . . and didn't stop for a while."

"Ahhhh!" they all yelled and squealed in delight.

"What did it feel like?" Marie asked. She was the most curious. Nohea had kissed a man before, several. She looked more proud than any of the others who were living vicariously through me at the moment.

"It felt wonderful," I admitted. "But it was also terrifying. I thought I might throw up or pass out. Do you think that is what it's always like?" I looked at Nohea.

"I don't think so, sweetie," she said. "I've only ever kissed boys, though, compared with William. You are in a totally uncharted territory right now. He is a real man." She giggled.

"He kissed me several times today, and it felt the same every time. Like I might pass out."

"Ohhhh." The room swooned.

"Was it kind of gross?" Marie asked.

"No," I said automatically. "It was definitely not gross," I said. "It . . . it was lovely. It was like I couldn't get enough," I explained. "He was gentle but also really passionate. It made my head spin but in a good way," I reflected.

The girls were enthralled, transfixed, hanging on every word. I told them all about the dance, about the other wives, about Theresa, and about the couples outside. I told them all about the tour, about tripping and William catching me.

"Only you would do that, Ruth." Elizabeth laughed.

"How embarrassing." Marie giggled.

"It really wasn't embarrassing," I said.

I told them about the bunks, about Will leaning over me on the bed, and about being in his room. I relieved the last two nights with them, and they ate up every word, and I loved telling it.

"I can't believe this is even you," Elizabeth said. "Who would've ever thought you would be like this? I really thought you would die an old maid."

"Hey!" I said, hitting her with a pillow.

"I'm sorry, but really, you've always acted like you hated guys," she said.

"I know," I admitted. "I really don't. I just don't want to be a silly girl floating from one to another. I only want to be with a man who really wants to be with me because he likes me, not because he likes the way I look."

"So you think William is different?" Marie asked.

"He is," I said certainty and lay back on my pillow, looking at the ceiling.

We stayed up a bit longer while Elizabeth told us about her night at the dance, about the sailor who danced with her and all the other girls in the room too, about Elsie spilling her drink on a sailor. We talked until it was late, and the girls had to go home. Elizabeth and Marie stayed and talked longer until we fell asleep in a disheveled heap on my bed.

8

Bright and early Saturday morning, I paddled out past the breakers. I turned over onto my stomach and paddled toward the beach, chasing a big swell, catching the lip of it; jumped on my board; and rode in the hollow. I repeated this several times, tiding in and paddling out. I was halfway in when out of the corner of my eye, I saw the bare chest of a haole standing on the beach. He was watching me. Normally, I wouldn't pay any attention to this discovery—an impressed onlooker was nothing unusual—but during my cut back, I looked up again to see who it was. It was none other than the breathtaking Lt. Cdr. William Wellington standing on shore. His chest was bare, tan, and gorgeous.

I was so shocked; my fin caught the top of the wave, flipping me and the board over and tumbling in the barrel. My leash broke free of my ankle as the wave crashed on top of me. I was rolled over and over in the wave. For a moment, I didn't know which way was up and which way was down. My legs flipped over my face, and I didn't know which direction to swim and which direction to fight to for air. By the time I reoriented myself, my board was on the beach, and I was on my hands and knees in the sand with the water to my waist. I checked my suit to make sure everything was still covered, adjusted my bottoms, and slowly, reluctantly looked up just in time to see William run over to me while saying, "Whoa! That was quite the wipeout! Are you okay?"

I felt like an idiot, washed up on the shore like a tumbled worn-out piece of driftwood. Did I have the courage in my pitiful state to look in the eyes of the man standing above me?

I didn't have to; he knelt in front of me, but I looked away.

"I am a disaster around you!" I said, trying to catch my breath. I was coughing up half the ocean.

William laughed and brushed the curtain of hair away from my eyes. "Let me help you up," he said.

He grabbed my elbow to help me up. My skin tingled under the touch of his warm big hand. *How can a simple touch send shivers down my spine?* I was irritated with myself for acting bashful, my heart swooning under his touch. *I'm such an idiot. Snap out of it!*

He grabbed my washed-up board while I attended to my hair, trying to straighten the tangled mess it had become. Sand coated the front of my scalp and hairline. I must have looked like a drowned rat. William sat on the beach next to me.

"I know what you're thinking," I said when I finally caught my breath completely.

"What's that?" William asked, relieved to hear me speaking.

"You're wondering how you can be with a girl who has such mad surfing skills," I said, teasing. "But don't worry, I'm sure you can keep up," I said, motioning to the board he brought. "I'll teach ya."

"You were doing pretty great until I startled you. Sorry about that," he said, laughing.

"What are you doing here anyway? How did you know I would be here? Are you stalking me?"

"I ran into Kekoa yesterday at the market," he said with a crooked smile. "And he might have told me where I could get ahold of a board so I could join you."

"Really?" I was surprised. "How long have you been here?" I asked.

"Just a minute or two. I watched you ride a few swells in. Now come on," he said, picking our boards. "Do you feel like going out again?"

"I don't know. I saw you at the tournament. Can you keep up?" I asked with a wink.

"Probably not, but I'll sure try. Do you need me to tow you out there?" He laughed.

"No, I'm okay now. I can make it," I said, grabbing my board from him.

We paddled out together. William's strong arms made long powerful strokes through the waves. I made two strokes to his one, but I didn't have trouble keeping up. I was in my element. We lined up, waiting for a wave.

"Ladies first," he said, motioning for me to go. I would have much rather stayed where I was resting and floating, but I had to redeem myself from my earlier wipeout, so I caught the next wave in, and William followed. We went back out and rode a few more. William had a few great wipeouts, which put me in fits of laughter. I lay on my stomach on my board, resting my chin on my hands and watching William wipe out again. Eventually, he joined me and floated on his back next to me, breathing hard from the swim. He put his arms behind his head; water sparkled off his chest. His shorts revealed strong legs. He had a muscular bulge right above his knees.

"This is my favorite part of surfing," I said, "just floating on my board, enjoying the peace of the ocean. It's the best part of my day."

"Is it okay that I joined you today?" he asked.

"Yeah, it's been kind of fun having company," I said, trying not to show how much I was enjoying it.

"Do you have company often?" he asked, trying to appear casual, but he wasn't fooling me.

"Just Kekoa. He joins me most days. Other than that, no."

We were starting to drift toward shore and about to be caught up in a swell, so we kicked farther out where we could continue floating and chatting.

"So no other men have joined you surfing. You say everything you do with me is a first. Why is that?" he asked once we were situated again. "Why haven't you had lots of sailors out here with you? You know, all those boys would think a beautiful surfing girl like you was the bee's knees. I bet they are lined up, dying to get your attention."

"Is that what you think?" I asked, very curious.

"What? Who? Me?" he asked. "What do I think?"

"Oh, you know, do you think I'm the 'bee's knees?'" I laughed.

"You already know I'm crazy about you. You're beautiful. I can't hardly keep my hands off you," he said.

My face burned red. I hid it under my arm so he wouldn't see my very pleased smile.

"That surprises you?" he asked. "You didn't expect me to be attracted to you?"

"Well, no," I stammered. "I guess I spend all my energy trying to avoid you guys I never really stopped to think about what you all thought of me."

"And why is that?" he asked. "You could go out with any sailor that hit this island. What is it you don't like about sailors?"

I thought a minute, swirling my fingers in the water. "Well, first of all, it's not that I don't like sailors. It's just most of the sailors are young boys fresh out of high school, looking for a good time. They are only here on the island for a short period of time." I paused. "You tell me. Why on earth would a young man be interested in spending time with an island girl if he's just going to be leaving in a few weeks or months? What could he possibly be interested in?" I asked, exaggerating my wonder. "Hmmm?"

"I think I see what you're getting at because I can think of a few things," William said without really answering the question. "But we are not all like that."

"True, so let's say a girl meets a more mature sailor who is interested in an actual relationship. What does that get her?" I looked at him steadily. "Either he is reassigned somewhere else and they break up, or they get married, but she can't be with him during all the months he is at sea. So either way, the girl is left alone and heartbroken," I explained.

"It doesn't have to be like that," he said quietly.

"I've thought about it a long time. My sister Evelyn is married to a sailor stationed in San Diego, and I think he has only seen their son a handful of times. Can't you see why I wouldn't want that?" I asked. "So I just try and avoid you yahoos. You're nothing but trouble," I said.

"I guess I can understand," he admitted, still serious. "So what are you going to do? Lock yourself in your house and swear off men altogether? That's not much of a life," he said.

"I'm here with you now, aren't I?" I said.

William smiled broadly.

"Yes, you are, and I'm glad for that. So what does that mean? Are you taking a chance on love?" he asked sarcastically.

"I don't know. This wasn't planned. I'm kind of mad at myself for letting this happen. I can't refuse you. You've kind of wedged your way in somehow," I said and blushed.

William's smile grew bigger than I'd ever seen before.

"I like that," he said, kicking closer to me. "I think I like being the exception," he said, "because heaven knows that I can't resist you."

I splashed water on him, whipping the silly smirk off his face. "Don't let it go to your head, Lieutenant Commander," I said, trying to look serious. I liked feeling in control, but I felt like I was falling. I was abandoning all my previous notions and betraying my standards. I was acting foolish like my sisters.

I stopped splashing him. After the laughter died down, we floated for a few moments in silence, basking in the sun.

He kicked his right leg and glided his board closer to mine so we were floating next to each other. We floated in silence a few moments before he casually pulled my board toward his and leaned in close so our noses touched. My heart leaped into my throat.

Our lips touched briefly before William yelled, "Whoa!"

Losing his balance, he capsized his board and disappeared under the water, splashing me in the process. William reemerged, soaked from head to toe, his board riding solo to the shore.

I laughed at him, hanging onto my board.

"Smooth, Lieutenant Commander, very smooth," I teased and whipped a drop of water off his nose.

"Look at what a pretty girl does to me," he said and reached up to finish the kiss he started. His lips tasted wet and salty. They were full and soft. My stomach flipped and turned again and again, and goose bumps spread up my arms to shoulders.

He hung silently onto my board, looking into my eyes. I drew circles on his arm with my fingers.

"Would you like to join me on my board?" I asked.

"Would I ever!" he said, smiling big. "Scoot back a little so I can climb up."

I sat up, straddling the board, and scooted my bottom toward the back carefully to make room for him. William grabbed the opposite side, gave one big kick, and pulled his upper half on the top of the board. He started to bring his leg around, but a large swell hit us, tipped the back of my board straight into the air, and knocked both of us off.

When I surfaced, my board and I were at least ten feet from William. William covered the distance with a few powerful strokes and folded his arms on the top of the board on the opposite side of me. I reached over and held onto his arms and erupted into a fit of giggles. We kicked farther out so we wouldn't be tossed around by any more swells.

"I'm glad you think this is funny," William said, laughing while we swam. "I was afraid you might be mad!"

"I . . . I . . .," I tried to talk, but I couldn't catch my breath. I was still coughing up salt water. "I . . . guess it was . . . just my turn to get . . . dunked," I choked out.

"I think we are out far enough now," he said, stopping.

"Yes, I think this is far enough," I said, finally catching my breath. We floated opposite each other, hanging onto the side of the board.

"Well, sailor, I must say you even look good soaking wet and half-drowned." I giggled. "Well, should we try getting on again?" I asked.

"Sure, let's do it at the same time. You go to the front. I'll go to the back," William said. We moved to the edges of the board. "Okay, on the count of three, pull yourself up. One . . . two . . . three," he said.

We both lifted our upper halves and swung our legs around the wobbling board. I straddled the facing William. The board teetered slightly; when we rose over a swell, I had to grab onto William's arms to steady us, and he held my waist. We were still struggling to maintain balance, so Will pulled me closer to him. I lifted my legs and rested them on his legs. We were facing each other in a loose embrace. William paddled us out a little farther so we wouldn't be disturbed by any more waves.

"There," I said. "I think we are finally steady."

William looked at me with another devilish grin. "Losing my board was the best thing that ever happened to me!"

I slapped his bare chest, and my face burned red. I felt so embarrassed to be sitting in such a position.

"I was just trying not to fall again," I said sheepishly. William chuckled and pulled me in close. I rested my forehead on his chest and let him envelop me in his safe arms.

William released his hold after a minute and looked down into my eyes. I couldn't hold his gaze long before I had to look away. I looked toward the harbor where I could see a few ships and smiled.

"All right," William said, breaking the silence, "what is going through that little mind of yours?" His mood was light and friendly.

"So what are your intentions, William? How is this going to end for us?" I asked.

"I'm not sure. All I know is I don't want to be without you right now."

"I'm just afraid," I said.

"What! Of me?" he asked, looking surprised. William put his finger under my chin and tipped it up until I was looking at him. "What are you afraid of, Ruth?" he asked in a whisper.

I was silent for a moment, not sure if I could make my lips form the words.

"I'm afraid . . . you're going to break my heart," I said and swallowed hard. "Honestly, that's what I've always been afraid of for forever, and it's why I stay away from you guys. But here I am, half naked with you, sailor," I said. "I don't see how this is going to end well for me." My eyes burned, holding back tears.

"Oh, Ruth, you worry too much." William sighed and pulled me in tight, hugging me hard. "The last thing I want to do is hurt you." William held my shoulders and pushed me back so he could look into my face. "Ruth, I promise, I have no intention of hurting you. I—"

"William, it's too late," I interrupted firmly. "No matter what you do now, I will be hurt. Don't you understand? It may sound ridiculous, but in the week I've known you, you've already taken part of my heart. If I never see you again, I will hurt. If I keep seeing you and it ends later, I will hurt. If we . . . If we . . ."

"If we get married," William finished my sentence. His face was steady, and he was very serious.

"Yes, if we end up together, you will still leave on your next assignment, and you will still break my heart." I looked away from him, too embarrassed.

"Ruth," he said finally with a sigh, "if you don't risk getting hurt or face a little fear, then you'll never live your life," he said finally.

I sighed; that was not very reassuring. William laughed like he read my mind.

"Ruth, it is true we've only known each other a little while, but I think we are both fully aware that this is not typical behavior for the two of us, correct?"

I nodded, looking down at my fingers. Again, William lifted my chin to look at him.

"Well, maybe there is a reason for that. I don't know about you, but I feel like I've known you a hell of a lot longer than I have," he said with a crooked smile; I smiled too. Just knowing he was smiling at me made my heart flutter.

"I had a great time last night, Ruth, and I'm having a great time right now. I don't know if I believe in soul mates or people destined to be together, but what I do know is every moment I am with you, I am wishing for more and more." I tucked my forehead under his neck, embarrassed and afraid of the next few words he might say.

"Ruth," he said, pushing me back again, "listen, I'm trying to tell you that I'm falling in love with you. I know that sounds crazy, but we don't exactly have the luxury of time. I am falling in love with you, Ruth Shepler, and I don't want to leave you any more than I can change the tide of the ocean."

I drew a sharp breath in, searching his face. He was serious.

This is so ridiculous! Two people falling in love this quickly? That's impossible, right? I searched my heart and mind for a response, but before I could think, I spoke.

"I'm falling in love with you too." It was just a whisper, barely audible, but it was the truth, and he knew it as well as I did. I sighed, feeling defeated and betrayed by my own emotions. How could I let myself say those words? How could I actually mean those words?

William kissed me softly. I wrapped my arms fiercely around his neck and kissed him back. It did feel good to say it, it felt even better to hear it, and then he said it again.

"I love you."

"I love you too," I whispered back.

I'd never felt this way before. I felt ecstatic and joyful but scared and vulnerable at the same time. I pushed the negative thoughts away and enjoyed the moment. He placed one hand behind my neck and the other on my leg. His large warm hand sent goose bumps up my thigh. His mouth opened slowly just enough for his tongue to graze the inside of my mouth. My heart leaped to my throat, and my whole body tensed up. My sister Evelyn told me about kisses like these, and it had always sounded so gross. Now it felt wonderful. I never wanted it to end. His tongue worked its way in and out of my mouth, possessing it, claiming it as his. He began kissing my chin and down my neck and my earlobes. Slowly, he pulled his head back and hugged me gently. My chin rested on his shoulder with my mouth next to his ear, and I stroked the back of his hair and neck with my fingers. We held the embrace for another moment and then let go.

I let my hands fall down to the side of the board, and William stroked my knees and legs while he steered the surfboard back out since we'd been drifting.

I looked up at him, smiling shyly, and then laughed awkwardly; I'm not even sure why I laughed.

"So . . .," he said with a smile, feeling a little awkward too. "There's no reason not to face the facts," he said in a serious voice, bringing me back to reality. I felt like my head was swimming in emotions. "Everything you've said is true. My time here is limited. I leave the end of January to go back to California to train some new recruits."

My heart leaped into my throat. I knew he would leave, but hearing the actual date cut me to my core.

"I'll be gone a while," he went on. I nodded slowly. "But after this next assignment, I can ask to be placed in a more permanent station, here perhaps, and like your father, I can retire from the navy. I'm up for reenlistment next year. I'm sure I can stay on the island until then, and I won't reenlist. I've always traveled because I had no reason to stay in one spot, but now I do. Then we could always be together." William looked at me. I nodded again slightly. That didn't sound too bad. "We have to decide though . . .," he said, trailing off.

"What?" I asked. William swallowed hard; now he looked embarrassed. "What?" I asked again, smiling, enjoying the turning of the table.

"We have to decide if we want to just wait for me to get back or . . ."

"Or what?" I really wasn't sure what he was trying to say.

"Or we could start a life together now," he said finally.

"You mean get married? Now?" I asked, shocked. "But we just met!"

"I know. We've been over that. Think about it." William smiled sweetly and linked his hands behind my back, pulling me in closer. "We could get married by Christmas, spend the whole month together, and when I get back, pick up where we left off."

That did sound nice.

Am I actually considering marrying him?

"But why? When you got back, we could see where we were then and then get married," I said, trying to sound sensible.

"Why!" he said. "I could think of a few good reasons!" he said fervently. "First of all, I'm not sure if I want to give up my position on the *St. Louis* for a girl who won't commit, who just wants to 'see where we're at.' If you don't want to marry me, then fine. Maybe I'll see you again on another trip through," William smiled playfully and whispered into my ear. "But you just got done telling me you loved me. Do you love me?" he asked sincerely, looking deep into my eyes.

I swallowed hard, searching my heart. "Yes," I said softly, "I just told you that." William kissed me softly and then continued on.

"Another reason we should get married now—so we can be together. We could live together, we would get a house on base, I could get an extended leave for our honeymoon, and we could spend the next month together. If we don't, I'll only see you the few hours I'm off."

"That does sound nice," I admitted. I couldn't believe I was actually considering this. I hid my face in my hands, trying to whip away the confusion. Just thinking about a honeymoon made my face flush red. I had no experience with men; holding William's hand made me nervous. Thinking about living with a man, doing who knows what, made me almost want to throw up. William pulled my hand away and tipped my head up to his. I looked away.

"I can't read your mind," he said. "What are you thinking?"

I let out a sigh and forced my eyes to focus on his. My face felt so hot and red I thought it was going to explode. I couldn't process this right now.

"I think it's time for me to go now!" I said. I couldn't look at him a minute longer. Thinking about a wedding night was too much.

I grabbed onto his shoulders, put my feet in front of me between his legs, stood, and dove headfirst into the water. Once I surfaced. I paddled hard to shore without looking back. I heard William call after me until a wave hit me, and it drowned out his voice.

When I made it to shore, I ran up the beach to the shower. Glancing behind me quickly, I saw William paddling in on my board. I grabbed my towel and soap off my bike and didn't stop again until I hit the shower. I breathed out a sigh of relief once I was hidden behind the small wall between the shower and ocean. It wasn't an enclosed shower, but the cement wall offered a small amount of privacy. I could at least hide my mortified face for a moment.

I turned the water on and rested my head against the cold concrete while the water washed the sand and salt off my back. The water was cooler than the ocean and felt refreshing and clean. I tried to digest every aspect of our conversation. What had just happened? William had been very sincere and logical. He was right; I loved him. I could not deny that. There was something very different about our relationship. Waiting for him to return from his next mission—who knows when that would be—seemed wasteful when we could be together now. But how could I allow myself to behave so foolishly? Only silly, immature girls marry someone they've just met. *What if William isn't who he seems to be? Maybe this is all an act?* I mulled the thought over in my head. *No, he is who he appears.* I couldn't lie to myself, but that didn't mean I was ready to get married.

I felt so confused, so torn between my heart and logic. I stood under the shower for several minutes, lost in my thoughts, before I heard William approaching. I could tell he was carrying both our boards; I heard him lean them on the other side of the wall. I waited for him to come around the corner, but he didn't. I listened as he moved around in the sand just a few feet from me, and I started to feel bad. Maybe I hurt his feelings running away from him like that. He had done nothing but be totally honest and caring to me since I met him. I shouldn't be hurting his feelings.

I reached up and pulled the hair tie out of my hair, leaned back, and let the water run down it. Once it was rinsed and I was sure it didn't look like a rat's nest anymore, I poked my head around the corner to see William leaning against the wall next to the boards. He looked deep in thought with his arms crossed, staring at the sand. His face was hard with worry, the serious pose of a sailor.

"Hey!" I said cheerily, forcing a smile. "I'm sure you have sand all over you too. Why don't you get in here and rinse off?"

William smiled slightly and hesitantly joined me behind the wall. William rinsed off while I lathered up my hair. I felt awkward standing next to him, soaping up, but I was trying to be open to his company. William turned around to facing the water and went about, scrubbing the prickly hair on his head and behind his ears, brushing the sand off, and rinsing down his smooth, muscular chest. I watched the muscles in his chest and arms work as he moved, and I couldn't believe that those perfect arms held me just moments ago. Why was I hesitating? Any woman in the world would jump at the chance to be William's wife, so why was I so reluctant? I wanted to, but something was stopping me.

William turned back around, catching me staring at him. He smiled and motioned for me to stand under the water. I leaned my head back in the water and let it run down my head and through my long hair. It always felt nice to wash off the sticky salt and sand. William rested his shoulder on the wall, and it was his turn to watch. I closed my eyes, feeling embarrassed seeing him stare at me. He still hadn't said a word since he came in. I didn't mean to hurt him.

"Your hair is really long," he said, finally breaking the silence.

I opened my eyes to see he hadn't moved but was smiling softly. He didn't appear to be so lost in his own thoughts, though there was still a worry line across his forehead.

"Yeah," I said, pulling up some of the ends and studying them. "I like it long, but it's really hard to wash the sand all out."

"I like it long too," he said. He still looked worried.

I stood motionless in the shower, looking back at him. I wanted to say something to make it right.

"Look, William, I'm really sorry. I didn't mean to offend. I'm just trying to take it all in. This is a lot for me . . .," I tried to explain, but he interrupted.

"No, no, no, don't be sorry!" he said. "I don't want you to feel bad," he explained. "I was just worried I had scared you. I don't want to do anything that makes you uncomfortable or upset. I'm afraid I pushed too hard. I'm the one who is sorry."

I breathed a sigh of relief and smiled up at him. I was glad I was standing in the shower, so he might not notice the few tears forming in the corners of my eyes.

"I am sorry," I went on. William opened his mouth to protest again. "No! Let me explain." I pushed. "I really like everything you said. I like you, I like the thought of me and you, and I like the thought of us being together. I just don't want to be foolish and mostly . . ." I paused, searching my feelings. William looked intently at me.

"Mostly, I'm just scared . . . of everything, William. I'm scared of making a mistake, I'm scared of falling in love with you, I'm scared of you leaving me now that I care about you so much, and mostly, I'm scared of . . .," I trailed off. I couldn't possibly tell him I was scared of the wedding night.

My face started turning red again. "I'm scared of abandoning everything I've stood for the last few years. This is not me, Will. I do not date sailors, I do not fall in love with sailors, and I certainly don't agree to marry a sailor four days after I meet him!" I was getting a little worked up, raising my voice. "I have to be me," I said, lowering my voice. "What if this is a huge mistake? What if we find out a year from now we don't really like each other? How could I live with myself?"

My heart was pounding and my head spinning thinking about all the questions and all the doubts plaguing my mind.

William placed his hand on the side of my head, stroking my hair, trying to calm me down, and smiled warmly.

"Shhh, shh, shh. Ruth, it's okay. Sometimes you just have to take a chance. I can't possibly answer all those questions. You just have to follow your gut. You're still you, and if you don't want to be with me, then don't. But if you do, don't let your prejudices or preconceived notions keep you from happiness. So you haven't dated sailors, so you don't fall in love and marry sailors, until now, until you met me," he finished, smiling sweetly.

I wrapped my arms around his waist and hugged him tightly.

William rubbed his jaw against my cheek and brushed his lips along my jawline. I held tighter onto him, trying to steady myself as goose bumps ran up and down my spine, reacting to the touch of his lips. He kissed my neck and under my ear. He kissed me along my jawline until he finally found my lips, and they locked together. Every time we'd kissed before, I thought it couldn't get any better, but every time it did. We kissed longer than ever before, only stopping momentarily for a breath. After several minutes, our lips broke, but William still held me tight. My hands rested on his chest, and his arms surrounded me, locking behind my waist, all the while the water streaming down on us.

"I think we are clean now," he said, running his fingers through my hair. He reached around me and turned the water off.

"I do trust you, William," I said. "I'm trying here. I really am. I want to be with you." I paused. "It's just hard, you know. I never in a million years thought I would fall in love like this."

William smiled and took my hand. "It's okay. I'm pretty sure I can convince you to marry me. Just look at what I've done a lot in just a week."

9

I skirted past my family, saying a quick hello before going to the back to change. William changed in the bathroom, while I went to my room. Once again, I stressed about what to wear. I didn't know what we were going to do today, which made it hard to decide what to wear. I never worried what to wear before. I couldn't decide if I hated or loved the way William was changing me.

"Love," I said out loud as I studied myself in the mirror. I let the word bounce around inside my head. William loved me? Could William really LOVE me? I loved William. It was so hard to believe. I gave up wrestling the thoughts in my mind and walked out of the room in a red dress.

When I walked into the living room, Daddy and William were both absent.

"Where are they?" I asked, looking around the room and out the window.

Mother smiled sweetly. "They are in the kitchen talking, dear."

"Oh," I said and started toward the kitchen.

"Actually, why don't you stay in here a minute and help your sisters with the dresses they are sewing? I'll check on the boys and make some lunch. You two must be starving."

Mother was acting very strangely. It was best not to argue with Mom, so I sat and started pinning the pattern to the fabric lying out between my sisters.

"This is a beautiful material," I said, rubbing it between my fingers.

"Do you like it?" Marie asked, excited.

"I love it. It's beautiful. What is it for?" I asked.

"Mom felt bad that you got a new dress, and we didn't. She is letting us both make a new one. They will be the same," Elizabeth explained.

"Matching?" I asked. "I guess that's kind of neat. They are going to be gorgeous. I love the color," I said, continuing to admire the deep red.

"Glad you like it," Elizabeth said.

"Why do you say that? You've never cared if I liked something of yours before," I asked. Elizabeth shrugged, and Marie busied herself cutting out sections. "Do you guys know what Daddy and William are talking about?" I asked suspiciously.

"No," Elizabeth said with a grin. "Don't you?" she asked.

"William came out of the bathroom and asked Daddy if he could talk to him for a minute. Mother nearly fell off her chair," Marie explained. "That's all we know."

I couldn't imagine what was going on, but I was pretty sure it had something to do with me. I pushed it out of my mind and focused on pinning and cutting the fabulous fabric, feeling a little jealous of my sisters. It didn't look anything like what they normally choose or what Mother could normally afford. It was thick and felt like silk or a blend of silk. It was a deep red with large flowers embroidered all over it in the same deep red, giving the dress an elegant texture. I wasn't sure what the pattern looked like yet, but it would be beautiful as anything.

We had nearly all the pieces cut before Mother fetched me for lunch. My stomach was roaring with hunger. Combined with that and my curiosity of their discussion, I leaped when she entered the living room, and I dashed into the kitchen. William was sitting casually at the table across from Daddy with his cap resting on his knee. I joined them, and Mother put a plate holding a small sandwich and a tangerine on it in front of both of us.

"Not much, Lieutenant Commander. I hope it's okay," she said.

"It looks great, Mrs. Shepler. I'm starved," William said gratefully.

"Me too!" I added. What were they just talking about in here? No one gave me a clue. William just smiled without answering.

We exchanged pleasantries with my parents while we ate. My eyes stayed curiously on William. I felt slightly awkward sitting there with William and my parents. Mom's face was beaming with excitement; she looked more beautiful than I've ever seen her before. Daddy maintained a casual air, though his countenance was light and happy, and he wore a broad smile on his face.

I cleaned my plate in a matter of minutes. Mother refilled my glass with fresh pineapple juice, which I slurped up quickly. William exercised better manners than me, eating slowly and not talking with food in his mouth. He carried the conversation, answering my parents' questions, while I focused on the contents of my plate and watched him skillfully navigate this potentially awkward situation. If he felt uncomfortable, he didn't show it. He smiled at the right times and had an air of maturity and playfulness, all while my parents scrutinized and observed him closely. Judging by my parents' reactions, he was passing with flying colors. Mother loved him the minute he walked through the door; Daddy appreciated his rank and loyalty to the navy. I couldn't think of a better man than William to bring home. How did I get so lucky without even looking?

"So what do you two have planned for the rest of the day?" Mother asked while clearing our plates.

I looked at William, not knowing the answer myself.

"Well, I have a few errands I need to see to, but I can come back this evening if I'm welcome," William answered.

"I thought you said you had the whole day clear?" I asked, confused and slightly disappointed.

"I did, but I remembered I said I needed to attend to a few errands," he said, placing his hand on mine.

It felt awkward in front of my parents. I looked out the corner of my eye for my parents' reaction. Daddy was studying the paper, but I noticed a small crooked smile sneaked across his face. Mother didn't hide her delight; she smiled proudly. I grimaced under their observations and pulled my hand away.

"Oh," I said softly, "do you need to leave now?"

"As much as I would like to stay, I'm not getting them done here." William wiped the corners of his mouth with a napkin before standing. "Mr. and Mrs. Shepler, thank you so much for lunch."

Daddy shook his hand, and William nodded goodbye to Mother.

"You will be joining us for dinner, though, right?" Mother asked.

"Yes, and thank you." William smiled graciously.

After offering the proper farewells, I escorted William through the living room, past my sisters, and out the front door.

"So what exactly do you need to do?" I asked once we were standing on the front porch.

"I just need to pick up a few things in town, and I forgot I was going to radio my mother today," he explained.

"Oh," I said, still confused, still wondering what happened in the kitchen while I was gone.

What did my parents say to him? Was that what sparked his need to go to town? Did he not want to be with me anymore? Maybe I upset him at the beach, and he changed his mind about us. I shook my head, frustrated that I allowed myself to be in such a vulnerable situation. How could I be so attached to a man already? I should have distanced myself more.

William looked at me sideways. "What is your little brain worrying about, Ruth?"

"I don't know," I answered honestly. "I'm just confused, again."

"Don't worry, sweet stuff," he said with a charming smile, tracing my jawline with his thumb.

Just as with all the other times he touched me, goose bumps ran up and down my spine, and my heart felt like it swelled inside my chest. He gently picked my chin and kissed me softly on the lips. Immediately, I felt reassured.

"I just have a few things I need to get done, okay?" he said sweetly.

"Okay." I sighed. "I'll see you later."

William held my hand in his and kissed the back of it gingerly before bounding down the porch and climbing in his car. He beeped his horn twice while backing up, and I waved goodbye. I felt like a foolish little lovestruck girl standing there, watching him drive away, but I couldn't help it. When he was out of sight, I let my head fall back and released a heavy sigh. What was wrong with me? I liked feeling this way but hated it at the same time.

I tried to smack the foolishness out of my head with the palm of my hand and then turned to walk into the house. I was afraid I was hopeless. The handsome debonair Lt. Cdr. William Wellington was going to break my heart. It was time to accept it and be prepared for the inevitable.

I felt completely lost without him. Whatever did I do with my time before I knew he existed? Hopelessly, I sat with my sisters and helped them with their dresses again. I heard them giggling and chatting around me, but I couldn't force myself to focus on the words. Mother came in and out, helping us piece the dresses together and instructing us on the assembly. It was a more complicated pattern than we've ever done before, so we needed a lot of guidance from Mom. I'm not a great seamstress, but I've sewn most of my own clothes. I can fake just about any pattern, but this one was more difficult.

I was focusing on the layout of one of the dresses when suddenly, I felt eyes looking at me. I looked up to see Mother, Marie, and Elizabeth staring at me.

"Ruth, Mom has said your name like five times. Did you really not hear her?" Elizabeth asked.

"Oh," I said. "Sorry, Mom, I don't know where my mind is."

"I KNOW where your mind is!" Marie giggled. "It's on Lieutenant Commander WELL-ington!" Marie swooned, placing the back of her hand on her forehead and pretending to faint.

Mother smiled and asked me politely to pass her the scissors I was holding.

"Why don't you take a break, Ruth? You look like you have a lot on your mind," Mom said while cutting loose threads off her piece of fabric.

"Oh, I'm okay, Mom," I said faintly. "I'm very curious to see how these dresses turn out."

"Oh, you'll see them, sweetie. I insist. Go get a breath of fresh air," Mother said. She stood and took the material out of my hands. "Now go on, get out of here. You've been sitting here for hours. Go stand up and stretch your legs."

"Okay," I said reluctantly. "Thanks." I stood, feeling a little confused, like I was being kicked out of my own house, but I was genuinely glad for a break.

I walked out back and up the hill behind our house toward a small forest of banyan trees. There weren't any homes or buildings behind our house. I could probably walk in and out of the vegetation for miles before reaching anything. I loved walking outside, exploring the rainforest, examining the plants and trees growing in circles overhead. Leaves bigger than my head hung off plants, roots, and vines crisscrossed the forest floor. I could spend hours exploring as in days past, but I felt tired, physically and emotionally, so I picked my favorite old banyan tree two hundred yards behind our house through a small clearing and climbed the spidery roots growing all around it. From the clearing, I could see the water and all the ships lined up on Ford Island. They looked like small bugs in the distance.

Moss carpeted the tree's thick branches, and the top must have been at least fifty feet over my head. It branched out like a giant umbrella, creating a thick canopy over the ground. I picked my favorite branch that was wider than my body and lay down on my back. I was at least fifteen feet in the air, staring up at the maze of branches and twigs above me, obstructing my view of the sky. I put one hand behind my head as a pillow and the other I rested on my stomach. I closed my eyes and listened to the sounds of the tree.

The longer and stiller I lay, the more I heard. The wind blew lightly, swaying the smaller branches, and birds were singing both near and far away. I forced myself not to think about the ants, cockroaches, and termites sharing the tree with me but pushed my thoughts back on Will. It wasn't hard to do. My mind was very comfortable dwelling on those thoughts. The sounds went further and further into the back of my mind. My body felt exhausted from the long days. My mind felt tired of mulling over the confusion the lieutenant brought, but I also felt happy, content, and complete like I'd never felt before.

I drifted to sleep moments later. When I opened my eyes again, it was getting dark, and the coqui frogs had already started singing. The shade of the tree made my surroundings even darker, so I lay still a minute to let my eyes adjust. I heard the sound that must have woke me up. I heard it again, someone whistling from below. I turned over slowly so I wouldn't fall and looked down. Standing directly below me was my smiling Captain America.

"Well, hello, Lieutenant Commander!" I said with a sleepy smile. William was wearing his uniform again.

"Hello, Ms. Ruth. Is this where you usually nap?" he asked. I let out a chuckle. "It appears I have some sleep to catch up on. I've stayed up a little late last few nights dreaming about a handsome man."

I started to get up off my branch, but before I could, William was up the tree. He stood on the branch below me and rested his back against the trunk of the tree. My branch angled upward slightly, so we were facing each other comfortably.

"Did you finish your errands?" I asked casually, resting my head on my arm.

"I surely did. What did you do, just sleep in this tree?" he asked, teasing.

"Yeah, just about." I yawned.

He laced his fingers in mine, resting on my stomach.

"Did you think any more about our conversation on the beach?"

"Yes. You are all I think about lately," I admitted.

Will smiled triumphantly. "That's great!" he said. He pulled me up and kissed me on my forehead. I could feel the warmth of his lips on my forehead even after he pulled away. My face started burning with embarrassment again as he looked steadily into my eyes. Surely I would never get used to being this close to him. I took an involuntary breath in.

He tucked a stray hair behind my ear, and I ran my thumb against his prickly cheek, dark from his five o'clock shadow.

"Are you okay?" I asked.

"Yes," he said plainly.

"You have a big fat worry line across your forehead," I said, tracing it.

"No, I'm great," he said, leaning back against the tree. "You're not the only one a little scared of this whole thing, you know, Ruth." He cleared his throat. "I've been in love before, Ruth," he said softly.

I swallowed hard, bracing myself for the following words. I felt sad knowing I wasn't the first person he loved and scared to hear why his past love didn't work out and about the heartache it caused the both of them.

"I've been in love before," he said again, speaking quietly. "But I've never felt this way about a person. I love you, Ruth Shepler," he said, leaning in closer again. "I know it's crazy, but I'm crazy in love with you. My whole soul aches to be with you. I've found the person I've been looking for my whole life, and she is sleeping in a banyan tree with moss in her hair." We both laughed while Will pulled a piece of moss out of my hair and tossed it to the ground.

Placing my hand behind his head, I pulled him to me and kissed him firmly on the lips.

"I've never been in love before," I whispered. "But I know that I love you." My heart leaped hearing the words myself. "I love you, Lt. Cdr. William Wellington. I didn't want to love you, I tried not to love you, I feel like an idiot for falling in love with you, but nothing can stop me, not even myself, from loving you. You're the person I didn't know I was looking for." I swallowed hard.

William smiled softly, leaned in, and nuzzled his nose against my cheek; his scruffy face scratched my chin. He smelled like sweet aftershave and mint. Goose bumps speckled up and down my arms as he brushed his lips across mine, teasing me.

"I guess that kind of sounds cheesy, huh?" I whispered in his mouth.

"No," he said firmly, "it sounds perfect." His lips met mine finally, and we kissed. It didn't feel awkward any more as our lips moved in and out against each other.

My eyes felt wet, and two small tears trickled down the side of my face. Will noticed and stopped kissing me to wipe them away.

"You're going to have to stop that, you know. The tears are falling so fast I can't keep up," he said, wiping the next streams of tears. "Your face is too pretty to be this sad," he said seriously. "Why are you crying?"

"I don't know," I said with a chuckle, wiping the corners of my eye. "I guess I never expected to fall in love, and I never thought it would be this scary. I still can't get over all the unknowns."

"There's nothing to be scared about. It's me. The last thing on earth I would ever want to do is hurt you," he promised. "Now stop worrying. Everything will work out. You will see."

"Ruuuuuuuth! Ruuuuth!" a voice called from below.

"It's Marie," I said in a whisper.

"Well, fun's over!" he said and kissed me once more quickly. "But we'll pick up where we left off later," he said with a wink.

William grabbed ahold of the branch and swung down easily. He turned around to help me down, but I was just moments behind him. He looked impressed.

"You're a surfer and a tree climber," he observed.

"Yes, but tree climbing is harder because I'm in a dress," I said with a grin.

"If only I'd looked up a second earlier!" he said, teasing me. I slapped him playfully on the arm.

I could hear Marie coming through the thick of the plants. It was nearly dark now, but my eyes were used to it.

"How do I look?" I asked quickly.

Will smiled. "Like an angel," he said sweetly.

"No, I mean, do I look like I've been crying or rolling around in a tree with a sailor?" I said with a laugh but anxious for an answer.

William took a step toward me, inspecting my hair and pulling bits of moss out of it.

"Turn around," he said.

I did so reluctantly as he brushed moss and twigs off my backside. His strong hands took long firm strokes down my back, and I blushed as he brushed over my bottom. When he was done, he turned me around by my shoulders, smiling.

"I would brush moss off you any day, darling. Now what should we do about your red eyes?"

William was wiping the corners of my eyes when Marie appeared from under a tree.

"There you are!" she said, looking slightly embarrassed discovering us. "Uh, Mom would like you to come for dinner now," she said, looking from William to me.

"Thank you, Marie." Will smiled. He didn't look a bit uncomfortable. "You lead the way." He motioned, taking my hand. We followed Marie over and under trees and roots until we reached the back door.

"Thank you for coming and getting us, Marie," William said as we climbed the steps of the lani.

"You're welcome." She smiled shyly at William. I think this was the most she'd ever said to him, to maybe any man; I wasn't quite sure.

Everyone was sitting at the table outside when we walked through the door, all smiling eagerly as we took our seats. William still held my hand as we crossed the lani and pulled out my chair for me to sit. I felt embarrassed by his attention in front of my family but also glad he felt comfortable doing it. My sisters eyed us curiously, and for the first time since I could remember, they didn't have anything to say.

"I see you found her, William," Daddy said after the blessing over the food.

"Yes, sir. Up that old banyan tree, just like you said," William answered, passing the rice around the table.

"What were you doing up there, Ruth?" Elizabeth asked.

William and I looked at each other and giggled.

"I fell asleep," I answered with a swallow of rice in my mouth.

"Well, that would explain why you brought half the forest home with you," Mother said, pointing to my hair.

I looked at William crossly and started shaking my hair out. Green foliage and twigs fell out and hit the floor. William laughed and looked innocently at me.

"What? It was dark! I did the best I could!" he said, picking more things out of my hair.

"I bet you have dozens of ants in there too!" Elizabeth teased.

"Shut your mouth!" I said, throwing a roll at her. She caught it quickly and threw it back. I dodged quickly, and it disappeared over the edge of the lani.

"Girls!" Mother said. "That's enough. I don't want you wasting food. You're going to attract the cockroaches."

We all laughed. Mother was a little cross, but the whole table was in good spirits. Elizabeth and Marie were giggling together. William smiled playfully while still picking bits out of my mess of a hair.

"So will we be seeing you again tomorrow, William?" Mother asked after the giggles stopped. "Perhaps you will attend church with us?"

"Unfortunately, I have duties to attend to tomorrow morning to make up for my leave today. I was hoping to come around tomorrow night and take Ruth out, with your permission, of course, sir," he said, addressing my father.

"Sure, sure," Daddy said. "If Ruth would like, she can go anywhere with you."

"I appreciate that, sir," William said with a nod.

I felt my family eyeing me as I pushed the food around on my plate. The girls looked at me curiously like they had never seen me before. like they were trying to figure out just how Will could like me. They looked at him, trying to figure out this strange male being in our home. They were all as curious as I was about what we would be doing tomorrow. I looked at Mother. She didn't appear to be shocked by any of the present events. She even looked like she knew William would ask me to go with him somewhere. Daddy didn't look a bit surprised either. My sisters looked as giddy and excited as Christmas Eve, and they appeared to know something I didn't. I looked up at William.

"Would that be okay, Ruth?" he asked. "Could I pick you up tomorrow night? We'll do dinner."

"Yes," I said weakly. "Of course, I would love to," I said, like I would say no.

I saw a large smile grow across my mother's face. I wonder if Mother knew we had kissed. I would die if she knew that. What if Daddy knew? Did he suspect? I felt ill thinking about it. If I did marry William, they would know I was going to have a honeymoon. Would Mother say something to me about it? I swallowed hard. My throat felt dry, my heart started racing, and my breathing got heavier.

"Are you okay, Ruth?" William asked in a whisper, but the whole table heard.

"Yeah," I said quickly and forced a smile. "I feel fine." I had to push these thoughts out of my head.

I took a drink of water and smiled.

"We can do something else if you would like," Will reassured. Mother looked worried.

"No, no, no," I said, shaking my head. "No, I really want to go." I patted William's knee without thinking about our audience. Will placed his hand over mine on the top of his knee and held it there the remainder of dinner.

Mother let out a sigh of relief. My sisters looked at me like I was crazy. I felt like I was crazy. I'd never been so emotional in all my life.

The rest of dinner was uneventful. Daddy and Will talked about a few things military. William asked Daddy if they were ever able to fly just passengers from Hawaii to the mainland. Daddy said it was rare, but on occasion, they arrange it. William thanked Mother for the lovely meal, and the girls and I cleared the table. When my family moved to the living room, Will announced that he needed to leave.

"I have an early shift, so I need to get back," he said, shaking Daddy's hand and tipping his hat to Mother. My family sat as Will took my hand and led us through the house and out the front door. We walked outside and closed it behind us.

"Thanks for a great evening," he said, pulling me into him.

"I'm sad you have to go," I said, wrapping my arms around his waist.

"Me too, but duty calls," he said. "I'll be back tomorrow evening, okay?"

"Yes!" I said quickly. "I can't wait."

"Okay then, I will see you tomorrow!" he said, kissing me on the forehead. He released his hold on me and walked down the steps. "I love you!" he called from his car.

My heart swelled at the words. "I love you too!" I called back, waved goodbye, and then floated back into the house.

10

I closed the door and rested my head against it for a moment before noticing my family staring at me. They were all standing in the living room.

"You LOVE him!" Elizabeth screamed. "We heard you say it!"

"Ohhhh!" I let out an embarrassed sigh and hid my face in my hands while my sisters danced and paraded around the living room, screeching with delight.

"Ruth's in love! Ruth's in love!" Marie chanted.

I flopped in the corner of the couch next to my quietly gleeful mother, and I hid in the corner.

"Did he kiss you again?" Marie asked, kneeling on the floor next to me. I didn't answer; I just squirmed in my chair.

"He DID!" Elizabeth said, joining Marie on the floor, both of them bursting into giggles.

"Tell us, PLEASE, Ruth!" Marie begged.

I took a deep breath. "A woman never kisses and tells," I said with a smug smile.

Both of them squealed giddily. Surprisingly, I felt the same way on the inside. I wanted to run around the room, yelling, "He loves me!" just like the girls.

"That's enough now!" Daddy broke in. "I will have none of this foolishness. I want everyone to settle down. It's time for my radio program, and you girls need to go help your mother with the dishes." Daddy tried to look firm.

"Oh, Daddy!" Elizabeth said, exacerbated. "Don't be like that. You can't expect us to settle down! Aren't you excited too?"

"I understand, Elizabeth," he said with a level voice. "I just don't want to hear about some sailor kissing on my daughter. Now I do expect him to be a gentleman," Daddy said firmly, looking to me. "Am I correct in assuming he is, Ruth? Should I continue to trust this man?"

I nodded slowly. I've never seen Daddy act this way before.

"I have a lot of trust in you, young lady, to behave as a young lady should. Am I the one being foolish?" Daddy looked very serious, and the room grew quiet.

"Yes, Daddy," I said. "I mean, no, Daddy. I mean, no, you are not foolish. We are both behaving properly," I said quietly. I felt hurt that I had to explain myself but also glad Daddy worried about me. I certainly didn't want him to restrict my time with William. I felt uncomfortable being at the blunt end of his firm stare. I wasn't used to Daddy being cross.

"I'm sorry, Ruth," he said, softening. "But you need to be careful right now. I understand that you are a young woman capable of your own decisions. It is clear to me the intentions of your gentleman caller, and you need to be mindful of your standards. Remember how you were raised, and act accordingly," he said regretfully. He didn't look happy about this conversation either.

I was confused. What was Daddy telling me? It was never openly taught to us what the right or wrong way was to behave with a boy or, in my case, a man. It was always assumed and never unclear that we were supposed to be "ladies," although the term was never defined.

"I understand, Daddy," I said quietly. I wished Evelyn were here to explain all of this to me. I don't remember what Daddy was like when she met her husband, Phil.

"I think I'm going to go to go help Mother with the dishes," I said, excusing myself.

I said good night to my parents and sisters after the dishes were done and went to my room and shut the door behind me. I lay on my bed, pen in hand, and let the words spill out on the paper. I told Evelyn all about William—how we met, the dance, meeting the officers, and even touring the cruiser. I told her I loved him and how scared I was. I asked her what it was like for her when she met Phil. I asked her how long it took her to decide she wanted to marry him. After two pages front and back, I laid my head on my pillow and fell asleep.

I woke up to the sun streaming into my room, the pen still in hand. Knowing it was Sunday, I dressed quickly for Sunday services. Sunday is the only morning I don't surf. My family attends a local Christian church with a mixture of local and Hawaiian members.

We all rode together in Daddy's car. The chapel is within walking distance, but Daddy never thought we should walk in our Sunday clothes. The pastor, Reverend Kaaloa, had been leading the services since we've been on the island. He is a close family friend of ours. He married my sister, and I expect he will perform the marriages for all of us girls.

It was a beautiful morning without a cloud in the sky. I sat on the pew with Mother on my left and Marie on my left. I tried to focus on Kaaloa's message, but my mind wandered, of course, to William. I shifted in my seat, searching for a more comfortable position. Mother was alerted by my fidgeting and put her arm around me. It was an unusual action for her. She wasn't normally the snuggly type. I felt uncomfortable sitting under her arm, but I wasn't thinking about William anymore. All I could think about was how weird we must look, mother and daughter snuggling on the pew in the church.

I let out another sigh, shifted under the weight of my mother's arm, and rested my head in my hands. Mom squeezed my shoulders and pulled me closer to her.

"Don't worry, honey, you'll see him tonight," she whispered in my ear.

How did she know that I was thinking about him?! Why did it bother me that she knew, and why was I upset that she was reassuring me? I let out a sigh, smiled at her, and changed my attention back to the service.

The rest of the service went on uneventfully. When it was over, I held back a minute to give Nohea and Elsie a few details of my date with

William. I met them in the back of the hall. My parents were waiting outside, so I only had time to say a few words.

"Soooo," Elsie asked. "How's it going?"

"Great!" I blushed.

"Are you still seeing him?" Nohea asked.

"Yes," I whispered as a few families passed us. "He surfed with me yesterday and ate dinner with my family."

"So it's going well then?" Nohea asked curiously.

I couldn't tell them that I was in love with him. They would think I was insane, so I just nodded.

"We are so incredibly happy for you," Nohea said, giving me a hug.

Elsie left with her parents, and I waved goodbye to Nohea and left through the back doors to my family.

The pastor was outside, talking with them on the grass. I walked over to the little group and shook the pastor's hand; he kissed my cheeks.

"Great service, Brother Kaaloa," I said.

"Thank you, Ruth. From what I hear, things have been going well in your neck of the woods," he said with a charming smile.

I looked at my parents, curious about what they were just talking about.

"Um, yeah, I'm doing well. Thank you," I said hesitantly.

"Well, you all have a pleasant afternoon," he said, turning to my parents. "Let me know when," he said to Daddy. "Aloha!"

"Aloha," we all said and walked to the car.

I rested my head on the side window of the car for the duration of the ride home and confined myself to my room once we got there. The day passed slowly as most Sundays do. I love Sundays for that reason. It's the only day when lying on the couch all day reading is acceptable, when afternoon naps are not only okay but also expected. It is most definitely the best day of the week. It is the only day we can rest and just be a family without working or feeling guilty about not accomplishing something.

I lay on the couch next to Daddy, reading a book, wondering what Sundays would be like with William. Would Sundays be this relaxed and comfortable, or would he be working most of them? Would there be such a thing as Sundays with William?

An hour before William was supposed to pick me up, I stood in my room, looking at my few dresses lined up neatly in my closet, wondering which one would be appropriate. I didn't even know where we were going. I settled on my knee-length yellow dress and pulled my hair back in a low ponytail. After applying a little lipstick, I was ready to go. I sat on the couch and waited. I was ready nearly twenty minutes early, so I had lots of time to wait.

"What are you two up to tonight?" Daddy asked.

"I don't know, Daddy. Honestly, I think I would be happy just doing anything with him," I admitted.

"It makes me very happy to see you happy, darling," Daddy said. "I'm really glad you are giving this guy a chance."

"Me too. I didn't think I would meet anyone like him."

We both smiled and went back to our books.

At five o'clock, there was a small knock on the door. My lips broadened into a smile as if it were a reflex.

"I'll get it," I said, stopping Marie, who was already on her way to the door.

I opened the door to a handsomely dressed Lt. Cdr. William Wellington who was standing on the other side in his dress whites, holding a single rose.

"Good evening," he said, politely handing me the rose.

"Hello, Lieutenant Commander. How are you?" I said, kissing him on the cheek and inviting him.

William removed his cap as he stepped through the door and nodded to everyone in the room, looking anxiously at me. Mom walked in from the kitchen, and Daddy and the girls were seated in the living room.

"Hello, everyone. We might be a little late tonight, General. Is that okay with you?" William asked my father.

"That is fine. You two have a good evening," Daddy replied.

"I hope you didn't eat yet," William said, turning to me.

"Nope. I'm starved," I said enthusiastically, anxious to get out of the house.

"All right, shall we?" William held out his arm for me to take. I waved to my family, and we went out the front door.

"How was your day?" I asked once we were outside.

"Business as usual. Yours?" he asked.

"Good," I said, stepping into the car as he held the door for me.

"So what did you do today?" he asked once he was seated in the driver's seat. He sounded a little nervous. I'd never seen him quite so nervous before, even on our first date.

"I went to church and just hung around," I said.

"Good."

"So where are we going?" I asked, trying to break the ice. He seemed a little nervous.

"I thought we would picnic on the beach. How does that sound?"

"Perfect. Very romantic, Lieutenant," I said. "What other plans do you have for the evening?" I asked.

"You will just have to wait and see," he said with a goofy grin.

"Oh, you are teasing me, huh?" I said, trying to break his serious mood. He smiled his toothless serious smile. He still looked tense. He gripped the steering wheel tightly and wiped his face with his hands. He looked deep in thought. I wasn't quite sure what to do or say. I suddenly felt really anxious.

"So what beach are we going to?" I asked.

"I thought we would go east a little, past Waikiki, where it's less crowded."

"Oh, that's sounds nice," I said and gave up prodding any further. I would just have to wait for him to lighten up, maybe when we reached the beach.

We were pretty silent for the rest of the drive. I waited for him to initiate the conversation since it wasn't working when I did. He never did except for a little small talk. About twenty minutes later, he parked the car in a small parking lot across from a beautiful secluded beach.

"You're right. It's not crowded here at all. I don't see a soul," I said, looking down the beach from our parked car.

"That's the idea," he said with a devilish grin. I was glad to see his personality coming out, but it made me nervous too.

"Stay there a minute," he said and walked around the back of the car, where he unloaded some things, and then walked around and opened my door. He had a basket in his hand and a blanket over his arm.

"This way, please," he said, gesturing to the beach. I got out of the car, and he bent and kissed me softly on the cheek. I think it was an effort on his part to ease the awkwardness we were both feeling. I was grateful he was making an effort, so I stood on my tippy-toes and kissed him one more time.

"Okay," I said, lowering myself down and feeling a little light-headed. I wondered if I would ever get used to kissing him. "Where to?"

"Let's set up under that tree over there," he said, pointing to a coconut tree about one hundred yards away.

"Sounds good," I said, and we crossed the street and walked the distance in silence.

William, dressed in his dress whites, looked devastatingly handsome but a little too dressy for the beach. I watched his shoes as he stepped in the sand, worried they were getting too dirty. His uniform was a crisp white, and I wondered if he would actually sit in the sand in them. I slipped off my sandals and carried them in my hand. I hate walking on the beach with shoes. I like the feel of the sand in my toes.

When we reached the designated tree, I sat and leaned on the base of it, while William spread out the blanket and pulled containers of food and a mug of water out of the basket and arranged them on the blanket. When he was done, he leaned on the tree next to me, our shoulders touching.

"I got one of the aunties at the market to make us a picnic. It's just finger chicken and rice, and I only brought one thing of water, so we will have to share," he said, handing me the thermos. William looked tired.

"I don't mind sharing," I said, taking it from him and stealing a drink.

William remained still next to me while I drank. I replaced the lid on the thermos and passed it back to him. I rested my head on his shoulder while he took a drink, and I studied the lovely picnic in front of me. He had really put a lot of thought into the evening.

With my cheek still on his shoulder, I looked up at him. He put the thermos down and looked down at me, waiting for me to say something.

"Do you still love me?" I asked with a goofy smile.

William let out a chuckle, and a big grin grew across his face. "Of course, I do. Why would you ask?" he asked, putting his arm around me. He looked amused. It makes me happy every time I make him smile.

"I don't know," I said, snuggling under his arm. "Sometimes this all feels unreal, like I'm going to wake up, and it will have all been a dream."

"It's very real, Ruth, and I'm not going anywhere. Do you still love me?" he asked with a laugh.

"Yes, I still love you," I said, and I leaned up and gave him a quick peck on his smooth cheek. "I have an idea. Let's go for a walk first!" I said, sitting forward.

"But we haven't eaten yet. I thought you were starved." He looked confused.

"Yeah, but I'd rather go for a walk first. Let's enjoy this beautiful beach," I said and scooted myself down by his feet, where I started untying his shoes.

William looked at me with wide eyes. I was a little shocked too that I was being so bold.

"What are you doing?" he asked.

"Well, you can't go for a walk in these fancy shoes. You will get them dirty," I said, and I slipped off one of his shiny black shoes.

I reached up his thigh and pulled off his perfectly placed black sock to reveal his bare toes and ankles. I did the same to his other foot while he watched me. I felt nervous and awkward, though I was trying hard not to show it. I'd never touched a man's leg before. His calves were strong and thick. They also felt hairy, which was an unusual feeling. After I put his socks inside his shoes, I rolled up his pant legs, uncovering his hairy sculpted calves. Pushing up his pant legs, I became very aware of all the places I was touching him, and I was feeling a little embarrassed, but I was determined not to stop now.

I placed his shoes next to him against the tree and reached for his top jacket button. I hesitated a moment before working up the courage to unbutton it. I didn't look at Will, afraid I would blush.

"Ruth, what are you doing!" he asked after I unbuttoned the top button and moved down to the next. They were thick buttons, harder to get off than any I was used to. He looked as shocked as I felt.

"You can't picnic on the beach in this confining thing," I explained, smiling at him, trying to hold back some giggles.

"I was trying to look nice for you tonight, Ruth," he said. "And look what you are doing to me!"

"You do look nice, Lieutenant Commander, but I want to be with Will tonight, not a navy man," I explained.

Will smiled, waiting patiently while I unbuttoned the rest of his crisp heavy jacket. I pushed his coat back over his shoulders. Will pulled his arms out, and I stood, folded the coat neatly, and placed it on the picnic basket, where it wouldn't get dirty, and I stood back to admire him.

Will sat with his arms resting on his bent knees in suspenders, a white T-shirt, rolled-up white pants, and no shoes. He looked fantastic.

The T-shirt revealed his broad shoulders and arms. It hugged his tight stomach, and he looked just beautiful staring up at me.

"There!" I said victoriously. "Much better! Now let's go," I said and held my hand out to help him up. He took it and practically pulled me down on top of him when he stood. My small frame was not near sturdy enough to support him. I pulled on his arm while we walked a few feet before I stepped behind him and jumped on his back.

"Take me away, Lieutenant!" I said, pointing to the ocean.

Will put his hands on my bare legs that were wrapped around his waist and started walking to the beach. I wrapped my arms around his neck and kissed it tenderly.

"You are full of surprises, Ms. Ruth," he said.

"I surprise myself, Will," I said. "It must be you." I kissed the back of his neck again and under his ear before I slipped down off his back and walked beside him.

We walked hand in hand, our fingers intertwined, toward the beach. I rested my other hand on his bicep and my head on his arm.

"See? This is nice, isn't it?" I asked, looking up at him. My cheeks were starting to hurt from smiling so much.

"Yes, this is very nice, Ruth. I'm glad you insisted," he said, smiling finally, looking relaxed.

We walked into the warm water and watched it lap over our feet. The sun was dipping into the horizon to the west of us, casting a glorious sunset over the water. I let go of Will's hand and wadded out deeper, pulling my dress up around my thighs and swishing my feet in the water.

"The problem with the ocean, you know," I said over my shoulder to Will, who stood with his hands in his pockets.

"What's that?" he asked curiously.

"I can never come to the beach without wanting to dive in. It's like it calls to me."

"Then do it!" he said enthusiastically.

"I can't get my dress wet!" I said, appalled at the thought.

Will walked up behind me and wrapped his arms around my waist.

"Well, you could just take it off," he whispered into my ear.

Shocked and appalled, I pulled myself out of his grasp and turned around to see him laughing. I tried hard to be mad and hold back my smile. I knew I ought to slap him for that. Instead, I reached down and splashed water on him.

"Oh come on, don't be like that." He laughed.

"Not tonight, Commander," I said threateningly as I walked back to the beach.

I glanced behind me to see him following.

"Rain check?" he said with a devilish grin, catching up to me and lifting me a foot off the ground.

I couldn't really be mad at him, and I was so glad he was loosening up, so I wrapped my arms around his neck and kissed his forehead.

"Rain check," I said quietly with a bashful smile. William looked thrilled. He kissed me square on the lips and spun me around a few times before putting me back down in the sand.

"Come on, if we're not going to skinny-dip, let's go eat," he said.

"Okay," I agreed, feeling happy and giddy again.

I sat on the blanket, crossed my legs, and waited for Will to pass out the food. He pulled the lid off a small container and handed it to me with a fork. He leaned against the tree next to me, holding a similar container. He propped his arm up on one bent knee and watched me. Inside the container was chicken and rice like he said. I used my fingers to pull out a piece of chicken and put it in my mouth.

"Mmm," I said. "Teriyaki—it's good."

"Glad you like it." He hadn't touched his food yet.

"What a beautiful sunset," I said.

"They always are here, aren't they?" he said.

"Yeah, pretty much," I said and took another bite of the chicken. Will still hadn't eaten anything. He just watched me eat. I took a bite of the rice with my fork and looked back at the water too. There were a few fishing boats a couple of miles out dotting the horizon.

With my eyes on the boats, I put my fork back in the rice and pulled up another bite. It felt heavier. I looked down to see why. Hanging from one of the tines was a gold ring dangling among the sticky rice.

I gasped and dropped the container of food. I stared at my fork, flabbergasted.

"Will?" I said in whisper. I was hardly able to speak or move. I didn't know what I was supposed to do.

William studied my face. He reached forward casually and pulled the ring off my fork. I watched him put the ring in his mouth and suck the rice off it. He turned it around in his hand, inspecting it. I didn't move.

The fork was still in my hand. I looked from him to the ring, trying to decipher just what was going on. The ring was simple, understated but a beautiful gold band with a small but very elegant diamond and with a few small diamonds across the top.

He sat on the blanket nonchalantly with his elbow on his knee, looking at the ring that was just on my fork. I waited silently, wondering if he was going to give it back to me.

"Ruth," he said finally, still looking at the ring, "if we have more time, I would wait a few months. But we don't have time." He looked at me finally. "And I love you. You're all I can think about. I hate being away from you. So instead of waiting a few months to do what I know I would do eventually, I'm going to do it now instead."

I nodded slowly.

William put the ring on his pinky and took the fork out of my hand, placing it on the blanket. He took both my hands in his. I scooted my feet underneath my bottom so I sat on my knees.

William bent on one knee.

"Ruth," he said, "I love you. I love you more today than I did yesterday. I'm sure I will love you more tomorrow and the next. I've been alone a long time, and now that I've met you, I don't want to be alone anymore."

I swallowed hard. This was a proposal!

"I've been waiting all my life to find a woman like you, and now that I've found you, I'm not going to waste any more time."

William pulled the ring off his pinky and held it in front of me.

"Ruth Ann Shepler," he said, "will you make me the happiest sailor in the South Pacific and be my wife? Ruth, will you marry me?" William held my left hand and pushed the ring up my shaking finger. He looked back up at my face, waiting for an answer.

My mind was racing. I swallowed hard, trying to make my vocal chords work. It felt like an eternity, although I'm sure it was just a few moments, before I was able to choke out.

"Yes . . . YES!" I said, gaining control of my voice, tears falling down my face. "Of course, I will marry you, William."

William smiled happily and pulled me up into a tight embrace. I wrapped my arms around his neck and slid into his lap. We kissed and hugged, and my tears wet both our faces. His hand caressed my face and neck as we kissed. He rubbed my back and up my sides. Goose bumps followed each surface he touched on my body. My stomach flipped, and I felt light-headed as our bodies were pressed against each other.

He kissed my forehead softly.

"I am going to take such good care of you, I promise," William said.

"I know. I believe you," I said in a whisper.

Slowly, our lips met again. William moved to my neck, kissing the nape of it. Goose bumps rose up and down my arms, and a chill shivered up my skin. William kissed my neck and jawline lightly and then back to my lips.

I let out a sigh, and William looked into my eyes.

"I like you," he said, smiling broadly.

I smiled big. I loved it that he liked me. I loved it that he loved me.

"I like you too," I said. "I like you enough to marry you!" I said, admiring the sparkly ring on my finger. We sat back, and Will handed me my food and started eating his finally. My whole face hurt from smiling. I'd never felt so happy. I rested my food in my lap and watched him.

"What?" he asked with a grin.

"We're getting married!" I squealed. "It is beautiful, William," I said, admiring the ring.

"I'm glad you like it. It was one of the errands I had to take care of on Saturday."

I looked back up at him and then to the ring.

"I'm getting married," I said under my breath and then looked back up to William. "To you!"

William let out a hearty, amused laugh. "Yes, you, Ruth Shepler, are going to marry me, William Wellington. Why is that so hard to believe?"

"I don't know. I don't know if I ever thought I would get married. And now I am!" I felt numb like I was in a daze. Nothing around me felt real. The last few days felt like a dream. I felt like at any minute, I would wake up, and none of this would have happened.

"Yes, now you are," William said, still smiling, taking a bite of his food.

"When?" I asked, suddenly serious.

"When are we going to get married?" William asked.

"Yes, when are WE going to get married?" I asked, still giddy with excitement.

"Well, when do you want to? Time isn't really on our side, so I was hoping sooner rather than later. I was hoping before Christmas," William said.

"Hmmm." I thought a moment. "Christmas is in a little over a week. That is really soon."

William nodded.

"What if we get married on the twenty-third?" I asked hesitantly. Was it weird that I was in a hurry too?

"That is a week from tomorrow," William pointed out. "Do you think we can put a wedding together that soon?"

I thought a moment.

"Honestly, I think my mom started planning it since I brought you home."

William laughed and nodded.

"Yes, I think you are right."

"Did you tell them?" I asked.

"Well, what kind of man would I be if I didn't ask your father's permission?"

"Oh, that's why Mother wouldn't let me go into the kitchen yesterday?"

"Yes, your father and I were discussing it."

"How did it go?" I wondered out loud.

"Very well. Your father loves you very much and wants you to be happy. He said if I made you happy, then I had his permission."

I smiled. William did make me happy.

"He then said he had never seen you as happy as you've been the last few days." William continued.

"He's right," I admitted.

"Your mother did a little dance right there in the kitchen when she heard my intentions. I had to swear her to secrecy. I knew I had to do it soon, or she would just burst."

I laughed imagining it.

"I can't believe she didn't tell me. She must be as giddy as I am!" I said, laughing. "I think we could pull it off," I said. "What do you think?"

"I will do whatever you want, Ruth. I'd marry you tomorrow if I could."

My cheeks blushed with embarrassment.

"A week isn't very long of an engagement. Will *I* be ready in a week?" I wondered out loud.

"Ruth," William said seriously, "I will give you all the time in the world. I don't want to push you."

"No," I said decidedly. "I don't think I will ever be more ready than I am now. Let's do it!"

"On the twenty-third?"

"Yes!" I exclaimed.

"Okay," he said. "Where? Your church?"

"No, I want to get married on the beach but by our pastor."

"Sounds fun. How about the reception at Hickam Hall? I can arrange it," William offered.

"That would be good," I said, getting excited. Just moments ago, we weren't engaged, and here we are, planning the details. My mind was reeling. I felt like I was on a roller coaster but a great roller coaster.

"You know, we better get your parents in on this planning," he said.

"Sure. I'm way too excited to eat anymore," I said, anxious to share our news.

"Okay then," William said and started packing up the picnic.

I helped put a few things away and grabbed his shoes.

"Sit back, mister. Let's get you dressed again," I said giddily.

William smiled and leaned back against the tree, both knees bent with his arms resting on them. I slipped his shoes and socks back on and rolled his pant legs back down. Sand poured out as I unrolled them. William watched and laughed while I worked. I tried to brush out the wrinkles and sand. I tied his shoes and looked up at him smiling at me.

"There!" I said and put my hand on his knees, leaned forward, and kissed him again.

I stood, grabbed his coat, and brushed off some of the sand. William stood so I could slip it up his arms. I stood in front of him and buttoned it up. I wasn't near as nervous as when I took it off, but now I felt a new array of emotions, imagining all the future opportunities to help him dress. My face flushed again thinking about it. I smoothed the collar and brushed the shoulders after it was buttoned.

"All done," I said and tapped his nose with my finger. William wrapped his arms around me and lifted me off the ground.

"I love you," he said.

"I love you too," I said quietly. "And we're getting married!" I squealed.

We walked back to the car holding hands. I skipped along beside him.

"I've become one of those girls I've always pitied," I said when we reached the car. William looked at me, confused. "But I like it!" I finished.

William smiled. "Get in, goofy," he said, holding the door for me, and we drove back to my house.

11

My nerves were making my hands shake. How on earth was I going to tell my parents? I've never had something like this to announce before.

"Nervous?" William asked after shutting the engine off.

"Yes. Weird, huh?"

"No, not weird. Normal. It will be fine," he assured me.

"What about your parents?" I thought suddenly. "When will you tell them?"

"I told my mom yesterday when we spoke, that I was going to ask you. I will call again tomorrow and tell her you said yes. My parents are thrilled. They've been waiting to hear this kind of news for a while," he said casually.

"When will I meet them?" I asked. I hadn't even thought about his family. How selfish. I wondered if they would like me.

"I don't know. Let's not worry about that now. First things first," he said and then hopped out of the car.

It was apparent that William was much better at this than me. My mind was scattered. I didn't know what to think about first. My thoughts were racing from one topic to another I couldn't organize a single event. William was calm and unflustered by any of it.

He opened my door and helped me out. "The only thing that matters, Ruth, is that we get married. Everything else and everyone else is just frosting on the cake," he said, taking my arm.

I nodded in agreement. That made perfect sense.

We held hands up the steps and into the house, where everyone was sitting in the living room as if they were waiting for us. When we walked in, Marie clicked off the radio program they were listening to, and everyone's attention turned to us. It looked like this would be easier than I thought. They looked like the already knew.

Mother's hand covered her mouth gently, bracing herself for the news. She must be scared I said no. I didn't know what to say. We stood motionless for a moment, holding hands, looking at my family, who were staring at us and sitting at the edge of their seats. William squeezed my hand, encouraging me to say something. I looked at him and then back to my awaiting family and then to the ring on my left hand, and it occurred to me what the easiest way to tell them would be.

I rose my left hand slowly for everyone to see the gorgeous new addition to my finger. "We're getting married," I said casually.

My sisters jumped off the floor, screaming, and ran over to me. We hugged and jumped together. Mother joined us just as giddy as the girls. They all grabbed my hand to examine the ring. I looked at William, who stood behind me, smiling proudly. I was beaming. I didn't know I was capable of feeling so much joy. I bounced and squealed as excitedly as my sisters as they bombarded me with questions.

"How did he ask? Where did you go? When are you getting married?" And on and on until Daddy cleared his throat, demanding order.

"Okay, okay!" Daddy said above the commotion, getting up from his chair. "Calm down, ladies. Take a seat and let's talk about this like adults."

The girls sat on the floor, and William and I sat on the couch next to Mom, who was rubbing my leg, smiling like a goofy schoolgirl.

"So you said yes, Ruth?" Daddy asked with a smile after the room was quiet. I could tell Daddy was excited too.

"Yes, Daddy," I said shyly, looking up at William, who held my other hand. I felt uncomfortable by all the attention but happy and joyful at the same time.

"So you two are getting married. William, I have to admit you must be quite the man because I didn't think anyone could charm my Ruthy," he said.

"Thank you, sir. But I assure you that it is her who has charmed me and captured my soul," William said modestly.

Marie and Elizabeth both let out a gasp and a few "Ahhhhs."

"Well, let's get straight to business. So when are we planning a wedding for?" Daddy asked.

I turned to William, afraid to tell my parents our hasty plans.

"Well, sir," William said, "time is not our friend in our situation. I am going to be deployed again to California in less than two months. I will be gone for some time, but then I plan on making Oahu a permanent residence."

Mother let out a quick gasp of excitement hearing we were going to stay local.

"We would like to be married soon so we can be together as much as possible before I leave," William went on. "With your permission, we would like to get married on the twenty-third. That is a week from tomorrow, Mr. Shepler." William turned to Mom. "Do you think we can pull off a wedding in a week?"

"I will do whatever it takes," Mother said gleefully.

"All right then, it is set. We will do it next week," Daddy said. "I will take care of offering invitations. Would it be okay, Ruth, if I deliver invitations face-to-face since there won't be time to mail them?"

"Yes, Daddy, that would be fine. I will type something up tomorrow," I answered.

"Mr. Shepler," William said, "if it is okay with you, I will organize the reception at the hall. I can put some of my men on it if the ladies can provide the decorations."

"That would be acceptable," Daddy said. "Now where are we getting married, Ruth?"

"I would like to get married at the beach, Daddy," I said, still beaming. I couldn't believe we were talking about my wedding, *my wedding*, the one I thought might never happen.

"I thought so, the one you surf at?" Daddy asked. I nodded. "We've already alerted the pastor. He just needs to be told where and when," Daddy said.

"And our bridesmaid dresses are nearly done!" Marie interrupted.

I was confused. Then it dawned on me.

"The dresses you have been working on are for my wedding?" I asked, putting it all together in my head. "They are perfect! How did you know that I would like those?" I asked excitedly.

"Mom knows you better than you think, Ruth," Elizabeth said. "Nohea and Elsie's moms have been making ones for them too."

I looked at my mother, surprised by her sneakiness. How did she know we would be planning this so quickly? "I picked up several wedding dress patterns and material yesterday. You just have to pick one, and we will get started," Mother said proudly.

"Will you take care of inviting all your guests?" I asked. "I'm not sure how many people you want to invite. I assume it's a lot, and I don't think I will have enough time to make them all an invitation."

"Yes," he said. "I'll take care of inviting the boys if you will make me six invitations to give to my fellow officers."

"Wow! Well, I guess we are really going to pull this off," I said.

"I will do what I can to help," William said. "But I'm afraid I will be a little scarce the next few days taking care of things on the cruiser."

I looked at him, confused.

"I'm going to try and arrange it so I have leave the next few months, but that will take some organizing and extra hours right now."

"You will have to find a place for you two to live," Daddy said.

"Yes, that too," William agreed. "I will have to get our new place set up and us moved into it."

"It will be a lot of work," Daddy agreed. "But we can do it. We'll have to get started first thing tomorrow."

We all sat silently for a few moments, thinking about our individual tasks. I was starting to feel overwhelmed. There were a lot of things to get done in just a few days. I could easily get stressed. I didn't want the details to ruin my good mood.

"I'm getting married!" I said, breaking the silence. Everyone laughed at me.

"Yes, sweetie, you are getting married," Mother said, kissing my forehead.

We discussed a few other particulars, and thirty short minutes later, I was saying goodbye to William again on the porch.

"I know a week is not long," I said, "but suddenly, it feels like forever. I hate saying goodbye to you."

"Me too," William said and kissed me on the cheek, holding my face in his hand. "Ruth, I forgot. Do you want to live on base or off?" he asked quickly.

"Oh, I'd never thought of that before," I said. What a weird question. It was weird to think that in a week, I wouldn't be living at this house.

"I don't know. I've always lived off base, but isn't that more expensive?"

William took two steps toward me, closing the few feet between us, and wrapped me in his arms. "Ruth, I've been in the navy for fourteen years with nothing to spend my earnings on. If you want to live off base, I can buy you something off base."

"Really?" I was surprised. I'd never even thought about money. Did William have a lot of money?

"Really," William said seriously. "I'm not rich, but I have a substantial amount of money saved up, enough to get you the kind of home you would like."

"Well, in that case, I would like to live off base," I decided. I felt selfish asking for it though.

"You got it!" he said with a smile and kissed me soft and smooth on the lips this time, making my stomach flip inside me. "Love you!" he said, squeezing me, and kissed me on the cheek and ran back to his car.

"I love you!" I called after him.

Once I was back in the house, I sat across from Daddy on the couch. Mother was in her room, digging out the material and dress patterns she'd talked about, and the girls were getting ready for bed.

"Daddy?" I asked.

"Yes, sweetie," he said, not looking up from his book.

"Daddy, I would really love it if Evelyn could be here, and I know William would never say it, but I think he would like it if his parents could come."

"I'd already thought of that, sweetie," he said. "I will see what I can arrange. I'm pretty sure I can get Evelyn here. I already talked to George on the base, and he said there are supply planes that come out of California all the time that I could get Evelyn on one. I was planning on looking into getting Will's parents here too. I can't promise anything. Wyoming is much more remote, but I will try."

"If there is anyone who could do it, it's you, Daddy. No one has pull like you do down there on base," I said, laughing.

"You got that right, toots!" Daddy said with a grin.

Mother came out of her room heavy laden with material and fabric so much that she couldn't see where she was going.

"Let me help you, Mother," I said, running over to her.

"No, no need," she said and dropped the bundle on the couch.

Hidden under the pile of fabric were several patterns she fished out for me. We sat next to the mountain of fabric and went through the patterns. She had about five of them for me to choose from.

"I bought all the ones I thought you might be interested in," she said. "And then I took a chance on this one," she said, handing it to me. The picture on the outside of the package showed a happy bride dressed in lace from head to toe. Her veil was one long carpet of lace streaming off her head. I only took one look at it.

"No, Mother, not that one," I said definitely.

"Well, it was worth a try," she said and handed over the other four. "I'll save this for one of the other girls." Looking at my choices, I realized Elizabeth was right. Mother did know me better than I thought she did. Each dress was simple and elegant, just what I would have chosen myself. I picked a lovely gown made of straight plain silk; short sleeves, which Mother said we could modify to a cap sleeve; a dipping neckline; and small train.

"I love it, Mom. It's going to be beautiful," I said, admiring it again.

"Yes, and easy to make. It's very simple. It looks like a glorified version of the dresses you wear every day." Mom sounded disappointed but not surprised.

I couldn't decide on any of the veils. They were all puffy and covered with lace and ribbon. Some of them had big bows on the top that looked like a second head. "Mother," I said tentatively, "I don't like any of these veils. They are all awful."

"I thought you would say that," she said with a sigh. "So what if we just made a simple lei po'o crown out of white plumeria flowers to wear in your hair?" she said.

"I love that idea!" I said, relieved. "Do you think William would agree to wear a tea leaf lei?" I asked.

"Oh, I don't know. You would have to ask Daddy if that would be appropriate since William will probably be in uniform."

"Daddy?" I asked, turning to him.

"I don't think that would be a problem. As for William, that boy will do anything for you, sweetheart," Daddy said with a silly smirk.

"Thanks, Daddy. Mom, I was also thinking. I love the train on the dress, but I really don't want it to drag in the sand—"

"I know. I was thinking the same thing," she interrupted. "We will need to shorten it," she said, studying the picture.

I was thrilled Mother was being so understanding. I always thought if I ever did get married, Mom and I would fight tooth and nail over every detail. Maybe the time crunch was a good thing. She knew we didn't have time to argue.

"What kind of shoes would you like to wear?" she asked while folding up some smaller pieces of fabric.

"I was wondering if I could go barefoot." I braced myself, waiting for her response. Surprisingly, she didn't react harshly.

"That would be fun for the ceremony on the beach, but you need something for the reception," she said casually.

"Oh, I don't know. Maybe just my sandals?" I considered.

"Nonsense!" Mom said. "We will pick up a nice white pair of shoes in town when we go shopping later," Mom said firmly. "Aha! This is the piece I was looking for!" she said, holding up a shimmery silk piece of white fabric. "What do you think? Is this the right material for your dress?"

I studied it for a minute and felt it between my fingers. "I love it, Mom. I think it will look simply elegant," I said completely honestly.

It was a fabulous fabric, much like the girls' bridesmaid dresses, only white. It was white with white flowers embroidered all over it. Daddy stood; I had nearly forgotten he was there.

"Well, ladies, I am off to bed. Don't stay up too late," he said, walking sleepily across the room.

"Night, Daddy!" I said with a wave and turned back to Mother.

"Well, let's get the pieces pinned tonight, and we can cut them out and begin sewing tomorrow. I bet we will have it done in a few days," Mother said.

She was enjoying this as much as I was. It was new and fun working with her without fighting. We spent the next hour pinning all the pieces of my dress pattern to the fabric. Mother told me a few stories about making her wedding dress and what her wedding was like. I was slightly curious about the wedding night but wouldn't dare bring up the subject. The thought of her and Daddy like that was disturbing.

"When we pick you up some shoes, we should also buy a nice nightgown for you," she said after a moment of silence, still studying the fabric and pins.

I didn't know what to say. She was right. I would need something to wear to bed other than my cotton pajamas. I would be mortified to shop for it with Mom though. I was mortified just talking about it and thinking about wearing something to bed with William.

"Oh, uh, okay," I said.

"Do you know what happens on your wedding night, Ruth?" she asked, still busy pinning.

This was the first time my mother and I spoke about a subject like this. "Mom!" I said, embarrassed and shocked.

"Ruth, I know it's hard to talk about, but I feel like it is important. No one told me, and I was clueless the first night with your father," she confessed, finally looking up at me.

"Mom, PLEASE!" I begged.

"It's true. All I knew was what my friend Maggie told me, which wasn't much," Mom went on. "I hid in the bathroom for an hour after I found out what we were supposed to do."

"UGH!" I groaned. There was no way to stop this.

"Just humor me, Ruth, and let me tell you a few things." I sat and put my head in my hands, hiding from the torture. "What do you know, Ruth?" Mother asked sincerely, folding her hand on top of the blanket of white material streaming across the table in front of us. I looked up at her.

"Honestly, I don't know much either, Mom, only what Evelyn told me." I sighed. "I wish she were here," I said, trailing off in thought.

"I know, dear, and maybe Daddy can get her here, but until then, talk to me. What did Evelyn tell you?" she asked.

"She said you have to be naked, and it hurts," I blurted out and hid in my arms again.

"Ruth," Mom said, rubbing my arm, "it's okay. Look at me. What else do you know?"

"I know what you told me a few years ago. That a man plants a seed in the woman, whatever that means."

"That is all right. You do have to be naked, and it does kind of hurt, but only the first time, and it is wonderful. I think you know enough, but listen to my advice, okay?" she said seriously. I nodded. "Follow your husband's lead, and just relax. If you tense up and get scared, it will hurt more and won't be any fun. You must trust him. Do you trust, William?" she asked. I nodded again. "Then you have nothing to worry about, dear," she assured me.

She went back to work, and that was the end of the conversation. The torture was over, but I didn't know any more than before. Why won't anyone tell me? I felt like an idiot. I went to bed that night wrestling with these thoughts. I didn't want to dwell them though. Mom was right. I trusted William. Everything would be okay. Mother was busily working on sewing the pieces of my dress together when I woke up that morning.

"Everyone is on their own for breakfast," Mother announced as I walked into the living room.

"Okay, Mom," I said.

"Ruth," Daddy said, emerging from the hallway. "Ruth, do you think you can have some invitations made by the time I get home from lunch? I'd like to pass them out at work today and deliver some to our friends on the way home."

"Sure, Daddy. I'll get started right away," I said.

The pressure was starting to build. I could feel it building up inside my chest. I could feel it from my Mother, from Daddy and growing in the pit of my stomach. *Maybe this isn't such a good idea.* Daddy left for work, and I made breakfast for me and the girls. Mother never left the sewing machine. She worked feverously like she was in a race. That was how I felt, like we were in a race with time.

"Mother, by any chance, do you have any nice paper for me to make the invitations with?" I asked her after breakfast.

"Yes, sweetie," she said without looking up. "I bought some pretty white paper and vellum on Saturday with some ribbon to tie them together. They are on my dresser," she instructed from the sewing machine.

I fetched the vellum and paper and sat at the typewriter with a loss for words. "Mom, I don't even know how to word this," I said. I was getting flustered before I even started.

"Go fetch one of Evelyn's invitations out of my scrapbook and type the same thing. Change the names and the date, of course," she said, still consumed with the mountain of white fabric laid out before her.

After I had Evelyn's invitation, it was easy. I copied the words and the same format over and over and over until I had a whole stack of printed paper on the table. I wasn't sure how many to make; my goal was fifty. Everyone else beyond that would need to be invited by word of mouth. It was time-consuming and taxing. Every time I typed the wrong letter, I cringed and spent several minutes trying to fix it, just to crumple it up and threw it away. Occasionally, my mother would interrupt me for a fitting of my dress. She would pin a sleeve or measure my waist, but for the most part, we worked in silence. By the time all the papers were typed, my sisters had joined me. They helped me tie the vellum and fancy paper together with a small white bow.

Mom was pinning me in my dress for the first fitting when we were interrupted by a knock at the door. I was so hopeful that it would be William; instead, Kekoa walked in.

"Kekoa!" I gasped. I had literally forgotten about him.

"Howz it, Ruthy?" he said. He had obviously just come from the beach.

"I am so sorry!" I blurted. "I totally forgot about surfing." How could I forget about something I had done every day for the last five years? Kekoa's face said he was thinking the same thing.

"Stop moving," Mom said through a mouthful of pins. She was trying to pin my sleeve on.

"Yeah, I missed you this morning. Whatz this?" he said, motioning to the dress.

"Uhh, it's a dress . . .," I stuttered.

"It looks like a wedding dress . . ."

I didn't know what to say. I didn't want to tell him. He shifted his weight back and forth awkwardly.

"It is," I said.

Kekoa nodded.

"Congratulations."

"Thanks." My heart was breaking. Why? Why was it breaking?

"Well, I can see youz busy."

Kekoa backed up, opened the door, and stepped outside.

"Don't worry about tomorrow," he said before shutting the door.

"Kekoa!" I called after him.

"Let him go, Ruth," Mother said.

"No!" I jerked away. "No! I need to talk to him!" I shuffled across the living room, trying not to tear the dress, but I opened the door just in time to watch him drive away.

He was gone.

When Daddy came home for lunch, we only had ten finished invitations, and Mom had finished the lining of my dress. "So how did you ladies do this morning?" Daddy asked at lunch.

"Good, Daddy," I said. "We have enough invitations for you to take to work."

"Great! I will be a little late getting home then since I'm going to drop some of them off. Will we be seeing William tonight?" he asked.

"I don't know, Daddy. I assume so, but he didn't say," I said disappointedly.

Daddy walked behind me and rubbed my shoulders. "Don't worry about it, honey. Remember, he is just as stressed as you are, but he has a whole fleet of sailors he is responsible for too," Daddy said and picked the invitations and left.

I sighed, knowing Daddy was right, but still feeling sad. My mind was worried about Kekoa at the moment. William didn't come over that night. The more time I spent without him, the more I wanted this week to be over already. Luckily, I had an enormous "to do" list, which was serving as a great distraction. Mother and I worked on my dress again all day while my sisters sewed buttons and embellishments on their bridesmaid dresses. We finished the final seams on my dress when Daddy came home from work that night. All that was left were my buttons and stitching up the hem as well as the final touches on my dress, my veil or lei po'o, and the decorations for the reception, which we hadn't even thought about yet. We were doing really well for time. How do you decorate the hall for a reception? I sat on the couch, talking to mother about the reception.

At 6:30 p.m., there was a light knock at the door. My heart leaped with anticipation, and I ran to the door in great hopes that it was him. I took a deep breath before turning the handle, preparing myself for disappointment in case it wasn't. I pulled the door toward me slowly, but before I could identify the person behind the door, my arm was seized, and I was pulled through the small opening outside with the door slammed behind us. It was William! He looked tired and as worn out as I felt. He swooped me up in his hungry arms, lifting me off the ground, and I breathed in his musky warm scent. I wrapped my arms around him tightly and let out a squeal of joy. He inhaled a deep breath, smelling my neck and hair.

"Oh, I missed you!" he whispered in my ear.

"I missed you too!" He found my lips and gave me a big exaggerated kiss, finally. He stumbled backward till he was leaning against the house, kissing me. We held each other for a few moments, trying to make up for the last day and a half of each other's absence. All my worries washed away with one embrace, and I was instantly reassured.

"Do you want to come in for dinner?" I asked after he put me down.

"Sure. I'll do anything to be with you," he said with a smile, tucking my hair behind my ear.

I opened the door a crack and poked my head in, looking for Mother. She was busily packing my dress away so William wouldn't see it.

"Thanks, Mom!" I said and opened the door wide enough for me and Will to walk in.

My family smiled and welcomed him. His presence was getting more normal for them and less embarrassing to me. My sisters didn't smile too big or giggle too much. Mother didn't stare at us or look too antsy. It was comfortable. It was nice. We made sandwiches for dinner since we'd been working all day and didn't have time to make anything else. William and I held hands under the table, oblivious to most of the conversation around us, until Daddy spoke up.

"I made some arrangements today, William," Daddy said.

"What kind?" I asked eagerly.

"Well, first, Ruth will be glad to know that Evelyn will be aboard a plane on the twenty-second and will be here that night," Daddy said casually.

"Really, Daddy! Yay! Thank you!" I said, running around the table to hug him. I was so excited he was able to pull some strings to make that happen.

"The other bit of news was harder to arrange," he said as I sat back. "But luck is on our side." Daddy continued. "I have a cargo plane stopping briefly in Cheyenne before continuing on to Oahu on the twenty-first. Do you think your family could be on that plane?"

"Oh, gee, Mr. Shepler." It was the first time I'd seen William speechless. "That is fantastic. I'm sure they would do everything they could to be there!"

"Well, talk to your folks, and let me know so I can inform my pilot. Their return flight is early on the twenty-fourth so they will be home for Christmas. We are very lucky. We don't normally have any of our planes passing through there. They will have to make a stop in Portland as well to load supplies. It won't be a very comfortable flight, but it will get them here."

I didn't know how Daddy did it. I was deeply touched that he would go to so much work for William. "That is so wonderful that you would do that. Not just Evelyn but William's family too! You are amazing!" I said, delighted.

"No problem, Ruthy," he said casually. "William is family now too. It's important his folks are here."

"Wow," William said, standing and shaking Daddy's hand. "I can't thank you enough, sir."

"My pleasure, William. If you would like, you may use our phone to call them," Daddy offered.

"You are too generous to me, sir," William said. "I truly appreciate this gesture. We'll call them after dinner. They will be so excited to hear. They were very excited to hear about our engagement. This will send them through the roof!"

After the table was cleared and the dinner dishes were put away, my family disappeared into the living room to give William privacy to call his parents from our kitchen phone.

I sat at the table with William while he waited to be connected to his parents. I nervously drummed my fingers on the table, worried about talking to them and eventually meeting them. I was very excited for William though. He looked giddy while he held the phone to his ear.

"Mother!" he said after a few minutes. "It's me, William!" He paused for a moment, listening to her on the other line. "Yes, everything is fine. I'm calling you from Ruth's house, so I need to make it short, but I have news." William smiled at me and took my hand. "Do you think you can get to Cheyenne on Friday? There is going to be a plane waiting for you to bring you here."

I heard screaming from the other line, and William pulled the phone a few inches from his ear. We both laughed.

"Dad," William said. His father was on the line now. "Yes, it's true, Dad. Ruth's father works with the Navy Air Corps, and he has made some arrangements. You just have to get yourself to Cheyenne." There was another pause. "Yes, she is sitting right here. Sure."

William pulled the phone away from his mouth and whispered to me, "Will you go get your father?"

I walked into the living room and asked Daddy to join us. When I returned, William was laughing and discussing a few more details, explaining that it probably wouldn't be a comfortable flight.

"Oh, he is here, Dad, just a moment. My dad would like to speak with you. Would that be okay?" he said to Daddy.

Daddy nodded and took the phone from Will. Will stood beside me with his arms around my waist while we watched Daddy.

"My parents are very excited. They can't wait to me you," Will whispered in my ear.

Daddy talked for just a moment, saying "You're welcome" and "My pleasure" several times. He told William's dad what time and where to meet the plane and that he was welcome to bring the whole family. He concluded by wishing them a good flight and then handed the phone to me.

"He would like to talk to you, Ruth," Daddy said and left the room.

My hands were shaking as I put the receiver to my ear.

"Hello," I said in a shaky voice.

"Hello, Ruth!" His voice was scratchy but kind. "I just wanted to hear your voice and tell you how happy we are to be getting a new daughter-in-law."

"Thank you, Mr. Wellington," I said.

"Please call me Richard. We look forward to meeting you. Please thank your father again for us."

"I will, sir. I look forward to meeting you too," and I handed the phone back to William, breathing a sigh of relief.

William's father had a kind voice, and it seemed like he shared the same gentle, happy nature as William. I'm sure that is where he learned it. I had to relax about meeting his parents. I had enough other things to worry about. If they are half as great as William, everything would be fine.

"Okay, Dad, we will see you in a few days!" William said. "Don't forget your swimming suit, and leave your boots at home. Tell Mom to bring a pretty hat! Have a great flight," and he hung up the phone.

"You look really happy, Will," I said.

"I haven't seen my family in a long time. I didn't ever think I would see my dad in Hawaii. It's going to be strange for them, ranchers from Wyoming in the middle of winter in Hawaii. It will be good for them. They are going to love you."

I was glad he was certain. We hugged again. I didn't think I would ever be tired of his hugs. I felt so safe and warm wrapped in his arms. It was getting late, and I knew he would have to leave soon, so I tried to enjoy it as much as I could.

"Will I see you tomorrow?" I asked.

"If you're not too busy with wedding plans," he said, pulling back to look at me, "I have a house I want you to come look at."

"A house?"

"Yes. I don't want to commit to anything without your approval. I think you will like it though. It's within walking distance of the beach. It has its own private access."

"It sounds lovely. Is it something you can afford?" I asked.

"Don't you worry about it. That's my department. Do you think you can get away after lunch?"

"Yes, I think so. How are things going on your end?" I asked.

"Good. It's a lot of work arranging for my absence, but I think it's coming together. The skipper is very excited for me and more than willing to make arrangements for my absence. Edward is pitching fit because he has to take up the slack for the next month, but that's just him. Everyone else is happy for us."

"I have a few invitations for you to take," I said.

"Great. I probably need to get going," he said regretfully. "Good ol' Eddie is watching the boys for me, and I'm gonna hear about it."

"I know," I said sadly. I hated saying goodbye. "I think this is longest week of my life," I admitted.

"I know. It will be over soon, and there won't be anything to get in our way," he said sweetly.

I got the invitations off the table and led him to the door for another goodbye. I wished we could go back to the beach again and be alone. It was fun to see him but not the same with all my family around.

"I think I might enjoy married life," I said once we were outside.

"You've just now decided this?" Will asked sarcastically.

"No, I'm just confirming a prior suspicion." I laughed. "Now don't let Edward give you a hard time. Tell him to knock it off," I said.

"Eh, he's harmless." William shrugged. "He can complain all he wants. We've all stopped listening."

With one more hug and soft kiss, William left again, and I went back into my house. It was weird thinking I would only be living here a few more days. It was hard to take in all the changes. I was really excited to get married but nervous about living with a man. I loved William, but living with him was certainly going to take some getting used to.

Mother announced that my dress was finished in the later the next morning, so I put it on for one last fitting.

"It looks beautiful!" Mother exclaimed once the back was buttoned up. I looked in the mirror. It was beautiful, long, sleek, and elegant.

"I love it, Mom! Thank you!" I said and hugged my mother for probably the fifth time since I reached my adolescent years.

"You are going to be a beautiful bride," she said through tears. "Now take it off, and we need to go shopping," she said, pulling herself together.

Mother left my room while I changed. I hung my dress up on my closet door, brushing a few stray hairs off it. It was a strange thought knowing that the next time I would wear, it I would be getting married.

When I joined Mother in the living room, she was giving the girls instructions on the last few steps on their dresses.

"I expect those to be done by the time we get back, girls," said, putting her hat on.

"Are they not coming?" I asked, confused.

"No. Just you and me, darling," she said, and we left through the front door.

Mother walked slower than me, so it took a while to get to town. It would take us longer to get home. That is why we did most of the shopping for her. This was a rare occasion for Mother, and we've gone shopping twice in nearly a week. If she had to go to town, she usually waited for an opportunity to take the car with Daddy.

"So what are we shopping for, Mom?" I asked. I had the wagon with me, so I knew she intended on buying more than just a few items.

"Well, we need to get some centerpieces and order a few flowers for your reception. William said that the hall had tablecloths for us to use, so we don't need to worry about that. I'm pretty sure you haven't thought about this yet," she said with a smile. "But you probably want to buy your soon-to-be husband a Christmas present. You probably won't have time to shop for one the day after you get married," she said, trying to look casual.

"Oh, you're right. I hadn't thought of that. I'm sure glad you're here to help me, Mother," I admitted.

She smiled and patted my shoulder. We have never been close. I think we were both enjoying the opportunity to be together and honestly enjoy each other's company.

We ordered some flowers from Auntie Rose, who was delighted to hear of my wedding, and we purchased some small figurines for the table centerpieces.

"What about the wedding cake, Mom?" I asked, startled at all the things I hadn't even thought of yet.

"Nohea's mother volunteered to make one. I still have the cake topper from Evelyn's wedding cake if you want, or we can look for another."

"No, I don't mind using hers. I really want to make this as simple as possible."

"I thought you would say that. Now let's go to Auntie Gwen's shop. You can look for a gift for William." She paused a moment. "You should also purchase a few nightgowns. If you don't have enough money, I can lend you some," she said, obviously uncomfortable to be bringing this up.

"No, I still have money left from teaching dance lessons," I said.

Auntie Gwen had a big Santa Claus face and snowman painted on the outside of her shop. Christmas in Hawaii was one thing I hadn't gotten used to yet. Sometimes people would light palm trees outside, which were beautiful, but the Santa decorations never seemed quite right. We hadn't had a Christmas tree since we moved here. They were very expensive to buy, and they always died within a few days. Some years, we cut out a paper tree and pasted it on the wall or used a big poinsettia plant to put our few gifts under. It was disappointing when I was young but normal to me now.

Once we were in the shop, Auntie Gwen raved about the excitement of my wedding. She had heard from the butcher, whose wife was friends with Elsie's mother, who told her.

"Do you have an idea what you want to get him?" Mother asked.

I'd been thinking about it since she mentioned it, and I was pretty sure I had an idea.

"I think I want to get him a pocket watch and maybe put a picture of myself in it. Is that too corny?"

"No, honey. I'm sure he will love that," Mother said.

We didn't need to ask Auntie to show us her pocket watches; she had been listening to our every word since we walked through her door.

She showed me her small selection. I chose a silver one with a simple design on the front.

"Would you like me to ask my husband to engrave it for you?" she asked.

"Yes, that would be a great," I said, but what would I have it say? I thought for a moment while Auntie Gwen found a pen to write it down. Finally, it dawned on me what I wanted to say, but I was embarrassed to say it out loud.

"Well, honey, what should I have it say?" Auntie asked impatiently.

I cleared my throat. "Um, to the man I didn't know I was looking for. With love, Ruth." Mother and Gwen both said, "Ahhh," approvingly.

"Normally, you would have to come back to pick it up, but if you wait a few minutes, I think we could get it done right now."

"Thank you, Auntie. That would be wonderful," I said.

Auntie took the watch to the back, where her husband and her lived, to have him engraved, leaving me and mom alone.

"Now would be a good time to look at a nightdress," Mother suggested.

"Yes, you're right. Do you mind if I look by myself, Mom?" I asked.

She smiled and looked relieved. She busied herself looking at the jewelry in the display case. The store was small and crowded with racks of clothes, but it didn't take me long to find the nightwear collection. I felt very fortunate not to have Auntie or Mother hovering over my shoulder while I browsed. I looked quickly through the hanging racks in fear that one of them would join me.

I wanted to buy more than one but couldn't even find one that I liked. They all had frills and fake white fur around the necklines and on the sleeves. I was pretty discouraged until I finally found a pretty silk cream gown. It was sleeveless, low in the back, and long. It would be cozy to sleep in; not too hot, which was important; and not frumpy or lacy. I thought it would look nice. I chose two more similar dresses in red and black. I tried hard to keep my thoughts off William seeing me in them, although that was the reason I was buying them, for him. I shook my head. This was very strange. I almost put them back, terrified of the thought of wearing them in front of him. They were seductive, not your momma's or little girl's pajamas. They were definitely made to be worn in a man's company. I held the red one up, wondering if I would really have the guts to wear it in front of him. What else would I wear? I certainly wasn't going to wear my holey cotton T-shirt I normally wore to bed.

I couldn't keep my mind from drifting to Kekoa occasionally. I needed to make things right with him. Was that even possible?

I took a deep breath, decided I had no other choice, and walked to the counter with them. Auntie met us there just a few minutes later with the pocket watch. She placed it in a handsome black box and wrapped a bow around it after I inspected the engraving. It looked perfect. I was very happy with it. I would just have to find a suitable picture of me to put in it.

I handed her my other purchases, and surprisingly, she rang me up without a comment. I was relieved. We thanked her for her help and left for home.

It took so long for Mother to walk up the hill that William was waiting for me in the driveway when we got to the house. It felt like the bag with the nighty in it was burning my hand as I walked up to greet him. I tried to smile casually and gave him a small kiss, but I was sure he sensed my hesitation.

"Just let me put this bag away, and we can go," I said, walking into the house. I threw the bag on my bed and ran back outside to join him again.

"Do you two want lunch?" Mother called to us from the door. I hadn't even thought of lunch. I looked at William to see what he thought.

"We'll grab something when we get back! Thanks!" he called back to her as he led me out the door. I was relieved to leave with him.

We drove down the mountain, turned right, and wound around the coast side. We drove for five or ten minutes before William turned up a small driveway shaded with trees and tall green coconut and papaya trees. The road opened up to a small white cottage. It looked just like the typical Hawaiian cottage, and it must have been pretty old.

"Wow, it's so cute, William!" I said as he parked to the side of the house.

"You wouldn't need to walk far for your morning surf," William pointed out. Through a line of trees at the front of the house lay a small beach.

"It's beautiful!" I said. I was getting very excited. "Let's go in. I want to see this place. Do you have a key?"

"No, the owner said it would be open," he said, and we both got out of the car and walked up the front steps.

It had a large lani big enough for chairs and maybe even a dining table. There were windows lining the front of the house covered with screen to keep the bugs out. The storm shutters were permanently nailed open. It was a beautiful view from anywhere in the house looking out to the ocean. It seemed too good to be true. It was old to be sure but cute. William opened the small wooden green door. It stuck for a second before William pushed it in with his shoulder. With the windows open, the house was brightly lit, open and friendly. It was small, basically just one large room. The kitchen counters lined the front right wall, and there was a sitting room just to the left. The room was empty, but I imagined the bed would go in the back left area with room for dressers and furniture. It was small but plenty big for the two of us.

I walked around, inspecting the kitchen and living space, opening cupboards, and running my hand down the counters. William stood in the middle of the house, watching me.

"I think this place is great, William! It's perfect and so cute! How did you find it?" I asked. I walked up and gave him a big hug.

"I have some good friends who helped me out," he said.

"Where's the bathroom?" I said, suddenly realizing I didn't see one.

"I was wondering when you would ask," he said and led me to the back of the house.

Between a closet and the bedroom space, there was a small door I hadn't noticed before. We walked through the door to a room with another small closet on the right and a sink and toilet to the left. William led me through the bathroom to another door, which led outside. Outside was a small square area with walls built out of beautiful rocks. The back and side wall were taller than me, but the wall on the ocean side was only as tall as my waist. I didn't realize what it was until I looked down and noticed the drain, and in the rocks on the back wall were two nasals and, above that, a pipe. It finally occurred to me what I was a standing in.

"This is a shower!" I said, staring at William in shock.

William chuckled and took a step closer to give me a hug.

"It's a shower with a beautiful view," he said, kissing my head, looking at me, not the ocean. I blushed and hid my face in his arm. "I can't believe it's outside!" I said.

I felt butterflies swimming around my stomach as we held each other. In just a few days, we could be standing here naked. I swallowed hard, and my forehead began to sweat. I had to push those thoughts out of my mind. I rested my head on William's chest and gazed out to the ocean.

"It's so beautiful here. I guess the only thing out here to see us are the bugs," I said, trying to warm up to the idea of showering outside.

"Do you still like it?" William asked.

"Yes, I love it. Do you like it?" I asked.

"Yes, I love it. Do you want to look at some other places, or are you happy with this one?"

"I don't think we could find a nicer place. Let's get this one, if that's okay. It's not too expensive, is it?" I asked. I worried I was being selfish. "We could live on base too if this is too hard."

"I told you, don't worry about the money. If you want this place, it's yours," he said, and he kissed me lightly on the forehead.

"Okay," he said, breaking away, "I need to go do some paperwork." William led me back through the bathroom into the main room. "We need to buy some furniture too. Do you have time to pick some out tomorrow?"

"Furniture?" I hadn't even thought of that. I worried about the money this would all cost him, but I didn't want to bring it up again.

"Sure, that would be fun," I said.

We drove back to my house, where he dropped me off so he could go fill out the paperwork for the house.

At home, we worked on folding the napkins in red napkin holders Mom found at the flea market. They were cute and would go well with the tropical red and green flowers that would be in the bouquets and around the reception hall. It was a mindless, time-consuming work that let my mind wonder and think. Mother, Elizabeth, and Marie worked along beside me. We chatted about the wedding and who would be there, how we were going to decorate and make the bouquets. It was an enjoyable conversation, but I found myself only half there.

I went to bed late that night without seeing William again. How could I miss a person I just met? How could I miss lying next to him in bed when I'd never lain next to him before? I missed him so much my heart physically hurt.

"I think our house needs furniture," William announced as he burst through the door the next day. "Actually, it only needs a bed, so how about we go shopping?" He grinned.

We went to the only furniture store in town to furnish our house. Mr. Murakami, the owner, met us at the door and led us through the store. We picked a dining table from the four available to choose from and moved on to dressers. Price didn't seem like an object to William as we discussed which one would suit our needs best. We picked one with four drawers, deciding the closet would have enough space for the items that wouldn't fit. We picked out a chocolate-colored couch with coffee and end tables.

The last item we shopped for was the bed. I felt really uncomfortable walking around the beds. William flopped down on one and looked up at me with a smug smile.

"Come on, try it out," he said, tapping the bed next to him.

"You are such a flirt," I said. Reluctantly, I lay down next to him, adjusting myself into a comfortable position. Mr. Murakami left us alone to choose. William rolled over and put his hand on my stomach.

"I love it," he said with a big smile, making me blush.

"It's nice," I said. "But I think this one is too hard," I said, trying to be objective and not swoon because I was lying next to him.

"Okay," he said, swinging his legs off the side. I started to sit up too, but before I could, William picked me up off the bed, cradling me in his arms.

"Let's try this," he said, dropping me on another bed and jumping over me to lie on the other side. I laughed so hard tears started forming in the corners of my eyes.

"What if I don't like this side of the bed?" I said, trying to look serious.

"Do you have something against that side of the bed?" he asked.

"No." I giggled. "I was just wondering. I have no preference." I giggled again.

"Well, let me see," he said, flopping his arm over me. "No, not quite," he said and then nuzzled his face into my neck, intertwining his legs around mine. "Yes, yes, I like this one. Very comfortable. What do you think?"

"Isn't it weird talking about this, thinking that we are going to share the same bed?"

"That's weird to you?" William asked with a teasing smile.

"yes! That's weird! How is it not weird to you? How is it that I'm the only person nervous about this? What if I kick you at night? What if I steal all the covers? What if you roll on top of me and crush me?" I giggled again, feeling more embarrassed. William smiled reassuringly and rested his head on his hand.

"You worry a lot, you know that?" he said, tapping my forehead. "Yes, it will be different, but it will be wonderful. I can't wait."

"How can you be so sure?" I asked seriously.

William looked at me, puzzled.

"Will, I am terrified. How are you not scared?"

"What exactly are you scared of? I thought you wanted this?" he said, looking hurt.

"I do!" I reassured. "Will, I'm nervous about the wedding night."

He stroked my face with his index finger gently and looked around to make sure we were alone. "What exactly are you worried about?" he whispered

"I guess, I just don't really know what to do," I said.

"Your innocence is one of the things I love about you." He smiled sweetly.

"So how are you so confident?" I asked.

"Well." William fidgeted nervously. He rubbed his head, looking uncomfortable and nervous. "Well . . . honey, remember how I said I am a thirty-year-old sailor?"

I nodded.

"Well, I wasn't always as refined or gentlemanly as I am now," he teased. "I was a young sailor at one time who succumbed to the temptations of girls' attentions. This is not exactly my first experience."

"What?" I said loudly, instantly quieting myself. "What?" I whispered. I had never considered that. Suddenly, I felt very self-conscious and scared. I scooted away from him.

He has been with another woman?

I didn't know if I should be angry or sad.

William looked concerned and a little panicky.

"I'm sorry. I hope I didn't upset you," he said quickly. "Maybe I shouldn't have told you that," he said, reaching for my hand.

"No . . . no . . .," I said, pulling away. "I guess I have to be okay with it," I said. But I wasn't okay—yet.

"So what do you think of this bed?" he asked, changing the subject.

"This one works for me," I said with a sigh. "And it looks like we only have one other choice," I said, pointing to a small cot across from us.

"All right, it's settled. Let's get it," he said, getting up. "And we can continue this conversation later." William's face was somber. He looked a little disappointed about my fear of our wedding night. I felt bad for bringing it up.

William pulled me off the bed, and we found Mr. Murakami to pay for our items. Two of his sons helped William load the couch, end tables, and dresser in the truck and followed us with their truck with the rest of our items.

I carried the couch cushions into our house, while the guys carried the heavy items. I watched them place the furniture around the house. With each item they brought in, it looked more and more like a home.

Once they set up the bed, I put on our new sheets, the sheets we bought together for OUR bed. I fluffed the pillows and put the thin white comforter on top. I arranged the few small decorative pillows William insisted on buying because he knew I wanted them, and I stood back to admire it. It looked cute and cozy; I couldn't wait to crawl into it.

William came up from behind me and touched my arms, startling me and making me jump.

"Whoa, you scared me!" I said, catching my breath.

"Sorry," he said with a chuckle, nuzzling his nose into my neck. I looked around our one-room home at the couch, end tables, dresser, and bed. It was all ours. It was an incredible feeling knowing this was the beginning of our life together. I sighed and leaned back into his chest.

"It looks great," I said.

"Mmm-hmmm," he agreed, nuzzling in my neck.

"Only four days and we will be living here!" I said.

"Yep, I can't wait," he said quietly in my ear. He sounded tired. We stood in silence for a few minutes.

He pulled my hair back, revealing my neck, and kissed it gently, sending shivers and goose bumps up and down my spine and arms. I giggled. More kisses followed, leading up my neck to the back of my ear. I felt warm butterflies circle around in my stomach, and I hoped he wouldn't stop. He turned me around, stroking my jawline tenderly with his thumb, leaning down slowly, and kissing me lightly on the lips. I pressed my whole body against him, begging for more, and he slowly lowered me onto the bed, lying on top of me. His kisses got deeper, more urgent, more demanding. It scared me but felt wonderful. I urged him on stroking his back.

"Are you still nervous?" he asked, leaning his forehead against mine.

"Huh?" My head was whirling.

"About our wedding night." He laughed. "I asked if you were still nervous. It will just be more of this," he said, kissing me softly again.

"Oh," I said. "No, I guess not. Where did that come from?" I asked. William smiled.

"You have no idea all that I've been holding back," he teased.

I giggled a little thinking about it. He took my hand and pulled me off the bed. We didn't say much as we tidied up. I think we were both trying to soak in the moment. I glanced at him, occasionally catching his eye, and he would smile at me. He was full of surprises. I tried to give William a big hug after he came in from throwing some plastic wrapping away outside, but he sidestepped me.

"Hey!" I said.

"Sorry, darling, but it's best right now while we are alone if I keep my distance from you," he said and kissed me on the top of my head. "I've exercised about as much self-control as I can muster." He crossed the room and leaned against the kitchen counter.

"Why?" I asked, putting my hands on my hips. I was puzzled.

"I can't believe you don't get it," he said. A huge goofy grin spread across his face. "It's taking all my willpower not to throw you on that new bed over there and rip off that cute dress of yours. I'm trying to be a gentleman here," he said.

I wadded up the moving paper I had just taken off the dresser and threw it at him.

"I can't believe you can talk that way without blushing, Lieutenant!" I teased.

"Get used to it, baby!" he said, chuckling. "It's only going to get worse after we get hitched!" he said, throwing the paper back at me.

I was glad William was set on being a gentleman but sad that he felt like he had to keep his distance from me. It made those four days ahead of us seem so much longer.

"Come on," he said, taking my hand, "let's go return that truck."

We closed up the house and climbed into the old truck. Instead of returning it right away, we decide to take a load of my things from my room to the house. I didn't have much, just a few clothes, a lamp, some pictures, and a trunk that I stored my knickknacks, books, and personal belongings in. All my things took up half of the bed of the truck. I left a few dresses and pajamas for the remaining days in my own house. I pulled the rest of the clothes out of my drawers and put them in a basket. William helped me pack my pajamas and shirts, but I paused at the top drawer containing my undergarments.

"Maybe I'll wait and pack that drawer later," I said shyly.

"Oh, come on, just throw it in there. Things are going to get pretty busy these next few days, and we won't have time. You're going to be sad when you don't have any undergarments." He paused a minute. "Then again . . .," he said with a twisted smile, "maybe you should leave the contents of that drawer. I wouldn't mind!"

"Oh you!" I said, appalled.

I opened the drawer and in one quick motion swooped up all my white delicates, including the new nightdresses I bought with Mom, and plopped them in the basket and covered the basket quickly with a pillow from my bed. William laughed the entire time watching me carry the basket to the truck myself.

"So when are we going to get your stuff?" I asked. I was a little out of breath from all the moving.

"I'll pack them up tonight and take it to the house tomorrow," William said. "I have even less things than you do. I have to keep most of my uniforms on the ship, and I don't own very many other things."

"Good! More room in the closet for me!" I said.

We drove back to the house and unloaded my belongings. I grabbed up my basket of clothes before William could and quickly unpacked the whites into the top drawer of my new dresser, while William wrestled with my trunk. He put it at the foot of our bed and looked up at me.

I was studying the dresser, trying to decide what to do.

"Which drawers do you want?" I asked. "How many do you want? Do we share drawers?" I felt silly for being so perplexed about a simple subject, but I was stumped.

"Just leave me one for my underclothes. Everything else I can hang in the closet," he said casually as he walked to the door to get another load.

My heart leaped just thinking about our clothes hanging neatly next to each other, his uniforms and my dresses. I puzzled a minute, wondering why such a thing would please me so much.

I left the second drawer open and unpacked my other clothes in the remaining drawers.

"Are you sure you don't need any more? Maybe a drawer for pajamas?" I asked when he came in with my lamp and a painting of a Hawaiian sunset.

"Nope, one is good. I don't have any pajamas," he said, winking at me.

I turned away from him smiling as my face flushed red. Would I ever get used to this teasing?

"I think you enjoy teasing me!" I accused.

"I sure do," he said, setting the lamp down. "You're just too darn cute blushing over there, angel."

When Friday morning came around, my nerves were shot. I wouldn't be able to see William until the evening when he brought his family, who were due to land around five o'clock.

I busied myself with the final wedding preparations. I helped my sisters hem their dresses and did a final fitting of my own. Nohea and Elsie came over, and all the bridesmaids put their dresses on. Mother and I inspected each seam to make sure everything was perfect. We made a few alterations to Elsie's neckline, which was sagging, and we took in the sides of Nohea's since it was a little big.

"I don't have a chest like Ruth!" Nohea laughed.

"Oh stop!" I told her.

"That is an easy fix!" Mom told her.

"Will is a lucky guy!" Nohea said.

Marie made a weird face, and Mother rolled her eyes.

"Take that off, Nohea, and I will fix it right now," Mother ordered Nohea.

"What about Evelyn?" Marie asked. "When will she try hers on?"

"She will be here tomorrow," I told her. I couldn't help but smile. "I'm so excited for her to get here. We're about the same size, so Mom fitted her dress to me."

Nohea, Elsie, and I went to my bedroom so they could change.

"Are you excited?" Nohea asked. "Just a few days!"

"I am! I'm also nervous. When I'm busy, I'm content, but when I'm idle, my mind races, and I worry about everything. I'm worried about meeting his parents and wondering what they will think of me."

"Oh, don't worry. They are going to love you!" Elsie said, grabbing my arm. Nohea gave me a hug.

"Don't worry so much," Nohea said. "Enjoy this. This is a great moment for you!"

"Thanks, guys! That means a lot. Mother tells me that all the time, but it's hard to believe. I just stare off into space sometimes because I have so much on my mind."

During one such episode, my mother caught me staring out the window, my mind wondering to every possible greeting and subject I might find myself discussing with his parents. She must have read the expression on my face.

"It's okay, darling," she said, putting her hand on my shoulder. "They are going to love you, dear."

I was grateful for her kind words but unconvinced. Hearing it from Elsie and Nohea helped a lot.

By the time 4:30 p.m. rolled around, I was a tornado running through the house, picking up thread and scraps of paper, trying to tidy things up. When I was finally satisfied with the looks of the front room, when every picture hung perfectly straight, the magazines on the coffee table fanned out perfectly, and there were no traces of any sewing projects, I moved to the kitchen to help Mother with the dinner preparations. I pounded out the dough for our dinner rolls with extra fervor and delight and quickly plopped them into perfect mounds on the baking pan. We didn't usually use our oven since it made the house so hot, but we were making an exception today for our honored guests. I was afraid they wouldn't enjoy the local cuisine, so steak and potatoes were on the menu. I hoped they never knew what length I went to find a potato on the island.

Shortly after 5:00 p.m., I heard the beeps of a car horn outside, and I knew it was them. I quickly whipped my hand on my apron after removing it. Looking at my mother, she answered my question before I could utter it.

"You look great, sweetheart," she said with a warm smile.

"Wait!" Elizabeth said, looking up from setting the table and running over to me. "You have some dough in your hair!"

"Thanks, sis," I said after she pulled a small chunk of sticky dough out of my bangs, and I went outside to greet our guests.

I stood on the porch, watching William as he helped his mother out of the car. His father stood silently, observing the trees surrounding our home. He was a tall man like William but a little heavier around the middle. His hair was gray, and his face creased and dark with years of work and worry showing across it. He wore black pants and a buttoned-up blue shirt. I guessed they were the nicest clothes this rancher owned. He looked out of place standing in the hot tropical sun. He looked like he belonged on a horse in Wyoming.

William's father spotted me standing on the porch first, and a great smile grew across his face, and his eyes seemed to twinkle. Instantly, he looked just like William. He had the same smile and same eyes. I thought he looked beautiful. I let out a relieved sigh.

"Well, you must be Ruth!" he said loudly.

"Yes, sir!" I said politely, walking down the stairs to greet him.

He put his left hand on top of mine as we shook hands, engulfing my small tan hands in his big rough, calloused ones. I noticed our hands were about the same color, only his were stained dark, probably from dirt and grease, but they were clean and warm.

"Well, I didn't think anyone could be as beautiful as William described, but now I see he scarcely did you justice!"

"You are very kind, sir," I said, blushing, and I stood on my tiptoes to kiss his prickly cheek. He looked startled when I lowered myself down.

"Traditional Hawaiian hello," I explained. "Aloha and welcome to Hawaii!"

He smiled shyly without time to respond before William stood next to me with his arms on my shoulders.

"Well, guys, this is Ruthy!" he said proudly and kissed me square on the lips. I blushed beet red, my face burning as I tried to look casual. Both William and his father laughed at my embarrassment.

"You're going to have to get used to it, dear," William's mother said, walking up to us from the car. I looked at her for the first time. She was much shorter than her husband but taller than me and had long dark hair, which was pulled back. She wore a long-sleeve cotton dress, and she too looked out of place in the island air.

"Ruth, this is my mother, Betsy, and my father, Charles," William said, his arm still around me.

"Pleasure to meet you too," I said, stepping forward to kiss his mother on the cheek. She too looked embarrassed by my affection, but I had no plans of changing my ways around them. I wanted to be true to myself.

"The rest of the family couldn't make it," William explained.

"Jonny and Christopher are both in the navy, serving on the East Coast, and Jacob and his wife had to stay behind to watch over the ranch," William explained.

"They would have loved to come," Betsy added, "but it just wasn't in the cards. We are so grateful to your father for arranging a way for us to be here," she said warmly. Her face was worn with wrinkles and worry that came, I'm sure, from age and stress of the harsh Wyoming winters, but she was stunningly beautiful. I felt self-concourse in her presence. She was trim and fit, and her eyes were a beautiful deep blue. I could only hope I would look that good at her age.

"I'm so glad you could make it," I said honestly. "Now why don't we all go inside? Dinner is just about ready."

William held my hand as we walked up the steps, and he never let go of me as I introduced his parents to my family. It seemed like he was being overly affectionate to me, showing off to his parents. It made me feel good that he was proud to have me as his fiancée.

"Well, I have to admit we've never seen William with a girl before, and you two certainty make a handsome couple," Charles said as we sat to eat.

"They do indeed!" my father chimed in. "We've been nothing but thrilled with the engagement," Daddy went on. Daddy was extra friendly and smiling. I think he was trying to put off a good first impression for me. "You've raised a fine young man." Daddy was all smiles and excitement since they walked through the door. The only people appearing bored by our guests were my sisters.

William's parents talked about their ranch and their other children. They reported their flight was enjoyable and thanked my father repeatedly for the arrangements. Mom and Daddy told them about a few places they should be sure to visit while they were on the island. Mother offered them some cooler clothes to wear while they were visiting. They tried to refuse but didn't insist for too long. They must have been really hot already.

The rest of dinner went smoothly. Mother and Betsy chatted and laughed while they cleaned up the dishes. Daddy and Charles moved to the living room and visited while Mother dished up some ice cream. William and I stood to the side, observing our parents, answering questions when asked, and snuggling while they were all distracted with each other.

William's parents were tired from the flight and four-hour time change, so they excused themselves early to retire for the evening. I lingered on the porch with William and his parents to say goodbye.

Watching his parents walk down the steps toward the car, I was desperate to keep them all there a little longer.

"Where are you all staying tonight?" I called after them.

"William set us up with a place on base," Charles called back with a smile and waved before he stepped into the car.

I turned to William standing next to me.

"Will I see you tomorrow?" I asked him, trying not to show my dismay.

"I don't think so, sweetheart. I need to spend the day with my parents," William said, brushing my hair behind my ear. He could see the sadness in my eyes. "But if you want, I can try and stop by . . .," he said, trying to make me feel better.

"No, no, no," I reassured him. "I'll be fine. I'll just miss you, is all. I like you, you know?" I added with a smile.

"Only two days and then you're all mine. We'll have all kinds of time," William said and squeezed me tight. I hid my face in his shoulder, feeling the lie behind his last statement.

We wouldn't have all kinds of time. Our time was limited.

12

Saturday morning arrived, and I begged Daddy to let me come with him to pick up Evelyn.

"No, dear, I have to finalize a few things with the pastor, deliver the remaining invitations, and I will get her on the way home for lunch," he said.

"Ugh!" I said, exasperated. "Come on!"

"Ruth," Mother interrupted, "stop arguing with your father. Surely there is something you need to do here."

"Fine," I conceded.

I bounced around the house for forty-five minutes or so, trying to occupy myself, before I gave up and left. I went out back to my favorite tree, my oasis from home, and plopped myself on the big branch.

I was picking mindlessly at the bark when I was startled out of my trance.

"Hey! Howz it, Ruth?"

Kekoa called from below me. He was a welcome sight. I jumped off the branch and scooted over to him, kissing him on the cheek.

"How did you know I would be here?" I asked.

"I juz know." He shrugged.

We stood awkwardly for a moment.

"Your father brought the invitation over yesterday. I had to come over and see for myself." He shifted his weight side to side nervously. "Are you dying?" he asked, crinkling his eyebrows and looking confused.

"No!" I laughed. "Why would you ask such a thing?"

"Then why? Why, Ruth? This isn't like you!" He was upset.

"What's wrong? Are you mad at me?" I asked.

"No, I mean, yes, I mean," he stammered. "I thought I had more time," he finished in a whisper and looked at the ground.

I stepped forward and touched his arm. He was shirtless again; his skin was warm and smooth under my touch.

"Kekoa?" I said his name softly. "What?"

"I know we never had anything, but I just always thought, I thought you waz my girl." He kicked some leaves.

"Oh, Kekoa, I am. I mean, I was," now I was stammering. "I didn't plan this."

He pulled his arm out from my grasp and turned his back to me.

"Well, I know," he said.

"Wait!" I said. He turned around. "You can't be mad at me for something I didn't know. I always thought there was something between us, but you never said anything! Shoot, you looked happy when I started to date him," I accused.

"I know. I just thought, you know, it was you. You didn't want to get married. I didn't think nothing would happen. I waz respecting your space. If I thought you wanted to get married, *I* would haz pursued you," he said.

"I'm sorry," I said. "I've made a mess of things. I feel terrible."

"If I had?" he trailed off.

"I would have," I said.

For a moment, I felt a tinge of desire for him. Would he be easier? It would be easier to be with him, so much less complicated. I pushed the thought out of my mind. *No, it wouldn't,* I thought. *No, I love William, William,* I repeated in my head. *William.*

I stepped forward, wrapping my arms tightly around his waist, and he engulfed me in his, resting his chin on my head and stroking my arm.

"I'm sorry," I said into his chest. "I do love you too. I will always love you," I said.

"But not as much as youz love him?" he said. I nodded. I felt him sigh, and then he pushed me away. "Well, I wish you every happiness. Youz deserve it, Ruth."

I stood on my tiptoes and kissed him on the cheek. He slowly pulled back and kissed me squarely on the lips, holding my chin with his thumb and forefinger. I knew I should pull back, but I didn't. I kissed him back. We lingered a moment before I lowered myself down.

"Sorry, I had to steal just one," he explained.

"I better get back," I said.

He stood with his hands on his hips, watching me as I walked back to the house. I had not expected this.

I raced through the house to the front porch. What had I just done? I rested my head in my hands, reliving the last few moments.

"Oh, Kekoa," I said out loud.

A few moments later, Daddy's car pulled up. I ran down the driveway. Evelyn jumped out with baby Isaac on her hip and sprinted to the porch. We embraced and started talking a mile a minute, and we never stopped.

"I'm so happy you're here!" I squealed.

"I can't believe you are really getting married!" she said. "I wouldn't miss this for the world!"

Her hair, identical to mine, was shorter now, cut to her shoulders. She looked older. She looked great, but it was apparent being a mother had aged her. Daddy used to call us twins, but there was a clear difference in our appearance now. She wasn't dressed in her typical Hawaiian clothes that I was used to. She looked more modern and more adult.

Daddy and I helped her with her things, and she carried the baby into the house. We spent the first few hours giggling and talking, catching each other up on everything we'd missed over the last year. Her baby, Isaac, was beautiful; Mother and Daddy couldn't get enough of him. They barely put him down long enough for any of my sisters to hold him.

She looked tired but happy. She kept gushing about her shock over my wedding news and how much she loved being married. I showed her my wedding dress, and she tried on her bridesmaid dress. I hugged her over and over; I could hardly believe she was standing there in our living room like time had never passed. We sat together on the couch, her in her red bridesmaid dress and me in my wedding gown. I rested my head on her shoulder.

"I can't believe you're here!" I said again for about the hundredth time. "I'm so glad you could come. It was worth getting married just to see you."

"How on earth did this guy get you to agree to marry him? And on such short notice."

"I don't know, Eve." I sighed. "I guess I just love him. That's all it took."

"Well, I'm very proud of you. You seem very happy," she said, rubbing my leg. "And when do I get to meet the guy!"

"Okay, girls!" Mother said, walking in. "Get out of those dresses now. We don't want you wrinkling them before the big day!"

We both giggled. Mother was all a flutter floating around from one task to another. She beamed with delight and happiness; she looked beautiful. Daddy remained aloof, trying to stay out of her way. Eve and I followed his example and kept to ourselves the remaining of the evening.

Late in the evening, around nine o'clock, there was a tap at the door. Evelyn looked at me curiously from the couch. "Could that be him?" she asked.

I didn't know.

"Who else could it be?" I didn't move, thinking briefly about Kekoa. I hadn't told her about him. Marie ran to the door, opening it to reveal a very tired-looking but dashing Lt. Cdr. William Wellington.

He stepped into the house, removing his hat. My mouth instantly formed into a smile.

"Good evening, ladies. Forgive me for coming over so late, but I did want to meet this notorious sister Evelyn, which I've heard so much about."

I jumped and hugged him. "I'm so glad you came! This is Evelyn," I said, hanging from him and motioning to her.

Evelyn stood to shake his hand and kiss him on the cheek. "Great to finally meet you. I didn't ever think I would shake the hand of my sister's fiancé." She laughed.

William laughed too. He looked exhausted.

"Sit down, Will. You look tired," I said, sitting back on the couch with Evelyn.

"Thank you. I am tired. I can't stay too long, or I will fall asleep," he said, sitting and resting his head on the back of the couch.

"Why are you so tired?" I asked.

"My parents don't believe in being idle. I've been running them around the island all day. Thank goodness for the time difference. They were tired and just went to bed," he said with a weary smile.

"Well, I am glad you came," I said, reaching for his hand.

"I am too." He squeezed my hand, lifting his head. "You do look a lot like Ruth," he said, looking between me and Evelyn.

"Well, I will take that as a compliment," Evelyn said politely. "I am the older, shier, less athletic version of Ruth," she said. We visited for ten or fifteen minutes or so. William asked about where Evelyn and her husband were stationed and asked for updates about the mainland. They played the name game to see if they knew any of the same people, but they didn't. Evelyn had to take a squealing Isaac to bed after a little while.

"I better go anyway." William sighed.

"Okay, I will walk you out." We stood on the pouch in silence for a moment.

"William . . ." I paused. "Kekoa came to see me today." I swallowed hard. How was I going to tell him?

Will gave me a crooked smile. "Did he profess his love to you?" He laughed.

I couldn't hide my shock. "How did you know?" I asked.

"It was pretty obvious. The guy has loved you for a while, I would guess. Everyone could see it. I expected something like this. Poor guy. I almost feel bad for stealing you. Almost." He laughed and pulled me in for a quick kiss.

"Well, he, he kissed me," I said quickly.

"Oh, he did!" Will chuckled again. "I didn't think he had it in him!"

"What?" I was confused. "You're not mad?"

"No, I know you didn't mean any harm in it. Just don't make a habit of it. Okay?"

I nodded.

"Wait. Did you kiss him back?"

I swallowed hard again and looked down.

"Ruth?"

"I didn't kiss him so much as I didn't stop him as quickly as I should. I should have slapped him." I felt so guilty.

He smiled again.

"It's okay, Ruth. Don't beat yourself up. Do you still love me?"

I nodded.

"You still want to marry me?"

I nodded.

"Promise not to kiss anyone else after we're married?"

"Yes." I laughed.

"I think we're good then!"

I said goodbye to him quickly after that. He kissed me tiredly on the cheek before walking to the car.

When I walked back into the house, Evelyn was waiting for me impatiently with the other girls.

"He is so handsome, Ruth!" Evelyn said. "I see how he was able to win you over! He is irresistible!"

"We've been wondering how she was able to win HIM over this whole time," Marie said.

"Hey!" I said, throwing a pillow at her.

"He is wonderful," I said, flopping down the couch and laying my head in Evelyn's lap.

"Are you nervous?" she asked curiously.

"Yeah, very nervous but excited too."

Evelyn slept in my bed that night. We talked until the late hours. Isaac shared the room with us. She got up a couple of times to tend to him. His sleeping schedule was off, and he was cranky and not happy being in a new place.

"Is it hard being alone all the time?" I whispered as she crawled back in bed after putting the baby down.

"Of course, it is," she said simply. "But the times he does come home, it's wonderful."

I sighed. I didn't know what response I was hoping for, but that wasn't it.

Eve put a hand on my shoulder to reassure me. "It's worth it, though, sis. I have a wonderful baby and a wonderful husband. Sure I'm lonely, but I would be lonelier without him. You don't want to live here with Mom and Dad forever, do you?"

"No," I said honestly. "But I also don't want to be alone."

"You would be alone if you didn't marry him. Don't you feel lonely now, even though you're with me?"

She was right. We had a great day together, but I missed William. I wished he were with us several times today so he could see how great Evelyn was and to laugh with us.

I nodded in agreement.

"See? It's worth it. He won't always be in the navy. You will have him all to yourself soon enough, and then he will be driving you crazy, and you will be wishing for him to go away for a time."

I laughed. I could hardly imagine that. "I hope you're right," I said. "Kekoa came over today," I said.

"Oh?" she said.

"He kissed me," I said.

Her head snapped up. "Ruth! Like a real kiss?" she asked.

I nodded.

"Well? Why? What did you do?"

"I kissed him back." I felt waves of guilt as I said it.

"Why! Ruth, you can't do that! Don't ruin this, honey," she said.

"I know. I feel terrible." I flung my arm over my forehead. "I feel terrible because I liked it. I would have dated him, you know. Hell, I would have married him probably!"

"What are you going to do?" she asked quietly.

"Nothing." I sighed. "I love William."

"Everything happens for a reason. If you had been meant to be with Kekoa, this would have happened before now," she said.

"I suppose." I closed my eyes.

"Did you tell William?" she asked.

I nodded. "Just tonight on the porch."

"What did he say? Was he mad?"

"Not at all really. He said he wasn't surprised."

"Well, I suppose that is true. We all could see it."

"Really? I never saw it. I didn't know he felt that way."

"Oh, Ruth," she said, closing her eyes.

The next morning, we attended church together as a family. I sat on the pew and realized this would be the last time I attended church as a single woman. I wondered if William went to church. I couldn't believe that was something we'd never discussed. I started feeling a little panicked. What else did we forget to talk about?

In the middle of my mental panic attack, I felt the weight of someone sit next to me and then put their arm around my shoulders. Startled, I jerked to the right to see who it was—William.

"Oh, you scared me! You keep surprising me!" I said, relieved.

"Who else would it be? I just can't stay away from you," he said, smiling broadly. William's parents were with him, taking their place next to him on the pew, looking like they were melting in the heat.

"Good morning!" I whispered to them. I couldn't say any more because the service began. They both nodded to me. Will's dad constantly wiped the perspiration from his head.

I sat next to William, feeling delighted and full of joy. He looked down the row and waved at Evelyn sitting next to me and flashed her one of his million-dollar smiles. She looked at me and mouthed the words "Wow!" when he wasn't looking. I felt happy and complete sitting there, our two families together. *Does life get much better than this?*

We parted ways after the service was over; we each had our individual tasks to attend to, but I was grateful for the small moment we had together. The countdown to the wedding was down to hours. My stomach jumped and my heart fluttered every time I thought about it.

My mind kept an ongoing mental countdown all day. *Only twenty-two hours and thirty minutes until I get married. Only twenty-one hours and forty-five minutes until our wedding. In twenty hours and fifty-five minutes, I will be a married woman!*

And so my thoughts raced on throughout the day. I was in a daze most of the day, walking around smiling and laughing between the occasional mental breakdowns.

"Where's my lei po'o, Elizabeth! I saw you wear it last night! Just what did you do with it? Are you trying to ruin my wedding?" I said dramatically.

"Ruth! It's right here," Evelyn said, fetching it from the cooler. "Calm down, sweetheart," she said with a laugh.

"Sorry, Elizabeth," I said quietly.

"I hope I don't freak out this bad when I get married," Elizabeth mumbled and slunk away to hid in her room.

"What is wrong with me, Eve?" I asked after Elizabeth left.

"Nothing," she reassured. "You're getting married tomorrow. You're entitled to a few bursts of hysteria. Get it all out now before your vows. You don't want to scare your new husband. You want to wait at least a few months before you flip out." We both laughed.

"I'm so glad you're here," I said again between giggles.

"Only sixteen hours until we get you hitched!" Marie sang as she walked into the room.

She had been helping me keep track of the countdown all day. The room erupted with squeals and giggles just like every other announcement before. Daddy let out a loud sigh, signaling he was tired of the game, but I didn't care. I was enjoying this moment. I rarely allowed myself to be so juvenile, and I liked it.

Mother was just as giddy as the rest of us. By 9:00 p.m., Daddy retired to bed, mumbling something about silly girls, while the rest of us sat around the dining table, which was a heap of flowers and greenery. We were making the corsages and bouquets for the wedding.

They were made out of small white orchids, one of my favorite flowers, while the bouquets were made of several small white plumeria flowers with yellow centers and green tea leaves as the base. They were elegant and simple. I loved each one. We each made our own, and the girls helped me with William's parents. We laughed and giggled late into the night. My mother told fantastic stories of her youth, which none of us girls had ever heard before. If I didn't look right at her and only listened to her voice, I imagined her as a young bride eager and nervous on her own wedding day.

By the time my head hit my pillow, I was exhausted, my eyes heavy with sleep, but my mind was restless. I tried desperately to calm it so I could sleep, but my thoughts raced in and out of my head. I slept in patches throughout the night, waking often and never reaching a deep, restful sleep. I was relieved when the sun finally peeked through my window, signaling that it was an acceptable time to wake.

I sat up straight in my bed and looked down at Evelyn, who was waking beside me. When her eyes opened, she looked up and smiled.

"You're getting married today!" she said gleefully.

"I'm getting married today!" I yelled back and hopped onto my feet, jumping on the bed. Evelyn joined me, the two of us practically grown women jumping on the bed, giggling with delight. Elizabeth and Marie, obviously hearing us from the hall, ran in and joined us in the fun. We ended in a heap on my sagging bed.

Isaac, who was sleeping in a basket across the room, sat up and smiled at me, looking just as excited as I was, and he let out a happy yelp too. We all laughed.

"I got to get ready!" I declared with urgency. "There is so much to do!" And I ran out of the room, practically knocking Daddy over on my way to the bathroom.

"I'm getting married today, Daddy!" I said and kissed him on the cheek.

"I know, darling," Daddy said, forcing a smile, but he looked slightly melancholy. I didn't have time to ask him what the trouble was; I had a mission and raced into the bathroom.

Nervous energy was running through me so much I could barely hold my brush still to comb out my hair. I knew I would never be able to apply my own makeup. It wasn't long before I'd enlisted Evelyn and Elizabeth in my preparations. Evelyn twisted and curled my hair on the top of my head, while Elizabeth painted on my eye makeup. My job was simply to sit still. It was a really hard job for me to do. Mother ran in and out of the bathroom, readying herself and shouting orders to

Daddy. Daddy didn't have a chance in hell at getting into the bathroom, so Mom sent him to shave at the kitchen sink. Isaac sat on the floor of the bathroom, banging two brushes together and giggling with the infectious excitement of the room.

"I'm out of here, ladies! I can't take it anymore!" Daddy announced, peeking into the bathroom.

"Oh okay, Daddy!" I said under Evelyn's arm.

"Don't forget the guys' boutonnieres!" Mother called from the bedroom. "And the ribbon that goes on the chairs!" Mother left the bathroom to inspect Daddy. He was wearing his uniform as most of the men at the wedding would be and looked dashing. Mom smoothed down his collar and gave him a kiss on the cheek before he left.

"I think we are done!" Evelyn announced, handing me a mirror.

I peered into the mirror. All my long brown hair was piled the on top of my head with large curls falling out around my face. "It looks great!" I said, delighted. Eve had pinned a few flowers on top of the pile of hair and placed the lei po'o on my head so I could see the whole do. My makeup was subtle but elegant, simply perfect.

"You girls did wonderful! I love my hair, and I love my makeup! Thank you so much!" I said.

"You're welcome," Elizabeth said. "Now get up! We have to get ready now!"

I gave them each a quick hug and got out of their way. Mother followed me to my bedroom, where she helped me get dressed and button the millions of buttons down the back of my wedding dress.

I stood in my mother's room, admiring the spectacle looking back at me in the mirror. If I didn't know any better, I would mistake the reflection in the mirror for a sophisticated, elegant woman. I looked like a bride. My hair was beautifully piled on the top of my head, accented with flowers, holding the lei po'o perfectly like a crown. My dress was smooth and white, hugging the curves of my hips, and flared out at the bottom. The cap sleeve and my shoulders flowed together down my arm as one, my tan skin the only distinction between me and the dress. A small white pendant my mother gave to me hung around my bare neck, adding just a touch of shimmer. I looked good, I admitted to myself.

"Time to go! We're going to be late!" Mother called from the door. I took one deep breath, grabbed my bouquet, and headed out the door.

Daddy had a driver take us down to the beach. We hid behind the tree line just before the sandy beach, five girls in dazzling, shimmering red dresses and one simple bride. It was hot; it was not yet ten in the morning, but the sun was beating down on our little party, but none of us paid it any mind. We took turns peeking through the leaves and bushes at the crowd gathering on the beach. Daddy must have set up one hundred white wooden chairs before anyone arrived, and he and five groomsmen were busily setting up more to accommodate the growing crowd.

"Who knew so many people would come to your wedding!" Marie said, pulling back a large leaf and peering through the bush to see. "I can hardly believe it."

"I can," Evelyn said. "It's all Daddy. He has a lot of friends, locals and people in the Army Air Corps. And by the looks of things, the lieutenant has a lot of friends too," she said.

"Let me see!" Nohea insisted, taking her turn to spy on the crowd. Elsie giggled with delight as she peered over Nohea's shoulder.

"There are a lot of people, Ruth. Take a look."

They stepped back to let me have a turn peeking through the brush. The commander and his wife, along with the other executive officers, were seated in the second row on the right. Behind them were many men I didn't recognize, all in white uniforms. The left-hand side was speckled with more uniformed officers, their wives, and local islanders. William's Dad was helping set up more chairs, while his mom stood in the back with my mother, greeting late arrivals. It was a beautiful sight with the white chairs, white uniforms, white ribbon strung among the rows against the pure blue of the ocean, which was acting as our backdrop. The chairs faced the ocean with nothing to impede the view except a small white archway decorated with flowers and tea leaves for the pastor and us to stand under. I swallowed hard. This hasty simple wedding seemed to be turning into quite an event. I pushed back the anxiety rising in my chest.

"I think everyone is here because they can't believe Ruth is getting married," Elizabeth said. "They just want to see it for themselves. No one can believe it!" She laughed. I knew she was teasing, but it was true. From what I knew about William, the same might be said of his guests.

I watched as Kekoa took his place up front with his ukulele. He graciously agreed to play the wedding march for me. I felt the tinge of guilt again.

There were no signs of the wedding starting. People were still visiting while ambling to their chairs. The pastor was hidden somewhere, along with William, and Mother and Daddy were still working the crowd. I turned to Evelyn.

"All these people came to see me get married?" I swallowed hard.

"Oh, sweetie, calm down. You look as pale as a ghost," Evelyn said, taking my hand." I felt dizzy. I was getting married—right now.

Evelyn took both sides of my face with her hands.

"Just calm down. Everything is going to be okay. Now bend over, rest your elbows on your knees, and drop your head. Take a few breaths. Good, good. Keep breathing," she said, stroking my back. "Now look." She pointed through the trees.

I peered through the trees to see William, perfect William, dressed in his fancy white uniform escorting my mother and his down the aisle. I watched him lead them to their seats, where his dad was already sitting. In a matter of moments, the party had turned into a wedding without me noticing. The pastor was already in place at the front, and William turned around next to him and faced the crowd. I squinted, trying to study his face. Did he look nervous? Scared? No. He was cool and confident, smiling at the hushed crowd, his hands folded together. It wasn't fair. He had years of training in remaining calm. I was just a young foolish girl.

When I turned back, Evelyn was gone, and in her place was Daddy.

"Daddy!" I said in a half sob and flung my arms around his neck. Daddy didn't say anything. He simply patted my back and let me have my moment.

"It's time, darling," he said, and I released him. "The girls and the groomsmen are already making their way around the trees. We need to catch up."

I nodded silently and walked with Daddy arm in arm down the edge of trees to join the rest of the party standing in the opening. I could see less of the crowd from this position than I could peeking through the bushes. Kekoa started strumming his ukulele, and it began. As Kekoa hummed along with his beautiful Hawaiian song, two by two, the wedding party departed around the big tree we were hiding behind and disappeared down the aisle.

First were Marie and one of the navy officers in the gunnery division, whom I'd never been formally introduced to, and then Nohea, Elsie, and Elizabeth, all with men I'd neglected to meet. Finally, it was Evelyn and Gunnery Sergeant Galloway. Evelyn gave me one quick kiss on the cheek before she left on Gunnery Sergeant Galloway's arm. I gripped Daddy's arm tighter, wondering if I would ever be able to let go of it.

Kekoa's song stopped, and Daddy turned to me. "That's our cue," he said with a smile.

This was it. I wanted to say something to Daddy that would tell him how much I would miss him and how hard this was for me, but all that came out of my mouth was "I love you, Daddy."

"I love you too," he said and led me around the big tree. Tentatively, I placed one foot in front of the other, making my way toward them. From the front, I heard the captain's booming voice.

"Atten-hut!"

White-uniformed officers lined the inner two rows all the way from me to the front. They all snapped to attention, their hands saluting. Daddy and I walked between the row of military men. Daddy's eyes remained fixed forward, while mine searched the crowd and sailors saluting us. My sisters and friends stood ahead of me in a row in glorious red, while the men stood the right in a curtain of perfect white. My heart beat quickly, and I was breathing heavily, feeling overwhelmed by the scene, until my eyes happened across William.

He was looking right at me, smiling his perfect smile, his eyes willing my feet to keep moving forward. I had nearly forgotten why I was here. I was here to be with William, and there he was, just a mere ten steps ahead of me. I wanted to run the rest of the way down the aisle to stand next to him, but Daddy held me back. As if a reflex, my mouth formed into a smile, and I looked deep into his captivating eyes. We covered the remaining gap between me and William just as Kekoa finished singing. I never looked at the pastor. My eyes were fixed on Will. I heard the pastor said something, and Daddy said, "Her mother and I do." I pulled my eyes away from William briefly to look at Daddy as he placed my hand in William's and took his seat next to Mom.

William squeezed my hand once and whispered, "You look lovely, my angel."

I can't say that I heard a word the pastor said. I think he rambled on about love, the combining of two families, and a union sanctified by God, but I can't swear on it. I looked at William, and he looked at me. I never once let my eyes stray from his. At one point, we turned to each other and promised our lives to each other. William placed a beautiful band on my finger to go with my engagement ring, and I slipped a simple gold one onto his. I held his hands tightly and rubbed his fingers, thinking I would never let go. At another point, we both said, "I do," as part of another promise to each other. Finally, the ceremony was over, signaling the end with "You may kiss the bride." William's smile grew a few more inches before he grabbed my waist and dipped me backward, kissing me. The crowd cheered, and my face was red by the time he pulled me up. We turned to the audience and waved as the captain called the men to attention again. I caught a glimpse of Kekoa before we ran down the aisle. My heart hurt for a moment. He was clapping slowly, but he wasn't smiling. We waved to family and friends along the way and holding tight onto each other's hands.

Once we were around the big tree and behind the bushes, William picked me and kissed me again, much more passionate than ever before. I giggled over and over, wrapping myself around him.

"I love you! I love you!" I said between kisses. Finally, he set me down again.

"I love you too, Mrs. Wellington, and now you are mine!" he said with a devilish grin.

13

By the time we joined our guests in the hall, everyone was seated, enjoying their meals and visiting with one another. We waited outside the double doors, holding hands and kissing, until we heard our cue from the announcer.

"Let me announce for the first time Mr. and Mrs. Lt. Cdr. William Wellington!" the announcer called from inside the hall. Chills shivered up and down my spine hearing our names together as one. *Mrs. Lt. Cdr. William Wellington.* That was going to take some getting used to.

The doors swung open, and we entered the hall, greeted with cheers and applause. My face hurt from smiling so much. I waved to everyone and held onto William, who was grinning as big as me. The band began playing immediately, and I didn't have time to even locate my family before William was leading me around the hall in a slow waltz.

It was hard for me to care about anyone else in the room other than the man smiling back at me. I was very aware of the room of eyes watching us twirl around the dance floor.

"We did it. We really did it!" I said under my breath. "I can't believe we are married!" I said excitedly. William smiled back at me.

"Yes, we are married. You are my wife," he said, looking happy but calm and collected, whereas I felt frazzled, ecstatic beyond belief, and nervous.

William was professional and still looked like a lieutenant commander, just a lieutenant commander in love. I wished I could pull it together more like William, but there seemed to be no use fighting it. His maturity and gracefulness among the pressure must come from age and experience. I was afraid I looked like a silly little girl standing next to him. If I looked like, either William didn't notice or he was good at acting oblivious.

When the song ended, William dipped me, and for the finality of our couple dance, he kissed me softly on the lips. My mouth returned to its usual huge smile, and William pulled me upright, and the music began again.

"Go find your father," William instructed. I searched the room with my eyes, clueless to his location. William pointed him out across the room. Daddy was already walking toward me.

William found his mother and began dancing with her as Daddy and I twirled around the room. Daddy smiled sweetly at me, but his eyes looked sad.

"What's wrong, Daddy?" I asked.

"Oh, it's nothing, sweetheart. I'm just having a hard time watching my little girl grow up," he said, forcing a smile. "I'm very happy you found someone so perfect for you, but I'm disappointed. I thought we would have a few more years."

"I know. You're not the only one, Daddy," I said with a laugh. "But I'm not going far away."

"I know, but you are growing up," Daddy said sadly.

"Sorry about that. There really isn't anything I can do to change that," I said, shrugging.

"I know. It's just hard on your old man." Finally, an honest smile crossed his face.

After William danced with my mother and I danced with his father, the floor was opened for the rest of our party. My sisters and friends were in heaven dancing with a new sailor during every song. It made me smile watching everyone have so much fun. William and I sat at our table, eating some of the delicious refreshments William arranged for the party. Our parents and the skipper and his wife sat at the same table with us. We didn't visit much. The music and noise from the party was too loud to allow for that. William and I remained in our own little world, smiling and laughing together.

At one point, we were summoned over to the cake table. Nohea's mother made us a beautiful cake decorated with flowers to go along with the decorations. It looked so wonderful I almost didn't want to cut it.

William and I fed each other a small piece while the crowd watched. I smeared a bit of frosting on his nose and then kissed his lips before he could whip it off. He rubbed his nose across my cheek, sharing the frosting. We all laughed, enjoying the playful banter, and then the cake was served to all the guests.

I looked around the room occasionally, surfing the crowd for Kekoa. He wasn't there. I had asked him to play at the reception too, but one of his friends was there instead. It made my heart hurt that he wasn't there.

The afternoon waned on, turning into evening, and slowly, guests began to leave. I was busy thanking everyone for coming and thanking my friends' parents for all their help before they left. I was visiting with a table of my father's friends when William approached me.

"It's time to go," he whispered in my ear, standing behind me, touching my elbow.

"Really?" I asked, looking up at him, puzzled. I really hadn't thought about the party ever ending.

"Yep, your parents are starting to gather everyone to wish us off. So say your goodbyes," he said politely.

"Oh okay," I said, tentatively studying William's face. He looked relieved that the party was over. I felt nervous and uneasy. I had really been enjoying visiting with all our friends, meeting his acquaintances, and hosting the party with my new husband by my side.

I excused myself from the table and walked with William across the room. Sure enough, most of the guests were outside. Mom and Dad were standing by the door. I gave them each a hug and kiss and thanked them for the wonderful party.

"Once you go out the doors, throw your bouquet, and then you two can be on your way," Mother said, dabbing tears from her eyes.

"Oh, Mom, don't cry!" I begged. "I'll see you in two days for Christmas."

"I know." She let out a heavy sob and hugged me again. "We love you, sweetie!" I looked at Daddy, confused. Mother rarely showed me any affection, and there I was, holding my weeping mother in my arms with spectators looking on.

Daddy shrugged and smiled weakly before taking Mom's shoulders and pulling her off me. They stood somberly together, embracing each other, as William and I walked toward the door. We embraced William's parents before exiting, thanking them profusely for coming. It was sad to leave them, not knowing when we would see them again.

The crowd cheered as we made our way toward the car, making me smile and forget about my heartbroken parents behind the door. We stood on the steps in front of the crowd; the girls all jumped, screaming, when I turned around to throw the bouquet. There was a moment of chaos and scrambling when the flowers reached the crowd. I could tell for a moment who caught it until finally, I saw Elsie's outstretched hand above all their heads. In her hand, she held the prize, my beautiful bouquet. And that was it for me. I was married, the wedding and reception was over, and I'd tossed away my bouquet. I felt relieved and blissfully happy.

William took my hand and led me down the steps. We ran through the crowd as they threw rice on us and to the car decorated with balloons and pop cans. William acted annoyed that his car was decorated, but I think he enjoyed it as much as I did. *Just Married* was written in shaving cream on the back window. I would enjoy driving through town with that on the back. William helped me in my seat, shoving my train into the car so he wouldn't shut it in the door, and then he made his way around to his side. I rolled my window down and waved to my sisters. Evelyn was leaving tonight. A pain ran through my heart when I thought of this. She pushed her way through the crowd and gave me a hug through the window.

"I love you, sis!" she said.

"I'll miss you!" Tears were forming at the corner of my eyes. "I love you. Thank you for coming."

"You're welcome." We let go and looked in each other's eyes. "Now have fun!" she said with a wink and kissed my forehead.

I turned around as we drove away, watching my friends and family wave and blow kisses behind me. When we turned the corner, I sat facing forward and looked at William, who was looking at me. We smiled, and William grabbed my hand.

"It's just you and me now, angel," he said, squeezing my hand.

14

When we pulled into the driveway of our new little cottage, I swallowed hard. I was happy but very nervous. I didn't want William to know how nervous I was.

"Stay put," he said with a grin, putting the vehicle into park. I watched William walk around the car and open my door.

"Mrs. Wellington," William said, offering me his hand.

"Lieutenant," I said with a smile, letting him help me up. I shut the door behind me, grabbed onto his shoulder, and jumped into his arms. "Take me away!" I said, laughing.

"My pleasure," he said and carried me up our steps and into our cozy one-room home, planting a kiss on my lips as we passed over the threshold. He set me down a few feet in the door and kissed me again.

I looked around at our little house. It looked just like it did when we left it, although I thought it would look different for some reason. It was only 6:00 p.m., hardly time to go to bed, but I wasn't sure what we were going to do now.

William took off his jacket and walked to the closet to hang it up.

"I had Gunnery Sergeant Galloway fill our refrigerator yesterday. I thought we might get hungry," he said from the closet. He was loosening his tie as he walked into the kitchen, where he opened the fridge. "I don't know about you, but I didn't eat much, and I'm starved. Would you like a sandwich?"

"I am starving, now that you mention it." I stood awkwardly in the middle of the house, smiling, while William worked in the kitchen.

I was impressed he was willing to make me food. He worked in the kitchen in just his undershirt and dress pants, while I stood motionless in the middle of the room in my wedding dress.

William looked up from the bread and meat that lay in front of him and smiled at me.

"Uh," I said, stepping toward him, mustering my courage, "I would like to take my wedding dress off before eating, and I'm really tired of wearing it." William's smile grew even bigger as he looked up and down my dress. I laughed nervously and turned around. "But I can't unbutton all of these buttons, so I will need a little help." I bit my lip, pushing back the heat of embarrassment burning under my skin.

William laughed nervously too. It never occurred to me that he might be nervous about tonight too.

"Well, I would love to help you with that problem!" William said, abandoning the sandwich. I turned around. He started at the top, fumbling his way around each tiny button.

"There are a lot of them," I pointed out after standing there a few minutes.

"No kidding!" he said, frustrated, crouching over to inspect them better. "I've never seen buttons like this before. What is with the tiny string around each of these obnoxious round buttons? A person could die undoing these!"

Nervous uneasiness grew in my tummy as each button was undone, revealing more and more of my slip. After each pop, I felt my dress loosened, and it slipped down my shoulders.

"That is the last one!" William announced at least five minutes after he began. "I've freed you from your dress!" he said triumphantly. I felt William run his hand down my back, along the opening of my dress over my slip, and then he hugged me from behind and kissed my neck. Goose bumps shivered up and down my skin.

"Thank you. You are my hero. Without you, I would have to be buried in this," I said with a laugh.

"My pleasure," he said, laughing in my ear and releasing me from his arms. I could feel William's eyes on me as I walked across the room until I disappeared into the closet.

I stood in the closet, wondering what on earth I should put on. I always thought I would change right into my nightgown, but it was too early for that. I slipped out of my dress and slip, terrified that William would come through the door at any moment. I hung my dress carefully next to his uniform jackets and pulled one of my silkier dresses over my head. It was cozy and soft. I always thought it was one of my prettier dresses.

When I walked back out into the main room, William was outside on the deck with the sandwiches and two glasses of water. I walked out the door to find him sitting at our patio table nibbling on his sandwich and smiling at me. He looked breathtakingly handsome in his tight white shirt. It hugged his arms, and I could see the definition of his muscles through the front of his shirt. My sandwich was next to his. Instead of sitting in the chair next to him, I sat right where I wanted to be, on his lap.

"Well, hello, angel," he said, surprised as I swung my legs across his lap and put my arm around his neck. He held my back and pulled me in for a kiss. "I think I like you here," he said.

"Well, I figured. We're married now. I can sit wherever I'd like, right?" I giggled.

"Damn straight you can!" he said, chuckling.

I reached over, grabbing half of my sandwich; tucked myself into his chest; and began nibbling on it. William finished his sandwich and wrapped both his arms around me.

"This is nice," I said, looking at the ocean. "I'm enjoying the company and the view."

"Me too," William said quietly. Without a word, he put his finger under my chin and tilted it toward his face, kissing me with more force and determination than ever before.

I dropped my sandwich, oblivious to where it landed, and wrapped both my arms around his neck. Chills and butterflies in my stomach were the only things I was aware of other than William's lips. Nervousness no longer wracked my body. My mind was consumed only by William and being wrapped in his arms and kisses. He stood, taking me in his arms, knocking his chair over. He carried me into the house, letting the door bang closed behind us, and placed me on our bed. In less than a second, he had his shirt off and was lying on top of me. I still didn't feel nervous. I felt excited, happy, complete, safe.

He lay carefully on top of me, his bare chest smooth and muscular burning through my thin dress. I laughed nervously.

He propped himself on his elbows on either side of my face and slowly kissed my lips over and over. I wrapped my arms around his neck and surrendered to him. His hand traced down my body, sending goose bumps up and down my spine. He reached between to my thighs and parted my legs, moving between them. I took an involuntary breath in as his fingers passed between my legs. His hand stopped at my breast, cupping and massaging one.

I had never been touched in these places. It felt wonderful and terrifying all at the same time. He continued kissing me but moved down to the nape of my neck and shoulders, and then pulling down the collar of my dress, he released my breast, letting it spill out the top of my neckline. I was breathing heavy; my heart was racing. I didn't know what I expected, but this wasn't it. He was tender, loving, and passionate, but I felt like my heart was going to explode. He kissed my nipple, his tongue licking and caressing it.

"Oh!" I said involuntarily.

He chuckled, mouth full of boob.

"Are you okay?" he asked, pausing from the kissing and returning my collar to the original position.

"Uh-huh," I said, but I really didn't know. "I, I just . . ." I had no words.

"Well, I like to have a little fun before we get right to business." He laughed. "Are you ready for me?" he asked between kisses.

I really didn't know what he meant, but I nodded yes anyway. Will pulled himself and stood at the end of the bed. Reaching for his belt, he began loosening the buckle, his eyes on me the whole while. I lay on the bed motionless, scared, excited, but mostly just excited. I had no idea what I was supposed to be doing. I propped myself up on my elbows, observing him. His trousers loosened around his waist and dropped to the floor, leaving him standing in just his white boxer shorts. I tried to remain casual and calm, but I was probably doing a lousy job.

Tracing both hands down each of my legs, he found my underwear and tug at it down with his fingers. I involuntarily grabbed his arm, stopping him.

"It's okay, love," he reassured me, kissing me on the forehead. "Do you trust me?" he asked.

I nodded. He slowly pulled my panties off, my dress still covering me. He discarded them onto the floor and then reached for his own waistline. With a wink and a smile, he dropped his boxers and stood before me naked.

My mouth dropped open. I had never seen a naked man. Never. I was speechless. Will laughed. He grabbed a small towel from the dresser. Kneeling between my legs, he instructed me to lift my hips. I obeyed. He placed the towel underneath me, his hands brushing against my bare bum.

"I'm sensing you aren't ready to be naked just yet," he said. My mouth was still gaped open like a fish. I felt like an idiot, but I couldn't do anything to change it. I shook my head. I really wasn't.

Will laid me back on the bed and began kissing me again. My dress still covered all my essential parts, and I slowly began to surrender to him again. I let my legs soften and fall farther apart. I stroked my hands down his back and up his neck to his hairline. My heart slowed, and my mind began to relax. This wasn't that bad, I told myself. This was wonderful.

He stopped kissing me long enough to ask "Are you ready?"

"Yes," I said, catching my breath. Ready for what, I wasn't totally sure.

"Okay, this will help, I promise. Stay with me, okay?"

I nodded hesitantly.

His left hand slowly started, pulling up my dress. I breathed heavier, not knowing what about to happen next.

"Relax," he whispered into my ear. I nodded again.

His hand followed my thigh up in between my legs to parts never explored by any person. Parting the lips, his finger slowly entered my body.

"Ahh!" I said, my legs involuntarily clamping around him.

"Shhh," he whispered into my ear. "Relax. Breathe. It's okay."

I took a few breaths and let my legs relax again.

"What are you doing?" I asked.

"I'm preparing the way." He laughed.

"What?" I was so confused.

I breathed heavier and heavier. I felt light-headed. It felt so good. How could this feel so good? Suddenly, he had two fingers pressing inside me.

"Aw!" I said.

"It's okay," he reassured. "Just relax, love. You can do it. I'm bigger than this," he explained.

Understanding washed over me. He was indeed "preparing the way." How was he going to fit inside me? I tensed again.

"Don't think too much about it." He laughed. "It's supposed to be enjoyable." I laughed. This was most definitely the weirdest thing I had ever done.

"Okay, I'm trying," I said.

"I know you are. You're doing great," he said.

"Uhhhhh," I said again.

"I can't wait any longer, love." He sighed.

He pulled his fingers out, and I instantly missed them. He pulled my dress up around my waist. I was completely exposed. I felt extremely vulnerable. His penis was huge, bigger than before; hard; and sticking straight out.

"It means I'm ready," he said, stroking himself.

"That will never fit inside me!" I said.

"Yes, it will," he said. It almost sounded like a growl.

He lowered himself on top of me, resting on one elbow to the side of me. He put his fingers back inside me.

"Relax. Shhh," he said.

I felt his penis on me, urging its way inside. Placing each of his elbows to the side of my face, he rested his cheek on mine, kissing my ear and whispering to me.

"Let your legs fall to the side. Just like that. Good," he encouraged. "Tensing up will only make this harder. You must relax."

I nodded quickly. A small tear ran down my cheeks.

"I won't come in until you're ready," he reassured.

I nodded. "Is this the part that hurts?" I asked.

"Yes," he whispered. "But I won't force myself. It doesn't have to be bad. You just have to let me."

"Okay," I whispered.

His hips began to rhythmically move on top of me, pressing his penis harder in me. I felt the lips part and the head of his penis enter.

"Oh my!" I said.

"Are you okay?" he asked.

"Yes," I said between breaths.

"Take a deep breath," he instructed.

I obeyed, breathing in.

"Now let it out slowly," he said.

Slowly, I released the breath I was holding. As I did so, he steadily pressed himself into me.

"Ahh, ahhh!" I couldn't hold it in. "I'm sorry," I said immediately.

"It's okay," he reassured.

"Uh-huh," I said. My eyes were watering. I felt his girth stretching my insides.

"Aw, don't move, please. Don't move," I begged.

"Okay," he said breathlessly. "Remember, relax. Let your knees fall back down. You can wrap your legs around me if you'd like."

I hadn't realized I had tensed up again. I obediently wrapped my legs around him, crossing them in the small of his back. He plunged a little deeper.

"Aw," I said again.

"I will hold still as long as I can," he said. He was breathing heavy now. I nodded. "Take a few deep breaths." I did so, exaggerating the rise and fall of my chest, trying to calm myself. What a strange feeling—he was inside me. Will's hips began moving slightly with each breath I took, pressing in and out of me. My breaths became shallower and quicker. His movements quickened with my breath, pressing himself deeper inside me.

"Oh god," I said involuntarily.

"That a girl," he said, smiling. A great wave of satisfaction grew across his face. His hips moved faster and faster. His eyes glazed over. Pleasure, he was taking such pleasure in this, and I realized so was I. I was happy that I was the one making him feel this way.

"Ohhhh," he groaned and thrust himself deeper than ever before and held himself there.

The room spun momentarily, and I gasped, my body convulsing under his until he released and fell motionless on top of me, breathing heavily.

After a few moments, he lifted himself on his elbows. His hair was tousled, and sweat gleamed on his forehead.

"Are you okay?" he asked.

"Yes," I said.

"Are you sure? You were really tight."

I laughed. "Yeah."

He laughed. "I'm going to pull out. It's going to be a little mess. Is the towel still under you?"

"I think so," I said. I really had no concept of my surroundings, of anything other than him.

He pulled himself out, leaving me empty. Standing at the end of the bed, he gave me his hand and helped me up. I felt a little wobbly, a little sore. I brushed my dress down over my legs and looked at the bed. There was a big red bloodstain on the towel.

"That came out of me!" I asked.

"Yeah, you okay?" he asked again. It was almost gruesome.

"That is a lot of blood," I said. "It didn't hurt that bad."

"Well, that's a relief," he said. "I'm sorry it hurt. I tried my best to be gentle." He kissed my head and rubbed my arm. "Let's get you cleaned up," he said, taking me by the arm and to the bathroom.

"I had no idea this was so messy," I said.

"No one talks about this part," he said after washing his hands. "Would you feel better with a shower?"

"No, I would like to go back to bed." I was a little embarrassed to admit it.

"I will give you a little privacy," he said and left me alone to clean up.

I changed into my nightgown after cleaning and looked in the mirror. I didn't look any different, still the same girl in the mirror, but I felt different. The great mystery had been revealed. I had sex. It was weird, wonderful, and nothing like I thought. I brushed my hair. It was snarled and tousled from the bed.

15

Neither of us left the bed until morning, when my growling stomach nudged me toward the kitchen. I rolled over, flopping my arm and leg around the half-naked man lying, still sleeping, beside me. I kissed his lips a few times until his eyes finally opened. William moaned sleepily, kissing me back.

I left him there to wake up, slipped on my nightgown, and wandered into the kitchen. I cooked up some eggs, but strangely, there wasn't any rice in our house.

"I don't think I've ever eaten eggs without rice," I said as I handed him his plate. William was still lying in bed but propped up against the wall. He wore nothing but a small sheet. I folded my legs and joined him on the bed. I was wearing one of the nightgowns I had bought for these moments with William.

"Yeah, sorry about that. Those of us from the mainland don't always think of rice," he said between bites.

"Well, I guess I can live a few days without it," I teased. "I can do anything I want now. I don't have to eat rice again if I don't want," I said, acknowledging my realization out loud.

"Well, you might have to when we eat with your parents, but you're right. We can do whatever we want now. It's just you and me and our new life together."

"I think I like that! This marriage thing just keeps getting better and better!" I said, laughing a little nervously, thinking about the intimate hours we spent together last night.

William laughed at me, but I was enjoying myself. I'd never felt so free or alive. I didn't realize I ever was restricted before, but all of a sudden, I felt unbound. "This is what it's like to be a grown-up!" I announced.

William laughed. "You're cute," he said between chuckles. When he finally stopped laughing, he put his plate down on the bed and leaned over to pull me toward him. He kissed me a few times, still laughing.

"No, no, sir," I said, knowing where the kissing would lead. "You have to let me eat. I'm famished over here!"

"Oh okay. I suppose." He accepted, picking his own plate back.

"Later," I said with a smile, feeling a little guilty.

"So what shall we do with our day?" William asked when my plate was almost clean.

"I don't know. What do you do the first few days you are married?" I asked.

"Well," he began with a devilish grin. "Nothing I want to do involves getting out of this bed, and you are wearing way too much clothing for the activities I have in mind, but I suppose we could do a few other things."

"Like what?" I asked. "Not that I would mind spending most of the day in bed," I added.

"Well, we could go try out the surf on our own little beach," he suggested.

"I would love that! I hadn't even thought of that! How great is it living right on the beach? I won't even have to ride my bike to surf!" I was so excited.

"Yep," he said. "I knew you would like that. It's a public beach, of course, but I don't think very many people use it, so we should be all alone." William flashed his devil grin again.

"Well, let's go!" I said, jumping out of bed and grabbing my suit out of the top drawer. "What are we waiting for?" I asked, looking back at him impatiently as he remained motionless on the bed.

"What?" he asked innocently. "I'm watching you get dressed," he said again with the sly smile.

"Oh jeesh!" I said hopelessly.

He lay back with his hands behind his head, staring at me. I pulled my nightdress over my head, wadded it into a ball, and threw it at him, covering his face. William laughed and pulled it off.

I did feel so awkward standing nude in front of him. I hadn't done that yet.

"Are you sure you don't want to just come back over here?"

I dressed quickly and ran out the door, giggling the whole way.

By the time I fetched our boards from around the side of the house, William was walking down the steps of the porch in just his swim shorts. *Will I ever get used to his handsomeness?* He looked gorgeous. He grabbed his board from under my arm and walked with me through the small path that led through the thin line of trees between the beach and our house. Neither one of us had stepped foot on the beach. We were too busy with the hustle and bustle of moving in.

It was a lovely little spot with the trees lining all around it, curving into the water on both sides, creating natural privacy. There were big rocks in the water following the line where the curtain of trees ended at the water's edge and continuing out into the water for one hundred yards or so. It was a much smaller area than the beach I usually surfed on, but it was cozy and secluded, which I liked.

"It is like we have our own private beach," I noted as we walked through the surf. "I love it. This alone makes our house worth the buy."

"I knew you would like it. It's why I showed you the house in the first place." William continued.

We paddled out and rode a few waves in. The rocks prevented the waves from being very big, but I still loved it. I could always go back to the other beach when I wanted a bigger challenge. This would be perfect for most mornings, so secluded and serene. That is what I looked most forward to when surfing anyway.

"I won't have to wake up as early anymore," I said to William when we were waiting for a wave. "I mean, I will have to wake up early enough to make it to class once school starts again, but that won't be too bad."

William smiled a softer smile, like the realization of real life saddened him. I didn't like it either. Shortly after classes resumed, William would have to leave. I didn't like thinking about that. I wanted to pretend that this would be the rest of our lives, soaking in the sun and waves and enjoying each other all night long.

As if reading my thoughts, William said, "Don't think about it. Let's just enjoy the now." I nodded.

William slid off his board into the water so he could be closer to me and kissed me, trying to erase the sad thoughts in my head.

We floated in the water for hours, taking breaks to lay on the hot sun, wrapped in each other's arms, kissing. Our bodies were covered in sand and salt, but it didn't bother either of us.

We jumped off one of the large black rocks. William even talked me into skinny-dipping for a few minutes. I worked up enough courage to jump off the rock naked but was too terrified of an unexpected visitor to do it again.

We treaded water naked, our bodies intertwined together. We made love in the ocean, on the sand, and again in the ocean.

Around two o'clock, we went back to the house for lunch. I was also worried about William getting a bad sunburn. He wasn't as tan as me. After lunch, William pulled out a small poinsettia plant from his truck.

"I picked this up a few days ago thinking it could act as our Christmas tree," he announced, setting it on the coffee table.

"I love it! Our house is definitely missing a little Christmas cheer," I agreed and ran over to the top drawer of our dresser and pulled out the wrapped box I had for him inside. I skipped over to the coffee table to put it under the plant. I placed it next to another small wrapped box William sneaked under the plant while I was fetching his gift.

"You got me a present?" I said, gently picking the small red box and looking up at him.

William smiled down at me angelically. "Of course, I did. Do you think I would forget to buy my angel a Christmas gift?"

"I didn't know," I admitted.

"You have to wait until Christmas though," he said, taking the box from me and putting it back. We both sat on the couch, and I snuggled into his chest.

"This is the best," I declared, wrapping my arms around him.

"It is," he said, snuggling into my hair.

"I wish it could stay this way all the time," I said quietly, playing with his hands. They were so much larger than mine. I put our palms together. My fingers only reached to the second joint on his fingers. William slid his fingers between mine, holding them tightly. He was silent for a moment, probably thinking about my last comment.

"I'm sorry it can't be this way forever," he said somberly. I immediately felt guilty for bringing it up.

"I'm sorry. I shouldn't have brought it up. I'm grateful for the time we have now." I turned my head to look at his face. He was serious, thoughtful.

"No, you don't need to feel sorry. That is the way you feel," he assured, still serious. His chest felt tight under me. "I'm glad you like me," he said with a laugh, lightening the mood. "I would be sad if you wouldn't miss me when I was gone."

I turned around and kissed him gently. "I love you. You're the best thing that's happened to me. I can put up with a little . . . temporary separation. You're worth it." I smiled.

The rest of our day we spent lazily around the house, snuggling. We took a walk on the beach after cleaning up in our fantastic outside shower, and then we took a nap. It was the most perfect day. We didn't accomplish anything, we didn't see anyone else, and we didn't feel guilty about it.

16

The next day, we saw William's parents off. We stood afar off the landing strip, waving to them as they walked up the stairs to the jet. William's mother held the small Christmas gift I gave her under her arm and waved madly and blew kisses to us as they walked away. I gave her a set of woven placemats I made out of palm leaves and told her they would brown but would be good for years. I could see she was still crying. She hadn't stopped since we began hugging our goodbyes. William's father had very few words. He embraced me and William and wished us luck. We promised to visit soon.

"That was not near long enough," I admitted to William as we watched them leave.

"No, it wasn't," William agreed. "I am grateful to have the time with them though. Pa had to get back to the farm."

I nodded silently, wondering if we really would ever see them again and realizing what a tremendous sacrifice William was making by being with me.

Christmas morning came without any fanfare or the usual giddy squeals of excitement like Christmas mornings at home. It was quite the opposite of all my Christmas pasts. We lingered in bed, drifting in and out of consciousness, until my stomach eventually drove me out and into the kitchen again. I didn't even remember it was Christmas until William sauntered into the kitchen with his sleepy eyes.

"Merry Christmas, my beautiful bride," he said with a smile and a kiss on my cheek before grabbing a cup from one of the cupboards.

"Oh! Yes, Merry Christmas, sweetie," I said, remembering. "First Christmas together!"

"First of many," William added, dishing himself a plate. The thought made me smile. I wondered where we would be next year at this time.

I eyed the small gifts under our little poinsettia plant during breakfast, curious what William got for me but more curious what William would think of his gift from me.

"Come on, let's open those presents you keep eyeballing!" William said, standing to clear the plates after we finished. I skipped over to the couch and waited anxiously while William rinsed the plates.

"Come on, come on, come on! The dishes can wait!" I called to him.

"I'm coming, you silly kid," he said, walking over to the couch.

"Open mine first!" I said, waving it at him until he sat next to me. I placed it in his hand for him to open it. William smiled and looked at me curiously. Leaning back on the couch, he opened the end of it while I watched him anxiously.

"Okay, I feel weird with you watching me like that. Why don't you open yours too?" he said, fetching mine and putting it in my lap.

"Okay, we'll open them at the same time."

I slipped the ribbon off the end of the package, only looking up at William once while he opened his. Under the paper was a small black box. I pulled the top of the box, revealing a beautiful oval silver locket. I picked it by the chain to inspect it closer. It was clean and simple with an elegant daisy engraved on the front. I was speechless for a moment until I looked up at William holding the pocket watch, which looked amazingly similar to the locket in my hands. We both laughed.

"If I open this, am I going to find a picture of you in it?" William asked.

"Yes." I giggled.

"Great minds think alike," William said, leaning over and kissing me.

I opened up the locket to see a small picture of William. He was in his navy uniform with his cap placed squarely on the top of his head. He looked handsome and perfect, just the way I would want to remember him.

"I thought the picture was a little over the top, but my mom said you would like it best that way," he explained.

"I do! I love it! I'm so glad your mom told you to put the picture in. It's exactly what I would pick for myself."

I unclasped it, and William helped me put it on. The weight of the locket on my neck felt comforting, a little reminder of William. I fiddled with the locket between my fingers and waited for William to open his pocket watch. He rubbed his thumb across the face of the watch, admiring the workmanship. He opened it up and watched the second hand tick around the white face of the clock. I looked up at his face and watched his eyes move to the picture of me that my own mother picked out of me.

"I love it. The picture of you is beautiful. I'll keep in my front pocket always."

"Really? I wasn't sure it would be allowed," I said.

"Of course, it is," he answered. I rested my head on his shoulder and snuggled against him. "Merry Christmas," I whispered.

"Merry Christmas, angel," he said, resting his head on mine.

And that was all we said. I knew the months he would be gone I would hold onto the locket like an anchor, helping me hold onto these first few weeks together. I wondered if William would do the same while he was away. A felt a lump building in my throat but pushed the tears away. Now was not the time to cry about the future; now was the time to enjoy the present.

After getting a little distracted by the bed, we went to my parents' house at about four o'clock that afternoon. The first few moments standing back in my house with my new husband by my side felt awkward. What was my family thinking? Were they wondering about our last few days together? Just thinking about what they were thinking made my face burn red. I couldn't look Daddy in the face for the first hour or so. It killed me to know that he knew I was no longer an innocent little girl.

Dinner was nice; Mom made traditional roast pig with sweet potatoes and rice. We had pleasant conversation, most of it unspoken. My sisters whispered and giggled between each other across the table, shooting me sideways glances and embarrassed grins. William asked about Evelyn, if she made her flight home. Mom asked us if we liked our place. We told her it was nice, and we really enjoyed living on the beach. We cut the evening short, leaving at seven o'clock. I was glad to leave and escape to our quiet home. Strange how the place I called home for so long felt strange and uncomfortable. After I walked through our doorway, I felt at peace and happy in our private sanctuary.

The days rolled on quickly and slowly all at the same time. We didn't leave the house often, only a few times to shop around the market and once we attended church with my family. I lost track of time; I often got confused and didn't know what day it was, sometimes even what time it was. We stayed up late and slept in until the sun was high in the sky. We lay out on the beach and soaked in the ocean, and we made love anytime we wanted day or night. It was wonderful. We were blissfully happy; it felt so much like a dream I knew it would end. Nothing this wonderful could last forever. Each day, I got to know William a little better. I anticipated his facial expressions, favorite phrases, and behavioral patterns. Our lives synced together naturally. I didn't question if this was the way most marriages worked; I was just grateful that things we're working out so well for us.

The first few nights we shared a bed were awkward. I wanted to sleep in his arms, but it felt strange and uncomfortable with another person next to me, but just a week or so later, my body molded next to his, and I doubted I could sleep comfortably without the weight of his body next to me anymore.

I still wasn't used to dressing in front of him. I felt awkward and self-conscious, but it didn't stop me from doing it. He took such pleasure in watching me that it gave me joy and made me laugh. Often, he would wrap his arms around me mid-dressing, kissing my neck and rendering it impossible to pull my dress over my head.

January 5 came, much to my dismay, and a resemblance of a real life full of responsibilities began for our new little family; I went back to school. It was my last semester, so I should have been relieved, but I looked at it as an evil stealing my precious time with my new husband. I wanted to withdraw from the semester and start back up in the spring, but William insisted I continue. William started putting in a few hours back on the cruiser while I was at school, but he was always home before me. The skipper was being very understanding, giving William as much time with me as possible. Usually, when I got home, he was working on paperwork at the outside table. I asked him a few times what he was working on, and his answer was always "Training material."

We never fought, a fact I knew would change with time, but it didn't look like we would be allowed that time. We adjusted to a normal life reluctantly but smoothly. We surfed early every morning, parted ways by eight o'clock, and reunited by four o'clock, instantly resuming our leisurely lifestyle wrapped in each other's arms.

William's deployment was set for January 26. The date haunted my mind each time my eyes crossed a calendar. I pushed the thoughts of his departure out of my head and focused on the now.

In the third week of January, our last week together, twice I slept through our morning surf. Both times, William woke me with just enough time to dress and make it up the hill to class on time. I usually rode my bike to school, but on those two days, I was so late William had to drive me.

"Why are you so tired, angel?" he asked me while driving me for the second day in row.

"I have no idea," I answered honestly, "but I've been tired all week."

"I've noticed you going to bed early too," he pointed out.

"I don't know why. I'm sorry. I don't want to spend our last moments together sleeping." A wave of sadness rushed over me. "Maybe I should take today off, and we can have a long weekend together before you leave."

"That would be nice," he said gently. "But I need to go in and make my last preparations on the ship," and that was all we said about that.

I came home as early as I could, but when I got there, William wasn't home yet. I was instantly disappointed. He must have meant it when he said he had things to do to prepare. I didn't know what to do while he wasn't at the house, so I flopped on the bed, instantly falling asleep.

I felt William's weight on the bed beside me. It felt like minutes later when I forced my eyes open. I could tell it had been at least an hour.

The sun was lower in the sky and shining straight into our west-side windows.

"Still tired, huh?" he asked with his brilliant smile. I let out a sigh; every time I saw him, my heart would swell. I really loved this man.

"I think I just don't know what to do without you here. I better get used to it. I don't think I can sleep for six months straight." I laughed, rubbing my sleepy eyes.

"No, I doubt not." William laughed. "You will have to find something else to do without me, and it better not include near as much naked time. I would become insanely jealous!" He laughed and then paused for a moment. "You know, you don't have to stay here all alone. You can stay with your parents if you would like." I looked into William's somber face. His mood grew more serious. He lay on his side with his head propped on his hand. I rolled on my side, mirroring his pose.

"I don't like to think about it, Will," I remarked.

"I know." He accepted, reaching for my hand. "But we kind of need to. I'm leaving in two days."

A single tear escaped out of the corner of my eye. William reached up and wiped it away.

"I think this place is going to be really sad without you here," I admitted.

"Well, you don't have to stay here all alone if you don't like. If you do stay with your parents, though, I want you to make sure to help pay your way. Pay for some groceries, and make sure you aren't a burden to them. I don't want your father thinking I can't take care of you," William said evenly.

I nodded. "I understand."

"As long as we are on the subject, I have some more things we should talk about." William picked a small stack of papers off the kitchen counter and then walked back over and sat on the bed. I straightened up so I could look at the papers he brought over.

"This is all our bank information," he explained. "I get paid on the twentieth of every month. The check will be mailed to you. You will just need to take it down to the bank. Do you know how to make a deposit?" I nodded. "I put your name on the account a few days ago, so you shouldn't have any trouble. If you do have any problems, contact this person on base," he said and handed me a piece of paper with a phone number on it. "Cheryl is our payroll and accounting. She knows me well, and she will help you with any problems that might occur." I nodded again. "The house is paid for, so you won't need to worry about any of that, but you will have to pay the utility bills. Do you think you can do that?"

"Yes, I know how to pay bills," I answered.

"Are you sure? Because I can arrange for someone else to take care of them," he offered. He looked more serious and businesslike than I'd ever seen before.

"No, I'd like to handle it," I confirmed.

William smiled, looking pleased. "That's what I thought. With the bills paid," William continued, "you should have about $125 dollars left. I'd like you to put at least $75 in our savings account." He handed me a paper with his/our savings account information on it. "And the rest should be enough for groceries and other household items you might need. If there is ever something you want to get that is a little more than that, you are welcome to. I trust your judgment. I would just like us to have a good amount of money saved now while it is just the two of us and the navy is paying my expenses. It's the best time to build up our nest egg." William looked to me for a response.

"I understand," I assured him. "I will take good care of everything and keep saving. This is more than enough money for just me."

"Good," he said with a smile and kissed me on the forehead. "Now I will be very hard to get ahold of." He continued. "If there is any emergency, your best bet is through Cheryl on base. The first three weeks, we will be running exercises at sea, so I won't be getting any mail, and I will periodically be out from then on, so don't worry if you don't get any letters for small stints at a time. You can mail me letters here though." He handed me another paper with an address in California. "I will check the mail as often as I can, and I will write you as often as possible too."

I nodded. I felt sick to my stomach looking over all the paperwork in front of me.

"I know this is hard, angel. You must remember that I love you and I don't want to leave. You know that, right?" I smiled slightly, holding back more tears. "You're not the only one who doesn't like this, but I must do my duty. I hope you write me. I will be looking forward to your letters," he said, taking my hand in his.

"I will. Of course, I will write! So . . . how long?" I asked.

"Not sure yet. We are usually deployed for at least six months. Do you have any other questions?" he asked.

"No, I think I understand everything."

"Great," he said, gathering the papers up. "Let's put it aside then." William stacked everything neatly, walked over to the dresser, and put all the papers in the top drawer.

"Now let's not talk about it any longer. We have two days left together. Let's make the most of it," he announced and jumped on top of me and smothered me in kisses.

The weekend flew by. Every hour felt like a minute. We didn't leave the house except to surf or walk on the beach. Monday morning came, and I cursed the sun for rising. When my eyes opened, William was awake, and I could hear him through the wall on the other side, showering. I sauntered sleepily through the bathroom, slipped off my nightgown, and joined him in the outside shower. He smiled when he saw me. I hugged him tightly under the steady stream of water. He looked stressed. His face and words gave a cheery "Good morning," but his eyes revealed his agony inside. Small drops of water were wetting the corner of his eyes. This was the closest I'd ever seen him get to crying.

"It's going to be okay, honey," I assured him. It was my turn to be the comforter. His eyes looked far off, focused on the greenery surrounding us. I gave him a tighter squeeze and shook him a little, trying to get his attention. "Hey!" I said, forcing a smile. "Are you okay?" Slowly, he looked down at me and brushed my wet hair to the side.

"Yeah," he said quietly, "I just don't want to leave you." I was startled to see him so upset. I'd been so wrapped up in hating that he was leaving me I didn't think about it being hard for him to leave me.

"It's going to be okay," I reassured him.

"I'm sorry I have to leave you here all alone," he uttered quietly, tucking his chin into the corner of my neck. "I've been thinking lately, and I'm sorry. Maybe you were right. It is easier not to fall in love when you know the person you love will leave you." I could see a lump forming in his throat. "Maybe it wasn't right of me to push you into this. I feel really selfish."

"Oh, now just stop!" I insisted, pulling his forehead down against mine. "You know I love you, and you didn't push me into anything. This is exactly what I wanted. I would never trade our last month together for anything. I can put up with a little separation. This is just goodbye for now." William nodded slightly. "Will, I love you! And I'm going to be just fine! Yes, I will miss you, but I can handle this. Do you believe me?" I asked him.

William looked off again toward the ocean.

"Lieutenant?" I said forcefully. He looked back again to me.

"Yes, I believe you. I know you will be okay. But will I?" He smiled again, this time it was more genuine. "I've gotten used to having your cuteness around! Those guys on the ship are going to be awful sore on the eyes after living with you. Not to mention that cot is going to be real cold and lonely."

I laughed. "I love you, William Wellington." I hugged him tight again.

"I love you, Mrs. Ruth Wellington." He leaned down, kissing me passionately. "I do have one question," he said.

"What is that?" I asked.

"I'm curious, and I want to know before I leave . . ."

"What!" I couldn't imagine what he was about to ask.

"Well, you've been really tired lately . . .," he trailed off.

"Yes," I asked curiously.

"And I don't know much about womanly problems, but we've been married over a month, and you haven't said anything about 'that time.'"

"No . . . I haven't," I said, starting to understand what he was getting at.

"Do you think you might be pregnant?" he asked tentatively. "Oh! I can't believe I hadn't even thought of that!"

When was the last time I had bled? It was two weeks or so before we were married.

"I am three weeks late! You're right! Oh my goodness, do you think I might be pregnant?" I asked again, grabbing my head.

"Well, that is what I am asking you!" William laughed.

"Well, I've never been pregnant before," I gasped. "How should I know? But I guess maybe I am." I felt light-headed, happy, confused, and excited.

The possibility of a coming baby was all we talked about while we dressed. William dressed in his dress whites in preparation for departure and gathered up the few things he would take with him. He stood in front of the mirror and placed the pocket watch in his front breast pocket over his heart and put his cap on his head. I stood in one of my sundresses, watching him button up his coat and straighten his uniform.

"If I am pregnant, I will look different the next time I see you," I marveled, rubbing my stomach.

William turned around and took two steps toward me. He rubbed my stomach with one hand and held me close with the other arm.

"You will look beautiful," he declared, kissing me again. "Don't worry your pretty little head about that."

"Are you excited about the thought of me being pregnant?" I asked.

"Extremely," he stated, beaming. "You will make beautiful babies."

"Well, I'm excited about it too," I said and stood on my tiptoes to kiss him.

"Well, my dear, we can't procrastinate this any longer. I need to go," he said reluctantly.

"Okay. May I come with you? I can call Daddy and have him pick me up at the harbor."

"Sure. I would like that," Will said, gathering his things.

We drove to town mostly in silence. We said a few occasionally, things about when he came home and the possibility of a baby. Already, I was grateful for the distraction the baby was providing for me.

"I feel giddy and excited right now instead of sad and depressed like I thought I would be," I admitted as he winded down the hill toward the base.

"Well, I suppose that's what children do for you." William smiled.

"What if I'm not pregnant?" I said, feeling a weight of anxiousness. "What if I lose the baby?" I felt another wave of panic.

"We will deal with that if it happens, and I'll come back, and we will make another one." William smiled devilishly. I playfully smacked his arm. "Don't worry about that either. Just take good care of yourself while I'm gone," he said, squeezing my hand. "I know you have connections with the hospital staff, but remember, you have navy insurance. If you need any help with that, call Cheryl. Make sure those doctors take good care of you."

"I will," I said quietly.

William parked the truck next to the other navy-issued vehicles, and we got out. William pulled his things out of the back of the truck and put them on the ground.

"Once we get to the ship, I have to be Lieutenant Commander Wellington, so we better say our goodbyes right now." I stood in front of him, looking up into his handsome face.

"I don't know what to say," I admitted.

"I know," he conceded, stepping toward me and sweeping me into his arms. He picked me, so my feet were off the ground, and squeezed me tight.

"I love you, Will," I whispered into his ear. "I will miss you so much."

"I love you too, and I will miss you more than you could ever know," he said. "You take care of yourself."

My chest started to heave with great sobs. I pushed it back with all my might, vowing to be strong. I wouldn't let him see me fall to pieces. I wanted him to know I would be okay.

"Make sure you take care of yourself and come home soon," I pushed out between sobs. I gained control of myself, and we kissed. We kissed passionately and sweetly. This would be our last memory together for a while, and I wanted it to be a good one.

He set my feet back down to the earth, brushed the hair out of my face, and kissed me again one more time. He retrieved his bag from off the ground, and we walked hand in hand toward the dock. We passed the large ships moored along the row until we reached the *St. Louis*.

There was a crowd of departing seamen on the dock in front of the ship, waiting for the same deployment. William leaned down one more time, kissing me tenderly as we walked. I stopped, knowing I had come as far as I was allowed. William squeezed my hand and looked at me one last time. Silent tears were pouring down my face. I willed them to stop, but they would not.

"I love you," he said simply, and I thought I saw his eyes water. He kissed the back of my hand and then continued on toward his men. My chest heaved once more with a large sob. I forced myself to hold on a little longer. *I will not come apart here!* I vowed. I simply could not do that to Will.

I stood motionless watching Will walk away from me back to his life before he met me, to the men and boat he loved so dear. He stood in front of his men and called them to attention. They quickly took formation, standing in straight lines in front of Will. He called out a few orders I couldn't hear. They all saluted, and he dismissed them. They formed a line and walked orderly toward the ship. One by one, they crossed the gangplank and disappeared into the boat's belly. William trailed behind them, carrying his bag and stopping slightly before stepping on board to wave once to me. I waved wildly back, surprised that he acknowledged me again. I blew him a kiss, and he tipped his hat once before stepping into the black abyss behind the doorway of the boat.

And then he was gone.

17

I walked back to the parking lot numb. I wanted to curl up into a ball right there at the water's edge and sob my heart out, but I forced myself onward. At first, I wanted to chase after Will and beg for one more kiss. I had waited a moment thinking he might run back out, knowing realistically he would not. Once I knew that was the last I would see of him, I wanted to run home, far away from the wretched sea that stole my husband. I forced myself to focus only on the steps I was taking, one in front of the other. I didn't trust my mind to wander to anything else but the ground in front of me.

Dad was waiting for me in the parking lot. I had hardly seen him in a month; he looked almost like a stranger to me. Nonetheless, upon spotting him, I ran into the safety of his arms. Daddy held me silently and let me cry. I didn't cry the heavy sobs I was burying deep in my chest. I sobbed silently in his shoulder for a few minutes until I felt a small release in the pressure building under my eyes.

"Do you want to come home with me?" Daddy asked once I'd regained control. I thought a moment, not knowing what I wanted.

"No, I think I want to be alone for a bit," I answered. "But do you think you could come get me after work? Is it okay if I stay with you guys for a bit?" I knew I wasn't ready to spend a night alone in my house.

Daddy dropped me off at home, telling me he would be back at 5:30 p.m. I thanked him, waved goodbye, and walked slowly up the front steps after watching him drive away. I opened our front door with only the sound of the creaking door to welcome me. I stood in our small living room, looking around the empty house. Even though I'd spent time alone in our house before, William's absence seemed to permeate every corner. I stepped inside slowly, looking around as if expecting to see something new. Everything looked the same except the couch was missing William in his usual spot. I looked at the table where William usually drank his coffee, and his usual chair there was empty too. I walked over to the bed and fell face-first on my pillow. I reached my hand out to the empty space beside me and let the tears flow. I cried big, heavy, ugly sobs into my pillow. I cried until my chest hurt and my eyes were dried up and there was nothing left to do but sleep.

Daddy woke me up at five thirty in the evening by shaking my shoulder. I could see the concern in his eyes, but he didn't say anything. He silently helped me gather my things and get in the car, where we drove to the house in silence.

Once in my old house, I started to regret coming. Maybe it would be better to suffer in silence. Maybe it would be easier not to have to face people right now. Mom, upon seeing me, instantly threw her arms around me in a motherly embrace. Nothing feels as comforting as being wrapped in my mother's arms.

"Mom," I said in a deep sob.

"It's okay, sweetie," she said, pushing me back and catching a few tears streaming down my cheeks. "Come on, let's sit down." Mom led me to the couch and cradled me in her arms and whispered soothing words.

"It's going to be okay, honey," and "This is going to get easier." The rest of the house left us alone while I wept. I cried until I felt silly and foolish for being such a baby.

"Sorry, Mom," I said, wiping my tears. "I think I'm going to be okay now."

"I know you will," Mom said, reassuring me. "I'm sorry it has to be this way for you. How about some dinner?"

"That sounds great. I'll help," I offered.

The girls were hiding in the kitchen with Daddy. Everyone looked on edge when I walked in.

"I'm okay." I sighed, exasperated. "You don't have to look at me like that."

"We know, sweetie. We're just worried about you," Daddy said.

"Thanks, Daddy. I'm going to be fine. It's just hard. I really love him, you know."

"We ALL know, Ruth," Marie said, giggling. "We haven't seen you since Christmas. Nice of you to come around."

I ignored her leading comment and chose to help Mom with dinner in silence.

After dinner, I walked out back to the old banyan tree. It felt like a lifetime ago that I was last here. I climbed the tree and into my old spot on the large branch. I could see all the way out to the ocean. Searching the shoreline, I noticed a dark image making its way out to sea. Surely it was William's cruiser. He had said that it would take all day to prepare the vessel, and they were the only ones scheduled to leave today. I watched in silence as my love sailed away. *How did I get here?* I wondered. Just a few short months ago, I was perfectly content going to school, living with my parents, enjoying life with my friends, unaware of Lieutenant William Wellington. How could one person's appearance in my life turn it from completely content to pure torture? It would be torture living without him, and yet I had to endure it. I had no other choice.

I stayed two nights at my parents' house. Home was a nice cushion for my grieving, but I didn't like staying there. It felt weird sleeping in my old room and seeping back into my old habits. It felt like William didn't exist, like it was all a dream, so I moved back to our cottage. It was lonely, but at least I could see William around every corner, and I was reminded of our short life together. I wanted to write to William right away the minute he stepped on the boat, but I knew I would only write sad things, and I didn't want to worry or upset him, so I waited until my mind was clearer. I went to class every day, surfed the mornings I could pull myself out of bed, and ate dinner with my parents a few nights a week. Routine was my friend; surfing and distractions became my life again. My heart hurt, but I kept going on. What other choice did I have?

Waking up in the morning felt harder each day. I started wondering if I was seeping into a real depression. I had never felt this tired before in my life. My body felt so heavy I could hardly move it in the morning.

By afternoon, I was dead on my feet. I looked at my patients' beds with such jealousy. I wanted to curl up right beside them. While I put sheets on a bed, I would pause briefly and rest my head on the mattress as I reached over the bed to tuck in a corner.

I stopped by Nohea's house on the way home from work one day and plopped on her wicker swinging chair on the porch. I kicked my legs up and rested my feet on Nohea's lap while we rocked. There was a soft breeze offering a much-needed relief from the relenting humidity. Nohea had such a soft spirit to her; I loved being in her company. It was so easy to be with her. We just rocked and visited. Her mom came in and out and offered us lemonade and then sat to join us.

"Well, I think I better get going," I announced. The sun was starting to set, and I needed to start walking home before it got dark. I swung my legs off Nohea and stood. A sharp, stabbing pain followed. It shoot through my abdomen and rocketed through my uterus. I tried momentarily to pretend it didn't hurt, but I couldn't hide it. I clutched my side and slumped back down onto the chair.

"Ruth, what's wrong?" Nohea asked, concerned.

"Oh," I gasped. "It's nothing. I don't know. Just a pain," I explained.

"Ruthie dear," her mom said with a very worried look, "does it hurt just inside of your hip bone?"

"Yes," I said, surprised. "How did you know, Auntie?"

"Do you think perhaps you may be pregnant, Ruthie?" she asked. Auntie was a midwife. She has delivered hundreds of babies.

"Uhh," I stammered. "I don't know. Maybe," I conceded.

"Well, if you're pregnant, that would be a very common pain caused by the stretching of the uterine wall." She looked at me sideways with a curious smile.

"Oh okay. If, if I was pregnant. Is there anything I could do for it?"

"Not really. Just stand up slowly. Same with rolling over in bed. Just go nice and slow."

"Thank you, Auntie. I'm going to go home now." I stood slowly this time.

Both Nohea and Auntie gave me very curious and little goofy grins as I walked away.

February 14, 1940
My dearest William,

It's Valentine's Day. I'm thinking of you, and I hope you are well. I think of you often, all the time actually. I believe you will be in California soon, and I hope your exercises at sea went well. This is my first letter I've formally written, though I've written many in my head. I talk to you every day, all day long, in my mind. I tell you about school, about my family, about the beautiful surf the winter waves are bringing in, but I haven't been able to put pen to paper just yet. Most of my thoughts are sad and desperate for your company, and I don't want to upset you. I want you to focus on your work and the great responsibility you carry, but know that I love you and miss you desperately. The house is quiet, and the bed is lonely. Nothing is as lovely without you. The view from our house is not as pretty, the smell of the hibiscus isn't as nice, but I am content, and I am carrying on.

School is going well. I am doing rounds at the big pink military hospital on the hill. I enjoy it. It's nice to help patients and to get my head out of the books. I'm still tired every morning, and I take a nap nearly every day. I believe I am pregnant but haven't gone to the doctor yet. On top of the fatigue, I am nauseous nearly all the time. I've missed class once this week because I couldn't leave the bathroom. I can't keep anything down, not even water. Last night I dreamed of drinking water. I was so thirsty. I don't tell you things to complain. I'm not even upset about the sickness. I'm glad to have a reminder of you. I haven't told anyone. I kind of like the little secret growing in my belly that only you and I know about. I kind of hope it's a boy. I would like to have a little William Wellington running around the cottage. Do you have any baby names you are fond of?

I love you with all my heart. I hope you write soon.

All my love,
Ruth

I patted my belly and sealed the letter. I would take it to the post on my way to work. I delivered my letter and began the walk up the hill. It was an unusually humid day, even for Oahu, and I was nearly drenched with sweat by the time I walked through the busy doors of the hospital. I was over an hour early for my rounds. My shift didn't start until 1:00 p.m. I had done it intentionally. I thought it was high time I found out for sure if I was pregnant. I made my way to the maternity ward, weaving through the busy hallways and around patients and their beds. The humidity had caused a larger number of sailors to suffer from heat stroke. There were many red-faced, dehydrated seamen behind each curtain.

I nearly lost my nerve after seeing Elaina, largely pregnant now, standing behind the desk in the maternity ward. She called out before I could sneak away.

"Ruth!" she said. "How good to see you! I haven't seen you since the wedding! How is married life?" She continued as she rounded the counter and embraced me. "How are you holding up with the men gone?"

"Oh, I'm good," I said. "And look at you!" I gestured to her belly. "I can't believe you are still working!"

"Oh, I do very little here." She waved away my astonishment. "And it is such a good distraction, you know? Your mind is a lonely place to be when you're waiting for a husband and a baby," she added, rubbing her bump. "It's so great to see you! I've thought of you so often. I saw William a few times after you were married. He looked so happy!"

"Oh, thanks, those were wonderful couple weeks . . ." I sighed, reflecting back at those blissful days.

"I know. It's hard, dear," she said, squeezing my shoulder.

"How about you? How are you doing? I mean, here I am, feeling bad for myself, and you are going to have this baby at home!" I suddenly felt very foolish. I wasn't the only person feeling alone, and she was bearing it so much better than me.

"Oh, it's never easy, but you learn to get by. Now what can I do for you? I didn't see you on rotation down here."

"Well . . .," I stammered. "I, I actually wanted to see the doctor . . ."

"Ah yes, I see." She smiled. "Right this way." She motioned.

I followed Elaina into one of the small exam rooms. She took my blood pressure and listened to my heart. She didn't ask any more questions about why I was there. She talked about Sarah and said that Theresa had a nervous breakdown after the boys left. She asked if I had received a letter, which, of course, I hadn't. She hadn't either. Hearing that made me feel relieved.

"Dr. Albright will be in in just a few minutes," Elaina said and pulled the curtain behind her. I waited for several minutes, swinging my legs nervously at the edge of the cot, trying to decide how to even ask the doctor if I was pregnant.

"Well, how are we today, Mrs. Wellington?" the doctor said, startling me a little. He had a very deep, alarming voice. "Elaina says you are newly married."

"Yes," I confirmed.

"And how is married life?" he asked as he sat. He was a very tall man with balding gray hair.

"Good," I said, "I—"

"You are here for a pregnancy test, I assume?" he asked, interrupting me.

"Yes, I—"

"Nurse!" he yelled. Elaina waddled in.

"Yes, Doctor," she said.

"Pregnancy test," he said and handed her the file and left the room.

I looked at her, a little confused.

"He's a little abrupt but a good doctor." She sighed. "Now take this to the bathroom and give us a sample." She smiled sweetly, handing it to me.

I filled the specimen cup and put it on the tray where Elaina had instructed me to and walked back to my small cubby to wait.

Elaina entered a few minutes later, closed the curtain behind her, and turned around, revealing the silliest grin I'd even seen.

"You're pregnant!" she said with a little hop.

I didn't say anything; I just stared at her, searching her face for some hint that she was kidding. I knew I was; I had to be. Why else would I be nearly three months late? Hearing it confirmed was a little surreal.

"You're pregnant!" she repeated, grabbing my hands.

"I'm pregnant?" I gasped.

"Yes, dear! Welcome to the club!" She embraced me tightly. Without me knowing it, I began to cry.

"I'm pregnant! I can hardly believe it!" My whole chest filled with joy. I hadn't realized how much I wanted this baby until this moment. "I'm going to have a baby!" I said excitedly.

"I'm so happy for you two!" she said, sitting on the cot next to me. She wrapped an arm around my shoulder, squeezing me tightly, sharing this life-changing moment with me.

"Would you like the doctor to come back in and answer some questions?" she asked a few moments later.

"No, I'm good. I have to start my shift in a few minutes."

"I will walk you out." She helped me gather my few items and walked me through the entrance to the maternity ward.

"Please don't tell anyone. I really want to tell William first."

"Your secret is safe with me! Now we are all having lunch this Saturday at my house. Come! Please say you will come!" she begged.

"I will come," I promised and left her with the grumpy Dr. Albright and went to my side of the hospital.

I would be working under Nurse Turner today. She was an older lady in charge of the nursing students. Her husband worked on base. She had just enough experience to make her really impatient with all her naive young nursing students.

"Ruth, you're late," she snapped as I joined rounds.

"Yes, ma'am, I'm sorry." She was much shorter than me, I had to look down to make eye contact, but she was no less intimidating.

"Don't let it happen again."

"Yes, ma'am."

I was assigned to three severely dehydrated seamen and spent the afternoon cleaning up their vomit, nearly adding some of my own to the mess, and checking their IVs. My mind was consumed with the idea of carrying a baby. It was all I could think about. Nurse Turner had to correct me a few times as she found me staring off into space.

"Hey, dreamer!" she called. "Your patient is puking again!"

I quickly grabbed the bedpan and put it under the young sailor's chin.

"Sorry, doll," he said as I wiped his chin.

"No worries, sailor. Let's just get you well." I soothed.

During my break, I sat and wrote William another short letter.

William,

   I realize you will be getting this letter shortly after the last, but I can't contain myself. We are expecting! Elaina was my nurse, so she knows, but not another soul. I wanted to tell you as soon as possible. I am so very excited! I must go. I can hear Nurse Turner tapping her foot as I write this.

Congrats! My love, Ruth

It was a frivolous use of a stamp but well worth it in my mind. I would mail it just as soon as I was off. I folded the paper and tucked it into my jacket and went about finishing my shift.

I walked to my parents' house after I mailed the letter. It was hard not to share my glorious news with them at dinner, but I wanted to keep it a secret just a bit longer. I wanted William to at least have a chance to find out before the rest of the world. Daddy drove me home that night. I kissed his cheek before I stepped out of the car, and my precious secret and I went to bed that night, smiling from ear to ear.

I went to Elaina's that weekend for lunch as she requested. I had a few fluttering nerves as I knocked on the door and listened to the laughs of the women on the other side. Elaina answered and pulled me right into the party.

"We are so glad to see you, Ruth!" Sarah said, giving me a kiss on the cheek.

The captain's wife was there as well, and Theresa was on a stool in the kitchen, picking at her fingers. She looked up and gave me the hint of a nod. Sarah introduced me to Beth, who was new to the base. Her husband was a lieutenant on the USS *Tennessee*. She held a baby in her lap and gave me a warm hello. Her husband was serving. I sat next to her and across from Sarah while Elaina handed us each a water.

"So you live off base?" Beth asked.

"Yes, I always have. I love living on the ocean. I can see how the camaraderie of living on base would be nice," I added.

"It's important we stick together," Sarah said. "If you ever need anything, we are here for you."

"That's so nice. Thank you," I said.

"How are you holding up?" the captain's wife asked. I wished I could remember her name.

"Pretty well," I said. "The first few weeks were hard, but I'm keeping busy with school. I will graduate soon."

"That's lovely, dear. Unless your husband is like mine, this is only temporary." She giggled.

"Oh, Ginny, you poor thing. I don't know how you've done it all these years," Sarah said, handing her a sandwich. Ginny, that was her name!

"I can handle all the alone time. It's the heat I can't stand!" Theresa grumbled as she joined us on the couch. "I just want to get off this wretched island. Ruth, living here your whole life, you must be nuts," she accused.

"I love it here," I said.

"Like I said, you're nuts."

"How much longer will you work?" Ginny asked Elaina, changing the subject.

"Oh, not too much longer. Theodor wants me to stop, but I really like to be busy. I hate to sit around, waiting for my husband and a baby."

"I don't blame you," Beth commented, patting Elaina on the knee.

"Theodor said that William will retire after this. Is that true?" Sarah asked.

"Yes, he wants to settle down. See if he can stay on base. He said he only stayed in the navy because he had no reason to leave," I explained.

"Well, we are very happy for you," Sarah offered. "But the boys will be sad. They have been a team for so long."

"They sure have," Ginny agreed. "Theodor keeps it light when things get serious, William always knows how to get the men to do just what they want, and Edward drives them all nuts!"

Everyone laughed. Theresa didn't look happy, but she wasn't going to cross the captain's wife. The rest of lunch carried on much the same. It was a relief to be with the ladies who shared similar trials. A few hours later, I reluctantly left the ladies and began my short walk home, detouring a little ways to walk through the shops. I wandered around the stands to buy some fruit from my favorite aunties.

"I think youz need to add some lilikoi to your basket, Mz. Ruth," a deep voice said from behind.

"Kekoa!" I exclaimed and embraced him. "I haven't seen you in so long!"

"Aye, youz been a stranger."

I nodded, a little embarrassed. "Well, let's change that! I haven't been to the big beach in so long. How about we meet up Saturday?"

"I didn't know youz still surfed!"

"Haha." I punched him in the shoulder. "Of course, I do. Could never stop."

"All right, I will see you Friday."

I smiled the whole way home. I hadn't realized how much I had missed that big burly guy. It had been months since I had seen him after seeing each other nearly daily. He was so comfortable. I had missed him.

Sleeping was getting increasingly difficult over the past few nights. Rolling over was causing sharp pains in my side. They were so painful it would cause me to cry out and grab my side. On top of that, I woke up one night to my calf morphing into a hard rock, which also caused me to scream. Once I flexed my foot hard, it started to ease. When I asked Elaina about it, she said it was normal. She said I was suffering from leg cramps and that the pain in my side was from my muscles being stretched from the baby growing. It didn't make it hurt less but was comforting to know what was happening. I made sure to go slow and easy when I rolled over.

I beat Kekoa to the beach on Saturday but didn't wait before I took a few waves. I had gotten used to the little surf at home, and it felt exhilarating to take on the big waves. I could feel a small bump as I lay on the board. It was very subtle, but it was there.

"Heya, Ruth!" Kekoa said. He was standing on the beach. I paddled in to greet him. We hugged and kissed each other on the cheek.

"You're late!"

"Yeah, sorry 'bout that. Let's do this."

We ran out through the surf and paddled out together. It was just like old times.

"I missed this!" I said.

"Me too," he said with his goofy grin. "Now come on, ladyz first."

I caught the next big swell, paddling hard as it built behind me. I grasped the side of my board, pulled my feet under me quickly, and stood quick. The sharp pain in my side returned and was sharper than ever before.

"Ahhhhh!" I screamed, doubling over, clinging to my side.

I fell headfirst into the swell. I wanted to straighten up and swim to the surface, but I was paralyzed. I kicked a few times, but it did no good. I tumbled over and over in the surf. I didn't know what way was up and what way was down. I had been rolled in the surf many times, but this was the first time I felt helpless. I couldn't move, I couldn't straighten up, and I was curled in a ball, rolling uncontrollably. My chest was burning, desperate for breath. How long had I been under? Where was the beach? Surely I should be rolling onto the beach soon. Just as I was about to give up and surrender my consciousness, a lifesaving hand grabbed my arm and pulled me out of the abyss into glorious air. I coughed and choked relentlessly as Kekoa carried me to shore. He laid me on the beach, and I spit up salt water and coughed some more.

"Ruth! Ruth! RUTH! Youz okay?" Kekoa said over and over, patting my back.

I began to get control of my spasms and finally focused on my rescuer. He looked terrified. I patted his tense shoulder.

"I'm . . . I'm okay . . ." I coughed.

He placed his forehead on mine and wrapped me in his enormous arms, cradling my limp body.

"I'm okay," I repeated, more clearly this time. "I'm okay. You saved me," I said, patting his chest. "You saved me," I repeated. "Thank you for saving me." I rested my head on his chest, catching my breath. He was so comfortable.

He kissed my forehead, my cheek, and my hand that he was holding in his.

"You scared me! What happened? You just fell off your board! Iz never seen you do that!"

"I, I got a cramp."

"A cramp?"

"Yes, right here," I said, pointing at my side.

He released me, letting me lay flat on my back to see where I was pointing. It felt great to stretch out. I lifted my arm over my head, stretching out further. Kekoa lightly touched my side where I was pointing.

"The pain goes from here by my hip bone to here, just under my belly button," I explained. "It was so painful I couldn't move." It still felt tender.

He looked at me, puzzled. "I will take you to the doctor." He began to scoop me back up in his arms.

I shook my head. "No, no." I pushed myself free. He touched my side again, examining me. His brows crinkled, confused.

"No, I'm taking you . . .," he insisted.

"I'm pregnant, Kekoa," I admitted.

He withdrew his hand quickly like I had burned him and then gingerly placed it back down, this time on my very tiny, hardly noticeable bump. My heart fluttered under his warm hand. I sighed. *Now he knows . . . before William . . . I told him before William.*

A small tear fell down my cheek, and my bottom lip trembled.

Kekoa rubbed his jaw with his hand, his eyes transfixed on my belly. He looked like he was going to cry too.

I covered my eyes with my arm. I couldn't look at him. He gently pulled my arm away and looked directly into my eyes.

"He got you pregnant and then left you all alone!" he said sternly. "He got you pregnant and left you!" he yelled it this time. He picked a rock and threw it across the beach.

He got up and stomped away. I covered my face with my arms again, trying not to cry. Why was he so severe? After a few moments, I slowly sat up, reorienting myself. Kekoa was pacing by the water's edge. I wanted to leave. I wanted to be home. I stood slowly. My legs were weak and barely able to move. I searched for my board. The water was lapping over it, pushing it down the shoreline. I wanted to leave it, but I couldn't. I walked as quickly to it as I could in my hobbled state, trying to stay out of Kekoa's sight. I put the board under my arm. My plan was to walk home. Hopefully, Kekoa wouldn't stop me. I wasn't halfway across the beach before he was behind me, wrapping his arm around my waist and pulling my back against his chest. I tried to push away, but it was useless.

"Give me your board," he whispered in my ear. He ran his hand across my stomach before taking my board from me. He put it in the back of his pickup and instructed me to get in.

"Youz not walking home half drown and in your . . . condition."

We drove home in silence. He put my board in the shed and walked me inside. He stood awkwardly in my living room. He had never been in our home. It was as if I could read his mind as he scanned the room. He was picturing William there—William standing in the kitchen, William sitting on the couch, and William lying in the bed. I could see the anger boiling underneath his stone face.

"Thank you, Kekoa," I said softly. He nodded stiffly.

"I needz to go. Will youz be all right?" he asked. He wasn't looking at me.

"Yes, I will be fine." I took a step toward him; he stepped back. "Could, could you not tell anyone? No one knows yet." He nodded again. "William doesn't even know yet," I added quietly.

He stiffened.

"Yeah." He shrugged. "Ruth?"

"Yes?"

"Don't surf alone," he said and then left abruptly. He was gone. I never thought that would be the way our day would end. I shook my head. Things would never be the same between us. Why had it not sunk in before? I was so naive.

I did surf alone after that but only on my shallow beach. There wasn't much harm that could come to me there.

February 30, 1940
My angel Ruth,

I am so very excited. Your letter confirming our good news arrived before your first letter! Can you imagine my excitement and also my anguish after receiving such a short note? I am well. Training exercises were successful, and we've made port in California. I met the new enlistees this week. I don't know if it's just me, but they seem lazier and weaker than any of my trainees before. My patience and tolerance for their apathetic behavior is at an all-time low. I suspect it is me, not them. This used to be my life. This used to be what I lived for, but my heart isn't in it anymore. My heart is at home with you in our cottage, looking into your deep blue captivating eyes and your beautiful, contagious smile. This is merely a job for me now.

I'm terribly sorry you are sick. I wish I was there to help you feel better. Maybe a doctor could help? I don't have any ideas for baby names. Please stay well and take care of yourself and our little baby. I worry about you. I miss you terribly. My cot is cold and empty as is the days which have made up this last month we've been apart. I send you all my love.

Lieutenant Commander William Wellington

The moment I finished reading his terribly short letter, I began writing to him.

March 13, 1940
Dearest William,

I was so excited when your letter came today. I shouted for joy! I'm glad you are well, and I'm also glad you miss me. I am well, and so is our growing baby. Mom and Dad know about our little secret now. They came over one night to visit and caught me sleeping on the floor of the bathroom. I had to explain why I was so sick. You are welcome to write your parents and tell them the good news. Mom went with me the next day to the doctor. His name is Dr. Albright. He's a stocky, balding, imposing man. He was rude and short with me and not at all gentle. I do not like him one bit, nor do I like being a patient waiting in those cold sterile rooms in the military hospital. I much prefer being the nurse. He told me there was nothing much he could do for the nausea. He told me to eat crackers and lie down as often as possible, and then he was gone. I do not wish to go back. Nohea's mother is a midwife and has delivered hundreds of the local babies. I think I will talk to her. Mom says that is what she would do too.

School is going well. I only have a few months left before I can be employed as a real nurse. I'm anxious for it to be over. I'm glad you pushed me to finish. It is working as a great distraction from my constant sorrow due to your absence. Sometimes I feel like the walls of our cottage permeate with the feeling of your absence. I hope work gets easier for you. You are good at what you do, and I know the navy needs you. Know that I love and miss you every day.

All my love,
Ruth

I gathered my belongings to go to town. I wanted to mail it right away. I hurried to town and mailed it off and then went to my parents' house.

"I finally got a letter from William!" I announced as I walked in the door.

"Finally!" Elizabeth gasped. "Now maybe we can get a relief from your moping."

I chose to ignore her. I was much too happy to have my mood ruined. They all gathered around as I read the letter to them.

"Well, that was awful short!" Maire said disappointedly.

"I doubt he has a lot of time to write," Mother said kindly. Marie was right though. That was what I thought too. "Don't be disappointed, honey," Mom added. I nodded.

"So can I join you for dinner?"

"Of course!" Mother smiled. "Daddy should be home soon. Let's get ready."

I read the letter to Dad at dinner. He said the same thing, that it was a good letter and he probably didn't have a lot of time to write.

Daddy offered to take me home, but I declined. There was still plenty of light, and I loved the walk.

When I reached my porch, a dark figure sitting on the rocking chair startled me, but I immediately recognized it as Kekoa.

"Howz it, Ruth?" he asked. It was near dusk, and I could barely make him out under the dark Lani.

"It is good. How is it with you?" I asked.

"Fine."

He stood to greet me as I walked up the steps.

"Would you like to come in?" I asked.

"Yeah, sure," he said nervously.

He still looked uncomfortable standing in my house. He was wearing a shirt, which was very uncommon, and his eyes looked wary.

"Are you okay?" I asked.

"I just had to apologize after what I said on the beach. Iz didn't mean to yell at you. I really juz hate to see you hurt and . . . and I handled it poorly."

"It's okay. Here, please sit down."

We sat sideways on the couch, facing each other. He made my couch look tiny. I placed one of my hands on his arm.

"I'm sorry if I did anything to upset you. You are my very good friend. You know that, right?"

He took my hand in his and stroked the back of it.

"I miss you so much, Kekoa. I never thought our friendship would be affected by this so much. You are so dear to me," I said sincerely. "What is it, Kekoa? You look so sad."

"I am sad. I miss you too."

My swelled to hear him say it. I was glad he missed me.

"I just don't understand. Thingz waz so great until the haole showed up. He scooped you up and rattled your brain. How can hez do such things in such short time and then leave you like this!" He gestured to my stomach.

"What do you mean?"

"Ruth!" He was looking agitated again. "Youz never been fooled by the navy boyz before. Howz it he can fool you so?"

"Fool me? What are you talking about? I was not fooled!"

"Don't you see youz totally changed?"

"I have not."

"Youz always made fun of the girls chasing the sea monsters. You never showed any interest . . . I thought . . . I thought you would be my girl," he admitted.

"I did too," I said softly, "but we went over this before." I touched his shoulder. "It just wasn't meant to be for us."

"That's not okay for me!" He placed his hand on the back of my head gently and pulled me close. He spoke softly. "I tried, I'm trying, but I can't. I think about youz all the time. I tried not to see you, but I see you in my dreams. And I get so angry thinking he marched in your life, stole you from me, got you pregnant, and then left you! How can I watch you suffer? I would never leave you. Do you believe me? I would never leave you."

"I do. I know you never would."

"Let me take care of you." He kissed my cheek close to my ear. "I love you, Ruth. Let me love you." He kissed my other cheek. "Let me cherish you." He kissed my chin. "Let me be with you." He kissed the corner of my mouth. "I am a fool for not saying this sooner. I thought I had time. Please let me fix this. Let me be with you."

I wanted to. Oh, I wanted to surrender to him. I was so lonely. He kissed me softly on the lips. It felt so good. It felt so good to be cherished and to feel loved. I loved his big strong arms. I loved his soft full lips on mine. I kissed him back, harder and more demanding than his kiss. He responded, pulling me into his arms. Maybe he was right . . . Maybe we could . . . No . . . No, we couldn't . . . No . . . William . . . No . . . No!

"NO!" I said out loud and pushed him away. "Kekoa, no." I stood. He looked heartbroken and confused. I couldn't blame him. I was being terribly confusing. I hated that I was hurting him—again.

"Kekoa, I know we could have a lovely life together. I could love you. I do love you," I admitted. I bit my lip, holding back the tears.

He pulled me in gently and kissed my belly. He buried his face in my stomach. I stroked his hair.

"But I am married," I said quietly. I took a breath. "We missed each other," I said softly. "We missed our chance." I pushed him away and sat back. "I don't know why, but we did. We just missed each other."

"How can youz say this? You stay here alone all day. He is three thousand milez away. Youz are here, carrying hiz baby."

"I know!" My heart was racing; my eyes were burning. I hated hearing these things. I knew them to be true. "I know!" I repeated. "There is nothing I am more aware of right now than his absence and my loneliness. It's all I think about." I heaved a heavy sob and covered my mouth to stifle it.

"So you will chooz this loneliness over being with me?" he whispered.

"That is not the choice I am making," I said firmly. "I am choosing to stay faithful to my husband, to that man I love."

"But youz just said you loved me!"

"Yes." My lips trembled. "But I didn't promise my life to you, and you didn't ask me to!" I accused. "You never asked me! You never made any kind of effort or insinuated that you had these feelings! And now, now when I am married AND pregnant, you are asking me to be unfaithful to the man who did!"

"If I had . . . If I had done those things . . .," he trailed off.

I nodded.

"I would have," I answered.

"I didn't know. I thought that . . . I thought youz weren't ready, and I didn't think youz would because . . . because I am . . ."

"Hawaiian?" I asked. He nodded. "But I love Hawaiians." I sighed. "I don't think we were ready, but perhaps we would have gotten there." I took his hands in mine. "I am so sorry."

He dropped my hands. His eyes were watering.

"I'm going to go."

"Kekoa—"

He put his hand up to stop me.

"Kekoa—"

"I shouldn't have come."

"No."

"Goodbye, Ruth," he said and let the screen door slam behind him.

Every encounter with him had been so painful. How could someone who gave me so much happiness now caused me so much pain?

April 14, 1940
Ruth,

    It's been nearly a month since my last letter. I've been out to sea. I just now received your last letter. I will write my parents next and inform them that we are expecting. I'm glad your mom knows now and can help you. I'm sorry to hear you didn't like your doctor. I trust your judgment of your care, so do what you feel is best.

    Days are still long here. I don't get the thrill I used to while leading and teaching the men to be proficient gunnery engineers. I got in an argument with the other lieutenant on board, Edward. You met him at the dance. I do not like that man. He is not honest. He is deceitful and boastful of his false accomplishments. He is not a good leader and a poor example to the men. Skipper is pushing us to improve the morale of the men, but I find that hard when the morale among the officers is so low. I know I am partly to blame for this situation. I am not happy here. I'm testy and short with the men. I am not acting as my right self. I don't want to be here. I want to be home with you, experiencing life with you and watching your belly grow. I love you with all my heart. Take care of yourself.

Lieutenant Commander William Wellington

May 3, 1940
Will,

I'm sorry about the argument you had with Edward. I remember him well. I eat lunch with his wife and the other wives nearly every other week. I've really enjoyed getting to know them, but Theresa is always unpleasant. Elaina had her baby last week, I'm sure you know by now. She had a little boy, and he is so cute. Don't pay Edward any mind. He is an unhappy person, and I believe unhappy people want everyone around them to be miserable too. Don't let him get to you; that means he wins. I hope you find some happiness in your work. I hate to think of you being so unhappy. Focus on finding joy in your work. Don't worry about us. We are fine. I miss you, but I'm getting along. I would be doing much better if I knew you were more content.

I helped deliver a few babies during my maternity round at the hospital. I even worked with Dr. Albright. It was awful. The hospital doesn't let anyone in the room with the mother. It was just her and I most of the time and occasionally another nurse. Dr. Albright gave her some medicine that knocked her out. She was pretty much unconscious the first sixteen hours of her new baby's life. I was the only one who held the baby until its mother came out of her drug-induced state. I won't be a part of that for my own delivery. I talked to Auntie Gwen, Nohea's mother. She's agreed to help me deliver the baby at home. I hope that is okay with you. I'm grateful to the navy for offering medical care for me, but I think I will politely refuse it.

I am happy to inform you that I am no longer ill. It is as if one morning I woke up well. My appetite not only returned but has also increased. I'm still very tired, but I'm back to surfing every morning and enjoying feeling good. I'm trying to take advantage of these last few months before my belly grows large. I have a small bump growing noticeable only to me. It hides neatly under most of my clothing. Occasionally, I

feel the baby fluttering inside me. It's an exhilarating feeling
knowing there is a tiny person growing inside me.
I love you with all my heart. Stay safe. Be happy.

All my love,
Ruth

I didn't think I would ever tell him about Kekoa. I knew he had some sort of idea of Kekoa's feelings anyway, and I didn't need to give him anything else to stress about.

I visited Elaina often. She looked beautiful. I hoped I looked so good after having a baby.

"How are you today?" I asked one day as I let myself in.

"Oh, fine, sleepy. Darrel didn't sleep much last night. Thanks so much for bringing us dinner."

"My pleasure. I'm happy to help." I took Darrel from her and sat on the couch. "Is it hard to do it alone?"

"I think it will be hard no matter what. Of course, it would be easier if he were here, but I would still be this tired."

"You always have such a cheery attitude. I hope to be as strong as you. Luckily, William will be back by the time our little one gets here."

She smiled softly.

I held Darrel while she showered, and I helped her fold some clothes before I went back home. I stopped at the post office and found another letter from William waiting for me. I read it while I walked home.

May 16, 1941
Ruth,

Things are getting easier, and I'm working on finding happiness here. I don't know how I feel about you having the baby at home and not taking advantage of good medical care, but like I said before, I trust you.

I have a bit of good news. I will be able talk to you about it soon. We are wrapping things up here. We will be running our last war exercises starting this next week, and then we will head back home. I won't know the exact date of our arrival until it is too late to contact you. All I know is it will be in the middle of June. Unfortunately, I have some bad news too. The admiral has one more assignment for me before I will be reassigned permanently to the islands and retire there. I will be overseeing the training of another group of enlistees. It won't be as long as this assignment, but I know this news will bring much disappointment to you as it has for me. I will only be home for a week before I will deploy again. I am so sorry, my darling. I wish it didn't have to be this way. Again, we will have to focus on the positive and enjoy the week we will have together. I wish I were there to hold you right now and I didn't have to tell you this in a letter. Please don't be angry. I can't wait to see you again, my love.

See you soon,
Will

My hands were shaking, and tears were streaming down my face. I ran the rest of the way home, and I sat on our bed, rereading the letter. This couldn't be right! I must be reading it wrong. How could he be deployed again? He said this was the last! I was so close to having him back just to have him ripped away again! I was furious. How could William go along with this so easy? How could he not be angry? I'd been counting down the days for June, telling myself I just had to make it until then and now. Now I had to double that time! My heart hurt. I was angry, and I felt sick to my stomach. I hated the navy for doing this to me. My husband was going to miss the birth of our first child. What more could they take from me?

I thought of Kekoa. He was so angry with Will for doing this to me. I was beginning to feel angry too.

18

Gradually throughout the month of May, my anger waned, and anticipation for William's arrival replaced it. I couldn't change the way things were, but I could make the best of the good moments. I eagerly anticipated William returning home. I worked extra hard the last few weeks of class just to distract myself from the raging excitement racing through me every time I thought of William coming home. When classes ended the first of June, I had nothing left to entertain my mind. The days dragged on. I surfed a lot, though my belly was getting uncomfortably large. Each day I paddled out in our little cove, I wondered if it would be my last for a while. I spent a lot of time at my parents' house and visited with my old friends Nohea and Elsie, and I napped a lot.

The days lagged by slowly; June 12, June 13, June 14, June 15, and June 16 all slipped away with no sign of William. I was on edge every minute, looking at the door, anticipating him walking through it, but he never did. Just when is the middle of June anyway? When on earth would he show up? I felt like I was going to crawl out of my skin with anticipation.

Nohea and Elsie visited me often. It was such a feeling of freedom and adulthood to have them, who were still living at home, come over to my own house. They caught me up on recent gossip. Nohea had a steady boyfriend. He was in Kekoa's band. Elsie had her eye on a particular sailor.

"If it weren't for you two, I think I would go mad!" I exclaimed one day.

"We missed you. It's like you disappeared for a month after you got married," Elsie relented.

"Well, we hardly ever left the house," I admitted.

"We're glad to have you back." Nohea giggled. "We will understand when you disappear again."

On the seventeenth, I went to work for my normal shift. The head nurse was on one today, ordering us around and blowing up over the smallest issues. She sent me to check the vitals of a poor sick sailor and began laying into some poor nurse on her first day who didn't file a patient's discharge papers correctly.

"How are we feeling today?" I asked the half-conscious sailor lying on the cot.

"Just great." He coughed. "You come here often, toots?"

I laughed.

"Every day." I listened to his heart and took his blood pressure. He was pale. I checked the IV drip.

"How long you been here, sailor?"

"Just arrived a few days ago, spent more time here than on the ship."

"Well, this is a fun place to hang out."

"Yeah, great place to pick up chicks." He coughed again, leaned over the side of the bed, and threw up all over my shoes.

"I'm so sorry," he said and puked again. "So sorry."

"It's okay," I reassured, wiping off his shirt. "You done?" I asked just as he threw up again, this time in the bedpan I handed him.

I started cleaning up the floor and my shoes. This is a normal part of any nurse's job. The stench was terrible, worse than any vomit I had ever cleaned up. I gagged several times and hid my nose in the corner of my elbow, but I couldn't hold it any longer, and I puked all over the floor, adding to the disaster. I was mortified. I turned quickly to scoot out the door, slipped in the vomit, and fell back first onto the floor.

I came to with the head nurse hovering over me and Sarah right at her side.

"Are you okay, Ruth?" Sarah asked.

"What the devil happened?" the head nurse demanded.

"I . . . I slipped." I tried to sit up.

"Easy does it, Ruth," Sarah ordered.

I could feel the vomit seeping through my hair into my scalp.

"I think we should have her checked out," Sarah said.

"I think she just needs a shower," the head nurse snorted.

"No, we definitely need to have a doctor look at her," Sarah insisted.

The head nurse looked at her crossly.

"She's pregnant," Sarah explained.

"Ugh, Sarah!"

"Sorry, sis," the head nurse said, shrugging. "She was right to tell me. Let's get you to a room."

Sarah helped me into a shower and had a change of scrubs ready for me when I got out.

"Did someone check in on that sailor? I feel bad we just left him," I asked while redressing in a fresh new uniform.

"He's fine. It's covered," Sarah assured.

Dr. Albright examined me. I wasn't cramping, and there was no bleeding, so he sent me home to bed.

I couldn't sleep on my stomach anymore; it was too uncomfortable, and I worried about hurting the baby. I chose to sleep on my back most of the time, although that was getting uncomfortable too. The weight of the baby squished me. It made it hard to breathe, but I wasn't ready to give up that position just yet. I hated sleeping on my side, and the day was soon coming that the side would be the only bearable sleeping position. So I lay on my back and propped up on three pillows, with a light comforter over me. I closed my eyes, preparing to enjoy my favorite part of the day, and let myself drift peacefully off to sleep. Just moments later, I was asleep, dreaming of William and life without the navy, a life where it was just me, him, and our soon-to-be child.

Shortly after falling asleep, I felt myself rising back to consciousness. I heard a rustling in what felt like the distance, followed by weight on the bed. A warm hand on my belly jerked me instantly out of sleep, and I grabbed defensively for the hand on my stomach.

"William!" I whispered, relieved. William was perched above me, in the flesh, the same dazzling smile and piercing blue eyes, only they were more beautiful than I remembered.

"Ruth." He exhaled. He kissed me sweetly before he lifted my shirt and kissed my belly.

I placed both hands on the side of his face and lifted his lips to my own. We kissed passionately. I missed his lips. I had forgotten how soft they were, how good he smelled, and how comfortable I felt wrapped in his arms. I flung my arms around his neck, and I cried tears of pure ecstasy and happiness.

"You're here! You're finally here!" I exclaimed between kisses.

"I'm finally here," he said, relieved, in his warm, deep voice. I missed his voice. He slipped between the covers with me, and that was where we stayed until late the next morning, holding each other tightly.

"It must be nearly noon," I said, snuggled next to him.

"I don't have anywhere to go, do you?" Will asked with his familiar grin.

"No." I giggled. "I don't have anywhere to be." William was rubbing my ever-growing naked belly. "I think it gets bigger every day," I moaned, embarrassed.

"It's beautiful. You're beautiful, prettier than I remembered." The baby rolled inside me. I looked from my stomach to William, wondering if he felt it. William had the silliest grin I'd ever seen. "Did you feel that?" he asked excitedly. "It moved! There is something inside there!"

"Yes, of course, I felt it. Apparently, you did too." I laughed. I was so glad he could share this wonder with me.

"That is amazing," he observed. Just then, the baby kicked me hard in the side. "Wow! Did it just kick you?" All I could do was laugh and nod.

"I'm a little worried. It's a strong little thing," I said after the laughter faded.

"Auntie said I shouldn't expect him to come until the end of September. Just imagine how hard he will kick then! Just imagine how big I will be then."

William's smile slowly disappeared. "And I will miss it all," he said.

"Oh, why did you have to bring that up?" I said, trying to tease, but my voice was at the edge of tears.

William moved his hand to my face. "I'm so sorry I have to leave again. If there were any way I could avoid it, I would . . ."

"I know," I said. "This is the way it has to be." I swallowed hard. "Let's just make the best of the time we have." I smiled weakly. "I'm glad you are here with me now."

"Me too. And I will be back in December, and I won't have to leave again." We kissed again and wiped each other's tears, both vowing not to dwell on his impending departure.

Just as expected, the week flew by. We eased back into our familiar lazy schedule sleeping in, lounging on the couch, taking long showers, and soaking in our blue front yard. Surfing was off the schedule, my belly was just too big, so we settled for swimming, snorkeling, and walking on the beach, if they were possible. I fell in love with him more each passing day. My tummy alone was entertainment enough for the both of us; watching the baby move and kick inside me offered us hours of delight. It was like he had never left. I loved him even more than before. He was the missing part of me. Any doubt I ever had was completely gone. I had made the right choice.

On Wednesday, we joined the other officers and wives for dinner at the captain's house. Ginny was the most gracious host, greeting us at the door. She showed me right to a chair, which I was very grateful for. I sat next to Elaina and doted on her baby. Theresa was, of course, there as well as Elaina. The boys gathered and sat on the other side of the room. The mood was very light and that of a joyous job well done. They were laughing and sharing funny stories of the new recruits. William beamed with pride whenever the topic of our upcoming baby came up. He eventually joined me by standing behind my chair, resting a hand on my shoulder.

"Well, I'm afraid this is the end of our glorious leadership," the captain announced as we sat around the table. "Let us make a toast. Raise your glasses. To friendship, comradery, and seasick sailors. It's been an honor to serve with you. Cheers."

Our glasses clinked together. I was a little sad to see this chapter of William's life come to a close.

"Will there be someone replacing William?" I asked.

"Oh, I'm sure," declared the skipper. "There will be one for us all. That is who we are training next week."

I was puzzled.

"Did ol' Will not tell you?" Theodor asked.

"It just never came up," William said. I thought I saw a hint of pink flush on his cheek.

"Been a little preoccupied, boy?" Edward said with the first smile I'd ever seen on his face.

"Theodor has retired as well," the captain explained, "wants to stay home with his new baby." Theodor gave Elaina a little squeeze. "Edward is moving back to the mainland, and Commander Gibbons is being reassigned to the *Oklahoma*. We are going back to train our replacements, not as the commanders anymore."

The mood shifted to a little melancholy. It was the end of an era. I felt immediately sad for them.

"I won't be going back," Gibbons explained. "I already started on the *Oklahoma*, and boy is my work cut out for me!"

"A change in command is always difficult," Theodor said. "Your boys will adjust."

"I can't wait to go back to the mainland," Theresa said. "I have to wait until Edward is reassigned, though, so after they are done training." She rolled her eyes.

I nodded.

"So we are all still on hold until you are done with this last training?"

The whole table nodded.

"But it won't be the same," the skipper explained. "We will have to step back, let the new command learn and make mistakes. It may be the most difficult mission we've been on!" The skipper laughed.

"That is the truth!" William chuckled.

We stayed a half hour longer before parting ways and going back to our home. The men, minus Commander Gibbons, would be back to work in just a few days.

On the last full day with William, I stood at the end of the bed dressing while William watched. "I think your stomach has grown since I got here last week."

I looked down at my bare tummy protruding over my pants. "Things are starting to get a little tight too," I said, pulling my shirt over my head and stretching it over my stomach. "I'm wearing trousers today just because I think it might be the last time I can wear them."

"Do you need to buy some more clothes?" he asked.

"I don't know. My dresses should cover me most of the time. How big do you think I will get?"

William laughed, got out of bed, and walked over to me. "I think that you might need a few new dresses just in case. Let's do something crazy and leave the house. We can go shopping. At least buy you a new swimming suit. I've noticed you need a new one of those already."

"Leave?" I asked and smiled, wrapping my arms around his neck. "I don't know if I can leave and share you with other people."

"Just a quick trip. It could be fun," he said, smiling.

"Okay. It might be nice to get out for a minute," I admitted.

William dressed, and we drove to the market. It was nice to be out in public. I held onto William's arm and smiled and nodded to everyone we passed. I was enjoying it more than I thought. The last few weeks, people were noticing my pregnant belly, and I was happy to have a husband on my arm. We mingled around the farmers market and bought some fruit before going into Auntie's shop.

Auntie Gwen was delighted to see us, raving about her surprise the minute we stepped through the door. William bought me two cute dresses. They were roomy but not too unflattering. We also bought a swimming suit and fabric for me to make another dress. "In case you grow even bigger than the new dresses," William said. It was fun to shop with him and let him spoil me. I've never been able to go to a store and shop like this. We made almost all our clothes growing up, only buying a new outfit for special occasions. I could tell William felt better knowing he was taking care of me and helping me when he couldn't be here for the coming months.

On the way back, we passed Kekoa, who was unloading a cart for one of the marketers. He looked at us for just a moment, long enough for William to nod. Kekoa nodded slightly before diverting his eyes. I instinctively covered my belly. It was such an "in your face" reminder of the pain I caused him.

"Have you seen much of him?" William asked casually.

"No, not at all." I sighed regretfully. William squeezed my hand.

"I'm sorry," he said.

I shrugged. What could I do about it? I had already spent so many hours fretting about a problem I could not fix.

We went home and unpacked my new treasures, and I thanked William for buying them for me. We didn't leave the house until noon the next day when he was scheduled to depart. Our goodbye was much the same as six months before. He said goodbye in the parking lot, I choked back the impending sobs, we kissed and held onto each other as long as we could, but this time he leaned down and kissed my belly goodbye too.

"I love you, Ruth," he said, resting his forehead on mine. "I'm so sorry I have to leave." I nodded; I was unable to say anything through my silent tears. "Please take care of yourself and the baby and call me when you have her." William always called the baby her, while I called it he. "I don't care what it costs. Do you understand?" I nodded again. He handed me a paper with the base's phone number on it. "You can call me before you have her too if you need. Don't be shy. I'd pay $1,000 to talk to you for one minute."

"I'll call, William. I'll write too. Don't worry, everything will be fine. I'm in good hands here with Mom and Auntie, and I pray every night for you, for me, and for the baby."

We kissed one last time before walking him down the dock. He waved to me before disappearing through the ship's door, just like last time. I stood frozen, waving goodbye to my husband again; my heart was heavy and stomach sick. Alone and pregnant—just what I never wanted, yet under it all, I was happy.

Even though the goodbye was just as hard as the first one, the empty house was easier to get used to. I slipped back into my usual solo routine, only work replaced school. I picked up some day shifts at the big pink hospital on the hill. It was nice making a little money, though we didn't really need it. I wasn't under the stewardship of Nurse Turner anymore, which was nice. I was able to live almost entirely off my earnings and save most of William's. It was a lonely but busy way to live.

June 26, 1941
Ruth,

I only just left you, and I can't mail this until we make port in a week, but I can't stop thinking about the way I left you standing on the dock big with our child. I can't express the depth of my heartbreak, that I am here, and you are there. I know this is hard for you as well. Please stay strong, stay healthy, and we will be together again soon.

Love,
William

July 15, 1941
William,

Hello, my love. I hope you are well. Thank you for your sweet letter. I promise I'm staying strong and keeping healthy. We will be together soon. That is all I have to hold onto now, hope for our future. It's what gets me out of bed in the morning and keeps me going all day long. I feel like our future is growing in my belly, and I dream of the days when the three of us are together again.

I've been working at the hospital full time. It's keeping me busy but is downright exhausting. I'm big now and can barely squeeze into my nurse's uniform. My pregnancy is obvious to everyone who sees me. The other nurses are kind and try to help me out when they can and encourage me to sit down a lot. I feel guilty for not doing my share, so I push myself harder than I should. Auntie says I probably only have two months left. I can't believe I have that long. I can't imagine the baby growing any bigger. I will try and work up until delivery, not because we need the money but because I need the distraction. It is not good for me to be idle. When I sit around the house with nothing to do, I think of you, and my heart aches. It is best when I come home tired and go to sleep right away and wake up and repeat the process.

Stay busy. Work hard. We will be together soon.

All my love,
Ruth

Most days, Daddy took me to and from work. I was just too big to walk all the time, and the heat was torture. I wanted to rip my skin off. I had never been so hot in my life. I constantly wiped beads of sweat off my forehead, and my lower back was always sticky and sweaty. I could feel the sweat rolling down my back and settling in the puddle of my low back. And night was the worst. As if wrestling with a huge belly while trying to sleep was bad enough, the heat made it completely unbearable. I despised sheets and blankets. I woke up several times in the middle of the night in a puddle of my own sticky sweat, my hips and back aching.

I visited Auntie and Nohea at their house for my usual two-week checkup.

"Ahh, Ruth, how are you, my dear?"

"Auntie, I am miserable," I whined as I kissed her cheek. "I wish I could bear this more gracefully, but I just can't!"

"Oh, Ruth," Nohea greeted, joining us in the living room. "Lie down here. I will fan you."

Nohea fanned my face and neck, while Auntie examined my enormous belly.

"You are huge, Ruth!" Nohea giggled. "This makes me want to rethink having children."

"You're not helping," Auntie intervened dryly. She was measuring my stomach. "You are measuring unusually large. You are extremely hapū."

"Tell me something I don't know." I sighed.

"It iz a good thing. You are growing a beautiful baby, Ruth dear. Big is healthy."

Nohea's father offered to drive me home. I refused. I was happy to walk today, and it wasn't far. Auntie said it was good for the baby and would encourage labor. I waddled down the hill toward town. A group of freshly cut sailors were huddled together at the base of the hill. I hardly paid them any mind except one darker sailor caught my eye enough to make me take a second look.

"Kekoa?" He didn't move. "Kekoa!" I yelled it this time. He turned away and tried to disappear through the crowd. I started running. I had to hold my belly as I ran. The bouncing pulled at my strained stomach muscles.

"Kekoa, stop!" I ordered. He kept walking away, weaving through the other sailors.

"Please!" I begged. "Please, Kekoa, stop!" I cried. "Don't do this to a pregnant lady!" I demanded.

He halted, but he didn't turn around. "Why are you making me run after you?" I asked when I finally caught up to him. I was panting.

He turned around slowly.

"Why do you insist on catching me?" he asked dryly.

"You cut your hair! I hardly recognized you. What have you done?" I scanned him up and down. "You joined the navy? What on earth would possess you to do a thing like that?"

"Why does it matter to you?"

"Why would it not! How dare you assume!" I was astonished that he would behave so curtly.

"I am not your concern anymore. Iz been gone for a month training, and youz didn't even know I waz gone! Isn't this what you like anyway?" He motioned to his uniform.

"What? No, I like you the way you are. Why would you do this?" I was near tears.

He looked down at my enormous belly; a wave of sadness darkened his face.

"Ruth, go home. Have your baby. Live your life. Don't worry about me. I have my reasons for joining. I wanted to do it," he said resolutely.

I was so confused but nodded numbly.

"I just never thought you . . . What ship are you on?"

"I'm serving on the USS *Arizona*. I'm very excited about it. It gives me a sense of pride." I didn't believe a word he said.

"Well, good luck."

Why couldn't I think of something better to say? My heart broke as I looked at him. Where had my precious Kekoa gone? I reached for him and hugged him awkwardly over my belly. I pulled him in tightly. At first, he remained stiff and did not move. And then he ever so slightly raised his arms and hugged me back. I kissed his cheek. It still felt like Kekoa's soft cheek.

"Goodbye, Ruth," he whispered in my ear and pushed me away.

He tipped his hat, turned around, and left—again.

I walked home sad, confused, and alone.

> *August 3, 1941*
> *Ruth,*
>
> *Hello, my angel. I'm always so happy to get a letter from you. It brightens my whole day. I find myself eyeing telephones on the rare occasions when I walk by, and I want to call you just to hear your voice. Phone calls are strictly limited to emergencies only. If it weren't for that, I would have called you a hundred times by now.*
>
> *I worry about you working so late in the pregnancy. Are you sure that is safe? I understand the need to be busy, but please be careful. Work is going well, better than last time. I'm training the trainer, which is enjoyable for me and something new. The men I am working with are good men. They love their country and work hard. I am busy, which helps me as well. The guys like to go out at night for a drink. I've joined them a few times, but I find most of the conversation juvenile and boring. The skipper, Edward, Theodor, and I usually stay back and spend the evening*

together. Edward is getting increasingly intolerable. I miss our late night conversations, and you are much prettier to look at than any of the boys. When I close my eyes at night, I see your sweet smiling face, I dream of you and the baby all night, and you are the first thing I think about when I open my eyes in the morning.

Take care, my love. I will see you soon.

Love,
William

August 29, 1941
William,

Thank you for worrying about me. Please trust that I am taking care of us. I've cut back my hours and only work a few days a week. It's more downtime than I want, so I spend it with my mom or Nohea and Elsie. I am very heavy now. I can only wear the few dresses you bought me, and I'm working on making another dress out of the fabric we bought together. It's very crowded inside me, and I have a feeling I'm not the only who feels this way. I can barely breathe. The baby moves less. Auntie says that is normal because the baby is running out of room. Anytime he stretches or moves an elbow, my whole stomach moves. His feet kick my ribs, and his whole body pushes down, and it feels like he is going to push his way right out of me. Sometimes when he kicks against my side, I grab his foot and push back. It's a fun game we play but pretty uncomfortable for me. It's getting harder to breathe, and I feel like my insides are all mixed up. Sleeping is horrible. I toss and turn all night. My back and hips hurt. The heat has never really bothered me until now. I hate clothing. It's hot and sweaty, and I feel like I'm on fire. Sometimes I wish I could crawl out of my skin.

I tell you things not so you feel bad or sorry for me. I just want you to feel a part of it and know what is going on. It's fun to feel the baby growing and moving inside of me, but I will be glad when it is over. I miss you, but sometimes I am glad you don't have to see me getting so large. I don't feel pretty. I hope I lose all the weight by the time you are home.

I'm glad you are busy. I miss you as well. You know that you are all I think about. I try to control my thoughts, but it is hard. Every day we are closer to our reunion. Stay strong. It won't be long.

All my love,
Ruth

I hoped my letter wouldn't upset William. I really wanted him to feel like he was a part of the pregnancy. If he were with me, he would be hearing me complain about those things every day. I was anxious and worried about the delivery, but I omitted that from the letter. The one thing that trumped my thoughts of William was worries of the baby's arrival. Auntie helped ease my concerns and practiced relaxation techniques with me, but that didn't take the worry away. Fear of the unknown was always upsetting to me.

19

August ended, and September began. The baby grew more each day. My stomach stretched to an unbelievable circumference. The human body truly is amazing. When September ended, and I was still pregnant, I thought I would lose my mind. Auntie came over the first of October to prepare my house. She brought blankets and towels, a bucket, and a few other things.

"I thought you said the end of September, Auntie! I've been pregnant for more than nine months! I think the baby is going to walk out of me soon."

"Be patient. You won't be hapū forever. The baby knows the right time. We must wait for him to decide when to come," she assured.

"But I can't stand it anymore! Isn't there anything you can do?" I begged.

"I thought you were nervous about the birth," she said with a wink.

"I am, but I would be willing to walk through fire to end this torture!"

Auntie laughed and rubbed my back. "It will be soon, love. Don't worry," she urged, and she left. She left me, and I was still pregnant. I was unbelievably frustrated. I cannot believe every person walking on the earth put some woman through this same torture. It's a miracle the human race isn't extinct because this is utterly brutal.

I spent most of the next day soaking in the ocean. The water cooled down my hot skin and relieved the stress on my back and hips. I floated on my back, calming my mind, and I swore to myself I wouldn't get out until the baby was born. I lay there for a couple of hours before I did get out. I dragged myself to the house and flopped on the bed, falling asleep instantly. I woke up the next morning as tired as I was when I lay down and mad that I was still pregnant. Every morning that I woke up still pregnant, I was disappointed. Was I ever going to have this baby?

I lay around the house most of the morning, considering going to Mom's house, but what would I do there? I would just feel guilty about my moping around. It was the third, William's birthday. I hadn't even written him a letter, wishing him happy birthday. I was so sure I would have had the baby and talk to him by now. It made me feel sad thinking about his birthday. I hoped somehow he was enjoying it.

By 1:00 p.m., I was back in bed, napping again, but woke up with a tightening feeling around my middle. It lasted about a minute and then subsided. I sat up so excited that this could be it. I felt another one a few minutes later and another a few minutes after that. I smiled and wandered around my house, not knowing what to do. Auntie said labor could last hours, even days. I knew this was just the beginning. They weren't painful yet, but they were consistent. I was scared with each passing contraction. I was worried that they would suddenly stop, but they didn't. They kept coming, each one stronger than the last. I didn't know what else to do, so I showered, hoping it would calm my nerves. By the time I got out, it was 5:00 p.m., and they were starting to get painful. I closed my eyes and breathed deeply with each contraction as they came. It wasn't anything unbearable, but each contraction seemed slightly more painful than the last.

I called Auntie to inform her that I thought it was starting. She said she would come over tonight after she put her kids to bed but to call her if things started to progress quickly. I didn't expect her to come over right away, but I was disappointed nonetheless, so I called Mom. She was more excited than Auntie and said she would hop a ride with her when she came in a few hours.

I was still alone. I wanted to call William. I stared at the phone, contemplating picking it up. I found the number he gave me and put it next to the phone. I wondered if it would be okay to call him. I knew he would like to hear from me, but would it be wise? I decided to write him a letter instead.

I squatted down by the bedside to get a pencil and paper out of the bottom shelf of the end table. When I was reaching forward, I heard a distinct "POP!" I stood quickly. Water gushed down my legs, creating a puddle on the floor. It scared me at first, it made me jump, before I realized what it was. More water oozed out. My bag of water had definitely broken. I did a little happy dance. I was really in labor now, and I mentally prepared for the contractions to get harder. Auntie said after my bag broke, they would increase in intensity. I didn't abandon the letter writing. After getting a towel and cleaning up the puddle, I sat at the table to attend to the letter, thinking it would work as a great distraction.

October 3, 1941
Dearest William,

Happy bir

I stopped, letting the next contraction wash over me. It was more intense than the last. I went back to the letter when it passed, just to be stopped after a few lines. I braced myself, grabbing the edge of the table. The next contraction hit before I was able to write any more.

And then another contraction started, tightening around my abdomen. The intensity of it increased far beyond any others before. I dropped my pencil and rested my head back while I waited for it to pass. The next and the next one came almost back-to-back, giving me little rest. I stood, abandoned the letter altogether, and started walking back to the bed, but another contraction hit before getting there. I stood in place, my hands supporting the small of my back, and rocked side to side, waiting for it to pass, but it kept increasing. My whole body began to shake, and I dropped to my hands and knees. That position felt a little more bearable. I breathed heavy and deep, trying to stay calm, but I had the overwhelming desire to rip my skin off and run screaming from my body. Once it finally ended, I frantically grabbed the phone and dialed Auntie's number.

"Come now, please! I'm scared!" I was barely able to utter the words before another wave tore through me.

"Aghhhhh!" I hollered. "Auntie, please hurry!" It was the most desperate plea I had ever made in my whole entire life. I wanted to yell "I'm going to die! Don't let me die alone!" but I couldn't utter another word. I just clutch my stomach and slumped against a chair leg.

Auntie assured me she was out the door and would be here in ten minutes. I hung up the phone, telling myself, "Only ten minutes, just ten minutes! That's probably three contractions." My hands shook with panic, and my mind entertained horrible thoughts. If labor lasted hours, even days, I would surely die. There is no way a person could endure this pain for much longer, and each contraction was worse than the one before. At the start of each contraction, I braced myself for the momentous task ahead of me. I forced the ugly thoughts out and replaced them with positive ones. "Just focus on breathing through this one, Ruth," I said it out loud as another started. I breathed deep and heavy. Each breath was heavier than the last as the contraction built in intensity. "Breathe out the pain!" I pleaded with myself. I was on my knees with my arms and head resting on the chair near the bed. I hadn't moved but a few feet since I made the phone call. I gripped the back of the chair as my body writhed in the electric pain I was experiencing. I felt the sudden urge to puke but forced with all my might to keep it down, fearing I would literally explode with the added pressure of vomiting.

I let out a loud yell as finally, the pressure crushing my middle started releasing and Mom and Auntie were at my side. I didn't hear them enter but threw my arms around Mom as she knelt beside me. I let an exasperated sob.

"Mom!" I blubbered.

"I'm here, darling." She brushed the hair off my face. "You're okay. I'm here. We can do this together," she encouraged me.

"No, I can't!" I tried to explain to her that this was the most desperate of all situations and that I surely was going to die.

"No, honey," she said firmly. "You can do this, and you will," she ordered.

She said it so firmly and convincingly I almost believed her.

They helped me move to the bed, but after one contraction lying down, I insisted on sitting up. I felt exposed and at the mercy of the birthing pains lying flat on my back, so I sat at the edge of my bed, my back in a C curve, resting on my mom's shoulder as she sat on a chair in front of me. I was barely aware of Auntie as she bustled around the room, gathering linens and other items. I heard her say, "This will be a quick one. She is nearly there." I was relieved to hear this. The thought of this horror lasting for hours was enough for me to want to give up the ghost.

I hid my shoulder in my mother's neck.

"Another wave is coming," I heard Auntie say, and this time she sat behind me, rubbing my back. "You can do it, Ruth. With each wave, you get a little closer. Your baby is almost here."

Baby? What baby? I thought. I didn't care about a baby anymore. All I wanted was for this torture to end.

"Breathe low and deep, Ruth," she instructed.

I exhaled low and deep just as she said. It did help. I sounded very primal as I moaned, and I suddenly felt relieved William wasn't there. I was glad he didn't have to see me like this. When the wave ended, I insisted on a new position. Mom's shoulder was too poky, and I was afraid I wouldn't be able to resist the urge to bite her next time.

Auntie put some pillows at the side of the bed for me to kneel on, and I rested my upper body and head on the bed. Mom knelt behind me and rubbed my back. Another contraction started. My whole body reacted to the pain. Not just one part of me hurt, but all of me hurt; my whole body tensed up, surrounding my center, pressing raw power through my middle. Yet again, this one grew stronger than the previous. I breathed hard and tried to relax the rest of my body. The pain was so intense. I wanted to kick my legs, move my arms, run away. I wanted it to stop. Tighter and tighter, the pressure grew until I threw my head back and punched the bed, screaming. It didn't help. It felt worse. The pain intensified even greater. How was I ever going to get out of this alive?

When the contraction ended, I let my head rest on the bed, so exhausted I fell asleep for a moment. When the next wave started developing, I promised myself I would handle this one better. I exhaled low and deep, focusing on keeping my muscles relaxed. Tighter and tighter, the pain encircled me. I curved my body around my middle. I exhaled harder, focusing my energy under the baby, until at the peak of my contraction, I felt a gush of fluid, and the baby's head drop down the birthing canal. It was so alarming I stood straight, stooped over the bed.

"He's here! He's here!" I screamed.

"Lie on the bed, Ruth," Auntie said quickly.

"I can't! I can't move!" I didn't know what paralyzed me more, the pain or the shock of the baby's sudden move. "It's coming now!" I yelled again. I could literally feel the baby's head. It felt like it was going to drop right out of me.

Somehow in my paralyzed state, they helped me onto the bed. Mom sat behind me, so I was leaning on her while Auntie worked between my legs.

"Okay, darling, you're going to want to push before the next contraction comes. It will make tearing less likely. I see the baby's head. It should only take a few pushes. Come on. We're almost there."

I was scared to death to push. I wanted the baby out so bad, but I was scared to push it out.

"I can't push! It's going to hurt!" I wailed.

"Come on, we're almost there. Just one push," Auntie reassured.

With one last deep breath, I put my chin to my chest and pushed. Immediately, the head popped out, and after that, an army couldn't stop me from pushing. It felt so good. One push later, the baby slid out, and I was left with the most wonderful feeling—the absence of pain.

I let my head fall back onto my mother's chest and soaked in the pure ecstasy I was experiencing. There was no way to explain the joy I felt. It was over. It reminded me of the feeling when I was sick and finally threw up, that feeling of release and relief, only a billion times better.

Auntie placed a small wet weight on my chest. I looked down at the wonder in my arms and saw William's eyes looking up at me. It had the same look of dismay and awe as me.

"It's a girl," Auntie proclaimed quietly, rubbing her and wrapping a blanket over her.

She was beautiful. She didn't cry. Her wide deep blue eyes searched my face for answers. No doubt she was as exhausted and shocked by the last few hours. I gently rubbed the side of her face and smiled. I was crying, crying from the pain, from the shock, but mostly crying tears of joy at the miracle in my arms. It was hard to believe just moments earlier, I was writhing in pain, while now, I was flying high with pure ecstasy.

"Hi, baby," I cooed quietly.

Mom brushed back my sweat-soaked hair and replaced a pillow for her spot. And then jerking me out of my glorious happiness was yet another contraction and the urge to push again. I tensed under the pressure and arched my back.

"Why?" It was the only thing I could say through my tears. It didn't really hurt that bad; it was just the frustration of the recurring pain that made me cry. "I thought this was over!"

"It's just the placenta, Ruth," Auntie explained. "You have to push the placenta out, but don't worry, its nothing like the baby."

She was right. It wasn't near as bad as the birth but uncomfortable enough that I had to hand Mom the baby.

"You did great, dear," Auntie said while cleaning up. "Only a small tear. It will heal nicely."

Mom wiped the baby down while I waited anxiously for her to hand her back to me. Once she was in my arms, again, I gazed with wild wonder at her. I studied her face, her hands, her toes. She was gloriously perfect.

"I can't believe she came out of me," I said in amazement.

"It's a miracle that never gets old," Mom said, sitting next to me and staring at the baby too.

"Isn't she supposed to cry?" I asked.

"She's just fine. She doesn't have to cry. She is probably just a content baby and is a little shocked by her experience," Auntie explained. "She looks wonderful. Shall we weigh her?"

Reluctantly, I put the baby in Auntie's arms. Auntie had a small scale that weighed the baby by hanging it in a wrapped cloth.

"She weighs seven pounds and three ounces," she announced. "A big beautiful baby. She will be hungry soon, Ruth." She gave the baby back, and I continued staring at her.

"What time is it?" I asked.

"It's 10:00 p.m.," Mom said.

"It's 1:00 a.m. in California. Can I call him?" I asked.

"He would want you to. There is someone on base who will answer and wake him." Mom pulled the phone as far as it would reach to my bedside and dialed the number I had set out. She asked for William and explained the reason for the call. She waited a moment and then hung up.

"Someone is waking William. He will call back in a little bit. You probably have time to shower if you'd like, and then you can feed the baby when you get out."

"Can I walk?" I asked seriously, doubting my abilities to get to the shower.

"We will help you," Mom said. I looked down at the baby. Her eyes were closed now, sleeping.

"She will be okay," Auntie said. "I'll clean her up while you are in the shower. Your mom will help you shower."

I set the baby on the bed for a minute and gingerly swung my legs over the side. Mom and Auntie both took an arm and helped me to my feet. I was surprised I was able to stand at all. We made slow progress to the shower. It was always a little strange showering outside in the dark. This time I was kind of glad for the dark so I couldn't see the blood running down my legs. I showered quickly, eager to get back to the baby and wait for William's call. Mom helped me dry off and slip a nightdress over my head. By the time I was dressed, Auntie had new sheets on the bed and the baby wrapped in a clean white blanket.

I settled in between the covers on my bed, feeling overwhelmed with the pleasure of sitting, and held my arms out for the baby. Auntie helped me attach her so she could nurse. It was strange and wonderful all at the same time. She was hungry. She ate like mad until she fell asleep from exhaustion. I wanted to lay my head back and do the same, but my desire to talk to William was greater.

Auntie finished cleaning up, kissed my cheek, and took her leave. Mom crawled in bed next to me. She said she would stay a few days. I was so grateful for her presence. I looked at her with clearer eyes in that moment, knowing that just twenty-one years ago, she performed the same momentous task to bring me into the world.

"I can't believe you did that four times, Mom. I don't ever want to do that again," I admitted.

Mom chuckled. "Oh, you'll forget. Your desire to have another will overpower your memory."

I smiled. I really doubted that.

"Thank you, Mom. I never realized . . ." I couldn't finish my sentence because the phone rang. I shifted quickly, wanting to answer, before Mom stopped me and got it herself. She answered politely before handing it to me.

"William!" I said excitedly.

"Ruth." His deep, clear voice was shaky with a layer of sleepiness.

"Happy birthday! You're a daddy!" I said with tears flowing freely down my cheeks.

"Ruth," he said again, this time with a sigh of relief. "How . . . how are you?" he asked tentatively. I could picture William clearly with sleepy eyes wearing his undershirt and trousers, sitting on an uncomfortable office chair in a dark sleeping office on base.

"I'm well, William. We are both doing well." As if on cue, she let out a squeal, followed by a soft cry. I shushed her softly.

"That's her!" William realized. His voice was shaking. I wondered if he was crying. I had never heard him sound quite like this.

"Yes, that is her. She is beautiful, Will. She has your striking blue eyes and cute nose. She has a full head of brown hair like mine. I've been staring at her for an hour now, trying to determine who she looks most like, but I can't tell. She looks like a combination of the two of us."

"That is wonderful, Ruth!" His voice was quiet. I didn't know what I expected him to say, but I waited for something.

"Are you okay, Will?" I asked.

"I'm great. I'm just speechless. I'm so glad to hear your voice. I've been very worried the last few weeks. Did . . . did the delivery go okay?"

I wasn't ready to talk about that yet, and I wasn't sure I ever wanted to tell Will how hard it was.

"It went well. It was fast, but we both did good." I paused. He was my husband; I should share more with him. "It was hard, Will," I said. "Not something I want to do again anytime soon." I laughed. I heard him chuckle too. "But it was worth it. She is perfect. I wish you were here to see her."

"I wish I were there too. Are you feeling okay?" he asked. He was sounding less sleepy.

"I feel fantastic right now compared to an hour ago." I laughed again. "But I am tired. Mom is staying with me for a few days to help me out."

"I'm glad. Be sure to thank her for me," he said.

"I will." I smiled.

"Should I let you go so you can sleep?" he asked.

"Heavens, no!" I said quickly. "I would stay up all night talking to you if I could. If you are tired, though, you can get off the phone."

Will just laughed. "Believe me, I won't be doing any sleeping for the rest of the night." I laughed too. "So what should we name the little bundle?" he asked.

"I don't know. I was going to ask you. I would like to give her a Hawaiian middle name if that is okay with you."

"That is a fantastic idea." There was another small pause. "I would like to name her after my sister."

"Dorothy?" I asked.

"No, Nora. She died when she was just a little over a year old. She got really sick the summer I was nine and died a few weeks later."

I waited a moment, listening curiously to the silence on the other line.

"I loved her," he explained quietly. "She was my little princess. I would like to name the baby Nora if you think the name is acceptable. You can give her any middle name you would like. What do you think?"

"I never heard about your sister," I said quietly. "I would love to name her Nora. That is a beautiful name." I studied the tiny face in my arms. "She looks like a Nora too." I thought a minute. "I would like her middle name to be Halia. It means sudden remembrance or to remember a loved one. I've been researching Hawaiian names," I explained.

"Nora Halia Wellington. It sounds beautiful, Ruth. I like it," he said.

We spoke for another twenty minutes or so. Not about anything in particular. He sounded a million miles away, but it was so nice to hear his voice and share this tender moment with him. I wiped the tears off my cheeks and swallowed back a sob. We both knew it was time to get off the phone, but I couldn't bear to say the words.

"I love you, William," I said quietly. Mom shifted next to me in bed, still trying to give me privacy.

"Ruth, I love you more than life itself." William cleared his throat. "Ruth . . . I miss you, and I'm sorry I'm not there with you. My absence isn't just hurting you anymore. It's hurting both of you. I'm sorry I'm not there . . ."

"Will, you will be here soon." I wanted to stop him. I could hear the pain in his voice. I wished I could make him feel better. "William, it's going to be okay. You're not the first father to miss his child's birth. You will be home soon. She will still be little, and she won't even know you we're gone."

"I know," he conceded. Silence followed. "I know I'm not the first father to miss the birth of his baby, but I never wanted to be this father." He cleared his throat again. This time I knew he was crying. "I'm so glad you are both well. I can't wait to meet her."

"It won't be long, Will. You will be home soon," I reassured him. "We are going to be fine. I promise to take care of her."

"Take care of yourself too, Ruth. I need you both," he urged.

We held on for a few silent moments before uttering a tearful goodbye. I hung up the phone slowly and sunk down in the bed, putting Nora between me and Mom. Mom rolled over and scooted closer to me and the baby, wrapping her arms around us, holding me while I cried. I cried myself into a deep sleep, only to be woken a few hours later by a whimpering baby. I was so tired the crying confused and disoriented me. I wasn't sure where I was, what was going on, or even what time it was. In the dark, I couldn't find the source of the noise. Mom calmly sat up in the bed and picked the baby, holding it against her chest.

"Ruth, Ruth, wake up, sweetie. The baby is hungry," she whispered.

I sat up and took Nora from her and attached her to my breast. I fell asleep a few minutes later. Mom woke me up when it was time to switch sides and then again when it was time to lay her back down. We repeated the same routine twice again that night and late into the morning. At eleven o'clock, Mom woke me up to eat breakfast. I sat in bed scarfing the delicious eggs and toast while Nora slept beside me. I couldn't remember a time when I'd been so hungry.

"Mom, this is delicious," I proclaimed between mouthfuls. Mom was in the kitchen, cleaning up. She laughed at my remark.

"Thank you, but I think you're just really hungry. You worked hard last night, and nursing tends to deplete you pretty fast."

"Mom, I'm really glad you are here. I don't know what I would do without you," I said, feeling so grateful. Mom wore a knowing, prideful smile.

"It's my pleasure, sweetheart."

Nora started fussing next. Mom walked over and picked her before I had a chance to get to her. "Finish your breakfast. Nori can wait."

"Nori?" I said, surprised.

"Yeah, don't you think it's a cute nickname?"

"Yeah, I do." I smiled thinking about it.

"Do you want me to go pick up a bassinet for the baby to sleep in?" Mom asked.

"Hmm." I thought a minute. "I hadn't even thought of that. I kind of like her sleeping with me," I acknowledged.

Mom and I had already bought blankets, diapers, and a few outfits for the baby, but I hadn't thought of anything else.

"I know, but there will be a time when you will want her to have her own spot. It's good for the baby too. Now that we know it's a girl, we should get some girly outfits. Maybe I'll run to town and buy some fabric for a dress." I laughed.

"I think she is a little small for a dress. All she really needs is some shirts and diapers, Mom."

"Oh, every little girl needs a dress," Mom said, doting on the infant in her arms.

Mom went out later that afternoon to buy groceries, leaving me and Nora alone. We managed just fine, but it was strange, just the two of us. We slept most of the time. I was still exhausted. I didn't think I was ever going to feel rested again. Mom returned a few hours later with Dad, groceries, and baby clothes.

"Oh, Mom, you didn't have to do that," I said when she held up the cutest pink bonnet I'd ever seen.

"Oh, I wanted to," Mom confirmed, smiling.

"I love it. But next time, I insist you let us buy it. William wants to feel like he is helping, and finances is the only way he can right now."

Daddy came in carrying a bag of groceries.

"Hi, Daddy!" I called excitedly from my bed. I was really happy to see him.

"Hey, darling. How are you?" Dad put the bags down on the table and walked over to my bedside. "Let me see this beauty," he said, sitting and holding out his arms. I picked Nora and handed her gently to him. Daddy folded her gingerly into his arms, cradling her against his chest. He looked natural and comfortable sitting there holding the tiny infant. "Oh, Ruthy, she looks a lot like you did as a baby." Daddy's smile grew bigger, and he looked over the moon with happiness. "Mom says her name is Nora?"

"Yes. We named her after William's late sister."

"It's a beautiful name. She looks like a Nora too. How are you feeling, sweetie?" he asked, not taking his eyes off Nora.

"I'm good, Daddy. Just tired," I admitted while watching him hold my daughter. Daddy reached out and squeezed my hand.

"What do you think about being a mom?" he asked. I thought a minute.

"It's pretty overwhelming, Daddy. I love it! But I'm feeling the weight of responsibility," I answered honestly.

"It's pretty big, isn't?"

"Yeah. This is big," I said.

I'd been feeling the weight of the responsibility of another human depending on me all day. I felt it most during the hours Mom was gone. It was just me right now. William was three thousand miles away across the Pacific. It was just me and Nora. My parents were here now, and they would always support me, but this was my baby, my responsibility. I was in charge of raising this little girl, teaching her, protecting her, feeding her, comforting her. I was all alone.

20

October 10, 1941
William,

 It's an amazing thing. Every day Nora changes a little bit. Her face is filling out. She spends a few more minutes of the day with her eyes open, but her sleeping pattern at night has yet to improve. I can stare at her for hours, and it amazes me that we created her. I can't believe she was inside of me! She is such a miracle. She sleeps for a couple of hours before waking up, wanting to be fed. It's exhausting, but luckily, I don't have much else to do. I catch up on my sleep at strange hours during the day. Mom stayed with me for six days. She was only going to stay five, but I begged her to stay one more. She said it was good for me for her to leave and that she would check on me every day, and she has. She always brings groceries with her when she visits, and she runs errands for me, getting me diapers and clothing for the baby. I insist that she uses our money when she shops for Nora. Mom has taken to calling her Nori, which I think is really cute. Before I had Nori, I thought I would go back to work, but I don't know if I can now. I don't think I could bear to leave her, even with Mom. She is my life. Every minute of every day revolves around her. Is she hungry, is she tired, does she need her diaper changed? Those are my thoughts when I'm not thinking of you, but usually, my thoughts of you and her are *intertwined. I can't look at her sweet face without thinking of you.*

I miss you terribly and wish you were here with me. I'm counting down the days until our reunion. I hope you are well and finding ways to focus on your work. I don't want us to be a distraction to you.

All our love,
Ruth and Nora

I barely had time to sign our names before Nori's squeal become so demanding I had to save her from the bed. I had hoped I would have time to write to Will and take a shower, but it appeared I would not have time for the latter. I scooped Nori up and plopped on the bed to feed her. I was still in my pajamas and hadn't fed myself yet, and it was after 10:00 a.m.

"Oh, Ms. Nori, will you ever sleep long enough for me to do anything? I can't even remember the last time I left the house."

I thought she might fall asleep after feeding her, but those little blue eyes popped right back open. I tied the blanket around my waist and tucked Nora in kangaroo style, and together, we walked out to the beach, me still in my nightgown. It felt so nice to be outside and feel the sand between my toes. I could see the very edge of Battleship Row. For a moment, I thought about Kekoa but pushed the thought back.

"Soon, you will meet your daddy, little one," I said to the little papoose swaddled around me.

"Ruth! Ruth!" My slightly frantic mother was calling from the house.

"I'm here!" I called back. "We're here!"

"You gave me a fright," Mom said as we joined her on the porch.

"Just went for a little walk, is all."

"Well, let me take Nori so you can get dressed." Mom laughed at me.

"Thanks, Mom." I chuckled and handed Nori over and took the most delightful shower of my life (second most, at least).

"How about we take the two of you up to the house?" Mom suggested once I was dressed.

"That sounds like a great idea," I agreed. "As long as I still get my nap."

"I think we can manage that," she offered.

"Ruth is here with the baby!" Marie shouted as we walked in the door.

"Hello, everyone!" I said.

"Ruthy! Bring that baby over here," Daddy directed with a smile, holding out his arms. I placed a sleeping Nori into Daddy's big arms, sat on the couch next to him, and rested my head on his shoulder.

"Don't hog the baby too long, Daddy." Elizabeth pouted. "We want a turn too."

"Ahh, wait your turn, silly girls," Daddy said firmly and then continued doting on Nori.

I closed my eyes and let the house swirl around me, and when I opened them, the room was just a bit darker, and it was just me and Daddy.

"Have you heard from him?" Daddy asked after I had been awake a few minutes.

"Not since we talked on the phone after having Nori."

"Hmmmm." He thought. "Well, I'm sure you are all he thinks about."

I nodded. "This is hard, Daddy. I was right to be scared of it before, you know, when I didn't know him and was afraid of men."

We both laughed.

"Yeah, it will be worth it, dear. I promise."

October 30, 1941
My dear Ruth,

> *I'm not going to lie. The news of Nora's birth distracted me greatly. I've been walking with an extra skip in my step since we talked. I understand why Theodor acted like such a goof when his son was born. I told all the boys that morning that Nora was born and showed everyone the small picture you sent of her. She looks beautiful. Just like a little angel. I think about you too every day. It is hard for me to focus on work. I think about how you are doing I try to picture what Nora looks like each day, but mostly, I dream about what it will be like when we are all together. I'm so proud of you*

handling all of this by yourself. Stay strong, be safe, and take care of my two little angels. I'll see you in December.

All my love,
William

I was sitting on my bed, feeding Nori, while I read his letter. She looked so much bigger than just a few weeks ago. Will was missing it. I knew he would, but watching it happen was so much more painful than I thought it would be. I had spent more time with Nori than I had with my husband. Things I knew would happen but still so hard to accept.

I laid the sleeping Nori down and picked a pen and paper. My shower would wait.

November 10, 1941
William,

> *I am feeling better. It's amazing what a month of recovery will do. I haven't started surfing again, but I'm hoping to next week. I took Nori for a dip in the ocean yesterday. She cried, she didn't really like it, but I'm sure she will come around. Mom still visits a lot, at least every other day. We visit her and Daddy several times a week. Daddy is so cute with her. He dotes over her and cuddles her every chance he can. Dad has offered several times to let us stay with them, but I like our cottage. It makes me feel closer to you. When I'm at my parents', sometimes it feels like you never existed. I sent a picture of her to your parents too. Your mom wrote back and thanked me for it.*

> *Nora still changes a little bit every day. She has a soft cry and a pretty voice. She wakes me up each morning with a beautiful cooing voice singing "la-las" and "fa-a-fas." It's beautiful and sweet. It melts my heart every time. December is only a month away. We look forward to your arrival.*

All our love,
Ruth and Nora

Nori and I dropped the letter off at the post on our way up to visit Elaina and Sarah to have a play date, but really, Nori was too small to play. She was passed from lap to lap around the room and doted on and kissed.

"Not too much longer, ladies. The boys will be back." Sarah abated after handing a hungry Nori back to me.

"I can't wait," I said, exasperated.

"Hang in there, Ruth." Elaina smiled. "We're almost there. And he's promised more than any of our husbands have. He quit the service as soon as he met you. If your husband hadn't quit, I think mine would still be in it. He wouldn't be retiring."

"Mine too," Sarah said. "We owe you a big thank-you. Our boys are coming home because of you."

"I never thought of that. I should be more grateful." I really should be. He was doing everything to be with us permanently.

> *November 18, 1941*
> *Ruth,*
>
> *I wish you could take a picture of every moment I'm missing. It saddens me. I feel like I've already missed so much. Things are winding down here. I'm confident in the men I've trained. They will carry on very successfully without me. I will be reassigned to Pearl Harbor, overseeing the training of new enlistees stationed on the island and free to live at home with you and Nora. We ship out tonight, and I expect to get in on the sixth. I won't be released for leave until the seventh. It won't be long now. We can count down the days of our reunion. I send you all my love. Kiss our daughter for me.*
>
> *William*

It had been a long five months, longer than any I've known before, but finally, at long last, the wait was almost over. The next few weeks I spent preparing for William's arrival. I wanted everything to be perfect. I bought a bassinet and blanket for Ruth and laid her down in it more and more often so by the time William was home, she would be comfortable sleeping by herself. As of lately, Nora had become really attached to me and didn't like it when anyone else held her. I feared she would be shy of William, so I took her to Mom and Dad's more often so she could get used to being held by other people. Daddy spoiled her and made the silliest faces I've even seen him make. I took her to Nohea's and Elsie's and down to the dance studio, where I used to teach. I even took her to the hospital once to meet some of my friends from school. It was hard to stick to it. I liked sleeping with her. I liked it that she only wanted me, but even more, I wanted her to accept her father. So I forced myself not to scoop her out of her bed and lay her next to me when I was lonely. I stood back when she cried and let Mom soothe her occasionally.

We spent more time on the beach. I dangled her toes in the surf, and we lay in the shade of the palm trees and played in the sand. Nora was still very young. She couldn't sit up yet, roll over, and do anything other than eat and sleep, but my life revolved around her. I was glad she was still so small. I didn't want William to miss any of those important milestones. Most mothers willed and pushed their babies to grow, but I had plenty of time to do that. Now I wanted to freeze her in this moment. The first day she smiled back at me when I changed her diaper, my heart broke. I laughed and cooed at her, so delighted to see her beautiful grin, but I hurt because William missed it. Not only did he miss it, but he also wouldn't be walking through the front door in the evening after work so I could recount her victory. I wanted someone to share her triumphs with who would be just as excited about them as I was. Soon, I would tell myself over and over, we will be together soon.

The days crept by slower and slower the closer to his arrival date, but I waded through each one until finally, the calendar flipped to the day of the sixth. Knowing he was on the island was like torture. I paced around the house, wiping and re-wiping every surface, straightening every shelf and cushion futilely, trying to occupy my mind with something, anything else. All day long, I wondered what he was doing. Was he in yet, was he back on the *St. Louis*, was he reporting back to the skipper, was he eating lunch, was he sleeping? On and on and on, the questions racked and tormented my mind until I fell into a restless sleep late into the night.

Nora woke me at four thirty, and I couldn't fall back asleep. It was a Sunday morning. William said he would be home today, but he hadn't said what time. How long would I torture myself until he finally arrived? Nora could sense my edginess. She was extra fussy. I had a hard time soothing her because I couldn't soothe myself. I showered while Nori slept because I had nothing else to do. The sun was still hiding under the water, and there was barely enough light to see. I dried off and dressed, giving up on sleep altogether. By seven thirty, I was outside, pulling my bike out of the shed. I tied Nora around me with a long blanket. She rested tightly against my chest, sleeping. Nora and I had traveled this way several times. We rode up to Mom and Dad's. They weren't home, of course. They had already left for church. I couldn't imagine sitting in a pew right now. I parked my bike in the shed and walked out to the old banyan tree. It was a little awkward to climb it with Nori tied to me, but I managed. Sitting on the old limb, I could see Battleship Row. I could see William's ship.

"Look, Nori! That ship wasn't there yesterday, and it is today! That's Daddy's!" I chirped. "Oh, Daddy, when will they release you?"

He was so close, so close.

We sat for several minutes, probably over a half hour, before I started thinking about climbing down. I hadn't made it off the first branch before the sound of a plane roared overhead in the direction of the base. I looked up to see what kind of plane it was, if it was taking off or landing on the airfield. The only thing I noticed about the plane was the rising sun emblem on the side of the rushing plane.

"The Japanese!" I said under my breath.

Instinctively, I pulled Nora close to my chest, just before my ears rang with the sounds of explosions. I stood motionless as the horrific scene played out before me. There wasn't just one Japanese plane; the air above was filled with the little devils. The sky was speckled with aircraft all soaring toward Battleship Row. We were under attack. The first row of planes dipped their wings and dropped what could only be bombs. No, it couldn't be a bomb! Right? And then a massive explosion followed. I was far enough away that I saw the fiery balls splash across the water and then heard the sound of the explosion that followed. And then one hit a battleship. The sound was deafening. The impact was horrific. Fire and smoke filled the area that used to be the battleship. I could not, of course, see or hear anyone on the ship, but I knew people had just died. I felt an actual physical pain in my heart.

The roar of planes overhead was like nothing I had ever heard.

"No!" someone yelled. It was me screaming. I didn't recognize my own voice. "No, no, no!"

I watched helplessly. Where was William's ship? My eyes frantically scanned the water, searching. There was so much smoke I couldn't see it anymore. The smell of diesel and gunpowder burned my nose. I tucked Nori under my chin and held her tight to my chest. I used part of her blanket to cover my nose and mouth. The bombs didn't stop. Over and over, the island was pummeled. The whole island looked like it was on fire. I could feel the island crying. Our peaceful beautiful island was being destroyed.

I wanted to get out of the tree, but I knew if I got down, I couldn't see anything. I gripped onto the trunk of the tree and held on for dear life.

Japanese bombers flew above, dropping torpedoes. They just kept coming. Then the machine gun fire began. It rained down from two directions.

Bombs continued falling over and over. There was never a break or a pause in the noise and fire. The sky was darkened with planes. Would they ever stop, or would this continue until every ship was destroyed? The smoke parted momentarily, and it appeared that a plane was making a run on the *Utah*. I could see William's ship still standing next to the *Utah*. The wing dipped and straightened again, and a torpedo hit. Then another plane and another hit. The smoke circled again, and I couldn't see anything again.

I jumped out of the tree, clinging tightly to Nori. Nora didn't cry. She tucked herself into my chest and held motionless against my heaving breasts. I ran through the trees and into the driveway and started running down the road. I didn't know where I was running to, but I had to do something. I had to get to William.

Dad caught me halfway down the hill. He grabbed me by the shoulders. I tried to push past him.

"Ruth, no! No, you can't go down there!"

"I have to! Let me go!" Mom grabbed my other arm.

"Come on, Ruth, you can't go!" she yelled. People were running all around us. It was chaos.

"Please!" I sobbed. "Please!"

"Ruth, think of Nori. We have to get to safety! You could be killed!"

I let them drag me back to the house. Dad guided us to the back of the house and into the crawl space. Daddy pulled Nori out of the blanket and cradled her against his chest. Mom, Elizabeth, Marie, and I clung to one another under the house and sobbed. I cried and cried until there were no tears left.

Suddenly, the roar stopped, but my ears were still ringing. It was silent except for the sounds of people shouting.

"Stay here," Dad said and handed Nori back to me. He came back a few minutes later. "Come on out. It appears the bombing has stopped. It's time to start organizing help parties in the neighborhood."

We gathered in the street just outside our house. Dad took charge.

"Ladies, gather all the bandages, blankets, towels, and anything you can think of to take to the hospital. They will be overwhelmed. All the men with me. They are going to need help recovering bodies and getting injured people to the hospital."

I was numb. This was not how my day was supposed to go. I had looked forward to today for so long. How could this be happening? Where was William? The world was spinning around me. Surely I was dreaming.

"Ruth, Ruth!" Daddy was standing in front of me.

"Yes," I said softly.

"They need you at the hospital," he directed.

I shook my head. How could he even suggest it? "No! No! I'm going with you! I have to find William!"

"We will find him, dear." He took me by the shoulders again. "Ruth, I will find him. Mother will take Nori. They need you at the hospital. You have to help."

I nodded. I knew he was right. But it felt so cruel to expect this of me. I sobbed and handed Nori to Mom.

"Mr. Maumau is taking a load to the hospital. Hop in with him."

"Okay. Find him, Daddy," I begged.

"I will find him." Daddy tried to shut the door of the truck.

"No!" I pushed it back. "I can't do this, Dad! I can't go! I can't do this!" I was screaming.

"You must, and you can. You are an incredibly strong woman, Ruth, always have been. Now show it. You are needed." He kissed me on the forehead and shut the truck door.

The hospital was already buzzing with people running to and fro, and hardly any patients had arrived. They were preparing for the inevitable arrival of hundreds, maybe thousands. We were hastily organized into groups and given shouted commands. There were no "Thank you for comings" or "We are so glad you are heres." No. You were here. Now get to work. It was overwhelmingly clear that I had never been in a situation as dire as this in my life.

The patients started to arrive, by the truckloads. There weren't enough stretchers to carry them all in. There wasn't enough of anything. Volunteers carried them in the hospital, in their arms, cradling them like babies, their shirts covered in sailors' blood. They set them anywhere and everywhere.

There were bloody, moaning men lying on stretchers, lining the hallways and on the floors, and sitting in chairs. I was momentarily stunned by the horrific scene.

Someone tossed a roll of gauze at me and shoved a man on a stretcher into my hip. I didn't see the person who rolled the man at me, just the bloody crying sailor in front of me. And suddenly, I was a nurse again. I checked his vitals. He was conscious.

"Where does it hurt the most?" I asked.

"My leg," he moaned.

I looked down at the torn trousers and bloody tissue hanging from the knee where his leg used to be. His leg was gone. I quickly tied a tourniquet and rushed him to the surgery center.

I didn't know how long I worked. The men never stopped coming. An endless row of injured people surrounded us. I saw Elaina across the sea of people up to her elbows in some guy's intestines. We held eye contact for the briefest of moments, trying to comfort each other.

Anyone who was remotely conscious, I asked what ship they were on. Most of them couldn't answer, but those who did never said *St. Louis*. They said *Tennessee, Michigan, Philadelphia*, but no *St. Louis*.

I had never seen so many grown men cry, but then again, most of them were still just boys. The head nurse asked me to sit with one young boy. I was holding the bandage on his guts while he shook and shivered in convulsive tremors.

"It's okay," I offered. "It's going to be okay." His trembling hand raised slowly and touched my arm. "I got you. You're, you're . . .," I tried to explain.

"Huhhhhhhh." He was gurgling, and blood was leaking out the side of his mouth. I rolled him over so he could cough up more blood and rolled him back onto his back and listened for more coughing. He didn't make any noise. I listened closer. Nothing, he wasn't breathing anymore. I slowly lifted my hands off his belly. He jerked one more involuntary time. My hands and apron were covered in his blood and the blood of others. My shirt was dripping with milk. I hadn't even thought about Nora this whole time. She must be hungry. I was so engorged.

"Take five, Ruth! Get cleaned up!" the head nurse yelled from across the room.

I took off my apron and washed in the basin. I stepped over body after body, trying to get to the door. How could I just walk past these men? But I did. I needed a break.

Mom was waiting outside. I didn't even ask how long she had been there; I just took Nora in my arms and sat against a tree to feed her. Another truck full of wounded sailors was pulling up and behind it an ambulance from the airfield. The airfield had been obliterated as well.

"Has Dad found him?" I asked.

"No, no, honey. But he's looking." She stroked my hair.

"Anything about the *St. Louis*?"

"No, nothing."

"This is horrible. I've never seen anything like this before, Mom. Do you think he's okay?"

"I have no idea, honey." She put her arm around me and pulled me in tight. "I sure hope so."

Mom said she was going to bring Nori back before bed, and I went back into the hospital. I found a clean apron in the back of the linen closet. A couple of other nurses were changing out their aprons as well, and I overheard them talking.

"One of the sailors I was bandaging said one of the ships went down entirely. They don't think there were any survivors."

"What ship?" I asked abruptly. "I'm sorry to interrupt, but did he say what ship? Please," I begged, "it's important."

"Uh, I think he said the *Arizona*."

A wave of relief rushed over me that she didn't say the *St. Louis*, but it was instantly replaced with horrific grief.

"Kekoa, no!"

I dropped to my knees.

"No! No! No! What is happening!" I cried.

"Oh, honey," the nurses surrounded me. "Did you know someone?"

"Uhhhhhhhhhh! Noooooooo!" I sobbed into one of their shoulders. This wonderful stranger held me tight while I wailed. The grief was paralyzing. It couldn't be true. It was not true. It had to be a mistake. Not Kekoa.

"Was he your husband, dear?"

"No," I gasped. "Friend. I don't even know if my husband is alive."

"Oh, sweetheart. There, there." She let me cry for several minutes. The other nurses left. When my sobbing quieted, she urged me to stand.

"Honey, I'm so sorry. But there are hundreds of other friends and husbands out there that need our help. We need to go help them now. It is horrific that this happened. There will be time to cry later. Now is the time to be strong." I nodded. "Take a few minutes and get back in there." She squeezed my shoulder and left me.

Oh, Kekoa, no. No, not possible. He was so angry the last time he saw me. Was this my fault? He wouldn't have joined the navy if it wasn't for me. It was my fault. Did he suffer? Did he cry out like the men here in the hospital? I couldn't think of him suffering. I leaned against the wall and clutched my breaking heart. I pulled the empty bin from against the wall and threw up in it.

21

I was still crying when I went back to work. I didn't care. No one else did either. No one paused to say "Oh, dear, are you okay?" or "What is wrong? Here sit down and rest. You've had a difficult day." No. We were all experiencing the most difficult day of our lives. We all had tears, tears we never thought we would weep. Our whole lives had changed in moments. Did I ever have a reason to cry in my life before this moment? I can't imagine I did. Yet I have cried before. Every pain I had ever felt in my past was nothing. Nothing. It was nothing. I was angry with myself. How could I have ever felt any need for sadness or disappointment? I was an utter fool. My blessed, soft, easy life I was living until this moment mocked me as I went bed to bed to dying men, men who had mothers, wives, sisters, friends. My tears flowed silently down my cheeks. I didn't even try to wipe them away.

I was assigned to triage. I sorted the wounded into three categories. The first being mortally wounded, they would not receive any care, only made to feel comfortable if possible. I placed a big black X on their chart at the foot of the bed large enough for everyone to see and know to move onto the next bed. For the first dozen or so, my hand shook as I did it. I looked at each burned and bleeding soldier as I did it, knowing I was placing the seal of death on them. Luckily, most of them were unconscious. This made it easier. The sailor who was both sopping wet and charred black and bloody and burned into an unrecognizable human form, his X was excruciating to write. He was wet from jumping off his ship to escape the bombing and scorched because the water he jumped into was burning from all the oil spilled. Could he be William? He was so burned. Who could tell? But then he writhed in pain. He yelled at me, begging for release from his pain. He didn't sound like William. Could he be? The worst part of that X, he could be saved. He could be saved in a hospital that was not overwhelmed and with a medical staff who could devote all the time and energy to his rehabilitation. We could not do this for him. It was better for him to be given a sedative and slip slowly away. But who was I to make these decisions?

The second category was the severely wounded, who were sent straight to the doctors. I drew a circle with a large exclamation point in it, indicating attention now And lastly, the not severely injured. Those with just minor cuts, missing fingers, and minor burns were quickly bandaged up and would have to wait. I drew a star on these charts. They would probably be tended to by volunteers and untrained individuals.

The men kept coming. The trucks never stopped delivering bloody, battered, injured, hardly recognizable men. What did it look like at the harbor if this was what they were sending to us? Where was Will?

And then the unimaginable hell I was living in got worse. The injured civilians started arriving. Children! Babies! Oh, the babies! They were placed on stretchers in twos and threes. There were not enough beds. They sat on the mothers' laps, who sat on the floor, awaiting, wailing for help. All instincts pointed to save the children, help the children. But no. Priority to the sailors. What? "Yes, Nurse, this is war. Help the sailors first." Who said that to me? I don't even know. War? WAR? War. This was war. Our beautiful peaceful island. War.

I still helped the children. How could you now pick up the precious four-year-old girl off the floor who was on the beach with her Auntie when the bombing started and her whole right side was charred, and her beautiful long black hair was singed and pasted to her face? How does a person walk by that? I do not know. I helped the children.

"What ship were you on, sailor?" I asked that question over and over. Still, no one said the *St. Louis*. I don't know how long I worked. My back ached, my feet hurt, but I couldn't stop. So many people needed help. I smiled at them through my tears, trying to give some sort of comfort. I wasn't very convincing. The hospital reeked of blood, smoke, and oil. It was stifling and rank. I was on the brink of delirium when I thought I recognized a voice of a man in the bed behind me.

I blinked, trying to clear my eyes. Could it be? No, but it was.

"Edward!"

He flinched at his name and looked at me.

"Ruth, hi." He cleared his throat and looked away. His chart had a star on it, a star written in my handwriting. I hadn't noticed?

"Edward!" I yelled it this time and ran to the front of his bed. I remembered putting the star on his chart and thinking, *This sailor isn't hurt. He should get out of this bed.* A doctor explained he was an officer and jumped off his ship as it started pulling away from port. His ship was the only one to get out of the harbor to pursue the Japs. And he jumped from it.

"Edward!" I said again. Everything started falling into place. "You, the *St. Louise* is the one that got out!" It was a question and a statement.

He nodded.

"William, did you see William? Is he okay?" I wanted to reach into his brain and extract all his knowledge. Why wasn't he saying anything? "Edward, tell me!" A few nurses looked up momentarily as I yelled but did nothing else.

"I don't know," he said slowly.

"When is the last time you saw him?" I demanded.

"We were both on deck." He spoke painfully, slowly. "We had a view of the whole harbor when the planes started roaring overhead. We all looked up, thinking they were friendlies, and then everything started exploding. Ships were being torn apart right in front of us. Shrapnel flew everywhere. Fire erupted out of nowhere. It was chaos. Men were screaming. Men we knew were running to and fro. I saw my friends get hit, their bodies being torn apart and flung in different directions right in front of us. They were jumping off their ships into burning water. We knew we were next. I was frozen." He looked away. "William did not freeze. He shouted orders and organized the men for counterattack. I thought he's a fool. We were about to die." He sighed. "So I jumped off the ship. I swam to shore and watched my ship sail away."

Shame. Shame was all that showed in his eyes. He was a coward, and he knew it. I wanted to scream at him and tell him he was a fool. But there was no need. He knew it.

I backed away slowly. I had nothing to say to him.

Mom was outside, waiting for me with Nora in her arms. I had no idea what time it was. It was dark. Daddy was there too.

"I'm being sent home for the night," I explained. Daddy walked me to the car. I nursed Nora as he drove us home. The whole island was in shambles. Palm trees were broken, and debris was scattered everywhere.

"I feel so guilty leaving. There is so much to do."

"You are no good without rest. It's good to come home," Mom said.

We walked warily into the house and sat in the living room in a stunned silence. What could we say? What could be said? Elizabeth and Marie sat on the floor. I don't think they had ever sat that long in silence before. They were dirty and exhausted. Daddy wouldn't let them all the way down to the harbor, but they had spent the day helping locals in the shops by the harbor, pulling injured people out of the rubble and picking up the destroyed shops.

"Did you find him, honey?" Daddy said, breaking the silence.

I nodded.

"The *St. Louis* was the only ship that was able to launch after the attack. No other ship broke port. They pursued the Japanese cruisers. That is all I know. The good news is he is most likely alive, for now." Daddy sat next to me and took my hands in his.

"He is alive," he repeated.

"He's alive," I said. "But he is pursuing the Japanese and hasn't returned." Daddy nodded slowly. "So he might not still be alive."

"There is a good chance he is still alive," Dad encouraged.

"Well, at least that's something," I said. But I had little hope after all the carnage of today. So many deaths, so many wounded. It felt selfish to even hope that William was alive. What had I done to deserve not losing my husband? Surely I was no more deserving than any other widow tonight.

"God, where are you?" I whispered as I climbed into bed.

How could this happen to our little island? How is it decided who lives and dies? Is it all an accident, by chance? Does God choose? Does he have that much control that he chooses who is skewered through by shrapnel or drown trying to escape the flames? Or does God just sit back and watch in horror like the rest of us? Why had I never thought of these things before? How could I be so blissfully naive and blind to the cruelty of this world? Do I even believe in God?

I do believe in God. I've seen him before. All around me. I saw him in the beauty of the island. I saw him change my heart so I could fall in love with Will. I saw him every time I held and looked my daughter in her eyes and wondered how I created such a thing. Simple, I created her with God. There is a God, yes. I told myself there is a God. But where was he now?

I don't think any of us slept that night. We sat around the breakfast table that morning red-eyed and wary.

"I'm going to go back to the hospital," I said. The table nodded. "If you think you're up to it," I said to Marie and Elizabeth, "we could use some extra pairs of hands."

"No! No way!" Marie said. Her eyes were wide with fear. "There is no way I can . . . I can do that. All the blood . . ."

"You wouldn't have to do anything like that."

"What would we have to do?" Elizabeth asked.

"There are a lot of men that are hurt and can't be tended to. They need a kind hand, someone to talk to, someone to give them water," I explained.

"How about Elizabeth and I go and Marie stays and watches Nori?" Mom suggested.

"Would you be up for that, Mom?" I asked.

"I will drive you all up there," Dad suggested, "and come check on you around noon with Nori."

"Would you be okay with that, Marie? Will you watch Nori?" She looked so relieved she wasn't being summoned to that hospital.

"Yes, yes, absolutely. Just feed her before you leave."

Dad dropped the three of us at the front of the hospital. I directed them to the stretchers full of men just outside the doors of the hospital under a large tent.

"Over here," I said, walking them to the canopy. "Just check on each of them, see if they need anything. Some of them only want someone to talk to. There will probably be more that join them."

Elizabeth tentatively approached a young man lying on a stretcher against the far wall. She touched his arm, and the man stirred.

"Can I get you anything, sir?" he moaned and lifted his hand slightly. She had to bend down to hear his response.

"He says his bandage is too tight. He wants me to loosen it," she said, turning to me.

"I will help you," I said. "Watch me. You can do this for other men."

I unwrapped the cloth from around his head, revealing a gaping hole in the side of his skull. I could see his brain. I looked at Elizabeth, willing her not to gasp or even flinch with my eyes. I grabbed her hand as she tried to step backward. Her mouth hung open. I shook my head ever so slightly and continued to instruct her on how to redress the wound.

We put new gauze over the hole and the oozing tissue and wrapped his head with new cloth.

"There, sir. Does that feel better?" I asked.

"Yes," he moaned. "Thanks."

I guided Elizabeth back to the font of the tent. "What was that!" she demanded. "You said I wouldn't have to deal with things like that!"

"I know. I'm so sorry. He must, he must have been put there because there is no hope."

"No hope?"

"There is nothing they can do to save him," I explained.

"Nothing!" She was appalled. "They left him to die?"

"It appears that way."

"That is terrible!"

"It is the way of things. It's the way of—"

"War . . .," she finished. Her jaw was set. "Are we at war, Ruth?"

"It appears that way," I said again.

A few tears started to stream down Elizabeth's face. I pulled her in and embraced her.

"Talk to him. Ask him about his family. Try and get him to remember happy times so he can die with happy thoughts. Ease his last few moments on earth. Offer him a tender touch."

I went into the hospital, leaving Mom and Elizabeth alone in that desperate tent. I checked on them a few times. Mom bustled about, trying her best to smile as she fed the men water and adjusted their pillows. Every time I peered into the tent, Elizabeth was near the dying man. The last time I poked my head in, she was sitting by the man, holding his hand.

"Dad's here. Do you all want a break?" I said as I entered the hot tent. Flies were starting to make their way in and buzz throughout the area.

"Oh great. I need a break," Mom said, relieved. She wiped her forehead and left to find Dad.

I placed my hand on Elizabeth's shoulder. "You coming?"

"I think I will stay. He was just telling me about his dog and his little brother, Peter," she said. She didn't let go of the man's hand. His breath was shallow and labored.

"Okay," I said. "Are you sure?"

"He doesn't get a break. Why should I?"

Here is God.

I sighed. The thought washed over me like a comforter. Here is God. Elizabeth's newfound strength and comfort was the hand of God.

She stayed with him all day. Late in the evening before going home, I checked on the two of them again. Her head lay on the bed, resting on his arm. I felt the man's pulse. There was none. I went to find the men in charge of the moving the dead and told him that we had another body. I motioned for them to wait when we got to the tent. Placing my hand on Elizabeth's shoulder, I tried to wake her.

"Elizabeth . . . Elizabeth." Her wary eyes met mine. "You did great, Elizabeth. I am so proud of you. Now let's go home." She shook her head sleepily and tried to protest. "Honey, he is gone. You did well. Let's go home."

She looked at the men waiting by the front of the tent and then at the hand she held in hers. She gingerly pried his fingers out of her hand, and then she looked at me and released a heaping, desperate sob. I pulled her into my arms and guided her a few feet away from the deceased sailor. I nodded to the men, who swiftly made their way into the tent and carried the sailor's stretcher out. Elizabeth sobbed louder as they lifted him out and took him away.

"I didn't even know him. How can I be so sad?" she asked as I led her to Daddy's car.

"You have a good heart, Elizabeth," I said, patting her hand.

"I wish I could have done something to help him."

"He didn't die alone. You were a great help today," I reassured.

I tucked her into the back seat and held her head on my shoulder. No one said anything. There really were no words.

Marie and Nori were asleep on the couch when we got home. I scooped Nori out of Marie's sleeping arms and took her back to my room, so relieved to feed her.

I couldn't sleep again. I tossed and turned all night while Nori slept peacefully beside me. I had helped so many men in the last two days, pressed my hands into their gaping guts, and reinserted their intestines with my fingers. I had cleaned and wrapped more wounds than I could count. I had cleaned up vomit, blood, and feces. I heard men cry, writhing in pain, making noises I had never heard before. Was this Will's fate? Was he in the same condition? The thought horrified me. I felt ill anytime my mind pictured Will bleeding, dying, or crying. Where was he? Would he come back? I was so busy during the day that I was able to push the thought of Will to the back of my mind, but lying in bed, it was helpless.

The sun wasn't quite up before I gave up on sleep and wrapped Nori to my chest and started the walk to my house. I hadn't been home since the attack. I needed clothes for both me and Nori. The crisis was subsiding slightly at the hospital, but I was still needed. I would go back again today, and a fresh change of clothing and showering in my own shower sounded heavenly.

The streets looked foreign, not like the streets I'd walked nearly all my life. The whole energy of the island had changed. It felt different. Desperate. Sad. Even the plants and flowers looked sad. I unconsciously kept looking up to the sky, looking for a plane. I'd never been scared walking the streets of my island. I felt nervous. I held Nori tightly, even though no one else was out.

As I rounded the corner of our narrow driveway, chills ran down my spine. Something was off. I walked slower. And then I saw it. I stood in front of our house or what used to be our house. It was destroyed, a complete loss. The porch was completely gone. Nothing left but small bits of white wood pieces. Half the roof had fallen in. It had clearly been hit by a bomb. Only the back wall was still standing. It was nothing but rubble. It had never even occurred to me that I would find it this way. I should have. We live right next to the water. What if we hadn't left early that morning? We would have been here. We would have died. The thought never occurred to me.

Here is God.

I didn't cry, not yet. I'm sure that would come. For now, I was stunned, shocked. I gingerly walked through the rubble, clutching Nori. I moved a few things as I went. Our couch was out in the tree line; the table had disappeared. The farther back in the rubble, the more things I found. The bomb clearly hit the front. I lifted a few pieces of rubble and found Nori's bassinette completely intact. I dusted it off. It was completely untouched. A few more feet away was our bed. It was covered in debris but appeared intact. I surveyed the entire scene. Debris was everywhere. Our entire home, the life we had just started, was destroyed. My back hurt from carrying Nori. I dusted the bassinet off entirely and gingerly placed her in it. All my dreams of Will coming home, laying Nori here in her bassinet while we slept in our bed, were gone. They would never happen. Nori slept peacefully without a care in the world.

I found our radio a few feet from the house. I picked it and turned it on. It worked. There was still music in the world. That felt wrong. Music. I dropped it in the sand. It kept playing its happy tune. I didn't care. My life was destroyed.

I walked to the waterline and surveyed the scene. The water was littered with floating pieces of ships, metal, dark patches of oil, and debris. There were still fires burning. Parts of ships were sticking out of the water while other parts sunk. *How many men are still in there?* I thought. I walked along the rocks and looked down Battleship Row or what was left of it. How would our little island recover from this? We'd been utterly destroyed. I walked along the rocks all the way out to the edge. I didn't want to keep looking. It was unbearable to see the fine ships destroyed. But I couldn't stop. I was searching, searching for Will. Where was he?

When I finally turned back to the house, I had my answer. He was standing in front of the house.

"Will!" I screamed, but he couldn't hear me, not from this distance and not over the sound of the waves. "Will! Will!" I continued screaming his name as I ran.

The black lava rock was so unforgiving, so sharp it took all my concentration not to fall as I scurried over the terrain. I could barely move faster than a walk. I felt like I was in quicksand. The world was moving in slow motion. I watched him do just what I had. He gingerly made his way, searching the debris. The thought "He thinks I'm dead!" hit me like a bolt of lightning. I yelled louder. My heart broke as I watched him. *He thinks I'm dead!* "Will!" *Oh, why can't I move faster!*

He dropped to his knees, poor man. Come on, legs, run! He rested his head in his hands. I thought I saw his shoulders heave in a sob. I finally reached the sand. I could properly run now.

Will's head snapped up. He heard something. He was so startled it caused me to stop too. What did he hear? He ran over to the bassinette. Nori must have squealed. I stopped and watched him scoop her up. He carefully placed one hand behind her head and one under her bottom, and he cradled her in his arms. I had dreamed of this moment so many times. This was never how I imagined it.

He was wearing dirty trousers and a torn white shirt and suspenders. The last few days must have been awful for him. He looked at her tenderly and gently pulled the blankets back to look at her face. My heart swelled in my chest, finally seeing my child in her father's arms. I bolted toward him.

He turned, and I could see his face. He was weeping.

"Will," I said. "Will." I was so tired from running I could scarcely get enough breath to yell loud enough for him to hear. "Will, I'm here." He looked up, finally.

"Ruth!"

"I'm here!" I ran, closing the one hundred feet between us, and I bounded through the rubble of our home. I threw myself at him. We embraced with Nori tucked into his elbow. He smelled so good, like metal and sweat.

"You're alive!" he said.

"You're alive!" I said. I kissed his cheeks, his lips, his forehead. I rubbed his arms and wrapped my arms around him, trying to take him all in.

We held each other and wept. *How is this even possible?* I thought. *How did I get so lucky? Am I dreaming?*

"What happened?" I asked finally.

"I was just about to ask you the same thing," he said, motioning to the rubble that used to be our home. "It is so good to see you. I thought you were dead," he choked. He rubbed his free hand along my face and behind my neck and pulled me in for a thirsty kiss.

"Oh, I missed you," I whispered. "I see you've met your daughter."

"Yes, for a moment there"—he swallowed hard—"I feared the worst when I found her and not you."

I nodded.

"I feared the same thing for you."

"Well, all is well with both of us, considering . . . And she," he said to the wiggling little Nori, "she is beautiful. How did you both escape?"

"We were at my parents. I couldn't sleep that night," I explained, "knowing you were coming in, so we weren't here."

"Well, for that, I am very glad. You are the prettiest little angel," he said to Nori. "Forgive me for putting you down, but I have to properly love on your mother."

He set Nori back in the bassinet and engulfed me in his arms. With our home, our lives, and our future shattered around us, he desperately kissed me. Holding me tightly into his chest, we held onto each other in the most grateful of embraces. We both wept and kissed each other over and over.

We sat on the beach together, Nori in his arms, our destroyed home behind us. He wrapped his arm around me and kissed my head.

The radio was still playing. President Roosevelt's voice interrupted the song.

"December 7, 1941—a date that will live in infamy."

Even the trees appeared to be listening. The waves sounded hushed.

"The United States of America was suddenly and deliberately attacked by the naval and air forces of the empire of Japan."

Japan, I wanted to spit at the sound of their name. Never have I felt such anger boil in the pit of my stomach.

"The attack yesterday on the Hawaiian Islands has caused severe damage to American naval and military forces. I regret to tell you that very many American lives have been lost."

He said it so simply. How could such a horrific event be paraphrased down to one sentence?

"No matter how long it may take us to overcome this premeditated invasion, the American people in their righteous might will win through to absolute victory. Hostilities exist. There is no blinking at the fact that our people, our territory, and our interest are in grave danger. With confidence in our armed forces, with the unbounding determination of our people, we will gain the inevitable triumph, so help us God.

"I ask that the Congress declare that since the unprovoked and dastardly attack by Japan on Sunday, December 7, 1941, a state of war has existed between the United States and the Japanese empire."

We sat in silence. We were at war. The people who destroyed our island would not be allowed to terrorize us without retribution. Evil will not be allowed to reign. God is here. He is in us. God didn't allow this to happen; evil inflicted it on all of us. Evil exists, but God has an army too. And his army doesn't lose.

Three days ago, my biggest worry was getting my husband home. Oh, how sorry I felt for myself then. What a burden that was. It completely consumed me.

I am a different woman now. Now I will willingly send my husband back to war, to fight for our country, to fight for peace, to defend the United States of America proudly.

And I will go back to the hospital.

Lightning Source UK Ltd.
Milton Keynes UK
UKHW010204070220
358308UK00001B/52/J

9 781796 085495